Shula and the Goat̴ ̴ ̴ ̴̴̴

This first edition
and winner of the 2016
Quassa Gold Award for
Literary Fiction
to my new friend
Van
With Best Wishes

McCauley Grange

6th Sept '17

To Dannii for her unwavering enthusiasm and unconditional support.

Also in memory of my cousin Kath.

Shula and
the Goats from Tala

McCawley Grange

Delgany Publications

British Library Cataloguing in Publication Data
A catalogue record for this book is available from the British Library.

ISBN 978-0-9567605-1-7

Typeset by Amolibros, Milverton, Somerset
www.amolibros.com

This book production has been managed by Amolibros
Printed and bound by T J International Ltd, Padstow, Cornwall, UK

About the Author

McCawley Grange was born in York in 1940. At the age of ten he emigrated with his family to County Wicklow, Eire, whereupon the family began to suffer financial hardship. Leaving school at thirteen years of age he worked in the building trade, then as a hotel worker and gardener and on his return to York in 1956, successively as a linesman, factory worker and builder.

At age seventeen, following a row with his father, he left home for London, where for a time he lived and worked with the Irish labouring fraternity. Returning to York, he joined the Fire Service in 1962 and after twenty-five years left the service with the rank of Assistant Divisional Officer. Following this, he spent two years with the Voluntary Service Overseas (VSO) organization building 'low cost' housing in Kenya.

Now retired, he lives in York with his wife, two children and four grandchildren employing much of his time playing golf and writing. *Shula and the Goats from Tala* is his second book. Of his first book, *Some Lessons in Gaelic:* 'What we loved about the book – apart from its gripping story – is the rich array of colourful characters'. *York Born & Read*

Prologue
Nairobi, March 1975

*B*lack kites circled above the city, the birds effortlessly suspended on early monsoon winds. To the north, clouds gathered
above the Aberdare range, not threatening but full of promise.
Soon, the sweet-sour air of the city would be clear and fresh and
its environs, the mulched volcanic soil, would be fertile again.

Inspector Sam Wamiru shrugged off a feeling of irritation as he
crossed the courtyard to where a young constable waited behind
the wheel of a jeep. Wamiru had just left the newly appointed
Chief-Superintendent's office where he had been greeted with
a false smile and a crushing handshake. 'Insecurity,' Wamiru
muttered as he eased into the passenger seat of the jeep. The
new chief was small for a policeman but well-spoken: too full
of friendly pretence. A charade, an affectation from his colonial
days; superiority all too firmly atop of any managerial agenda
he might have brought with him from Nakuru. Overblown, like
a fruit with worms inside.

The constable at the wheel of the jeep was young, slender and
unknown. 'Kitonyi, sir,' he introduced himself, before edging
nervously into the chaos of Nairobi's traffic.

'Garissa Road,' Wamiru said. The words a request rather than
an order, he felt uncertain, looked grumpy and knew that the boy
was nervous. Nairobi was no city for nervous drivers.

'I know it, sir.'

'Do you know Katamara village?'

'No, sir, I am new here from Mombasa but already I know Garissa Road.'

'Pass Thika Town and keep going until I tell you when to turn off.' Wamiru knew the village, knew the hospital and most of the people there, but did not know why he was being sent. The chief had been vague. All he had told him was that 'something serious' had happened close to the hospital and people would be waiting for him there. Was this new man from Nakuru trying to unnerve him, put him to the test? Well, he had a pad and pencil, a young constable as witness, and years of experience. The new chief was going to have to do better than this.

The driver started making conversation; talking about the coming rain, hoping it would be prolonged and steady. His driving was proficient and Wamiru had decided already that he liked at least one of the new kids on the block. 'It's here now,' the driver said with a smile as large raindrops began to splatter on the dusty windscreen. As the jeep pulled into the teaming current of Tom Mboya Street, the inspector's attention was caught by a *Daily Nation* placard and his immediate thought was to tell the driver to pull over. But the traffic was heavy and the young man was still nervous. Did he need a national newspaper to tell him something he already knew? No, in his heart he knew well who the body was and his heart was heavy with all the things he kept in there. All action must come from the brain, never from the heart; a Kenyan policeman cannot survive unless he knows that rule. *BODY IN THE MORTUARY IDENTIFIED,* the placard read. The body was that of his friend and things bothersome and burdensome moved from his heart to his gut. He felt sick.

His friend – the last time he had spoken to him was on the steps of the Nairobi Hilton Hotel. He was off duty at the time but, knowing that J.M. was due to leave a conference, Wamiru had waited for him to emerge. Embracing warmly, the words they spoke were few but friendly and they agreed to have a few beers together later that day to catch up. That was weeks ago and his friend had not been seen since.

2

A charismatic man, Josiah Mwangi Kariuki had been a *Mau Mau* freedom fighter, eventually to become an assistant minister in Kenyatta's government, a man destined for great things but far too outspoken. He was overtly critical of Kenyatta's extended family and their penchant for dealing in gemstones and trading in land purchases; it would have served him better to have behaved circumspectly, kept those things in his heart, but he was a politician, not a policeman and he had to appeal to the masses. And appeal he did. His cry of *'land for the landless'* rousted the people to his cause and his, all too public, mantras made him nationally loved but too outspoken to survive. Loose cannons are dangerous to fledgling governments and a facially disfigured corpse had been found by a *Maasai* herdsman in the Ngong Hills; now the corpse labelled *'Unidentified African Male'* had been identified.

The rain increased and the driver kept talking but Wamiru was not listening. There would be an investigation, the people would demand it. So would the police, the government and the establishment and there would be a cover-up. Would the new Chief Super be involved in the cover-up? Of course he would: a man made for cover-ups. Wamiru had been angry at what had happened and he had shown it. He should never have shown that he knew so much. Should never have told a superior, never have threatened to go to the newspapers. Now, what he should have kept in his heart was in his gut and it was churning and a false smile and a false handshake had sent him to an incident without telling him anything about it.

The rain was heavier now and the wipers worked frantically on the rain-lashed wind screen. On Garissa Road, the pot holes of the short rains had been filled and tarmaced over but this was the start of the long rains and the pot holes would return in days. Kitonyi slowed the jeep. All traffic slowed except for the honking, laden *matatus*, busses underwritten, as they were, with divine indemnity; 'JESUS SAVES' and 'TRUST IN JESUS' emblazoned on their roofs, hellbent on adding to the carnage that was Kenya's roads. The faster they went the more money they made. Monsoon rains were good for business.

Thousands of miles away, the rain had started with southerly winds in the Indian Ocean; strong sea breezes growing stronger as they pressed towards the coast of East Africa. Over the ocean a measureless raft of moisture had been drawn up by the sun and cooling, had lowered to a thick, black shapeless stratus which would soon become the long rains. When the clouds reached Kenya they emptied on the coastal towns of Malindi and Mombasa and then the clouds swept inland: a leaden mass stretching all the way between the Sabaki and the Tsavo rivers to the south and the great Tana River to the north, before they advanced to saturate the Tsavo plains and beyond to the Chyulu hills. Torrents of rain would soon be reviving the temperate Rift Valley, the central highlands, the cities, towns, villages and their environs, a weight of water thundering down from the Aberdares and the Ngong Hills to swamp the grasslands. Instantly, little fresh streams would multiply, to muscle their way through the loamy ground to gorge streams and tributaries until they swelled and rolled to join the Galana and the Sabaki rivers; back to the Indian Ocean; back to where the rain began. In all of Africa, nothing is as welcome as the coming of the long rains.

'What is your name?' Wamiru shouted above the thunder on the roof.

'Constable Kitonyi, sir, new here from Mombasa.'

'Your Christian name?'

'Peter, sir.'

'Peter, we are going to a hospital in a village called Katamara. It's a hospital and school run by Catholic nuns, "The Missionary Sisters of the Precious Blood" they're called. All the new chief would tell me was that something serious has happened.'

Peter Kitonyi, his head thrust forward, stared motionlessly through the windscreen. Only his lips moved, 'You know this place well then, sir?'

'Last year I was sent there to investigate the death of a child.

He was found hanging from a window cord.' Wamiru lowered his voice, he appeared to be musing and Kitonyi had to tilt his head to hear what was being said. 'It was a mystery. An accident, it couldn't have been anything else. Only God knows how that little boy came to die.'

'One day, I might be in charge of such an investigation,' Kitonyi said wishfully.

'The children there are badly handicapped. Maybe it's another child but whatever it is, it must be serious or I wouldn't have been called for. A local boy, a corporal called Adonis, he would be dealing with it.' Once again Wamiru seemed to be talking to himself.

The driver switched off the demister so that there would be no need to shout above the rain. 'Or maybe a *musungu*: a dead white at a hospital, very serious.'

Wamiru disliked intensely the inherent inferiority of the man's remark but silently he agreed. If murder was involved then a dead white at a hospital would be very serious indeed. Colonialism had gone, but unfortunately residual inequality remained.

'Are there *musungus* at the hospital?' the driver asked with a glance sideward.

'The nuns are Kenyan but there are three whites,' Wamiru answered. 'Two English guys are building a new accommodation block for the nuns. I've met one, Charlie Carter, but I've never met the other. And there's a nurse, Jennifer Collins from Ireland—' He was going to say more but stopped himself.

'Maybe it is the *musungu* woman who is dead,' Kitonyi suggested sombrely.

Wamiru could not reply for this *musungu* woman inhabited his mind. She had done so since the day she asked him, quite blatantly, if he had another woman – and etched in his mind were eyes that clearly hoped, then briefly shone at his denial, reminding him that she was single too, inviting, and awakening in him, once again, the urge to bond with a woman. He had lost his arm. With his arm his confidence had gone too and only bitterness remained. The bitterness was diminishing and he knew

5

in his heart, that with this woman at his side, it would soon be gone. She was a puzzle. Entering Kibera to aid a sick woman is tough. But she was weak too. A trembling, weeping weakness because of what was assailing her at that time. He had helped her to overcome her problem and she had done something just as great for him; helped him in overcoming his. His mind went back to the suddenness of her question and the things, unspoken that had flowed between them at that moment: the stream of promise, honest, almost child-like, its flow unimpeded by the jutting rocks of vacillation and dilemma. That night in the Jaffa bar they had got to know each other, like each other, and they could build on that. In this lovely stream there was no perplexity. He thought he had lost her to Charlie but now he knew he hadn't. The next weekend he was meeting her for dinner in the city; there was excitement in her voice when she accepted. His first date for a very long time; he wasn't making a mistake this time. Surely he could never make that same mistake again.

'Yes, I am thinking it is her.' Kitonyi's jaw set grimly.

Wamiru looked out of the window into the streaming mist of rain. It couldn't be. It mustn't be. If this woman was dead, then hope had vanished from his life. Let it be no one. Let it be Charlie, or this Freddie who he had never met. Or maybe another child, no, no, another dead child found in the arms of Nurse Collins, not that. Anything rather than for him to have to investigate her again, question her about another child. His mind sprang shut like a trap, the concept too awful to contemplate.

'The body in the mortuary sir, I think it is Josiah Kariuki, did you see the placards?' Kitonyi had changed the subject.

'Yes, it is Josiah, I'm sure of it.'

'It was rumoured.'

'I knew him well. In fact, he was a friend of mine.'

'Then for the people it is sad but it is more sad even, for you.'

'Yes it is very sad for me.' Wamiru wanted to talk because he dared not think. Thinking made his stomach churn. He had done what had been asked of him and still managed to stay loyal to his friend. Over beers that day, J.M. had told him what might happen to him and who would be responsible. It *had* happened. Wamiru had tried to do what he felt was right: big mistake. He had gone to the Chief, the old Chief, and told him what he knew. The old Chief had understood but had retired suddenly, too suddenly, and now this new man, who he didn't trust, had taken his place. Those actions had not come from Wamiru's brain but from his heart, bigger mistake. Relax, he told himself; he was being paranoid.

To the left, they were passing the mist-shrouded town of Thika. Before them, to the right the cloudy mount of Kilimambogo closed on them from out of a drab sky; a bleak, wet landscape. Katamara village nestled at the far side of the mountain, another half an hour on the rain-swept road. Wamiru liked the young man hunched over the steering wheel, unblinking eyes fixed straight ahead. He was quite scrawny for a copper, his uniform too big for him. Who the hell had fitted him out? He didn't like the doffing of the man's cap to something his country had fought so hard to rid itself of but that would take time. Colonial days were not quite over for the *wanachi* but they were for Inspector Wamiru. But he liked the young man's innocence, his enthusiasm fresh from the unequivocal dogma of training school. How long before it was turned to cynicism by corruption? Did he have the right kind of heart, the kind to hide things in? He was thinking again, he must stop thinking.

'No respect, not even for police,' Kitonyi grumbled as a *matatu* overtook them, a wave swamping the jeep.

'See the mountain? That's Kilimambogo, Buffalo Mountain,' the inspector said, nodding across the driver to the right. 'In a while we'll pass Muka Tano, then the next sign will be to Katamara, then it's about two miles to the village. The road is black cotton and you know what that stuff's like. You're going to have to slow right down and drive real careful in this rain.' They drove on, no thunder or lightning, no fanfare, just slate-grey slabs of cloud assuaging the thirsty earth. 'Doesn't look much, does it, the mountain? but all the way south from here there ain't a bigger one. Next biggest mountain south is Kilimanjaro in Tanzania.' The inspector kept nodding at the mountain. 'Just over seven thousand feet, not much of a mountain really, but the people around here are mighty proud of it. You've got to be proud of something if it's all you've got.'

Kitonyi smiled proudly, 'Kilimanjaro, the highest mountain in Africa, and the next highest is Mount Kenya and me, I climbed it. How many Kenyans have thrown a snowball? Me, I've thrown snowballs from the top of Mount Kenya, imagine.'

Wamiru laughed. Kenyans did not climb high mountains. Why would they? Only stupid *musungus* and paid guides did that, but this scrawny policeman had. Good luck to him. The jeep shuddered as its wheels hit a rough patch of road, a pothole succumbing already to the rigours of the rain. 'How long did it take you to climb Mount Kenya?'

'It took three days and two nights. Even then, we did not make it to the highest peak. We needed special equipment for that, but we reached the snow.' Proudly, he talked of his adventure, sleeping under the stars and how he saw lions and elephants on the lower slopes. Then, as the rain continued unabated, they were signalling right towards the village of Katamara.

Here the dirt road was slick and dangerously slippery as Wamiru had warned and after engaging four-wheel drive Kitonyi struggled to keep the jeep at centre. Black cotton soil is impermeable and treacherous when sodden and it took almost three-quarters of an hour to reach the outskirts of the village. Nearing the hospital, the first building they encountered was unfinished. 'That's the building project the two whites are working on,' Wamiru told the driver. 'It's a new accommodation block for the nuns. It's a big building but I'd have thought they would have been further on with it by now.' Kitonyi slowed and stopped the jeep outside, eyeing the building which looked derelict and ominous in the rain.

'I need to relieve myself before we get to the hospital. Is that OK, sir?' the driver asked. Wamiru motioned that he would join him and Kitonyi jumped from the jeep and opened the door politely for his superior, spreading his jacket high above his head to afford protection for them both. The rain slammed into the jacket, cascading at either side in streams.

Together they picked their way over higher ground towards the doorway of the building. It was then that Kitonyi noticed the flapping left sleeve of the inspector's jacket and jerked his eyes away.

'Don't tell me you didn't know,' Wamiru laughed. It was impossible to stay together under one jacket and with one hand he pulled the collar of his own jacket above his head. 'I thought everybody knew.'

Kitonyi was dodging puddles a couple of paces in front of him. Upright, he looked even scrawnier, his uniform even bigger. Even his trousers were too big.

Kitonyi murmured apologetically, 'I didn't know, sir.'

'Sam Wamiru has only one arm: only one-armed copper in the whole of Kenya, maybe in the world. Even in Mombasa it is well known that Inspector Sam Wamiru only has one arm. I can't believe you didn't know.'

They had reached the comparative shelter of the building and both men let their jackets fall down about their shoulders.

'I'm sorry, sir.' Kitonyi said. Then he ventured, 'Can I ask how?' he allowed the question to fade away, as if suspecting his superior's reluctance to answer.

'Happened some time ago,' Wamiru answered, jumping a large puddle to the shelter of a corrugated *mabati* section of roof. 'Maybe I'll tell you on the way back to Nairobi. See what time we get finished at the hospital.' He would tell him something, the usual; he would tell him that he got bitten by a spitting cobra.

They were both beneath the small, roofed area and, facing opposing walls, unzipped their flies. Wamiru thought it strange that this policeman had never heard of him. Maybe he wasn't as famous as he thought he was. He shuddered at the thought of what might lie in store at the hospital. Finished, he shook himself and looked around at the stark walls and the beginning of the roof. 'Something serious' had happened; the words resonated. Someone had been murdered, he knew it. He shuddered again. From this day things would not be the same for someone. Awful things happened in life, and sometimes so suddenly, so unexpectedly. A story was about to unfold and in one shattering moment he knew why the young policeman had never heard of him.

PART ONE

Jennifer

Chapter One

One year earlier

*E*xtract from a letter from Charlie Carter to his mother, dated sometime March 1974.

> *We've only had drinks together and a few meals in Thika and Nairobi so, Mother, don't be getting ahead of yourself. Her name is Jennifer Collins and she's a nurse at the hospital. She's Irish too and you know how you like the Irish. She's a really nice lady and we are very fond of each other, that's all, it's not serious yet so don't be going and buying outfits until I tell you. This is a great country and whatever happens when I get back home, I'll have a story to tell.*

Four women were wailing in the back of the pick-up, their heads sunk onto their chests. Through the open window the dirge was unintelligible, but unmistakeably a tribal lament for a dead baby they were journeying to collect. The petals from the flowers, tied in small bunches to the sides of the truck, were gone and the wind was now snapping at the stalks. The baby was in the

Thika mortuary, and Charlie Carter was willing to oblige. Charlie in a Ford pick-up, courtesy of The East Africa Aid Agency, had been much in demand since his arrival four weeks earlier in the village of Katamara, and was experiencing popularity, hitherto undreamed of. Benevolent by nature, when asked by a lady with soulful eyes and halting English to collect a baby for burial; well of course he would, and in doing so make himself even more popular and ever more so in demand.

He had never been to a mortuary before; what a story to tell when he returned home to England. He might even be able to get inside the building and see dead bodies laid out. In this alien country there were new experiences every day, and this was another. He saw himself in the pub back home talking to fellow drinkers. He was telling them about the baking hot day he took four wailing women to a mortuary in a town called Thika to collect a dead baby and the drinkers were gathered round, hanging onto every word.

The truck bumped and rattled over the rutted ground dodging and weaving around ruts and protruding rocks. The snaking lane was cradled in bush, thorn trees and sisal; scorched and listless and desperate for rain. The wheels churned the dust, raising it high, and in the still air it took long to settle. Hearing the wheels, small animals scuttled to the sanctuary of the rocks and dusty undergrowth until it was safe for them to venture out again. At one place the lane dipped to a dry stream bed which in a few days, would be a torrent heading for the Athi River. At the other side of the bed they had to slow then stop for a herd of cows and goats shepherded by a small boy. The herd passed and disappeared into the dust cloud caused by the wheels. The truck set off again and through a gap in the bush Charlie could see the river close by, it was running slow and sluggish; everything was stunned in the heat, even the mighty Athi and there was no sound other than the whirring of the wheels and the women wailing.

On the Garissa road the truck accelerated, the wind still snapping at the stalks and now drowning the plaintive voices of the women. To the right, the vast pineapple plantations of The Kenya Canning Company, to the left, grass and woodland where on his first journey on that road, he had seen giraffe loping along beside him. Charlie felt a comfort in his mind: drive to Thika: collect the baby's corpse then drive back to Katamara. Then, with the large part of the Sunday behind him, he could settle down by the river near the bridge and watch the hippos wallowing in the shallows until night began to fall.

His house was more habitable now that he had replaced the broken windows and rid the rooms of scorpions and those infernal jumping spiders that had unnerved him so those first few nights. A scorpion had escaped his cull, for only last night as he lay in bed and by the light of an oil lamp, he had seen one scuttling to disappear behind the skirting board. But he was becoming accustomed to scorpions; it was only the bats that bothered him now – every twilight bats in his living room- how the hell did they get in, and how the hell was he ever going to get rid of them?

Another man, Freddie Bristow, would be arriving soon to help him with the project; he would feel more secure with another man to share the house at night. Bristow was to spend three weeks in Nairobi learning the rudiments of the *Kamba* language, just as Charlie had done; time wasted, considering most of the locals spoke good English, and were a lot more colourful to listen to. How shame-faced Charlie had been, when asked by a local school-boy how many languages he was able to speak; he had answered, 'Why, one of course, English.' Were there others, others that mattered? Didn't everyone speak English, simply everyone in the world?

The new guy Bristow, would they see eye to eye? Working together was one thing but *living* together was a different thing altogether. Up to now all had gone well. To the villagers, Charlie, easy going and accommodating, and with a camera, a truck and money, was a prince among men. A pied piper to the children and an enigma to the women, the sudden introduction of another *musungu*, and a younger one at that, could well alter dynamics irreversibly. Well, there was nothing Charlie could do about it and he would carry on as he had begun. He would keep giving because it was his nature to give. Those who give of themselves receive in kind a tide of goodwill and generosity, it flows through them, to and fro, and the moment such a man as Charlie stops giving and conserves then his spirit stagnates and all the glory in him dies. Although in Charlie's case there were reservations with this philosophy: when it came to women, there had been an awful lot of giving, very little receiving in return and no glory whatsoever.

He slowed for oncoming traffic and glanced in his rear view mirror. The women still had their heads sunk to their chests but appeared to have stopped their lament; the heat gate-crashed through the open window and bludgeoned him. As he drove, he thought of his life in Katamara and was satisfied. The women of the village looked upon him shyly, unsure of his inclinations, he, in turn, looked shyly back, terrified of theirs, but time was on his side. The sisters at the hospital he came into contact with only when he wanted to, but Jennifer Collins, the Irish nurse, was lovely and he timed his shopping expeditions to the village to coincide with hers. But when he saw her, he avoided her, it was most unlikely that she had the time to want to stop and talk with him. He got on well with the village men and with the volunteers. He had been given rudimentary drawings to work from, a budget to work with and basic instructions on manpower: maximise the local workforce of volunteers and maximise the local elements of construction but minimise expenditure, and then he had been left to it. So Charlie made his plans for the construction of the accommodation block, natural stone for foundations and external walls, earth blocks for internal walls and sisal roof trussing. A decision on roofing materials he would leave to Freddie Bristow. Oh, and the plasterwork had to be a mixture of soil and whitewash.

Charlie's problem was, although he had qualified as a bricklayer at the technical college twenty years earlier, he had never laid, pointed or plastered a brick since. A building firm had employed him and through work-force expediency at the time, stuck him in an office, and, showing a flair for office work, there he remained. Charlie had the qualifications but not the expertise. Twenty years later, and still in the office, Charlie produced his qualifications and was readily accepted by the Aid Agency. In the universal spectrum of the payroll how many of us are similarly and fatally employed within the parameters of these bizarre dynamics? Guiltily, Charlie knew how much was to fall on the shoulders of the new guy, Freddie Bristow.

They were nearing Thika, famous for its flame trees, but it would be June before the blush of molten orange would be seen, and then only if the rains were good. Charlie had been told that there was nothing in nature as glorious as a flame tree's celebration of the rain. Once upon a time, and not so long ago, the town was ablaze with flame trees. Most were gone now, the few remaining in private plots and gardens, having escaped the enterprising *fundi's* axe; how ignominiously ironic for a gorgeous flame tree to end its days as charcoal.

The women were quite still, one of them directing him with hand gestures that there was no need to venture into town. The mortuary stood in its own grounds as an attachment to the hospital and was easy to find. Built in brick, the building was a modern single storey construction with a French tile roof, but its grounds were un-kept and in some places heavily overgrown, a brush of sisal, cactus and paperback thorn. Charlie parked the truck conveniently, then, following the women to the main entrance doors, was surprised to find them locked. The women in turn knocked on the doors without response and looking perplexed at the hollow resonance from within, they exchanged their concerns in their native *Kamba* tongue.

It was oven-hot and Charlie was irritated; this was an official hospital building and there should have been an attendant to meet them. Prior arrangements had been made with authorities for the women to pick up the body of the baby at a precise time.

If Charlie had one major complaint with his new Kenyan home it was the dilatory and perfunctory attitude of its officials, and notwithstanding its inherent corruption, this was a classic example. It was only common decency for someone to be there to meet them, and although he was not a man to make unnecessary fuss, he would find the person responsible and make his feelings clear. In turn the women knocked on the doors again but only the dead were listening. 'We'll wait at the gate,' Charlie said impatiently.

By the gate, they sheltered from the sun beneath a cabbage tree until a man approached. Charlie stopped him politely. 'We're trying to get into the mortuary, have you any idea where the attendant might be?' he asked.

The man answered with a toothless smile. He knew exactly where the attendant might be and pointed distantly in the direction of town, making a drinking motion with his hand.

'Drinking in a pub?' Charlie snorted.

The man emitted a wheezing giggle, his unsupported lips flapping noisily, 'He will be drunked up, Josephat all the time is drunked up.'

Claws of anger crept over Charlie's skin as if they were the talons of a raptor and he the flesh it feasted on. Who was this attendant and who were these ladies to be treated so discourteously? 'Wait here,' he told the women, 'I'm going to get him and drag him back here to do his job.' He found two pubs in the direction the man had indicated both of which also served as groceries and haberdasheries. The proprietors knew Josephat well as a regular customer, the second one implying that Josephat might be found in bushes.

''The Bushes', is that another pub?' Charlie asked irritably.

'The bushes, the bushes around the mortuary,' the shop-keeper explained.

Charlie prickled with heat and rage. If Josephat was in bushes in the grounds of the mortuary then he was fast asleep, otherwise he would have heard the knocking on the doors. This wasn't dilatory or perfunctory, this was dereliction of duty on a massive scale. The man would explain himself or be dragged by the scruff of his neck to the hospital and exposed to whosoever purported to be in authority. 'Look for him in the bushes,' he snapped at the women when he arrived back at the gate. There followed an immediate collective search of shrubbery until Josephat, unequivocally drunk, was found asleep in a thicket. Charlie hauled the spluttering, protesting decrepit to his feet and began to harangue him violently. 'How dare you, how dare you? You drunken fool. These ladies have come all the way from Katamara to collect a baby and you should have been here to meet them. Look at you,' he shook him, trying to bring him to his senses. 'Look at yourself. You are a disgrace, you—you—' In his gorge of indignation he was spluttering himself.

Josephat slurred a protest and tried to stagger back into the thicket but Charlie held onto him. The official was wearing a stained white tunic of office with the effrontery of a badge bearing his name pinned to the breast pocket. The thicket in which he sought refuge was littered with empty beer bottles. Charlie pulled him clear of the undergrowth and although resisting the urge to slap his face, he did not moderate his tone, 'These ladies have come from Katamara to collect a baby for burial. Now get those doors open. Understand me?' He then began half-pushing, half-carrying the man towards the doors of the mortuary, suspending further vituperation because of the effort and energy required. Heaving for breath, he propped the stupefied attendant against a tree until he regained composure. 'Pissed out of your mind in a bloody bush, what sort of a man are you? A disgrace to yourself and to your country, how can Kenya hope to re-build itself as a nation with drunken idiots like you holding responsible positions in the community, asleep, paralytic, out of their mind with drink?'

The drunk gurgled.

His bald pate frying, sweat streaming down his back, Charlie grabbed the man as he tilted away from the tree. He looked around for the women. They were waiting patiently and silently at the mortuary doors. 'Listen, the minute I get those ladies back to Katamara I'm going to return here and report you to the hospital authorities. I'll see you get fired, understand? I'll see you get the sack. Now open those bloody doors.'

Glassy-eyed and drooling, Josephat looked uncomprehendingly into Charlie's face. Gabbling something in an unknown language, he consented to be hauled up the mortuary steps. Ferreting in the pocket of his tunic, he produced a large key and, after waving it in the faces of the women, attempted to impale the door lock. Prodding with the key, he managed to locate the keyhole and with an elaborate twist one of the doors swung open inwards. Charlie entered first, the women following, with the drunk left slavering at the threshold. Charlie heard the door close and felt the women jostling behind him.

This was the story he could tell back home. The long, dimly lit rectangular room, the narrow aisle, the women crowding him. Somewhere in this eerie mausoleum a dead baby; the meagre light from latticed panels close to the ceiling; clearer now, the shapes of draped bodies at either side on stretcher-type beds. How many of the beer-swilling men of Tala, his home town, had ever experienced anything—? His senses exploded as he hit a wall of stench. He turned in panic only to hit a second wall, a wall of muttering women. He was trapped in a palpable well of putrefaction. This place had no refrigeration. A roasting day on the equator and he was in a room with dead bodies and no refrigeration. He began to wretch violently as he attempted to wrestle through the women. He knocked one woman to the floor and in his haste to escape he sprawled on top of her, he was clawing at her. Now another woman had fallen but he was on his feet and he was trampling on their bodies, trying to reach the doors. Falling sideways, he dislodged the leg of a cadaver; it brushed his face and emitted a cloying putrid gas; a gathering posse of decaying bodies prevented him reaching the doors. Hand clasped over his mouth, he vomited through his fingers but he was free. Somehow he had untangled himself from the women and the dead and had reached the doors. The closed doors: the locked doors. The drunk had locked the doors and was sleeping soundly in the thicket.

Doors from public buildings should be fitted with a panic bolt and open outwards, Charlie knew that much, but was a house for the dead a public building? Kenya had adopted the British infrastructure comprehensively, what of its building codes? Twisting the door handle, he flung his weight at the doors but they did not yield and he slumped into a pit of vomit and despair. In a safe-deposit of consciousness, a fragment of self-preserving intellect bolted through boundless horror to reach his reason. The doors opened inwards, he had remembered the key, and the lock, and the door opening inwards and he was outside retching into bushes and the sweet, sweet air of mankind's cradle would never taste so sweet again. Oh where was Josephat that innocent, much maligned attendant?

Josephat was staggering back to the sanctuary of his thicket and the oblivion of beer and sleep but before he could fall inside, Charlie was lurching after him. Eyes streaming, 'Wooooooooaaaaaaaa there my friend,' he called and caught him and held him but the hands that now held Josephat were those of understanding and togetherness. 'Josephat, I had absolutely no idea of the conditions you have to put up with. My friend, you have every right to be drunk, every right to be pissed out of your mind twenty-four hours a day, seven days a week. Oh Josephat if I had to do your job I would be exactly the same, drunk, pissed, paralytic. I called you a disgrace, far from it, you should be honoured for the job you do. Who else would put up with conditions like that?' He embraced the man whose glassy eyes were as uncomprehending as when first he was pulled from the thicket. Charlie thrust a ten Kenyan shilling note into the tunic pocket behind the badge, and finished, 'Josephat my friend far from calling for you to be sacked, please have a drink on me.' The attendant staggered backwards and on falling to the ground resumed the same state of oblivious repose as when they found him.

Hearing footsteps, Charlie turned to see the four women walking sombrely and sedately towards the truck, the mother carrying a baby basket covered with a white cloth. Immediately he felt disgust at his own frailty. They were leaving the mortuary with a grace contrasting every whit with his own wretched exit. His squeamishness epitomised the puny sanitised mode of the white-man and he measured in disgust the vomit down the front of his shirt against the dignity of the women, two of whom he had trampled underfoot. Sheepishly he joined them at the truck, expecting and deserving words and looks of recrimination, but was pleasantly surprised to be met with an ambivalence that suggested his unseemly conduct had gone unnoticed. One of the women gestured kindly that they were ready to embark and as he helped them to board the truck he reflected on the story he would have to tell the men back home; he wouldn't, it was a shameful story. He nodded towards the building: 'I'm sorry for what happened in there, don't know what came over me, this heat I think, really I came over quite poorly.'

'It not good in there,' one of the women understated in broken English.

'Not good,' Charlie agreed.

'Not good,' the other three women concurred in unison.

'Let's get back to Katamara,' Charlie said.

Back on the Garissa road the women started wailing again and the wind whipped at what was left of the stalks.

Chapter Two

*F*rom Katamara village to the mountain, a stone bridge spans the Athi and is built just high enough to avoid the raging river when in flood. Across the bridge a narrow path squirms its way up the lower slopes of the north eastern side of mountain to peter out in heavy brush. People are wary of going beyond the path because higher on the mountain, buffalo graze the grassland and leopards prowl the brush. At either side of the path, only wide enough to accommodate a single vehicle, there is heavy undergrowth, home to a multitude of unknown and unseen creatures, they are born and live their lives and die there beside the path and each in their own way make impact on the world just as we humans do.

Smaller paths converge and are used to traffic livestock from the smallholdings, *shambas* of squatters, those who have illegally settled on the mountain. The squatters take their herds across the bridge each morning to the fertile grazing land around the village and return them to their corals on the mountain before nightfall. The animals are usually shepherded by boys or old men and no one seems to know their names; they keep themselves to themselves, maybe out of fear of upsetting the locals who might try to get them evicted from their homes. About a quarter of a mile along this steadily rising path is the house of the *musungus*. An ex-colonial residence: it has always been home to whites and still is. Charlie Carter lives there. The house cannot be seen from the village or the bridge but anyone turning three bends on the path can see it clearly to the left, a two story building faced with stucco which had been painted white at one time. Trees of great variety surround the house and those at the rear, fever trees and slim pod acacia are higher on the mountain and sometimes chimpanzee can be seen in the branches. Sometimes these monkeys are very still, seemingly watchful, custodial.

Freddie Bristow would arrive soon and he and Charlie would live together until they had completed the building project; the new accommodation block for the Catholic nuns who ran the hospital situated across the bridge in the village.

When Charlie first arrived, the house and its wild surroundings did not beckon to him as strange and untamed places often do to a man. Another, perhaps this new man, might be more sensitive to the history and nature of the house and terrain; he might be intrigued by a house for whites built in such an unlikely place. He may enquire about the people who once lived there and those who may have died there, for it was quite an eerie place. But not Charlie: Charlie had no inclination to explore the house or the mountain. In fact, he thought it was a liberty to call that hump of Kilimambogo earth a mountain at all; how could it qualify when on a clear day the glorious snow-capped peaks of Mount Kenya could be seen from the porch?

No, what had gone had gone and Charlie was looking to the future, a new future. He had no inclination to probe the mists of time; the milieu of antiquity was lost on Charlie. This was do-mestic accommodation and what man would be concerned with history when on his first day he found an abode where he was expected to live for two years, almost derelict and colonised by cockroaches, scorpions, spiders and lizards? The odd snake too. Charlie's liked to think of himself as a pragmatist and his only thought was to make the house fit for human habitation, and this he did. He visited Thika daily for materials for repairs and poisons for infestation and within the first two weeks the house was liveable. Except for bats, he had not prepared for bats. They came, into what he called his living room, and went of their own volition and defied every measure he had, hitherto, taken to prevent their entry and rid the house of them. They unnerved him and he hoped the new guy, Bristow, would have more success.

Charlie Carter was forty-four years old and he hadn't done much with those years: no wife yet or children and no prospect of them either. He had lived in the Yorkshire town of Tala with a mother who forever badgered him to marry and settle down. Something had to be done; if life is going nowhere; change direction fast.

People warmed to Charlie, for although life had not been bounteous, he never felt the want to offload his misfortunes onto others. But the warmth of people is not enough. That was why he found himself fearful in a house on the side of a mountain in rural Kenya. Why, that first night as he had huddled on his bed, cradling his knees in terror of the scorpions and spiders, he asked himself what the hell was he was doing there? Well, although he didn't like to admit it, not even to himself, he was there in the hope of finding a woman. Rather than confront the bad choices he had made with women and try to remedy them, he just kept repeating them so that one was diluted in seriousness by the sheer volume of the others. Be they English or Kenyan, women were a big problem for Charlie. He was more afraid of woman than the creatures that had made his house their home.

The house had two floors. The ground floor consisted of two bedrooms, a living room, a washroom and a small, cockroach-infested kitchen. At one time it had hosted an internal lavatory next to the washroom, now non-functional, the water cut off and the compartment irredeemably disgusting. What now served as a *choo* was an enclosed hole in the ground, detached a few yards from the house and remarkably free of flies; a phenomenon which no one was ever able to explain. The upper floor, accessed by a termite ridden staircase, boasted two large rooms, which probably, at one time served as bedrooms: derelict and littered with small boxes, one large box incongruously propped against a wall. There was other assorted debris, all draped with dusty cobwebs. With glass broken, small dirt-streaked windows looked out over the river and the mountain, permitting only token light to infiltrate the murk. These rooms had a sense of foreboding about them, and having viewed them briefly, once, Charlie vowed never to mount the suspect staircase again. The ground-floor rooms were sparsely furnished, the agency providing only the bare necessities for living, but he had managed to make his bedroom homely with coloured photographs, taken with his own camera and magazine pictures of wild life and native girls pinned to the walls. *Kangas*, the brightly coloured shawls favoured by Kenyan women, were also fastened to the walls and others served as curtains for the window and drapes for the two easy chairs. As homage to the tribal land on which he now lived, a *Kamba* bow and a quiver of arrows along with tribal batiks were secured to the wall above his bed, with a mosquito net pinned to the ceiling, as if a fluffy cloud had drifted in from the mountain. The locals had assured him that mosquitoes around these parts could not survive the cold nights, ironic, as mosquitoes were the only tiny creatures he had come prepared to face.

To distract his mind from the fears of night he read, evident by the stack of books alongside his bed or else he would listen to local broadcasts on the wireless. Often he would take the truck into the village and drink beer with the locals to help him sleep, but most nights, before sleep, he would take time to read his books.

Anyone entering Charlie's room and noting his stack of reading material would perceive that the topmost was a *Bond* by Ian Fleming but on further inspection would find *The Velvet Stripper* on a colourful cover directly underneath. Conceptual subterfuge it might be, but Charlie had never purported to be a literary aficionado; unashamedly, his lettered inclination pulsed in the direction of entertainment and titillation. A middle-aged single man, alone in a third-world country, was he likely to have Emerson's *Conduct of Life, Society and Solitude* within easy reach of his bedside?

The laws in Kenya are quite benign, especially in application to travelling whites, but following extensive but discreet enquiries,

Charlie understood that the Kenyan nation did not hold liberal views on the possession of salacious material, so, not being a man to take chances, the stuff he smuggled through Jomo Kenyatta Airport was pretty mild indeed. A customs official had waved him through without question but had he decided to rummage through Charlie's bags he would have been surprised to find *The Confessions of a Dairy Maid* within the folds of *'a cleverly constructed thriller'* and *'a deeply moving examination of contemporary dilemmas'* eclipsing raunchy shenanigans behind the curtains of a London suburb.

There were genuine Westerns and Murder Mysteries within Charlie's bedside stack but the observer in his room could not help but notice, with a glance, which of the reading material was the most well-thumbed.

That first week in the house it was the 'dairy maid', long into the night, who distracted him from the fearful sounds of creaking timbers, shrieking animals and the silent scuttling of scorpions. The oil lamp he dared not extinguish even though its flickering, spectral light only added to his fears, the shadows it cast hosting unseen phantoms. He would find himself jerking his head from the pages of his book to try and catch them as they faded into faint penumbras. And the shadows of bats in the living room that he could not hear or see, they seemed to be able to flit through solid walls, always two but sometimes three or four, silent and sinister, appearing in the dusk of evening; what attracted them? Did they feed on gnats and midges thriving in the high, hot space beneath the ceiling? Desperate for sleep he would lay his 'dairy maid' aside and close his eyes but they were always there, all the more fearful for darting and feeding in the corners of his mind.

After a week he had grown a little more accustomed to the creatures with which he was besieged but he still abhorred them, especially the bats, even though they were always gone when he ventured into sunlight sweeping through the window. He needed someone with him, he hated being alone in the house at night.

The new man, when he arrived, would keep him company and together they could laugh at all his fears.

But there was already a compensation he was thankful for, from the first day of his arrival he was rewarded by the appearance of a brown, short haired *shamba*-dog that awaited him each morning on the porch, and was there again when he returned from work each evening. She was a sturdy bitch that wagged her tail and barked a welcome until she was fed a bone or left-overs from a meal. They were immediate friends and Charlie called her Brownie, not an inspirational name but then Charlie was not an inspirational man. Brownie's visits were a blessing to the lonely man and after each evening meal there was more left over on the plate than there was the night before.

Night had fallen and sitting at the doorway of his bedroom he watched for the bats. When they came, he could close the door and start to read; try to forget them. Tonight they were late, and he nurtured pale hope that they were gone. They had never been so late and he was about to retire to his bed when they materialized. Suddenly they were there with no gap or crack from whence they could have come, two of them forming instantly from the shadowy fabric of the room, swooping and whirling in macabre, lamp-lit spirals. Then came a gentle knocking at his door; no one had ever knocked on his door at night. Tentatively, holding the lamp at head height, Charlie anxiously opened the door onto the porch.

'Me I am Titus,' a voice filtered from the dark and through the bowl of light.

Lamp-light shifted shadows until a shape came into view: a black-clothed, diminutive form, a barely discernible face; a bright yellow balaclava on which was perched a black trilby hat. It was a music-hall caricature of everything small and comical, lost and vulnerable.

'Can I help you?' Charlie asked politely.

'Me I am Titus again;' the soft voice was laden with geniality and so was the obligatory handshake. The stature of a boy possessing a man's voice followed the handshake into the light. In his left hand was clasped what looked like a bow, arrows and an umbrella and as his right hand fell to his side he smiled twin rows of startlingly white teeth and Charlie, without compunction, welcomed him further inside the house.

'I wasn't expecting anyone,' Charlie said, 'you gave me quite a shock.' Above them, the bats circled and wheeled beneath the ceiling. 'These bloody things, I don't know where they come from, I want rid of them.'

The two men crossed the living-room floor to the bedroom whereon the little stranger began to disrobe. Charlie watched him, mesmerised. First the bow and arrows were laid aside and then the umbrella. The trilby was placed on a chair then the balaclava removed with some difficulty was laid on top. Surely someone was having a joke with him. This Chaplin-like figure then slowly and meticulously removed an overcoat, two jackets and a scarf, becoming smaller and thinner with each layer. This was the joke; a man was going to disappear before his eyes.

Charlie laughed, 'Please Titus, tell me who you are.'

'It is only me I think, and I am here to assist you by special dispensation.'

'Oh we are going to be friends I can tell,' Charlie chuckled. Titus was older than he had first thought, probably late twenties but completely self-assured for a stranger in a strange house. There was not a hint of shyness or discomfort about him and he radiated a familiarity for his new surroundings that Charlie envied. 'If you're here to assist me, then getting rid of those bats would be a great start.'

'Bats is OK except they shit,' Titus replied gravely from amid a pile of his own clothes.

'They can shit as much as they like as long as they shit somewhere else.'

'I will see to it. Bat shit is not good.'

Charlie started to laugh again. 'I still don't know who you are and why you are here. No please don't introduce yourself again, just tell me why you are here to assist me.'

'I am,' Titus began, pausing for theatrical effect, 'your *askari*.'

'*Askari*?' Charlie wondered.

'Soldier, guard, watchman, *askari*, I stay out on your porch each night armed with bow and arrows. I am to protect you.'

'If you're to protect me I think I'd prefer you inside the house,' Charlie quaffed.

'It is better I am outside.'

'To protect me from what?'

'Ants.'

Yes, he was being fooled. This ant of a man was here to protect him from his own kind. 'Ants,' Charlie scratched his head.

'And bandits.'

'Ants and bandits,' Charlie repeated the words slowly, weighing up the relative threat. 'And who's paying you for providing this protection?'

'I am being paid by the Co-Operative who owns this land and this house but I was sent here by your agency. "Go to *Bwana* Charlie," I was told, "and be vigilant at all times." Me, I do not sleep but be vigilant at all times and by the will of Almighty God my arrows will find their targets. This is a good opportunity for me because I have been without work for some months causing a wolf to nest outside my door and great problems of finance circle my family but now I am your soldier and God in heaven has smiled on both of us.'

'I think He has,' Charlie grinned. 'These bandits?'

'Bandits who roam this mountain for a long time now and are very bad; they will smash a great rock through your door at night to scare you, then rob, torture and murder you, often worse. But they very much fear an armed *askari* such as Titus.'

'Well, thank God for that. And ants?' Charlie asked dryly, knowing now he wasn't expected to pay for this tiny man's dubious protection.

The face of Titus grew grave. '*Bwana* Charlie, there is many types of ant in Kenya, around these parts, mostly fire ants and soldier ants and both is known to kill a buffalo, strip it to the bone. They come in a great army and you will see it before you leave this place. But outside on the porch I will be vigilant at their coming and warn you before they eat you up alive.'

'Yes I think you might be better outside,' Charlie conceded ruefully. And so for the next two hours they talked of ants and bandits and other creatures of the mountain night that might assail a vulnerable *musungu* without a watchful soldier at his door. And as they talked they got to know and understand each other and the spontaneous affection they had for each other grew palpable. Different worlds, yet of the same order, each in awe of the other's comforts and each the other's dread. Conversation was easy, and sprinkled with queries, laughter, answers and concern, as it was, it could have lasted until dawn. They moved from the bedroom to the kitchen, noting that the bats were gone and scattering cockroaches with their tread. Charlie drank beer and Titus drank tea, for no *askari* worth his salt drank alcohol on the job. Tenderness towards his new friend filled Charlie's heart and at midnight, and ignoring the little man's protests, he took one of his easy chairs out onto the porch and covered it with a blanket so that his *askari* could be warm and comfortable for what was left of his watch.

'No chair, no blanket,' Titus objected: comfort was not compatible with the diligence required for the vagaries of night. 'But God bless you a lot, Amen. Tomorrow I bring photos of my family. My first born in standard two and my last born a baby only and you will see that my wife Josephine is fine and my other two children is fine and pushing on with life. And when you visit my *shamba* we will kill a chicken in your honour and my wife will cook it for you and you will drink beer made with honey, which is very powerful, and you will leave my *shamba* drunk. So drunk in fact that I will have to escort you to make sure you do not fall from the bridge into the Athi and get eaten by a crocodile.' With this, Titus shook with laughter.

'It's a deal,' Charlie said.

'I'm interested in your *shamba* in England,' Titus said.

They moved back inside the house and Charlie showed him

photographs and Titus studied each in turn with progressive bewilderment before saying, 'And this is your mother in her *shamba*?' He spoke of an elderly grey-haired lady in her garden in the spring.

'Yes, that's my mother in her garden.'

'Then her garden is very beautiful. What is all the yellow?'

Charlie peered over his shoulder, 'Why, those are flowers, daffodils.'

'I have never seen flowers as these. They are very beautiful. Your mother sells them in the market?'

Charlie laughed, 'No, my mother never sells flowers in the market.'

'She sells them on the roadside?'

'No. She doesn't sell them at all.'

Titus was baffled. 'Then what does she do with them. Do you eat them?'

Charlie had to think. What did his mother do with all those flowers? She looked at them; that was all she did. She just looked at them from her kitchen window. He had never given that saffron blaze a single thought until now. But he was talking to a man to whom every clod of earth must be nurtured to produce, what use to Titus and his family is a field of yellow stone? 'She looks at them,' he answered a little shamefully.

'You don't eat them and your mother she doesn't sell them but just looks at them,' Titus repeated contemplatively and Charlie thought he sounded sad that *musungus* could countenance such waste. 'And for how long does she look at them?'

Charlie pondered, 'About three weeks I suppose.'

Titus could not understand a woman beholding proudly a wasteland of her making however gilded it might be, only colour; a wife and children cannot live on colour but then there were many idiosyncrasies of the opulent West he couldn't understand. His fingers shuffled through the intriguing photographs. 'And who is the people buried here?' he asked gesturing to stone bird-bath and bird-table side by side.

Charlie chuckled, 'They are not gravestones. The one on the left is a bird-bath, the one on the right a bird-table. They are there for wild birds. In England we're not allowed to bury people in our gardens.'

Perhaps Titus could just about grasp a garden full of worthless flowers but the bathing and feeding of wild birds was completely beyond comprehension; 'You bathe the birds?'

'Well not exactly, the birds come down and bathe themselves.' Charlie was struggling not to laugh at something quite pre-posterous. He knew that the corners of Kenyan *shambas* were consecrated for the dead of a family with small tombstones as testimony to their lives. Where better to bury a grandmother than in the bosom of her descendants?

But Titus had entered an alien world where people practised the most senseless things and he did not wish to show contempt but he did wish to understand a little clearer, 'And these bird tables, you put food on them?'

'Yes.'

'And birds sit down to eat?'

'Well not exactly.'

'You are bathing wild birds then setting out food for them to eat?'

'We feed them, yes,'

And suddenly Titus understood, and a huge smile transformed his face. 'Ah yes, I see, I see. The birds come down to bathe and eat and you shoot them. Your mother then cooks them and you have your dinner.'

Speechless, Charlie shook his head. Then they looked at each other and when their eyes met there was a palpable sense of accord and humour, a meeting of souls immutable and indestructible; how different their respective worlds were to one another. 'No, we don't shoot them, we don't eat them. Titus, it is the white world that is crazy,' and Titus understood.

Midnight came and went. They moved on to the porch and under the *mabati* roof Titus put on all his clothes again, even the ridiculous trilby hat upon his yellow balaclava. Charlie perched on the arm of the easy chair he had provided, inviting his tiny friend to sink down in its depths.

'Rest too easily and a man might fail at his job,' Titus scorned, twanging the string of his bow in preparedness for his vigil.

'Sit the night out warm, you don't have to fall asleep,' Charlie counselled.

Horrified at the imputation of the word 'asleep' Titus adopted a challenging stance against the black backdrop of the mountain. Charlie was striking at the heart of his profession, the integrity of his calling. 'That chair, it is too nice for an *askari* and I will not do it. It is my duty to remain vigilant and protect you,' the declaration was emphatic.

'Well there's tea and coffee in the kitchen, food too, just help yourself.'

'I will do it *Bwana* Charlie.'

It was a beautiful African night, still and bright with stars; the vast Kenyan sky brimming with stars, the great pale moon chief among them. The light of the oil lamp disturbed winged insects which buzzed and pinged the glass. Towards the river *a shamba* dog barked at fearful things and beyond the river in the village another answered its call. One part of the village had electric light, little wavering spots which kindled through the trees like fireflies. Charlie felt warm and happy to have a companion and for the first time he felt no fear of the night. 'When will it rain?' he asked.

'Tonight,' Titus answered readily, sniffing at the air. 'The moon can get no bigger now and as the moon gets smaller and smaller so it rains and rains. It is the rain that shrinks the moon. In the morning I will start pushing on with preparation for the harvest so that in future I can be keeping my head over water and my family in fine fettle, thanks be to God.'

'I am looking forward to the monsoon rain,' Charlie said. 'I've heard it is quite something to behold.'

Spurning the chair, Titus switched on his torch and extravagantly searched the porch before taking up a position, sentry-like, beside the door.

'Goodnight, Titus.'

'Goodnight, Mr Charlie, I think we are good friends.'

'I think we are,' Charlie said.

Charlie awakened. Dawn was not far off, the moon dim and sinking fast. He got out of bed, tiptoed across the living room and noiselessly opened the door to the porch. With the blanket wrapped tightly around him, Titus was slumped in the chair fast asleep and snoring gently. A light wind troubled the leaves and grasses but could not budge great arms of black cloud, blacker than night, that coveted the mountain. Charlie returned to his bed and soon he was sleeping soundly too.

When he awakened it was raining gently, not the thunderous monsoon rains he had expected. The blanket and the chair had been returned to the living room and Titus was gone.

Chapter Three

*B*efore Charlie's arrival at the construction site, a communications specialist from the Aid Agency had been seconded to the hospital to survey the area and generate goodwill among the locals. Her specific assignment had been to communicate with dignitaries in order to recruit sufficient voluntary labour to make the hospital accommodation extension a viable proposition. The specialist was efficient; volunteers being so plentiful that their living proximity to the site became the primary component of her selection criteria, thereby logistics and hurt feelings were dealt with in one fell swoop.

Upon selection, the volunteer force, consisting of approximately twelve men at any one time, was each expected to give a minimum of three months full-time work on the project, consideration being given to the upkeep of their own families. As it turned out, few of the older men were able to work more than the requisite three months but some of the younger ones (the youngest being Sammy, at twelve years old) gave their time unconditionally and many remained on site for the duration of the project. They shrugged their shoulders in explanation. There wasn't much else to do!

All personnel would receive a daily meal financed by the organisation and cooked on-site by the only female volunteer, an old lady called Mama Mary. Of course for all men there was the added incentive of training. Even after working for the minimum three months, a man could return at will to update himself on progress and avail himself of technological developments. By the time the building was finished, it was expected that each man, to some degree, would be proficient in all the aspects of alternative construction techniques. The only stumbling block, and it was a big one, was the man who was supposed to be doing the training.

As soon as work began, Charlie knew that he was to learn far more from his trainees than ever they would learn from him. Having built, or helped to build, their own houses *nyumbas*, they already knew about the methods and properties of wattle and daub and sisal construction. As Charlie talked to the men about the proposals, he was evasive when questioned on specifics. He knew about rendering walls with a mixture of earth and white-wash but had no idea how it was done. Having spent the last twenty years in an office, he had never handled anything more constructively dexterous than a Biro. And that very first morning, as he addressed his workforce on the properties of the soil necessary for stabilized block construction, it was pointed out to him that the site chosen stood on irredeemably unusable black cotton earth, but before he had had the chance to scratch his head in bafflement he was led to a nearby stretch of red murram, which the volunteers knew, was ideal for purpose.

So Charlie, having started with the less demanding digging and laying of foundations, would make the job last until help arrived. Acutely aware that in the fullness of time his limitations were bound to be even more exposed, he embarked on a programme of proactive ingratiation. He might never understand, let alone teach the complexities of third-world pan-tile manufacture but he could buy sweet-cakes at tea time and fussily take on the role of health and safety. How he fretted as shovels, spades and pick-axe heads diced with toes and ankles. Yes, unbelievably, most of the men worked on site in their bare feet. Charlie calmed only when he realized that the bare calloused feet of his native workforce were as tough and durable as rhino hide.

It had rained heavily over the last couple of days, the rain falling at night with the days that followed blistering hot. It had been a good week for Charlie, the best week since his arrival. The nights were no longer sleepless and the bats no longer fearful with Titus at his door. The men on site were in high spirits too. The foundations were finished and the building was now ready for construction. With the new man expected to arrive today or tomorrow, real progress could be made. To celebrate completion of the first phase, the men had stopped work in early afternoon. The day had been the hottest since the day of his best forgotten visit to the mortuary and Charlie was sweaty, dirty and tired as he began his weary walk back to the house. He was looking forward to a wash and a rest and, having stomached Mary's *ugali* and *githeri* at lunch time, something more appetising for evening dinner.

Already he had a lot to thank Titus for and teaching him the rudiments of cooking was high on the list. He smiled at the thought of the tiny soldier, heaven-sent to protect him from bandits and ants. The perception of a balaclava clad, trilbied joke of a man fitting an arrow to his bow as a deterrent to the dangers of the mountain struck him as ridiculous, but as a night-time companion he was priceless.

As he trudged uphill he reflected satisfyingly on his weight loss, everywhere except his middle. Oh, he might well complain about Mary's *ugali* which had the look, texture and redolence of partially solidified wallpaper paste, the taste too, and the watery cabbage which passed under the name of *githeri,* but the diet was doing wonders for his body. Maybe a pot belly was always the last to go. His physique was reacting well to his work regime also, he had taken to leaving the truck at the house and walking to and from work each day. He chuckled inwardly at what his mother would have to say when next she saw him. But he promised himself a good meal today. Yesterday he had bought meat, maize, potatoes and beans and with the liberal addition of herbs and the tutelage of Titus, he was confident that the whole culinary shebang would not be rendered inedible by the process of his cooking as it had been before. He would know tonight.

Crossing the bridge he began whistling. He was early and Brownie would not be waiting but, hearing his whistle, the dog would materialize by his side; where she came from Charlie had no idea but surely she knew where a good meal could be had. 'Brownie – Brownie,' he called into the bush. When there was no response he began whistling again. With the house in sight, he saw that a second truck was parked beside his own, it was the truck he had seen passing the site earlier. His stomach lurched with excitement. Bristow the new man was here. He stopped whistling and through the shimmering heat he saw a bare-chested man unloading goods from the truck. There was a girl at the upstairs window. She appeared to be watching the man below her. She would be from the agency and Charlie would complain to her about the state of the staircase and the upper floor. It was difficult to make out her features through the dirty glass but she seemed to be a lot younger than the woman who had accompanied him on his first day, and a lot prettier.

So who was this man who would share his life for the next two years? The last time he had been at the agency office in Nairobi he had heard that the new man also came from Tala. Some coincidence as Tala was a relatively small town, and Charlie, as he commenced uphill, wondered if perhaps he might have met the man before; he might even know him. As he neared the house he saw that the man was moving about in the back of the truck and the woman at the window had gone. He was tall, dark-haired and muscular, and, even at a distance, plainly younger than Charlie. Charlie grimaced. No wonder the girl at the window had been watching him.

As Freddie Bristow moved about the truck his actions had the effortlessness of an athlete 'Hey there,' Charlie called. Stripped to the waist, the man didn't tense his stomach muscles, the way most men do when approached by another male. He didn't have to; they stretched across his torso like a mobile iron grill. He

39

looked like the man Charlie would like to be and he felt a twinge of envy. Exuding confidence, Bristow was the antithesis of Charlie and Charlie's twinge redoubled to mistrust.

The new man vaulted from the truck and came to meet him, his smile as easy as his actions. They shook hands firmly. Was this man different to Charlie? Too bloody different, Charlie thought and his heart sank further.

'Freddie Bristow,' he announced in introduction, 'I know you're Charlie Carter. Understand that we both come from Tala, some coincidence.'

They looked each other in the eye.

'Yes, but I don't think we've ever met,' Charlie answered, all the time assessing the new man, figuring that he was every bit as good as he looked.

'Not from Tala really, got divorced and only moved to Tala about eight months ago,' Freddie continued, 'from Cravenvale, we won't have ever met. Excuse me, Charlie, but I'm in a hurry. Got to unload then take the truck back to Nairobi. Got to get back here tonight on a motor-bike they've given me, a *piki* they call it. Going to try and make it before it rains.' Wiping beads of perspiration from his brow with the back of his hand, he looked upwards at the mountain, and sniffing the air, continued, 'and according to the forecast, it's going to teem with rain tonight.' He jerked his head towards the house, 'God what a bloody dump,' and jerking a thumb towards the upstairs window, said, 'up there, holy Christ, as long as they don't expect us to live up there.'

Both laden, they walked towards the house together. A few items of furniture and parcelled goods remained to be unloaded. Freddie continued, 'Saw you working on site as I passed. Was going to stop but really, I didn't have the time. You can tell me everything I need to know tonight.'

Charlie said, 'Saw a truck pass, I wondered if it might be you. I won't be long in the shower. I've a couple of things I need to tell you before you set off back. Oh, have you seen a brown *shamba* dog, Brownie I call her? She's always here when I get home?'

Freddie shook his head. Charlie explained, 'I'm early but she'll be here soon enough, comes every morning, every evening without fail, see I feed her. Call her Brownie, the people around here don't give their dogs and cats names. People around here think I'm crazy. Now though, it's taken on, all the dogs are getting called Brownie, never seen so many confused dogs.'

Freddie laughed. Of course his teeth were perfect. 'Charlie, I've got to get back, I'll see you tonight,' he said hurriedly, apologetically.

'Ok, oh and we've got an *askari*, a night watchman, armed with a bow and arrows and an umbrella, cutest little fella you ever did see. Titus, you'll meet him tonight.'

With lithe grace, Freddie jumped aboard the truck. 'I'll tell you now, Charlie, I'm spending as little time in that bloody house as possible. The Agency has no right to give us such a grotty hole and I'll tell them when I get back. Upstairs', he shook his head. 'Christ.'

'You haven't seen the bats yet, I got rid of the scorpions but can't get rid of the bats,' Charlie called ruefully from the doorway, then, collecting soap and a towel, he made his way from his bedroom to the shower.

The washroom was a curved *mabati* construction accessed from the lobby of the rear exit door with a galvanised open tank on top. The tank was fed gravitationally by piped water from a small lake on the mountain and with the heat of the day the water would be warm. It was. With his clothes in a bundle by the doorway to the house, Charlie lathered under a steady stream, happy to see the dirty brown detritus of the day seeping into the soak-away beneath his feet. He heard the engine of the truck start up and remembered the girl from the agency. Freddie could have waited until he was finished in the shower. Charlie had asked him to wait; he wanted to meet with the girl, talk to her but she had been momentarily forgotten in the drama of meeting the new man. He wondered why she had not come out of the house to greet him; perhaps she was busy with something in Freddie's room. He was sure that he had never seen her before but would ask about her tonight.

Charlie had not known what to expect from the new man but he hadn't expected a Freddie Bristow. Freddie was just a little too perfect to be volunteering for work on a third-world building site. What the hell was he doing here? His dark hair curled about his ears and already his skin was turning an enviable, unpeeling bronze. Muscles rippled naturally beneath his skin when he moved and his hazel eyes were steady and assured. Although he had been undeniably friendly, there was a hint of arrogance about him but it could be confidence. Having little of his own, Charlie often mistook confidence for arrogance. Speaking educated English, with only mild expletives, Freddie's voice was easy to listen to and Charlie didn't feel threatened. Threat comes with competition or confrontation and Charlie instinctively knew that he could not compete with this guy. His hope was that they would get on together; they had to if they were going to live and work side by side for two years. Anyway, their differences could prove special. Disparities shared unequivocally would make each other whole and strong. The accommodation block was as good as built.

It was evening and the air had cooled. Heavy clouds were gathering ominously westward. Charlie watched them from the porch. Stacking high, they became top-heavy, spilling across the sky and the wind, which always came before nightfall, had brought them quickly to the mountain. The rain began to fall heavily, noisily on the *mabati* roof above him and he thought of Freddie Bristow speeding along Garissa Road on his *piki* and how wet he was going to be when he arrived. Presently, Charlie heard the *piki's* engine as it crossed the bridge.

Freddie effortlessly lifted the motor-bike into the shelter of the porch: 'Long way from Nairobi on a motor-bike on a shitty night like this,' he said, taking off his crash helmet. Together they started taking the contents of the panniers into Freddie's room.

'Titus will be here soon,' Charlie told him. 'He's here to protect us from bandits and ants.'

'Looking forward to meeting this Titus,' Freddie said, grinning. 'Did your dog turn up?'

Charlie had forgotten about Brownie. No, his dog hadn't turned up; strange. Freddie began taking off his wet clothes, shaking them outside on the porch. Rain hammered on the *mabati* roof and the men had to shout above its roar.

'She will turn up, she always does,' Charlie assured. 'She'll be here in the morning. The girl, this afternoon, you didn't wait. You didn't introduce me.'

Freddie looked blank.

'As I was coming up the hill, I stopped and saw you unloading the truck. There was a young girl in the upstairs window. I only saw her for a few seconds, the agency girl who was with you this afternoon when you arrived.'

'There was no agency girl with me when I arrived.'

'There was a girl, Freddie, I saw her.'

'I was on my own, Charlie. I don't know what you saw.'

'I saw a girl. She was at the upstairs window. She was watching you.'

Scratching his head, Freddie looked puzzled. 'Charlie, I promise you, there was no girl.'

Through the rain, they heard Titus coming up the hill.

Chapter Four

Charlie had arrived in Kenya during a period of political turmoil. The tragic and sterile years of the *Emergency Period* engendered by the *Mau Mau* uprising was long gone and the country had fared much better than anyone expected, certainly better than most other African countries, with their civil strife, insurrections and political coups. Charlie was inclined to think that it was more thanks to the co-operative and philosophical nature of its people than the political machinations of its leaders. Not that he concerned himself unduly with commerce and politics, but he read national newspapers and listened to the radio so he knew what was going on. What care had Charlie for the high price of oil and the stagnancy of the country's agricultural policy when he had cockroaches in his kitchen? Although, as he listened to arguments, he questioned himself: was he being unfair to Kenyatta and his KANU government? The country had enjoyed relative peace and stability during its ten years of independence and must take credit for steering a course of peaceful co-existence with both capitalism and communism and for having the sense to remain within the equable auspices of the Commonwealth. Charlie grinned. Kenya going through political turmoil; it was a Utopia compared to what he had left behind in the UK: inflation spiralling out of control, Irish Republican Army terrorists threatening to blow up its cities, a three-day week and piles of rotting rubbish in the streets. Miners' strikes, fuel shortages, power cuts and Edward Heath and Harold Wilson squabbling over a country swiftly going down the pan to the strains of T-Rex and a bizarre glam-rocker called Gary Glitter. Charlie didn't mind having to use candles; candle-lit dinners were fine if only he had someone other than his mother to share them with.

It had not rained for almost a week and the hot days and warm nights had hardened the ground and stiffened the rutted road so that when a police car, with two-tone blaring did not have to reduce speed as it passed the construction site towards the hospital, Charlie thought it must be the start of political rally. It wasn't. The men stood up from their work and muttered among themselves in speculation; what could have happened to warrant three policemen, one in plain-clothes, to travel with such urgency? These men would have come from either Machakos or Nairobi, usurping Corporal Adonis who, around Katamara was single-handedly responsible for law enforcement. This was not a political rally, neither was it a case of petty theft or affray; something grave must have happened at the hospital for that was where the vehicle was screeching to a stop.

Freddie Bristow had been on site for two weeks and Charlie had already relinquished responsibility to the new man as he had established himself, and amid a buzz of curiosity, it was Charlie who had been elected to walk to the hospital and find out what was going on. He was stopped at the gate by Corporal Adonis Musyoka whom Charlie knew as an ebullient man of many words, most of them self-congratulatory. Fully uniformed, his eyes obscured by shades with an unlit cigarette in the corner of his mouth, Adonis, stood, as always, with his pelvis thrust forward, a phallic symbol of authority in tangent with a manifestation of insecurity. Charlie was a little afraid of the corporal's reputation, as was everyone in Katamara. No doubt, there was little crime in the village for which the corporal must take credit but Charlie couldn't help but think of the policeman, as less of a custodian and more of a prick.

'A fatality,' Adonis confided, taking off his shades to let Charlie see the seriousness of the situation. Now, as the corporal would have everyone believe, there were many dark corners in the village of Katamara that were peopled by the demented and deranged, which were routine and grist to the mill to him, but in this case at the hospital there were 'sensitivities'. Sensitivities requiring a senior officer complete with investigating crew, attending from Nairobi. Adonis narrowed his eyes, not that he had much time for sensitive cases. Why only last month he had been required at another village to deal with the death of a wife at the hands of a drunken husband. 'Full confession in fifteen minutes, that was all the time it took me,' he explained ungrudgingly. Then, 'I have my ways,' he expounded with a sly wink and, when Charlie choked at the implication, he elaborated. 'There's electricity in that village. Only half of Katamara has electricity you know, Charlie, but soon it will be the whole village including my police station and my job of interrogation will be so much easier.'

Was the policeman serious? Charlie felt he was. 'Well thanks be to God for that,' he agreed uncertainly.

Adonis breathed on his shades, polished them with a handkerchief and examined his reflection.

'So Adonis, what's all the commotion at the hospital?'

Adonis spat the cigarette to the ground and glanced from side to side as if he feared being overheard. 'A young boy, Kennedy, has been found dead in the dormitory. He was found hanging from a window cord. I know of that boy, he's a crippled boy so how has he been able to put the cord around his own neck and throw himself out of his cot?' He began chuckling at the concept, 'Very suspicious, that kid was too much of a nuisance and it is my suspicion that someone has put that cord around his neck and pushed him from the cot.' He tapped the side of his nose knowingly and all mirth vanished from his face in an instance. 'Someone in the hospital has murdered little Kennedy and I have a great suspicion who it is. I should be dealing with this case. If I was dealing with this case it would be over already. I rang Nairobi and told them to let me handle it – but – sensitivities,' he ended regretfully.

'Oh you should be dealing with it, Corporal,' Charlie concurred agreeably, as he was expected to. The policeman replaced his shades and taking another cigarette from a packet he clamped it in the left corner of his mouth. Adonis never lit his cigarettes, Charlie wondered why.

'The Missionary Sisters of the Precious Blood are important people around this place and the person I suspect is important too, so it is men from Nairobi who are called.' Adonis began to elaborate through one side of his mouth. 'They have sent an inspector but I am to assist him the minute I'm done with preventing unauthorised entry. "Prevent unauthorised entry, Corporal Adonis," the inspector told me when he arrived. Then the inspector said, "I will need your help, as I have been told that you know everything thing there is to know." It is Inspector Sam Wamiru and he is quite famous. I will be his right-hand man. "You are my right-hand man," he told me. He needs a right-hand man because his left hand is missing. In fact his whole arm is missing.' Adonis began chortling. 'He is the only policeman in the whole of Kenya to only have one arm, the whole world maybe.' Now he was doubling up with laughter.

'How did he lose his arm?' Charlie asked curiously.

Adonis closed his eyes and grimaced, then, opening them, squinted to either side again as if any knowledge he had was not only painful but highly secret: 'A police mission when he was bit by a spitting cobra and left footing through the night to a clinic.' Somehow the policeman was able to transfer the unlit cigarette to the other side of his mouth by only using his tongue. Charlie was mesmerised by the oral dexterity. 'Too late, gangrene and an amputated arm,' the corporal finalised, removing the cigarette so that it would not impede uproarious laughter.

Charlie made suitable commiserating noises but did not join in the fun.

Straight-faced again, the corporal continued. 'He thought he would lose his job as well as his arm but a year later he was promoted from sergeant to inspector. I am now deserving of such a promotion myself as, on my very own, I have kept this village free from bandits ever since I arrived. Bandits fear Corporal Adonis. Once I worked in a slaughter house where I was very diligent and well thought of by my employers who were *musungus*. Now what I learn there I practise on bad men of this area and they fear me much, but sometimes I think maybe I should find a spitting cobra of my own so as to get justly promoted.' Adonis removed his unlit cigarette, wedged it beneath his cap and took off his shades, polished them again with his handkerchief then studied his reflection again, this time regretfully.

'Is life ever fair but it will come, Adonis, I am sure of it?' Charlie lamented. Then, 'You think it might be possible for me to have a word with the inspector when he has the time? It's personal, something I need to know.'

Charlie would prefer to see Adonis sacked rather than promoted.

The corporal's eyes clouded with suspicion. Was a villager and *a* white at that, about to go over his head? This was an affront. 'Any problems Charlie, you must see me first.'

'No it's not a problem,' Charlie assured.

But it was a problem and a mystery, and being both fascinated and repulsed by the corporal's law-enforcement rationale he was reluctant to confide in him on anything. Moreover, he had been forewarned that any favours bestowed by the corporal were sure to cost him money. 'It's just something I want him to look up for me in Nairobi.'

'Mmmmm, maybe I could use my influence,' Adonis considered portentously. 'Soon I will be in there,' he jerked his head towards the hospital, 'Inspector Wamiru will need me, he told me so himself. I have information but such information is only for the ears of the inspector. See Charlie, it is only me who knows who murdered that kid Kennedy and if the inspector listens to me I will solve the case. But when the time becomes ripe I will ask him if he will assist you and when I tell him that you are my friend, I am confident he will say yes and you will owe me a big service.'

'Thank you, Corporal. Please tell him that it will be a favour only and that it is not terribly important.'

Answering a call from the hospital Adonis squared his shoulders, sniffed purposefully and marched soldier-like towards the building.

Not terribly important? Either Charlie was still sane and keen-sighted or the heat was starting to affect his mental stability. Were there grubs inside his head? In Africa things could get inside you, pupating parasites. Were they feasting on his reason? Was he seeing things? He had agonized but he *had* seen a girl in the upstairs window of his house. Although relatively featureless she was young, slim and brown and she was living, moving, flesh and blood. Why hadn't Freddie Bristow seen her too? He was in and out of the house unloading possessions from the truck. It was impossible for him not to know that she was there, he had been upstairs himself, how could he have missed her?

'Was she pretty?' Freddie had laughed scornfully. Freddie had begun poking fun at him.

Charlie was irritated. 'I never got close enough to see if she was pretty but my guess is that she was.'

'Believe me, Charlie, if she was young and pretty, I'd have seen her.'

'Freddie you've got to believe me, I know what I saw and I'm not going mad. I stopped on the path and watched you through the bushes. I wasn't spying or anything, just curious. The new guy had arrived. I wanted to see what he looked like. And I wondered who the girl was. Thought she must have been from the agency come to help you move in. A woman from the agency came with me the day that I arrived. I thought this was another, a younger one, one I hadn't seen. These things were going through my head as I saw her. You had me doubting myself for a time but she wasn't a figment of my imagination. She was at the upstairs window and she seemed to be looking down at you.'

Freddie sighed. 'Well no one came with me. They gave me a key and a map and I was on my way. They told me to stop at the site and tell you I'd arrived but I didn't, I drove straight by, wanted to unload the truck and get back. Rain, remember?'

'She was wearing a light-coloured dress,' Charlie said despairingly.

Freddie put a hand on Charlie's shoulder. 'It was really hot that day, blistering hot and you'd been working hard. You left early. You were looking at me, at the house from a distance through bushes, seen reflections in the glass. You might have been suffering heat stroke, sun stroke or whatever it is.'

'I saw a woman, Freddie,' Charlie despaired, 'or a ghost.'

'There are no ghosts in Kenya. For Christ's sake, ghosts don't haunt mud huts. There isn't bloody room. What self-respecting ghost would be seen floating around a mud hut rattling chains? Chains getting tangled up with kids and dogs and chickens, it'd be apologising all the time for tripping over things.'

'Our place isn't a mud hut,' Charlie argued unconvincingly. But the issue was getting out of hand. He simply had to stop talking about what he'd seen or thought he'd seen: he was making a fool of himself. Whenever he raised the subject of the spectral girl, Freddie ridiculed him.

Chapter Five

*T*hey had been together five weeks now and, in spite of enormous differences in interests and nature, they were compatible both at home and on site. The workmen enjoyed Freddie's company; he was a hard worker and his knowledge and expertise were inexhaustible. He was a joker too, and although his surreal, sarcastic, English humour was completely lost on them they accepted him, rejoicing in his proclivity for fooling them with card and coin tricks but Charlie sensed that behind every prank there was a dash of spite. He was mad but then all *musungus* were mad, it was just a question of degree. Anyone who would travel thousands of miles to work in appalling heat for next to nothing must be mad. Charlie was mad, and Freddie was mad and there was speculation on site and in the village as to who was the maddest, no doubt about it, Charlie was.

Forget the girl, real or illusionary, she must not be allowed to disrupt their fledgling companionship, they had the best part of two years to spend together. Freddie had made it clear from the start: he would work on site yes, but no one should expect him to spend his free time in Katamara. The cradle of mankind had a lot to offer, from the Rift Valley to the Maasai Mara game reserve, from Lake Victoria to the Lamu Archipelago there was a lot to take in and he would take advantage. Charlie, on the other hand, was happy to stay in Katamara with the people. As Freddie had commandeered the truck Charlie really didn't have much choice.

It could have been the heat, for Charlie Carter was not a man to see ghosts, he was a down-to- earth Tyke who didn't believe in ghosts, fairies, unidentified flying objects and he wasn't too sure about God for that matter either, but in the interests of détente with Freddie he had decided to put the matter out of mind. But he found it difficult. It was quite possible that Freddie hadn't seen the girl but Charlie knew what he had seen; there was a girl in the house that day and whereas, hitherto, Charlie had had no interest in the house's history, he had now. Maybe Inspector Wamiru with access to archives in Nairobi could throw light on a mystery that was now bedevilling him.

With a bedroom/office provided until his investigation was complete, Wamiru couldn't sleep. It was night. He got out of bed, dressed and by the light of low-watt bulbs moved quietly along the corridors. Shadows like the branches of gaunt trees clung to the ceilings and walls and muted sounds whispered secrets from the portals of the sleeping building. The little boy's death was either an accident or deliberate murder. And if it was murder then it could only have been committed by Nurse Jennifer Collins. She didn't act like a murderess and could have no conceivable motive and from all the information he had accrued, the woman was devoted to Kennedy as she was to all the children in her care, yet he had a nagging doubt. She reminded him of Clara.

At every junction of the corridors, statues and portraits of saints eyed him suspiciously. A statue of St Anthony of Padua situated outside his bedroom door positively objected to him. And what was the significance of the coat of arms above the chapel door. It depicted a bleeding sheep. Earlier, Mother Veronica had eloquently explained that the image was the Lamb of God with a victorious flag and chalice, the chalice, a container into which the lamb's heart-blood streamed.

It was midnight and a nun was still about, a celibate, vocational thing on night watch, flitting about rooms and corridors like a hallowed ghost, rattling her rosary like a little castanet and fingering the ring with which she gave herself to God.

Missionary Sisters of the Precious Blood; the order, Wamiru had learned that day, had begun in South Africa. Their aim, in a spirit of friendliness and cheerfulness was to bring Christ to the Africans. Their original habit had been a red skirt, a reminder of the blood of Christ but the habit they wore now was entirely white, adorned only with a small, brass cross attached to a red ribbon. Red, blood red, Wamiru thought about it. If colonialism had a colour, it would have been blood red – colour has a profound and subliminal effect on everything; the religious order had changed colour, an unconscious shift to leave the past behind. 'Our mission field is the Kingdom of God and knows no boundaries,' Mother Veronica had told him that day, quoting Abbot Francis Pfanner, the order's founder.

They were sexless and manless, these women, but in their repudiation of self-indulgence they had found something else. There was genuine warmth in their relationships with the villagers and among themselves, a social and spiritual bonding and the perpetual half-smile on their lips evinced a secret knowledge, a faith he didn't understand.

Together with the twenty-bed hospital there was a school accommodating more than thirty physical and mentally handicapped children and a clinic, treating among other maladies, malaria, dysentery, infection, children's complaints and gynaecology. There was contraception advice too but that was dealt with by a doctor from Thika. The Holy Sisters wanted nothing to do with the prevention of babies. The building creaked and, from afar, he could hear the muffled cry of a small child, disturbed in slumber by a fearful dream.

Wamiru entered the chapel and sat on a bench in total darkness.

Was Kennedy's death an accident? Yes, but it was impossible for a child without the proper use of his upper and lower limbs to tie a cord around his own neck and throw himself from his cot. But he juggled the accident hypothesis with the equal impossibility that no one at the scene at the time could have the motive or inclination to do it for him. Corporal Adonis, although invaluable as a source of local intelligence, was proving to be a bumptious pest and his proposition that he be permitted to torture Nurse Collins until she confessed, Wamiru thought of as tasteless, but treated as a joke.

He stayed in the chapel for some time, wrestling with thoughts before tiptoeing back to his room. St Anthony of Padua eyed him balefully. And in the dim light, the lily he held in his hand looked like a sabre; it would surely smite him as his back was turned. He would avoid the venerated Franciscan if he could but he couldn't and closing his door quickly he reflected with grim irony on this saint being the patron of finding things. Maybe he should do a novena or whatever it was; help him find out what had happened to little Kennedy.

He tossed and turned. Jennifer Collins and Clara troubled back and forth through his reverie, until, outside his window, the world awakened. He fell asleep when the two women merged into one.

'Through my efforts, Inspector Wamiru is willing to see you,' Adonis had told Charlie.

In Wamiru's office, Charlie Carter introduced himself politely and, after apologising for his impropriety explained that he was doing a thesis for the East African Aid Agency on *The Provision of Adequate Shelter,* and if the inspector could find the time, could he possibly check the archives in Nairobi for any mention of the only colonial house on the mountain close to the village of Katamara. 'You know sir, anything of note that might have happened in the house in the past. You know, sir, background stuff.'

Wamiru warmly agreed and promised to communicate any information via Corporal Adonis. Charlie, in turn, would make discreet enquiries among the villagers for himself.

Leaving the office, Charlie paused at an open window and viewed through shimmering heat, the volunteers working on the digging of pit latrines. Distant pick-heads glinting in the sunlight, the muffled hacking of their chisel edges breaking through the baked black earth and the chatter of the men as they worked, that peculiar clacking of their *Kamba* tongues.

His innards lurched as Nurse Collins distracted his attention. She was leading a group of children into a play area. Those who couldn't walk she carried, one child at a time to join the others. She then formed a circle around her and the children sifted dust between their toes and gurgled at each other until the game was started. The nurse threw a ball to each child in turn, retrieving it herself when a child missed a catch or failed to return it properly. The children screamed and laughed and the nurse smiled as the contrary ball shot every which-way causing little dust puffs and eddies as it bounced and skidded on the ground. One little girl appearing mentally sound but had no legs, just stumps at her torso's end, It was she more than any other, who helped the nurse retrieve the ball. Hands on the ground, her trunk swinging between them, she giggled with happiness as she trundled back and forth.

Charlie beheld the woman below him. She was pretty, her blond hair bleached almost white was tied back severely in a bun and she wore little make up. Avoiding the sun's great heat as best she could, the skin of her face and arms was a soft, freckled, pink blending neutrally with a loose-fitting white frock. She didn't know he was watching her. This woman was not pretending to enjoy the company of these damaged children, her joy was genuine. What could possess a woman, probably not yet forty, to spend the optimum years of her life in an environment such as this? Did she not want to marry, have children of her own? What a wonderful wife she would make for someone. What a wonderful wife she would make for Charlie. Everyone knew that this woman was suspected of murdering a child. Talk was all around the village. How crazy people are.

She looked upwards towards the window and for a second their eyes met. Charlie jerked his head away and began to hurry along the corridor towards the stairway. She had caught him peering down on her. She would never speak to him now, ever. Charlie hated himself, she had caught him peeping.

Three days later Corporal Adonis informed Charlie that the inspector had found no mention of the house on file in the Nairobi archives, except that a house on the mountain close to Katamara had been used as a hunting lodge since the turn of the century. That was his house; there could be no other.

'Please thank the inspector for me when you next speak to him,' Charlie asked.

'I will do that, Charlie,' Adonis paused. 'What is it you are looking for?'

'I'm just interested in the history of the house.'

'If bad things have happened there in the past?'

'Yes, could be. Bad things, eventful things, things happen everywhere.'

'Many bad things happened in Katamara before I arrived and in the police station there is files going back a long, long time.' Adonis's eyes narrowed, inferring untold depths of archival villainy waiting to be unearthed and slits of light appeared as if a switch had been activated to all sorts of advantageous possibilities. 'Since my time here I have never seen anyone new in that house but that house always seems strange to me and a German family left, as if something was bad in there. Maybe I should look into things for you, Charlie' – a preposition left open, ready to be filled with whatever lurid fable was likely to prove the most profitable.

'Leave it for now, Adonis,' Charlie said prudently, 'it's not really that important.'

It was becoming more important. Last night, just before dawn Charlie had heard a peculiar knocking sound which hadn't been heard by either Freddie or Titus.

Chapter Six

*I*t was raining. It had been raining almost non-stop for twenty-four hours. The long rainy season was going out with a bang. Sitting at his desk, Sam Wamiru sighed. The phantom pain where his left arm had been was bothered him. It always did when he was troubled. The Nairobi brass wanted answers. They were under pressure from everywhere, most notably, the press. If the tragedy at Katamara hospital was a crime, why had no one been arrested? He examined again the notes, photos and sketches taken at the scene; nothing new. He read the autopsy report again, this time skimming through it: cause of death – compression of the arteries- neck markings – a distinct groove – little change in facial colour – the boy had not been hanging long. No one else had been in that dormitory room that morning. The windows were locked. Was some crazed nun on a mercy-killing mission? No. There was nothing more he could do. He couldn't question Nurse Collins again, not without new evidence. She had answered his questions a dozen times; same questions, same answers. Yes, there was something more he could do; get to know her better.

From a vantage point on an upper floor of the hospital she watched the Athi rising dangerously fast. Every year, twice a year, the bridge leading to the *musungu* house and the mountain was threatened and every year it survived. Over one hundred years earlier the little bridge had been cleverly thought out and constructed by craftsmen of the time. Every year since she had arrived at the hospital she had stood at the same window worrying about the bridge, the river bursting its banks and parts of the village being marooned, as had happened once before. A few years earlier the river had burst its banks and swamped the lower levels but, built on higher ground, the greater part of the village and the hospital had been spared.

She was worried and was beginning to feel depressed. Still under suspicion for the death of Kennedy, the inspector had told her not to leave the village. Yesterday in the marketplace, she had sensed people whispering and some, who she knew well, had deliberately avoided her. Mr Muinde, the hospital administrator supported her as did the sisters. But there was mistrust among the villagers. What could she do? She couldn't go from one to another protesting her innocence. But she had had her first conversation with Charlie Carter. She had opened her heart. She would have had to look vulnerable, *be* vulnerable before Charlie dared approach.

She had wanted to spend the weekend in Nairobi but even if the inspector allowed it, the *matatu* could not negotiate the road after so much rain. She wanted to keep her promise to the mother of one of the children in her care. Elizabeth was very ill and not responding to the medication she had brought for her. Kibera, where the woman lived, was a squalid shanti town on the outskirts of Nairobi, and in Kibera monsoon rains only made a bad situation worse.

She sensed Inspector Wamiru at her side and tightened. Not more questions. 'It's wondrous, isn't it, this rain?' he said. For the first time his approach was friendlier but her tension did not ease.

The rain hammered on the window and on the roof above them and the building groaned beneath the onslaught. Outside everything was grey, everything that should be green was a saturated, dripping grey. She tried a smile. 'A soft day,' as we say in Ireland.'

'Always found monsoon rains fascinating,' the inspector replied, joining her at the window.

Conversation would allay her anxiety. 'Look at the bridge,' she frowned, 'you would think that at any second it would be swept away. The river looks so angry at the bridge for standing in its way.' Each mighty swirl of water rose defiantly against the stone buttresses only to fail and thwarted, surge downstream, defeated.

Wamiru said, 'I was looking at some old plans. The bridge was built at the same time as the house on the mountain, the house where the two Englishman live. You know, Nurse, there was a little hospital here over a hundred years ago.'

The nurse did not answer. She could not go back in time. The present was too real, the future too uncertain. She did not trust the policeman's friendship. Her heart sank, yes, he was about to question her again.

Wamiru said, 'I know that you were hoping to go to Nairobi this weekend. Reverend Mother told me earlier.'

Surprised, Jennifer Collins inclined her body towards him. 'Well- I was – yes—' She gestured helplessly.

'I'm going to Nairobi and I'm setting off soon, before it gets any worse.'

She hesitated. 'But I thought—'

Wamiru looked the woman directly in the eye. 'Time I was candid with you, Nurse. I think Kennedy's death was an accident and I'm sure in my mind that you had nothing to do with it. I've put you through it I know. If you want, I'll take you into Nairobi and I'll bring you back tomorrow afternoon and on Monday I'll make my official report – accidental death.

Her voice flooded with relief. 'Oh thank God. It's been an awful time for everyone, not just me. God, I've hardly dared go into the village.'

Wamiru grimaced: 'One proviso though. See, I don't have the last word, any conclusion I come to has to be ratified in Nairobi. I must ask you to let me have your passport. Can you imagine the embarrassment should you decide to leave. Imagine my superiors in Nairobi… "Not only did the idiot allow her to get away; he drove her to the airport." '

'The woman's smile was grave. 'Oh Inspector, I promise you I'm not going anywhere. Except that a lady is expecting me and I would hate to let her down. I can get a few things together in no time at all. Oh I'm so grateful to you.'

'I'll see you at the front in fifteen minutes. I'll bring the car close up to the door.

'And your car can make it to the main road?'

'It has four-wheel drive.'

'That doesn't mean a lot to me.'

'Where does this lady live?'

'Kibera.'

The tires of the Ford sank into the black ooze, and finding friction, moved slowly forward. The wipers whipped at the windscreen as the car slid into the maelstrom and, with his head jutting above the dashboard, Wamiru wrestled with the steering wheel, so much more difficult with only one hand. By the outskirts of the village both knew that the journey was foolish and likely dangerous. Every yard of progress had the vehicle slewing sideways into the roadside gullies but it would be impossible now to turn back. It was either make it to the Garissa Road or abandon the car and return on foot. Already Wamiru was sweating profusely. 'God, this is a lot worse than I thought it would be,' he grumbled as the car began to broadside on the road, its wheels spinning ineffectually.

Jennifer Collins was helpless and said nothing, fearful of distracting the man from his task. How difficult it was with only one arm; how inventively did he use his stump. It wasn't until they reached the tarmac of the main road that she spoke. 'Dear God but you did a great job there, Inspector.' Breathing heavily, Wamiru took a handkerchief from his pocket and mopped his brow 'I said my prayers,' the nurse said, joining her hands in supplication.

Wamiru laughed. 'Well they were answered.'

Jennifer was joyful that he had warmed to her and she was no longer afraid of him. If they had ended up in a gully she would have learned more about him trudging back through the vortex; a man reveals more about himself in failure than he does in success. She trusted him, he would exonerate her and she would get her passport back.

The wheels were gratified at having solid ground beneath them and as the car geared towards Nairobi they hummed their appreciation. 'Kibera?' he asked, the word a question.

'You needn't drive inside the town.'

'I'd never get turned around.'

'You wouldn't.'

'You're not going to spend the night there, I hope,'

'I'm not. It's where my friend lives. She's the mother of one of the little girls at the hospital, little Paulina, the girl with no legs, you may have seen her, meningitis it was, when she was a baby. Oh it is so sad. Elizabeth, her mother, she's very, very ill and no one knows what's wrong with her. She has two other young children living with her and the poor woman is so ill she can hardly get out of bed. There's a good road down to the township, please drop me there.'

'I could wait for you.'

'Inspector, it's kind of you but I just don't know how long I'll be there. I'll stay a while then I'll get a bus into the city.'

When Wamiru pulled off the main road he stopped by rows of *mabati* and timber huts, spreading like stains along narrow alleys through which muddy rivers flowed. This was the outskirts of the shanti town Kibera, he had been in Kibera many times and he had never failed to leave without a feeling of disgust. Rain scythed through the sky as if to eradicate this sprawling monument to corruption and neglect. 'Nurse Collins, are you sure you don't want me to wait for you?'

They arranged to meet in Mfango Street at four o' clock the next day for the return journey. 'I promise, Inspector, I'm fine and thank you so much.' Getting out of the car and careful where she put her feet, Jennifer raised her umbrella ineffectually against the barrage and stepped into the mist. Two women standing dismally in a doorway had become agitated at the sight of the police car. Who was the passenger? Was it a landlord wanting money? A politician to close them down or would they be arrested? They disappeared inside. Wamiru watched and as the nurse reached the doorway the women reappeared and words were exchanged, then the nurse had vanished behind a mountain of steaming refuse into a saturated alley that would never have a name.

Efforts had been made by the townspeople to brighten windows with *kanga* curtains and roofs and timbers had been coloured but Wamiru could only think of an old hag with a ridiculously powdered, painted face. To the policeman, it was sheer madness; a white woman venturing into such squalid depths. It was dangerous. Certainly this woman was more in tune with the dispossessed than with the charmed circles cities have to offer to her kind but her manifestation of humanity bordered on recklessness. Who else did he know who would admit to having a *friend* in a place like this? No one. He knew of whites, who, in a show of disingenuous virtue would act the charitable charade but Jennifer Collins wasn't acting.

It had been almost a year now since Elizabeth had visited a doctor complaining of feeling unwell. The doctor had diagnosed malaria, a condition corroborated by a second doctor some weeks later. But it was not malaria; malaria reaches a crisis stage and people either die or recover, they don't get progressively worse over a period of months. Baffled, the doctors washed their hands of her and without funds for further treatment Nurse Collins took over, giving her quinine then, mindful of her occupation, treatment for syphilis. But nothing worked and the woman was going to die soon. Night sweats that drained her: a cough from which there was no relief and strange lesions which did not heal. When Jennifer opened the door of her hut she expected the worst but the bed-ridden woman was still alive and, awakened by the opening of her door, she raised herself a little and began coughing, a wrenching, consumptive expulsion of hopelessness. Getting her breath, she tried to smile.

Two little children played with a puppy on the floor. They looked up as the nurse entered and said, '*Jambo*,' in unison.

'*Habari*,' the nurse answered and traced her fingers through their wiry hair; children, innocent and blameless, soon to be orphans. Should their mother's ailment turn out to be endemic, there was going to be an awful lot of orphans. 'And how are you two today?' She cupped their little faces in her hands.

'Fine, fine,' they answered; not yet attending school, this would be one of the few English words that they knew and understood.

She wiped their noses with a tissue and the puppy barked and tried to bite her hand before skidding around the room excitedly. Moving to the bed, Jennifer sat on the side and dabbing at Elizabeth's brow, spoke words of consolation. The children joined her, looking earnestly into their mother's exhausted eyes. Presently the nurse got up from the bed and heated soup that she had brought in a container. The little girl and her younger brother, officiating diligently with a cup and spoon, took turns to feed their mother. The boy spilled soup on the floor and the puppy lapped at it greedily then raised its jaw and barked expectantly for more. Jennifer began tidying the room. Yes, Elizabeth would die soon of whatever it was that ailed her, her body was failing fast. Not so long ago, Elizabeth had stood with Jennifer on the hospital playing field as they watched Paulina racing after a ball, using only her hands. What, in the name of God, had befallen this poor woman since?

The family shack consisted of one room and a little kitchen and was remarkably clean, testimony of help that Elizabeth was getting from somewhere, so that all that was needed was the washing of some dirty clothes in a tub. Rain drummed on the tin roof and in one corner leaked into a plastic bucket that was about to overflow. Jennifer had brought food rations which she left in the kitchen and chocolate and soda-pop which she gave to the children. On a bedside table she left new drugs which the hospital doctor had prescribed and Jennifer had paid for. After explaining the dosage, she kissed Elizabeth on the forehead and was about to leave when the door opened and a young girl entered. So wet was she, that at first, she did not notice Jennifer but as the children ran to her, welcoming her warmly, she looked up in surprise and after obligatory handshaking she introduced herself, ' I am Elizabeth's younger sister, my name is Aisha. I know who you are. You are Nurse Collins because I have seen you before.'

It was Jennifer's turn to be surprised.

'Not long ago you had a *harambee* at the hospital. I was there with my poor sister. I didn't say hi, because, really, Nurse, you looked so busy.'

Jennifer laughed. 'Come next time and don't be shy.' The girl was tall and pretty, just as her older sister once was, she was, maybe, twenty years old. 'Elizabeth talked about you a lot. You were in a convent.'

'It was my wish to be a Holy Sister. I was very afraid to become like Elizabeth. When Elizabeth fell ill I left the convent, maybe now I won't go back. Nurse, I must tell you that my family, they congratulate you a lot on how you have been looking after Elizabeth and God will smile on you for it. And I must ask you about my little niece Paulina.'

Jennifer told Aisha how well her niece was doing at the hospital; how happy and vibrant she was and how inspirational to the other children. And Aisha told her that when the time came, Elizabeth's three children would be looked after by relatives and kept together as a family in Kangundo. Kenyan children are not neglected, extended families see to that. The puppy stood on its hind legs, clawed at Aisha's knees and barked.

'Oh we won't leave you behind,' the girl laughed, ruffling its ears. The drumming on the roof was less now, the rain was easing. Opening the door, she emptied the bucket which had begun to overflow.

Jennifer held Elizabeth's hand while Aisha, with the two children hanging from her skirt, attended to domestic chores of her own. When Elizabeth fell asleep, the nurse kissed her on the forehead again, feeling that it would be for the last time. It was.

She left then, contented in her mind that the sick woman was being looked after and the children would be cared for. It had stopped raining.

She found a cheap hotel and what remained of the weekend was pleasant. She had her meals in a nice restaurant, but as always, she caused enormous confusion among the waiters and chefs by being vegetarian. How could a human not eat meat? Meat was lovely, it was nutritious, good for you and there was plenty of it about. She must eat meat – protein. Tiring long ago with principled explanations she would finally say, 'Eating meat is against my religion…' Now that was something waiters and chefs could understand and they went about their business smiling and nodding to each other and they didn't bother her anymore. And mightily relieved that she was no longer suspected of the death of Kennedy, Jennifer slept well.

Inspector Sam Wamiru was waiting for her in Mfango Street as arranged. The late Sunday afternoon was hot and bone dry, as if it had never rained at all. The *matatus* honked, the street children pestered and the beggars begged; the city was back to normal. Leaving Nairobi behind, the nurse told the inspector about Elizabeth, Aisha and the children and the policeman scolded her for venturing into such an unsavoury precinct.'

'Inspector, there are lovely people in Kibera.'

'And there are not so lovely people too.'

'Like the whole world over then.'

With the city behind them, they entered an eruption of yellows, greens and reds encircled by an egg-shell sky; everything had been washed free of dust and was thrusting lustily with life. The pot holes in the roads had dried out already and the inspector swerved to avoid them. Roadside markets had sprung up with the sun and blazed with multi-colour as they sped past. As they closed on the town of Thika, the inspector said, 'I'm surprised that you don't wear a nurse's uniform.'

There was a moment's silence, then, 'The first things that will be found in hell are uniforms,' Jennifer answered.

Back in her room at the hospital Jennifer thought of Elizabeth dying in her bed of an unknown illness. The last time she had felt so sorry for anyone it had been for herself.

Chapter Seven

*T*here's something strange here,' Charlie told Titus. The sun was low and through the trees it speckled the white stucco of the house in crazy shadows. Titus faced the sun, its light catching his teeth gleaming marble bright. 'Last night, about three o' clock I heard knocking again and I couldn't tell where it was coming from. It's the second time I've heard it. Freddie didn't hear anything, did you?'

Titus thought hard before answering. 'About that time Mr Charlie, I was vigilant about the *shamba* and all was fine and quiet.'

'Who in the village should I see about this house?'

Titus pondered. 'The *Mzee*, in English it means old, wise man. He is the one. He speaks very little to anyone, he is what you call – I think – grumpy.' His teeth flashed again. 'And he won't speak at all in English. Once he swore that he would never use that language again. He is Moses Nyjonjo, the puncture *fundi* and he hates the English more.'

'I know that *mzee*. The man has cheated me already.'

Titus laughed. 'Always he cheats the white man. He will have charged you more than what was right.'

'The *piki* had a puncture, he kept waving his hand at me saying, "*Mbili, Mbili.*" '

'That is "two" in Swahili,' Titus smiled.

Charlie nodded. 'Two punctures when there was only one.'

'The whites, the English, they treat him very badly and he is still bitter.'

'I'm not surprised.'

Titus turned and faced the mountain, an eagle a tiny spot in the distance spiralled above its summit and detached itself from others. Titus' voice was far off as he spoke: 'Moses Nyjonjo, he came from up there. His family were squatters. When he was very young he left the mountain and came down to the villages. He was a good man who worked hard and soon he had a large herd of livestock.' In seconds the eagle was high in the sky above them and beneath them the chickens and all other tiny life had vanished. Both men watched the eagle's flight in quiet wonder. Titus continued. 'During the big trouble he was accused of being with the *Mau Mau* and all his livestock was taken from him. He says he was never with the *Mau Mau*, yet his livestock was still taken and when everything was over, he never got them back. Also he was imprisoned and beaten very badly, and in the camps he got cholera and very almost died. When he came out of prison he returned here but was poor. Now, for many years he had been mending punctures in the village and has no family. He is known all around the mountain not as Moses Nyjonjo but as the puncture *fundi*.'

Charlie strained his eyes at the sky the eagle had disappeared and the chickens were foraging again. 'Titus, talk to him. See if he knows the history of this house. Ask him if anything strange has ever happened here.'

'He is not a man to talk but I will do it.' The failing light caught resolve in the young man's eyes.

'But don't tell him it's me, a white, who wants to know.'

'Mr Charlie, I will do it.'

Freddie was visiting Lake Naivasha when Titus came to the house with a truly harrowing story. When the story was over Charlie did something that he had not done for a long time, he went alone into his bedroom, knelt down and prayed.

Titus was shocked to find the *Mzee* willing to talk. The *Mzee* began the story by talking about a reptile.

In his own words and with a passion Titus had never seen before, the *Mzee* explained that this reptile can live in all of us, providing room is made for it within our souls. And it can be seen quite clearly and rooted out, but only by those who understand its nature. It fears to be seen; hiding itself and hiding its mission, even from its host and it is well armed to protect itself, thriving best of all on that most destructive of emotions, jealousy. People will do most anything to rid themselves of the dreadful feeling of jealousy, and the reptile is there to advise them, to guide them, motivate them until they prostrate themselves. Then it has them and they can't escape; its mission is accomplished. But in jealousy the reptile has its biggest weakness, for it is in jealous eyes that it can be seen most clearly and thereby rooted out. Who has never seen the reptile in a pair of jealous eyes?

It was in Clarissa. It had lived in Clarissa since her childhood, from the day she first let it in and from then on, unbeknown, she had nurtured it lovingly. A battle raged within her and she was happy to let one side win. Its weapon was her desire to control, and the more she indulged it, the more it became entrenched. People who knew her and her fascination with dominance would say 'O that's just Clarissa,' and would give in to her, let her have her way, but it wasn't 'just Clarissa', it was something much deeper, entrenched. She was empowered by the defenceless, oh, the way they made her feel. Among the defenceless she was superior, beyond compare and her appetite for underlings was rapacious, for unbeknown to her, she was feeding a parasite which would one day eat her soul.

That day came when she learned that her husband, Johnnie, was having a torrid affair with a young native servant girl called Grace, who worked at a house in a far off village called Katamara on a slope of the nondescript mountain called Kilimambogo. And when she heard this devastating news, she did not cry or wring her hands in anguish and neither did she confront her husband. She just carried on her life as normal, caring for her home, engaging in the social scene, even busying herself in the affairs of a local church. And no one knew what she was hiding, what creature had asylum in her soul.

It was the year 1897 and it was from the family estate of Vale Royale, in the county of Cheshire that Hugh Cholmonderley, the third Baron of Delemere, on his travels first saw the fertile valleys and lush green highlands of central Kenya and found his *Shangri La*. It is possible that he and his retinue of friends and servants were greeted by *Kikuyu* herdsmen or bejewelled, bare-breasted *Maasai* maidens or by other tribal denizens who had no idea what it was they were about to welcome into their lives. Most men at some time during their life will have a vocation, a sense of their own destiny, but because of their circumstances, will be careful to keep it within the limits of their capabilities. But this is not the case with a man like Delemere; fabulously wealthy and an aristocratic member of a nation, controlling the biggest empire the world had ever seen. Why, such a man can indulge in whatever vocation takes his fancy and may see his destiny in anything he wants, even vast tracts of land to which he has no claim, countries even. So four years later when Delemere, a little red-headed goblin of a man, returned to the country and decided that he would become the unofficial leader of East Africa's entire colonial community, he did.

He was a stunted oddity but, as is often the case with such men, he more than made up for his lack of looks and stature with inexhaustible determination and drive. But he needed help, men of his own ilk, the only distinction being they must be white. And where should he look for them but to the gentry and minor aristocracy of his native land? And they heard him calling. A call to turn an African Eden into a colonial officer's mess; a call to the arrogant to dispossess the people and disregard fair play and his call was answered. Delemere was established and with vast possession of land, he was the largest of the *large men* and king of his domain.

And it was to this oasis of adventure, corruption and privilege that Johnnie Chance, the rootless son of Suffolk-landed gentry was enticed. Abandoning his share of the family estate, he joined up with his luminary and inspirational mentor in Nyreri, east of the Aberdares to a life of hard work and pleasure-seeking degeneracy. Johnnie Chance was personable, dashing and gregarious; his wife, although beautiful, was none of these but she was richer than her husband so she didn't have to be. Good-tempered Johnnie settled in quickly with the elite, social factions of the white community, the settlers and colonial officials, and having all the right credentials he soon became a dominant influence with both. Because the land he had acquired was more suited to grazing, he purchased livestock – cattle, sheep and goats, and learning from Delemere's mistakes and under his consummate guidance, the ranch prospered. Its success was due also to forethought and enterprise and Johnnie, who hitherto had spent a relatively feckless life, surprised everyone, none more so than himself, as to how hard he was prepared to work. He had taken a big risk leaving England, and the security it provided, for life in a new country but it was paying off.

Problems he resolved by facing them square on, pilfering of livestock by the dispossessed *Maasai* – one of the biggest problems – he rectified with single-minded charm offences; he had the natives eating from his hands and turning to his neighbour's farms for recompense. He also borrowed unreservedly from a stockpile of Delemere knowledge accrued during his years of trial and error. Predators could have been a big problem if permitted but Johnnie had been a huntsman all his life and whereas scarlet coats, brass buttons and pursuit of a fox with a pack of hounds was fun, confrontation by a four-hundred-pound lion was exhilaration beyond compare. But a safari hunt it wasn't. Joined by his equally enthusiastic peers, Johnnie was hell-bent on the wholesale slaughter of every predatory animal from Nakuru in the west,

Nyeri in the east and Naivasha in the south. A cavalry charge of happy white hunters cutting an indiscriminate, exterminating swath across the whole of the Central Highlands. They were led by a little red Barron, once mauled by a lion himself, who felt he had a score to settle. What a life for Johnnie, hunting game by day and women by night.

Clarissa Chance acclimatised differently but comfortably in her new social and elemental environment. These were people, by and large, plucked from one habitation to a similar one albeit a few thousand miles distant. Nyeri, the town of their choice with its cool air and morning mists was a home from home. It was as if they had never left the agreeable comfort of their peaceful English villages – why, in the early days, it would have been no surprise to Clarissa to see a rural English bobby on his beat or a postman pass her window on his bike. She joined the local women without becoming part of any sisterhood, restricting her activities to afternoon teas, genteel garden parties, formal dances and non-violent sporting events. Clarissa was wealthy enough to appear disdainful at times, haughty detraction an admirable quality to the circles in which she moved. But Clarissa did not ascribe to her new sociality entirely; she abhorred the incipient drug-taking and alcohol abuse among the white settlers and distanced herself from the overt wife-swapping she witnessed all around her; she would never swap her Johnnie. She was somebody and would continue to be somebody, providing she didn't involve herself in the grubby misconduct of her peers. Her voice had an ever-scolding, brittle quality and when she laughed or smiled it was without warmth yet she was not unhappy, these characteristics put her in charge, her poise and bearing, barriers preventing people getting close.

Domestic duties were carried out by servant girls under the direction of Big Evangeline, a devoted auxiliary from childhood and brought with Clarissa from her own family estate in Norfolk. Clarissa was not above helping out on the farm and with the live-stock, when required, but had no time for the game-hunting which so enthralled the menfolk. She loved her husband and admired him and would have children once maternal urges prevailed but until that time she would live her life as she had done in Norfolk. She had no great ambition but was content as long as she was captain of all she had. The captain of a becalmed ship bound for nowhere is still the captain. Becalmed, a ship should not founder on rocks but this one did.

There was a side to Clarissa which, although well known to everyone, only Big Evangeline was really party to. Their love of servants at their beck and call, and if the servants at home in England had been servile then the pretty, brown girls of Nyeri, desperate to hold onto fruitful employment, were positively submissive. And these girls were picked on unmercifully. Clarissa and big Evangeline combined to find fault and the more a girl tried to please, the more certain it was that things would not be right. And the girls they chose to work for them were not passive, lazy girls but intelligent, energetic and industrious girls whom by nature would always try their best. Apart from a managerial strategy a well-meaning girl is so much fun, while trying to please and programmed to fail, the girl was a plaything while those setting the tasks were in control of the game. Very unfair one might say but then Clarissa was paying them a wage. Now Clarissa never laid a hand on a girl and Big Evangeline was instructed likewise. Physical punishment would alter the dynamics of the game: no broken flesh or bones. So much more subtle and rewarding is the breaking of spirit. Spirit can be mended with a few kind words only to be broken again then mended then broken again; so elastic is spirit, so malleable, so wondrous a toy to play with. With errant servant girls apology was never enough nor was powerless pleading, remorse had to be wet-eyed with humiliation before Clarissa and big Evangeline's blood was heated up and when that blood began to tingle in their loins only then a girl might be forgiven so that she might fail again.

Now servant girls subjected to such relentless mental cruelty might be thought to be helpless; how could such defenceless creatures ever win? But they can. It is the inexplicable mystery of the universe that although fate cannot be prejudiced, it often seems to weigh in on the side of the weak. What if fate should find a pretty servant girl to fuck Clarissa's Johnnie; to have him wallow in her arms, to have him on his knees and rest his chin, dog-like, on her lap? It was fate that found one, not one of Clarissa's own servants but a kinswoman, an unwitting ally, not in Nyeri, but in a village called Katamara many miles away. Once again, fate had weighed in on the side of the weak but fate is also unbelievably cruel.

It just so happened that one of the best day's hunting Johnnie Chance had ever had was a leopard shoot on Kilimambogo. Not only the chase, stimulating and successful as it was, but the camaraderie afterwards, the new house on the mountain, the food and drink, the revelry and the pretty local girls who waited on the huntsmen, it was one girl in particular that captured Johnnie's eye. It might have been the wine and whisky and merrymaking that caused Johnnie to make an offer on the house, accepted amid laughter and boozy recklessness, but more likely it was the girl. There was an unwritten proviso on the deal; the house must be retained as a hunting lodge for use by any of the men, their guests, and their retinue for as long as the house stood on that hill. Johnnie had a proviso too, the young girl Grace, from a squatter family on the mountain, who had taken his fancy, was to be employed as caretaker at an unheard-of wage. The men clinked their glasses in agreement and the pact between Johnnie and the girl was ratified in bed before they left. Of course it should have stopped there but it didn't. Fate decreed that when the drink wore off, Johnnie's love for Grace did not and just as hate ruins everything so unrestricted love can do the same. They could not resist each other, they were besotted and as leopard hunting on Kilimambogo grew ever more frequent so did Clarissa's suspicions.

It was as if Johnnie had ripped the heart from her breast and twisted it fiendishly. She could have tolerated a little infidelity, covert and ephemeral with someone of her own status, after all, it was all around her but not a native, menial bitch whose only purpose in life was to be abused. Or maybe, deep in her heart, she felt that the loins of servant girls were more honeyed than those of the upper crust. But whatever reason for the outrage it was an unacceptable debasement at the hands of one whom she despised and one whom she loved dearly, a discordant fusion that screeched at hell for vengeance and she resolved that both would suffer in a most appalling way.

She did not let bitterness show and when she spoke to Johnnie she did not do so darkly. But she was careful not to let him look into her eyes because she now knew what was gleefully dancing there. Very quickly she decided what was to be done and with her man sleeping soundly beside her she made her plans. In the morning she told Big Evangeline her intentions and as the woman smiled grimly and agreed, other eyes rejoiced too because blind obedience to authority was its weapon too.

Johnnie was due to spend a week away with his cronies and be back home for his birthday so there was no great hurry, time to plan and prepare his birthday present. A trusted footman was despatched to Katamara with a camera. Cameras were new and quite unique in the villages of the mountain and girls were queuing up to have their picture taken, a girl called Grace was no exception.

Appropriately Clarissa hired a coach and horses. The coach was bigger than needed for two women but was fit for purpose. Arrangements were made for suitable accommodation for the women and for the horses to be exchanged for fresh ones at intervals along the way and the day after they waved off Johnnie and his cronies, they set forth upon their journey. Whilst the coach heaved and squeaked and the horses trotted gently, dawn slid slowly down Mount Kenya's peaks and tip-toed through the sleepy streets with robust day behind. What they had planned was going to be easy and they certainly were not going to answer to anyone for something so patently justified. But as the horse's hooves stirred the dust they agreed to be circumspect, why tempt jurisprudence, why have legal process snapping at their heels?

Sparing the horses and stopping regularly for themselves and for the horses to eat, drink and rest, they reached Thika by nightfall and after exchanging and stabling the horses at a hostelry, they retired to an inn for a restful night. Refreshed, they set off at dawn the following morning, arriving in Katamara in the early afternoon. As they sedately trotted through the village they nodded and waved to the people going about their daily business, causing not a stir. The villagers were accustomed to *musungus* in coaches and on horseback going to and from the new house on the mountain; only yesterday three men had cantered through the village, scattering chickens and children on their way to take up residence for the weekend. Clarissa knew the three men, friends of her husband, knew what time they would arrive and when they were due to leave, she also knew that Grace would be at the house to serve them. What she did not know was whether or not the men would be out hunting when they arrived. If they were at the house, or if, for some reason Grace was not at the house then the plan would be postponed. Clarissa did not want to wait for another day, hitherto her plan was working perfectly, but as the coach approached the bridge she worried just a little.

With the house in sight, Big Evangeline slackened the reins and the horses stopped and began nibbling at the grass. Alerted by the rattle of the coach's wheels a girl appeared on the porch, squinting in their direction. The women squinted back, slim and pretty as in the photographs, it was Grace. Big Evangeline jumped from the coach and with a disarming smile approached the girl with hand outstretched. 'Are the men about?' she called.

'No, ma'am, the men are out hunting.'

'Is anyone else in the house?'

The girl smoothed imaginary creases from her dress and lowering her eyes deferentially, said, 'No, just now there is only me, but—' At that moment Big Evangeline raised the hand of friendship, crunched it into a fist and struck the girl heavily above her ear, causing her to crumple unconscious to the floor of the porch. She then waved for her mistress to join them. The women did

76

not speak but looked about them to ensure they were not being observed.

To a thundering pain in her head and the sensation of water being sprinkled on her face the girl awakened to find herself wedged tightly, full length, into a padded coffin-like box, its lid sufficiently open to perceive the pale oval faces of the two women. In panic at what, inconceivably, had been done to her, the girl screamed and frantically tried to raise the lid but it was held fast and wedged just inches open.

'Hello Grace, I am Johnnie's wife,' one of the oval faces said.

Then the lid was closed and the girl understood a terror she could have never dreamed of. Then in indescribable relief the lid was raised again and in a tidal wave of air and light and hope, a voice again, 'I am here to punish you and you are there to punish Johnnie,' and then the lid was closed and a bolt was heard sliding in its keep.

The two women then carried the box which was quite heavy and awkward with the shifting of weight inside and, trying to ignore the pounding and kicking and muffled hysteria from within, they loaded and secured it on the coach. Climbing on board, Big Evangeline shook the reins and had the horses walk unhurried down the path towards the bridge. Briefly Clarissa thought to lift the lid again, a little more air and light, a little more hope, but dismissed the idea. They were crossing the bridge, only minutes and they would be in the village and the people would be nodding and waving again. Did she want them wondering about the coffin-shaped box and a racket from inside? The women were relieved; everything was quiet through the village, people waved, yes, and the two women waved back but with saturnine expression they avoided familiarity. They relaxed. Once outside the village, Big Evangeline shook the reins harder and the horses broke into a trot. There was no sound other than the dry, dusty whispers of the leaves and the choking sound of hooves cracking on the earth.

They did not speak a word or even glance at each other until they reached the Garissa Road and then they only spoke of mundane things: the heat of the day, the need for rest, water for the horses. They reached Thika after night had fallen where they registered again at the same inn and had two porters carry the long box of belongings to their room. Following a light meal they arranged the exchange of horses at the hostelry for the next day then, returning to the inn, exchanged pleasantries with the other well-to-do whites residing there. Yes they were returning to Nyeri in the morning, they had been visiting friends; yes the day was likely to be very hot again; they would set off very early because it was husband Johnnie's birthday; they must be back in time for the celebration.

Just as the dawn had slipped silently down the mountain peaks at their departure so did night on their return. There was no cloud and the white light of the moon spread across the heavens, dimming the stars and settling cosily on the quiet streets of Nyeri; on the little adobe houses and on the grand ones too. On the grandest of them all the servants greeted their mistress and her maid with spurious joy at their safe return. It was the master's birthday and sounds of revelry were coming from the dining room, the celebrants heedless of their homecoming. Big Evangeline and a servant carried the large box up the back stairway to Clarissa's bedroom with all the staff forbidden to tell anyone that they were back. Alone in her room Clarissa took some time to wash and tidy and compose herself before having a servant call her husband. She sat on a chair with one leg tucked under the other. On the dangling leg her shoe was loose; she rocked it back and forth. But she was not relaxed, her heart was beating madly as she heard his footsteps on the stair and faster as Johnnie appeared in the doorway, then she calmed, got up and kissed him and wished him 'happy birthday'. He was about to speak but she stopped him with a finger to his lips, the culmination of her actions must not be confounded by frivolous dialogue, needless distraction. She was about to show him how much she loved him and what she was prepared to do to keep him. His eyes rested quizzically on the box on the floor beside the bed then turned to hers for explanation. She smiled in inference of a present she had brought for him and gestured for him to open it. Bemused, he bent to release the bolt.

'It's Grace from Katamara, darling,' Clarissa said.

Did Clarissa, unhinged in her fever of sexual jealousy, imagine that the girl Grace would look in death much as she had looked in life; a pretty, frightened, fawn-like creature lying supine and restful in a padded box? Did she envisage an Ophelia, open-armed and upward-gazing in rapture at her lover's eyes, reminding him of what he'd lost. In all her cloistered life Clarissa had never seen a corpse; she could have no idea of what awaited her. What she did not expect was an expulsion of rank air so violent it made the body momentarily come to life. The body moved, the head moved. What she and Big Evangeline had put into that box did not have bulging eyes and purple skin and indescribable terror etched into its face. Overcome with the enormity of what she had done, Clarissa screamed and collapsed in shock, while Johnnie, his knees buckling, staggered backwards to the doorway. Trembling he cried piteously, 'Oh God, what have you done?'

What had she done and for whom? 'For you Johnnie, for you,' she was crawling to him and clutching at his feet.

'That's not Grace,' her husband moaned, 'it's her sister Shula.'

Chapter Eight

*H*aving prayed, but unsure of what he had been praying for, Charlie came out of his bedroom and in the living room sat at the table with his head in his hands; he felt lost and overwhelmed by horror. Titus came in from outside and sat opposite him and for a while they feebly counselled each other.

'It may not be true,' Titus reflected at length.

Charlie was some time answering. 'If it is true, then why isn't it all around the village? Why haven't you heard the story before? Surely the *fundi* must have told someone else a story like that.'

Titus' forehead creased in a deep frown. 'That man he will speak very little to anyone only mutters angrily to himself. I sat down with him and asked him if he knew anything about the house, anything bad that happened there. Truly I was very amazed for he lit his pipe and began telling me that story and he only stopped when the story was finished. That tale poured from him, it came pouring from his lips like a river. He told me that I was the first to ever to hear the story and that I would be the last.'

Charlie sucked his teeth. 'And God, what a story it is.'

'In fact, Mr Charlie I don't believe it to be true.'

'I do believe it's true, Titus. That poor girl she is still here in this house,' Charlie answered, 'I know she is, because I've seen her.'

Titus did not believe the *fundi* because the rural Kenyan has no concept of the abstract, no appreciation of the metaphysical; if it lives and can be eaten it is of value, all else is profligate and worthless.

He said, 'Even maybe if it is true, that girl is dead this long time, maybe how she died is true but she does not live here as a ghost – it is better to leave such crazy stuff alone.'

'Did the *fundi* know it was me, a white-man looking for the story? Charlie asked quickly.

'I did not tell him but he would know it. He will know that I am your *askari*. He seemed as if he didn't care. Seems he was ready at last to tell that tale'

Charlie raised his eyes, 'This reptile, Titus, he was talking about the devil.'

Titus nodded. 'He did not say, but surely he was talking about the devil.'

'Did he say what happened to Johnnie and Clarissa, to big Evangeline?'

'That *fundi* had nothing more to say,' Titus answered gravely.

'Then tomorrow go back to him and find out what happened,' Charlie said earnestly. 'Ask what happened to Johnnie, the two women, surely they could not get away with a terrible crime like that.'

'Mr Charlie, I don't think he knows more. I think if he knew more he would have told me.'

'Maybe he want's paying for the rest of the story.'

'It is well possible but I would not pay him.'

Charlie sucked his teeth again. Already he had learned that the generous *musungu* is anomalous and that it is the peremptory duty of every Kenyan, even those that are fond of whites, for such a man to be taken advantage of. What chance had he with someone who hated him, hated his nation, refused to speak his language? He shook his head. 'No, don't ask him for more of the story. Maybe I can find out for myself.'

'Someone else in the village might know the same story. There is many other old ones. It is just possible,' Titus advised.

'Say nothing more now, Titus, I don't want anybody else in the village to know about this house. I'll see the inspector with the one arm, what's his name? Wamiru? I'll ask him to look up his files again, see if he can find a Johnnie Chance.'

Titus managed a smile. 'They will think you even more crazy Mr Charlie. Maybe they say – now the *musungu* believes he is living with a woman dead for almost seventy years – better to say nothing.'

Charlie nodded. 'I'll go myself into Nairobi, go the public library there. Those White Highlanders are part of the history of this country there must be something about the Chances. And, Titus, there is no need for you to call me *Mr* Charlie'

'OK, Charlie, will you tell Mr Freddie when he comes back from Lake Naivasha?'

'I'll tell him a young girl was taken from this house many years ago and murdered. I'll tell him her name was Shula and that it was her I saw the day that he arrived here. He can laugh if he likes, I know what I saw and now I know who I saw.'

Charlie spent the afternoon in the market before returning home. It was almost midnight before Freddie returned. He told them that he had arrived back earlier but had been drinking at a bar in another village. He had been enchanted by Lake Naivasha, a freshwater lake with towering cliffs at either side. 'Open-ended, it was,' he continued lyrically, 'the wind whistling through.' And birds; never in my life have I seen so many birds. I was talking to another white guy there, an ornithologist. He told me that there were more species of bird on and around the shores of Lake Naivasha than in the whole of the British Isles.'

Charlie regarded his colleague with an admiration tinged with resentment. He had never met anyone quite like Freddie. His specialist attainments were remarkable. Quite simply he could turn his hand to anything. Whatever the trade or craft required, his proficiency was instinctive and with alternative technology he was innovative, learning from the volunteers and combining their age-old traditional methods with his own modern Western expertise. Yet he only ever talked of an academic background in electrical engineering. The agency knew what they were doing when they accepted him; they could not have got a better man. Freddie worked hard, harder than Charlie, harder than anyone;

yet this volunteer stint of his was a prolonged holiday as well and he made no bones about it.

They retired to the porch. Outside, with lamp light flickering in the quiet night, the night awakened, nocturnal creatures grew bold and rustled in the brush and in the overhead trees night-birds flashed their wing-tips in nameless pursuit of nameless things. Freddie opened three bottles of beer and, taking one for himself, handed one to Charlie and another to Titus.

'It is not good that I take drink on my watch,' Titus protested.

'Take it,' Freddie insisted, 'it will help you to sleep.'

'But I am vigilant at all times, Mr Freddie,' Titus puzzled.

'OK then, it might help you stay awake.'

Titus looked blankly to Charlie for explanation. Sometimes Mr Freddie did not speak understandable English. He took the bottle from Freddie.

Charlie did not respond neither did he take a swig from the bottle neck as the other two but appeared to study the label intently before levelling at Freddie and saying quietly and convincingly, 'Titus heard a story about how a young girl was taken from this house maybe about seventy years ago. She was murdered. They called her Shula and she was horribly murdered by mistake, she was mistaken for her sister.' He then related the full story.

Freddie listened intently but his expressions and body language evinced considerable scepticism. When Charlie had finished, he laughed, 'Think I'll maybe move upstairs?'

'Freddie you can laugh as much as you like but I saw that girl the day you arrived here. I saw her in the window. I'm telling you Freddie this house is haunted by that young girl, what do you think we should do?'

'Get a Ouija board,' Freddie said.

Chapter Nine

Wamiru was tidying up. 'An accident, Corporal, my official opinion, the coroner may come up with another but as far as I'm concerned there is no other explanation.' The man sitting in front of him did not look pleased.

In terms of knowledgeable intelligence Wamiru couldn't fault the man. Adonis had given him the pedigree and personal data of everyone at the hospital including the sisters and all regular visitors with the only background eluding him being that of Nurse Jennifer Collins, a point which clearly vexed him. Adonis was pushy, authoritative and irritating but, unfortunately, he had been needed for his exhaustive local awareness.

'I have told you about my suspicions, sir.'

'You don't seem to like Nurse Collins much,' Wamiru ventured, his words understated and nuanced with humour.

They were sitting at the table in Wamiru's temporary bedroom-come-office, all the accoutrements of his tenure packed and ready to go back to Nairobi, indicative of a satisfactory conclusion, a closure. Adonis thrust his jaw forward: 'There is more to meet the eye about that woman and one day I will know it.'

'There is not one atom of evidence against her,' Wamiru argued.

'What about the other kid, the first kid, the little girl who choked?'

The inspector shook his head. 'The same, Nurse Collins is with the children more than anyone else. She told me about the first child herself, I didn't have to ask her. "Inspector," she said, "soon after I came here, a little girl choked to death in my arms." She had been feeding her and suddenly the little girl was choking. She said, "I am a nurse and I should have saved her but I couldn't." Anything happens to a child then the first person on the scene is almost certain to be Nurse Collins. I've questioned her relentlessly about both deaths, I've had her in tears time and again but she's never wavered in her story. Corporal, I know when someone's lying and when they're not.'

'That woman, she make no attempt to revive that poor black kid, Kennedy, no attempt, just hands little Kennedy to a sister. Same with the little black girl, she just hands dead black kids to someone else.'

'Both times she was in shock. Sister Agnes told me that she was ashen-faced and trembling after finding that boy hanging. Those kids, some are terribly handicapped, they're much more vulnerable to accidents than normal children.'

Adonis thrust his jaw further forward. 'And the kid at Eka-racara, seems strange to me that every time that woman steps someplace a kid is dead.'

Wamiru paused, keeping his irritation in check 'I've investigated that death thoroughly too. I've been to the clinic in Ekaracara and interviewed everyone concerned, read every report. Nurse Collins was not even in the building at the time it happened. Not even in the village.'

Adonis shrugged his shoulders sulkily. 'Maybe if them kids was white kids, she'd a done more, saved 'em maybe.'

Wamiru didn't have to justify himself to a subordinate, certainly not one as wearisome as the corporal. He made to stand up, signalling that the exchange was over but sat back down again when Adonis said, 'An' she's a racist.'

The remark was worth a raised eyebrow. 'A racist?'

'A racist like that woman should never be a nurse.'

Wamiru shook his head. 'I've never met anyone less racist than Jennifer Collins. She gets on famously with everyone. Everyone loves her, the children, the sisters, the villagers, hardly a white face among the lot.'

Adonis put his elbows on the table and steepled his fingers. 'She doesn't get on with me, she is racist towards me. She doesn't like it that I am superior to her in this place and she should make efforts to please me as I am the law enforcement.'

'And that makes her racist?' Wamiru argued.

'Inspector, I want to like that woman but she makes it impossible. She refuses to look at me. Kind of turns her white nose up in the air when she sees me. Sometimes in the marketplace I look down on her, even smile at her, wanting her to look up to me so that we can smile together and say nice words to one another but no, up goes her white nose again as if she thinks that maybe I don't smell too good. That woman should fear me but she doesn't.'

'You're getting mixed up with respect and fear,' Wamiru explained dolefully, 'I'm afraid, a lot of policeman have the same problem. Corporal Musyoka, I'm sorry to have to say this but Nurse Collins probably doesn't look up to you because she doesn't like you. It's not racism, she just doesn't like you, have you ever thought of that?'

Adonis registered dismay. 'But I am law enforcement and it is her duty to like me, to fear me.'

Wamiru scratched his head and grimaced. 'I've also noticed that the Sisters at the hospital don't look up to you, they don't seem to like you either. Are they "racist" too'?

Adonis retracted his jaw and lowering his eyes, studied his fingernails saying almost shyly, 'That I understand, Inspector. Those sisters, they are holy and in looking my way they might be tempted.'

The inspector laughed. This man was priceless. He stood up and gathered his papers. Time he was back in Nairobi.

Charlie was troubled. He needed to share his awful story, he could only think of Jennifer Collins. He was in the marketplace, nodding and smiling and shaking hands but too preoccupied to engage in conversation. Wamiru had gone back to Nairobi leaving word that Kennedy's death was accidental. It was over for the nurse. He spied her beneath a hoarding. She appeared to be crying. This time he might dare to put a comforting arm around her, reassure her that her ordeal was over but he was not good with words to women and he wasn't any better at putting his arm around them either 'Good evening, Nurse,' he said instead.

'Charlie, please call me Jennifer.'

He was embarrassed to see her crying. Was she crying with relief? 'So it's over,' he prompted.

'It should be, Charlie, but I don't think it is.' Her face was uncharacteristically rigid, her eyes wavering, her lips trembling. There was a light wind and the air was cold in the shade beneath the hoarding. Charlie moved as close to her as he dared, wanting to warm her with his body, wanting her to burst into tears, then he might dare to hold her tightly with legitimate compassion. His story would have to wait. They moved aside to allow a woman to enter the shop. Jennifer looked hurt that the woman had not stopped to speak. She turned her head and, by resting it on the rough timber shop façade, hid her face from his. 'Inspector Wamiru, he has questioned me so much. I know he suspected me, the questions he's asked me, and over and over, the same questions. Charlie, I swear to God I began to think that I might be guilty after all. Anyway, today he told me officially that he was certain that I had nothing to do with it and that it was an accident. He told me that but he needs to tell everyone else.'

Now Charlie dared to grip her arm gently and say softly, 'Jennifer, of course people know you didn't do it. No one has ever suspected you. It's over. Maybe I should walk you back to the hospital.' Her shoulders were slumped and she yielded to the hand that held her and her vulnerability awakened in him the maleness long repressed by failure. 'So why are you crying, is it the thought of Kennedy?'

She was quiet then suddenly she blurted, 'Charlie, the people in this village still think I did it. The people are cold, they avoid me. They think I'm guilty. The woman in the shop now, the one that passed us, she knows me, I know her, her name is Mary. She didn't speak. It hurts me. They don't accuse me, I wish they would then I could defend myself. You can't defend yourself against a snub, a look—'

Charlie renewed his grip on her arm. 'No, Jennifer, you can't be right. The woman in the shop, she was in a hurry.'

'Charlie, I feel guilty, I know I look guilty and the more people avoid me, the guiltier I feel. I cry on my own and I cry publicly and I can't sleep, that's the worst, Charlie, I can't sleep. I'm emotional all the time, the Kenyans, they don't seem to understand emotion, not like we do. It's a bit of a luxury, don't you think, emotion?'

Charlie had never been so close to her before, the tears on her face, making noticeable the faint trace of freckles on her cheeks. 'You're upset, it's a reaction to all that's been going on. I'll walk you back to the hospital.' A film of sorry sunlight showed the way. It heralded roasting days to come. The woman came back out of the shop. '*Jambo*, Nurse,' she said.

Jennifer brightened. 'Oh hello to you Mary.' The woman was on her way. Charlie steered Jennifer from beneath the hoarding and out onto the street.

'No one believes you are guilty of anything. You're imagining things.'

Jennifer sniffed. The wind increased as it always did at the end of day. They walked slowly towards the hospital and to change the subject, Charlie told her the story of the girl at the window and Shula's murder and when he had finished, Jennifer surprised him by saying, 'The girl at the window. Was that when the bats left?'

Charlie was thoughtful.' 'They left when Freddie arrived. What made you ask that?'

Jennifer tried to laugh. 'The story's awful and I'm sure it's true. I remember someone telling me about you and the problem you were having with bats and then someone told me that they had left. It just came to me, that question, I don't know what made me think of bats.'

Charlie was more thoughtful. 'There was *a shamba* dog that would visit me every morning, and every evening. You know one of them little brown *shamba* dogs. I would feed her left-overs from the night before and she never missed. I haven't seen her either since Freddie arrived. I haven't seen the bats or Brownie since the day Freddie arrived.'

He had known for some time that it wasn't Freddie at all. The bats and the dog had vanished with the arrival of the girl at the window. Also the chimps in the trees, he hadn't seen them for a long time either.

PART TWO

Esmeralda

Chapter Ten

*E*xtract from a letter from Charlie Carter to his mother, dated sometime September 1974.

> *As I told you in my last letter, Mother, it's over between Jennifer and me, although we still remain good friends. She was very upset, I was too but also, as I told you, I've met this fantastic girl called Esmeralda. (See enclosed photos) I just never dreamed that I could ever get anyone as beautiful as Esmeralda. And, Mother, she loves me. She wrote me the most fantastic letter, I received it yesterday, she had pushed it under my door, can't send you a copy because it's too embarrassing. I'm so happy I just walk all day on air. This is it, for me certainly. When the project here is over I'm going to bring her over to England to meet you. I know you will just love her, everyone will, they will never have met anyone like Esmeralda. She's much younger than I am but native girls seem to go for older white men. Don't do anything yet but you might just be buying new outfits after all.*

Instinctively Charlie sucked his stomach in as far as it would go and held it taut. A heart-stopping girl in high heel shoes and a short, tight skirt was picking her way gingerly across the work-strewn site towards him. Straightening, he whipped a cap from his pocket and covered his bald head. With shy downcast eyes, the girl swept the ground at his feet and murmured demurely, 'I am Esmeralda.'

His spirit enraptured at the sound of her name; she had come back to him. The Esmeralda of his childhood; the aching vulnerability of a Cinderella; the loneliness of Gretel lost in the forest; the loveliness of Sleeping Beauty. The day the enchantment of a girl opened up to him with the delicacy and potency of every maiden in every story he had ever read or seen in movies. Rapunzel, her lustrous hair hanging from a turret window; the Little Mermaid, wistful on a rock, casting wounded eyes across the restive seas and the faces of the angels in a young girl's scrapbook; cherub girls with angel wings.

'Esmeralda,' he greeted, as shyly she raised her eyes to his. Ecstasy overwhelmed him, a second mystic girl? He exposed his dirty hands in apology that he could not take hers. It was mystical that she had come through all those years to appear before him once again.

Through centuries, his mind leaped back in time. She was crawling through the legs of the King's guards, guards being pressed by jostling gypsies. The guards began beating back the gypsies; she was a gypsy girl and she was bewildered and frightened. Fires were burning and flags were flying and bunting decorated the streets and she was at the centre of some great celebration. She ran away from the King's Guard and looked so alone and frightened in a city vibrant with the gaiety of jesters, clowns and tumblers. Entertaining a crowd, a play was being performed in an open theatre and next to it, in an open space there were ugly faces gurning through a hole in a wooded panel, the most grotesque, earning jeering cheers from the crowd. Cutpurses, finger-smiths and downright thieves slithered through the milling masses while drunkards called deliriously to Bacchus. It was Paris and a gypsy girl, followed by her pet goat, shrugged off her fears and began dancing through the streets to the jangling of her tambourine. Loose clothing swirled about her body and although later he was told that the imagery he had seen was in black and white, her dress, to Charlie, was crimson and her hair would always be a flaming crimson red.

Some words are beautiful to say, to listen to; some more beautiful than all others. The tongue caresses them, reluctant to let them fall on graceless ears. Only a poetic soul can understand truly the beauty of a word. Charlie was not a poetic soul but the word 'Esmeralda' made him feel like Captain Phoebus. Emerging from his trance he said, 'Well I'm really pleased to meet you, Esmeralda. I am Charlie.'

'I know who you are, Mr Charlie. I have heard.'

'And why are you here, Esmeralda?'

'For to be a monson,' she answered candidly.

'Monson?' Charlie repeated uncertainly.

'To build a house with bricks and stone for the Holy Sisters.'

Charlie laughed, 'A mason, a stone-mason.' He shook his head in disbelief. He could see her with a tambourine, not a hammer and chisel. He was aware that the men had downed tools and were gathering around, they knew her and she knew them, she was a local girl. Freddie was irritated and blatantly displeased that her arrival had stopped the men from working. Charlie could hear him muttering in the background. 'Working here on this site is not suitable for a girl like you. You don't know what you're asking for. I don't think—' Charlie was fumbling for words.

The girl looked crestfallen. Holding her hands together wistfully, she lowered her head and said, 'But I am a strong girl and very willing and God on high will look down well on you, Mr Charlie, if you give a willing girl a chance.'

'Well, there's nothing to stop you really,' Charlie said hastily, 'these men, I can see you all know each other, well these men are volunteers. No pay you understand, only a meal each day of *ugali* and *githeri* and the work is very hard.'

'But we Kenyan ladies are used to working hard and *ugali* and *githeri* we eat each day. It is, I think, our national dish. We Kenyan ladies live to have babies and work from dawn to dusk.' She raised her eyes slyly and said coquettishly, 'I was told with good authority – go and see Mr Charlie for he is well known to give a girl a chance—. All I need, Mr Charlie, is one chance in life.'

His brain running amok with confusion, Charlie said, 'I don't think this is work for women – girls – I—'

Esmeralda's face hung long and sorrowful, then straightened with righteousness. 'So it is men who get the work, yet around here it is the women who do it. You will see in good time, Mr Charlie.'

Charlie smiled bashfully and, lifting his cap, scratched at sunburned skin, flakes falling on his shoulders like tiny snowflakes. 'Well, yes, I suppose it's fine with me but I'd better have a word with Freddie.'

Freddie had overheard Charlie's simpering acquiescence and called disdainfully, 'Are you bloody mad, Charlie? No. Not likely.'

Charlie turned appealingly to him: 'She can't do any harm, Freddie.'

Freddie looked at Charlie with a mixture of derision and disgust. Charlie had taken his cap off and was holding it both hands in serf-like deference to the girl. He was sweaty, portly; so unsure of himself and so out of place on an equatorial building site. What on earth had possessed Charlie Carter to volunteer for such a programme? A pink candle of a man, slowly melting in the sun, what on earth had possessed the Aid Agency in choosing him? 'I know girls like her, you won't believe how much trouble they can cause.' Freddie bent to his trowelling task again, saying, 'Look, Charlie, you're supposed to be the co-ordinator, you're supposed to be the boss. If you want her on site it's up to you but just remember, you've been warned.'

Charlie turned back to Esmeralda: 'He said it's OK. And yes, a girl deserves a chance. When do you want to start?'

'Well. Now of course,' she answered, kicking off her high-heel shoes. Her teeth were large, even and very white, teeth like these were an invaluable asset, Esmeralda knew it. They were great for ensnaring men. Inwardly she congratulated herself; she had just ensnared Charlie.

Heart thumping with joy, yet Charlie frowned, 'Ok, well come into the kitchen. You'll have to sign some paperwork.' And in the kitchen, bending over the agency's paperwork, Charlie found out, that although no one had kept records of family births, the girl thought she was eighteen or nineteen years old, lived in the nearby village of Uamani and was unemployed. Maybe a tight short skirt and a sparsely buttoned blouse were not standard attire for Kenyan building sites, but who was Charlie to argue for he was a man already insanely in love.

'You will not regret this move,' Esmeralda said, touching her open lips then transferring a fingertip kiss upon his dome.

Then she was bouncing happily about the site, telling each man in turn of her new appointment. A position greeted with less than outright enthusiasm by Freddie, who grunted at her approach then overtly ignored her. The men smiled at each other ruefully because they all knew Esmeralda and her antics.

'You'll need a pair of gloves,' Charlie fussed, then wiping his hand, took her hand in one of his. 'You must protect those fingernails. And you must have suitable clothing and sound shoes for this kind of work. I hope you're not thinking of working in your bare feet as these men do. And when we get to roof-work, you'll need a hard hat.'

'But I have no money for those things,' Esmeralda complained and blinking her eyes rapidly, looked almost tearful.

'I'll see to it, don't worry,' Charlie promised, also making a mental note to improve the midday meal. He would have a word with Mama Mary; no reason why the work force could not have chicken or goat meat occasionally. Charlie cared not that the money would come out of his own pocket. Esmeralda's introduction to the rigours of building site work would be as gentle and undemanding as he could possibly make them: watch how a batch of mortar is mixed, how a brick is laid, how a stone is pointed; it wasn't necessary at this stage for her to actually *do* anything. And it was this latter functional principal that Esmeralda found the easiest to embrace for within hours a bitter Freddie knew for certain that the girl was not on site to work today and neither did she have any intention of working in the future because she wasn't even bothering to pretend.

The smiles of the site men lengthened as the day wore on. They knew of the contradictory forces at war within the mind of the young girl who had joined them and the wilful and capricious notions that wreaked havoc with her reason. They understood her fixation with Western magazines which sold her high hopes for herself because she knew that she was every bit as lovely as the models they featured but they also knew of the grim frustration of reality which denied her any chance of being one of them. And they winked and grinned at one another as they watched her flirting outrageously with Charlie and, bemused by Freddie's opposition, they waited to see what would happen next, because as long as Esmeralda was on site, something would.

'Bloody get rid of her,' Freddie hissed, pulling Charlie to one side.

'But we've got to give her a chance.'

'What chance? A chance for her to become a mason, do me a favour. I don't know what the hell she's here for but it certainly isn't stone-masonry,' Freddie snorted, spearing the point of his trowel into a heap of mortar then stalking off, ostensibly to measure a door opening in the stonework.

Charlie watched him go stifling a tide of unease. Freddie was over-reacting: why? He sensed Esmeralda close behind him and turning, felt himself blush as the swell of her breasts brushed his arm.

'Excuse me, Mr Charlie, but do you, by any chance, have a camera?' Esmeralda asked of him.

'Yes, of course, but it's at home.'

'I was thinking, a job like this should be photographed in its stages. How nice it would be for you in some years' time to look at photographs, saying – that day we did this and this day we did that and ooh look, that was Esmeralda, one of the mason's—
It would be nice and if you bring your camera, we could start tomorrow.'

'Esmeralda, that's a great idea, yes, tomorrow, of course.'

Bloody get rid of her, Charlie was trying to rid his head of Freddie's whisper.

After midday lunch and perhaps sensing a burgeoning antagonism between the two *musungus*, Paul Kutungu, by virtue of his age, the site *Mzee* and appointed ganger, took first Charlie and then Freddie to one side in turn, and explained the nature of a girl who was clearly going to come between them. Around the mountain Esmeralda was famous and infamous in equal measure. Her moods were legendary, vivaciousness to sullen despair; joy of living to woe and distress at life. She alienated would-be suitors from the villages who called her vain and proud, but the girl had a real fear of being shanghaied into a life of marriage, countless children and the drudgery of *shamba* life when all she wanted was the magazine life of a model, to which, she felt, she rightly aspired. The older men viewed her with a live-and-let-live pragmatism while the younger men lusted after her, but fearing rejection, always from afar. Of one thing, Paul wholeheartedly agreed with Freddie, Esmeralda definitely was not on site to become a mason.

And by late afternoon Charlie was thinking that Paul and Freddie just might be right but he didn't care. On one occasion, she was perceived holding up one end of a straight-edge (not a heavy one) and shortly afterwards she had taken hold of the handles of a laden wheelbarrow, puffing and blowing ostentatiously in a false attempt to lift it off the ground; an extravagant charade that had the site-men falling about in laughter, a manifestation of building work that was a joke to them and a bigger joke to her.

'You've made a huge mistake with her,' Freddie warned. 'Look at her, not only is she not working she's stopping the men from working.'

'She's on the books now and I can't see her doing any harm,' Charlie defended. An austere building site had bloomed for her being there; grey stone blossomed to her touch and the earth she trod gave off the sweet odour of optimism and was no longer a sombre black, the sky was bluer and the birds sang sweeter in the bush. Already she was healing erstwhile wounds of denial and negation still open and sore in Charlie's heart and already she was auguring promise of wonders to come. She did it with her voice and with her eyes whenever they were raised lingeringly to his. Before leaving site for the day, Charlie took her to one side. The site-men had begun to move off in different directions, each towards their *shamba* homes and Freddie was in the truck impatiently waiting for Charlie. He honked the horn.

'I couldn't believe my ears when you said your name was Esmeralda. I never knew of another girl called Esmeralda in all my life. Only in a film I once saw called *The Hunchback of Notre Dame*. In that film there is a gypsy girl called Esmeralda. I've never forgotten that film, and that name. It's such a beautiful name,' Charlie told her.

'I think it was my father, God rest him, who gave me that name, maybe he also saw that film,' Esmeralda said, kneeling down disconsolately, to clean caked mud from her feet.

'You cannot ask him then?' Charlie asked.

'He is passed away, this long time now because God loved him more and wanted him but my mother is still alive and glad of it with another husband who she has had this long time now. Life means a lot to my mother who is doing a bit well at the moment so I will ask her where I got this name and she will be truthful about it because she has a sincere heart.' She glanced over Charlie's shoulder to where Freddie was sitting, seething in the truck. She had not yet looked at Freddie eye to eye until now. Her eyes flirted, they lingered seconds longer than was needed and when she looked away sharply, the movement of her head was quicker than was needed. Signals she hoped Freddie would recognise. He did. He sniffed contemptuously and honked the horn again but Freddie's turn would come.

Charlie said, 'When I first saw you, you leaped out at me from that film. It was strange, as soon as you said your name

100

the opening scene of that film came back to me as if I'd seen it only yesterday, Paris and the gypsy girl leaping out at me as if I might catch you in my arms.'

Standing up, tossing her head back and clapping her hands, Esmeralda whooped with joy, crying, 'I leaped out of a film and landed on Charlie. Oh my God, Charlie, to leap out of a film and land on you is quite amazing.' Then she put on her shoes, brushed herself down and started to waltz towards the village.

Charlie hesitated, flicking unsure eyes between Freddie who had started up the truck and the girl whose buttocks rippled voluptuously beneath her skirt. With girls, especially beautiful girls, he was struck dumb and when he did manage to speak, he found himself saying silly things which he would later regret for days but today conversation had flowed easily and he wanted more. Nervous of spoiling things, but with uncharacteristic valour he took loping, purposeful strides and caught her before she reached the road, blurting, 'Miss Esmeralda. I could give you a lift. Uamani is a long way from here. I could go home, drop Freddie off and come back for you with the truck. It would be no problem, in fact—'

'It is OK, Mr Charlie. I am to visit my cousin here in Katamara. I will rest with her, even stay the night so that I am ready tomorrow for another hard day's work at the building.'

Freddie honked the truck's horn. The blast was longer, its tone exasperated.

Charlie dared to gently hold her shoulders, compelling her to face him. 'I just want you to know how nice it was to have you here today on site. It's good to have a woman working with the men, good for morale, you know, morale. You understand morale?' He was stumbling with his words, 'A tonic, you understand a tonic, it's not important how much work you—' He stopped talking, his mouth was drying up. If he was not careful he would plummet into a well of banality and negate all the positives of his day. Stop blathering or a great day would end like most other days with women; he would go home feeling stupid and depressed.

Freddie rescued him by driving past with a dissenting thrust from the engine. 'Bloody get rid of her,' he snarled through the open window, ensuring that the girl could hear him too. 'I'm going, I've waited long enough.'

The girl's eyes narrowed assiduously as they followed the dusty path of the receding truck. 'Oh Mr Charlie, you must inform Mr Freddie that I am only here to learn to be a mason so that soon I may be employed in Nairobi, on construction work where wages are somewhat better than in Uamani or Katamara, even.'

'It's OK, Esmeralda. I'm in charge here. I am the project co-ordinator. What I say goes. Freddie has no right to be rude to you.'

'Oh Charlie that is so good news, you see, it is so that I might help my family, who are burdened with the worry of a wolf forever at their door and it is my hope that you and Mr Freddie can promote me with a little cash in the very near future.'

Charlie's mind struggled with the unlikeliness and presumption of the girl's expectations; he couldn't find an answer. Clearing his throat in readiness for suitable words, he kept pace with her towards the village. 'I don't suppose you have ever been to my house on the mountain? The *musungu* house, have you been there recently?' He surprised himself with the question.

Esmeralda glanced backwards in the direction of the house and shook her head. 'That *musungu* house, no, never.'

'Have you ever seen me or Freddie before this day?'

'Never Freddie, and once only, I saw you driving through the village, but I hear of you a lot. Why you ask, Mr Charlie?'

'Esmeralda, please don't call me Mr. And it's nothing really. Once I thought I saw a girl at the window of the house, she might have looked a bit like you. I don't know who she was. Sometimes I think I might have been mistaken.'

'I have never been inside that house but of course I've seen that house many times and I don't like it. Once, a few years ago, after the German family left, I thought I saw the Virgin Mary.'

Charlie stopped her. 'The Virgin Mary, 'he gulped.

'Yes, I had a friend then. She lived among the squatters. I thought I saw the Virgin Mary as I was passing the house on my way to see my friend.'

'Where was she, was she at the upstairs window?'

'No, she was standing on the porch, like a statue, not moving, not speaking, not breathing, I was frightened and I hurried past. But I think I was mistaken because I never saw her since and I never heard again of anyone else ever seeing such a thing as that.'

The sun's rays began quarrelling with cloud, freckling the earth; light and dark where it was green, and yellow where the grass was sheltered from the rain. Lizards stood petrified on rocks as the two passed by, blinking and winking as if they all knew something Charlie didn't.

Chapter Eleven

*T*oo much of Kenya's rich and fertile lands had been given to the Europeans, forcing the native population to seek employment from the whites. 'Sequestration' it was called. What a lovely word the British courts of law had found as a substitute for 'thieving', Wamiru thought as, early morning, he set off towards Machakos to meet his friend. Of course it wasn't slavery, but it was dispossession and drudgery, a racial treadmill: people chained together by subservience. And emitting subliminally from the rattle of those chains came the whispered word – Uhuru – the Swahili word for freedom. The word became a song and the song spread to the towns and cities and became an octave higher until it was a strident cry for justice. The rebellion was slow but it was inexorable and from out of the White Highlands and from under the boot of the white people came the *Kikuyu* to inhabit the enclaves of Mount Kenya and The Aberdares and give birth to the *Mau Mau* and war against colonialism. By 1960, 100 Europeans and 14,000 Kenyans were dead, one of them being Sam Wamiru's father.

The Wamiru and the Kariuki families lived close by in the province of the Rift Valley and Sam and Josiah had been friends since childhood, hunting wild animals in the bush and playing football on the grasslands. They grew up together, they had even been together that fateful day in Nakuru when Josiah won his fortune at the race-track; money that would put him through his schooling and on his road to political success. Sam couldn't believe how quickly his friend had risen to prominence, why, for six years he had been Jomo Kenyatta's private secretary. Controversial and vociferous, there was talk of him, one day, being Kenya's president. Sam could never forgive himself for not heeding his friend's advice; backing the cert he'd got the tip for. How different might his life had been had he won the same amount. Anyway, they had gone their separate ways, Sam into the police-force where he would lose his arm and J.M. into politics, where, if he didn't moderate his reactionary conduct, would lose his life.

Sam was looking forward to meeting up with J.M. The politician was seeking re-election and Sam would help him how and when he could. But they would be drinking tonight, reminiscing, they would talk about the girls they had had and the trouble they got up to in the dusty streets of Kabati-ini. But first Sam would stop off at Katamara first.

Although she had known that Elizabeth was not for this world much longer, Jennifer Collins was still shocked and upset to hear the news that she had died. A cold morning mist clung doggedly to the mountain when Elizabeth's grandparents called for the child, Paulina. Kenyans revere the sanctity of family life and although the nurse was disappointed not to meet with Elizabeth's sister Aisha again, she was happy to see that Paulina was in good hands. Still she wept openly as she said goodbye to the little girl. Paulina was crying too, refusing to release hands that clasped tightly around the nurse's neck. Eyes closed, the woman whispered gentle promises in the girl's ear and the girl responded with choking sobs, a confluence of tears met where their cheeks pressed together and in the cool mountain air little clouds of vapour gathered above them from their united breath. Paulina would not return to Kibera but, together with her little brother and sister, would live with their grandparents in Kangundo and the nurse's gentle whispers were promises to visit soon. The little girl leaned backwards in the nurse's arms and tearfully demanded, 'When?'

'Next Saturday, one week from today,' the nurse said with a catch in her breath.

'But you won't know where I'm going to live,' Paulina wailed. The girl's head fell forward again and nuzzled in the nurse's neck and her little body shook with grief.

'I know where you are going to live, Kangundo, and I'll find you, I promise.' Paulina was a favoured child. Nurse Collins tried to treat all the children the same but although all children might receive equal gifts, equal attention, at least one will always receive unequal love. Through innate and indefinable endowment of nature and spirit, one child will be more lovable than all others. In Katamara Hospital, Paulina without legs was that child, and when she left with her grandparents in the *matatu* for her new life in Kangundo, Jennifer Collins fell into a deep melancholy. She went to her room and, although she fought against it, she felt herself drawn back to Ireland, to a happy time and to a deeply unhappy time. The unhappy time was the trough she fought to avoid but the departure of the little girl had triggered memories; she was falling in the trough now and her great fear was how long she would remain there.

A knock on the door interrupted her disquiet. She swivelled towards the door. 'Come in.'

'Good morning, Nurse. Hope I'm not interrupting anything.'

Shocked, Jennifer offered her hand. 'Oh Inspector, sorry, I was miles away. Please sit down.'

Wamiru, observing the woman's tear-stained cheeks, took a seat, saying, 'I've found you at a bad time. It's just that I was passing and I thought—'

Jennifer said, 'Elizabeth has died, remember the lady you took me to see in Kibera, she died last week. This morning, only fifteen minutes or so ago, Paulina, her daughter was taken to Kangundo by her grandparents. I'm sad because of it, that's all.'

Wamiru said kindly, 'That day we thought the rain would never stop. Maybe it's a blessing that the lady died. And her daughter, I remember you talked about her, the little girl with no legs, she's going to be well looked after?'

'Yes, Paulina will be well looked after. They said that Elizabeth died of natural causes triggered by malaria. Of course she did not, it was not malaria.'

'Malaria, so often falsely accused.'

Jennifer laughed feebly. 'If medics are unsure, it's always malaria. My God but wasn't one of the sisters telling me today of another young woman in Nairobi showing the same symptoms. Oh think of it, should it be some kind of epidemic.'

'Young women,' Wamiru said. 'It does not seem fair.'

'Is this world ever fair?' Jennifer asked the question, not of the policeman, not of herself but, bitterly, of some abstract arbiter of human justice.

'I was passing on the Garissa Road, I thought I'd call and see you. You were upset when I left you last and I find you upset again.'

'Oh Inspector, it will pass, things pass.' Jennifer then made a pot of tea and for the next half-hour they talked of simple things. Sam, of his childhood in the Rift Valley and of his boyhood friendship with Josiah Kariuki and Jennifer told of her life as a carefree girl in a small seaside town in Ireland where she was thought of as a bit of a rebel.

Wamiru laughed, 'Can't see you as a rebel somehow.'

'Does time not change us all?' Jennifer answered simply. It was time for him to go. They went outside. The sun's strong rays had burned off the reluctant mist and after the long rains the flora was full-flush and the green was giving up a lush, sweet smell of propagation.

'And everything is all right in the hospital now and the village back to normal? Wamiru asked as he was leaving.

'Oh everything is fine now,' Jennifer assured him as she waved goodbye. But things were not right at all. In fact things were so awful, she still couldn't sleep.

Chapter Twelve

Of all the villages around the mountain, the principal Sunday markets were in Donya Sabuk and Katamara and the people of the mountain converged on these villages in numbers. In the drinking houses and on the porches outside the drinking houses, the men drank and smoked, exchanged stories and argued their point and like men everywhere, they put the world to rights, knowing that they would never be called upon to do a thing about it – except perhaps to give their lives. Barefooted children dodged and played in the dust around the fruit and vegetable stalls amid a tumult of younger children vying for attention from mothers who only wanted peace, the children, too young to know what was wrong with the world and all too busy to care, creating a cacophony of chattering, like birds at sun-up. But, above all, market day was woman's day, a riot of batics, *kangas*, dresses and shawls. Amorphous and multi-coloured, green framed by distant bush land and the blue, cornflower sky.

Arm in arm, young girls approached the village of Katamara and in its shimmering periphery, they might have been skipping with rainbows and when they reached the market street with their beads swinging, their dresses swirling and their eyes flashing they called coquettishly 'Hi' and *'Jambo'* to the boys. And the boys were cool; thumbs tucked in their belts, cigarettes in the corner of their mouths they vied with each other for who was toughest, who was coolest who was most attractive to the girls. Sunday market in

Katamara was a colourful, carefree scene and it was at its centre that Corporal Adonis Musyoka took up his position of authority on the elevated decking of a pub, with the unlit cigarette in the corner of his mouth.

From the hospital, the Missionary Sisters came too, singly or in pairs, and sometimes, if she had not gone on a weekend visit to Ekaracara or Nairobi, Nurse Collins would accompany them but she was not at the marketplace today. The Sisters were speckled white and looked like swans coursing through the myriad colours of the market. Sometimes they stopped to talk and laugh and examine merchandise, bargaining frivolously as everyone did and the people they stopped to talk to were happy and proud to be seen talking to the Holy Sisters.

When he saw them arrive, it was Adonis' custom to stand out boldly on the decking and stretch the material of his trousers tight about his genitals so that they were more prominent through the fabric. He was teasing, enticing and it was rewarding for him to see that they dare not look his way; they were no more than women after all. Jennifer Collins did not look at him either and he responded to her distaste by putting a hand in his pocket and stretching the fabric even tighter. But she hadn't come today and it pleased him, things must be getting uncomfortable for Jennifer.

Did the sisters know that he was trying to provoke them? Of course they did, because they dropped shy eyes and he was pleased about it because that was what he wished them to do; if they didn't want to look his way then he would give them reason. When they neared, he laughed out loudly, provocatively; one or two of the nuns had tiny secrets that he knew about, and that, he felt, gave him dominion over them. He did not know of the white woman's secrets but she would have them and dark ones too and one day he would know them and use them. Many of the market people understood what he was doing and secretly despised him.

But today Adonis did not even notice the holy sisters. Today, not everyone was carefree. This policeman was unhappy and appeared decidedly indifferent to the noisy, iridescent spectacle around him. Wearing his customary shades, he stood, pelvic bone thrust forward but not for the benefit of the nuns. Standing on the raised porch of the pub in the centre of the market, today it was just force of habit. He looked as he wanted to look, like a commander grimly surveying a displeasing scene and barely acknowledging the forelock-tugging homage of some of the villagers beneath him. He appeared to have something on his mind. He had words on his mind and now, fully crafted in the smouldering forge of troubled cogitation, they were suitably memorised to give them credence when they landed. They were structured to land on a certain village girl, who had not been behaving as she should.

She would come. She always came to Katamara market on a Sunday afternoon. He saw her coming and she was alone; surprising, as she often came, arm in arm with other girls. Alone or in a group no one could miss Esmeralda waltzing into town. Esmeralda was a potent mountain brew. She never did anything particularly extravagant to attract attention, she didn't have to. Just bouncing from side to side of the dusty market street, talking, laughing, smacking outstretched hands to each in turn with people seemingly forming queues for the privilege. That was until she reached the corporal. '*Jambo* Adonis,' she greeted and mounting the porch, she made to slap a hand that wasn't there. No handshake, subliminally setting the tenor for an encounter.

Stern-faced and stiff-lipped in regulating a torrent, threatening to tumble from his mind, his tailored indignation was sufficient to cause the girl to lower her eyes uncertainly. Then he said loftily, 'Esmeralda, it is my duty as an officer of Kenyan law to confront you with what the *wanachi* are saying about you, and after thorough investigation on my part I know what they are saying to be true.'

Stepping back down from the porch she was silent awhile regarding him with dismay. 'Saying?' she queried, raising her eyebrows archly and allowing a frown to replace her ready smile.

She was wearing a bright yellow blouse and skirt with a blue sash around her middle. A red bonnet complemented red, high-heel shoes. Adonis hated to admit it, but she looked stunningly beautiful. He gulped. This girl always made him gulp, especially when he needed to remonstrate with her which was every time they met. 'There is much talk about you here in Katamara and in your own place of Uamani, in fact all around the mountain the talk is of Esmeralda and the disgraceful way she goes about her life.'

Her reply was not immediate and she stepped back another pace. 'Talking about me?' she said, wide-eyed with incredulity and, in placing one finger between her breasts, implied a 'me' that was both unwitting and beyond reproach.

Throwing his head up and looking down his nose disdainfully, Adonis spoiled his authority by gulping again but his words were well enough rehearsed to spill unstudied. 'It is you and a *musungu* that the talk is all about, the old man Mr Charlie who is reported in a daze for months, since the minute that he saw you. What are you thinking about, girl, strutting about a building site, bending your bum at every opportunity so that Mr Charlie is walking into trenches and bumping his bald head because he cannot take his eyes off you and the men thinking that at any moment he will have a heart attack? You girl, spending a whole weekends with him in Nairobi thinking that no one can see through the antics of Esmeralda when everybody can see through them except poor Mr Charlie who will return to England as a gibbering idiot with his heart broken by a jazzy *Kamba* chick,' and such was his expression of outrage, Adonis then raised his eyes, taking in the market and the people, some of whom had stopped to listen, it was as if he was awaiting some form of unanimous endorsement.

Esmeralda planted her legs firmly apart and glared. 'Talk, talk, talk,' she scoffed, gesturing right and left with an outstretched hand. 'Tis this way, tis that way, tis this way, with talk, talk, talk, I'm almost traumatized with exhaustion, me only working hard on that site for almost eight weeks now, so that the good sisters of the hospital might have someplace nice in the future to rest their holy heads.'

'Working hard,' Adonis sneered down on her, 'Working hard is me keeping this place free from robbers and bandits. Working

111

hard is having bad men fear me. "What if Adonis catch me?" they say and flee to other places to bandit there. But you- you-' he stuttered, words failing him. Swallowing his gall and finding some of the words he had lost, he continued, 'You never doing a finger of work 'cept strutting around in a skirt that gets shorter every day, posing this way, posing that way and work coming to a standstill with Mr Charlie taking photos of you and the men downing tools and falling over to get in pictures with you and the poor nuns of the hospital dying of old age waiting for a new place never to be built 'cos of the antics of Esmeralda.'

'Tis not true,' Esmeralda countered, stamping her foot. 'My poor fingers are almost to the bone already. And the weekend in Nairobi was in innocence, walking around the shops only, buying gloves for my hands and a hard hat so as not to damage my head.'

Taking his shades off to let her see the resolution in his eyes, Adonis, in a hushed voice, issued his coup de grass, 'The talk is that it is your wish to become the old *musungu*'s wife.'

If this revelation was designed to shock it failed, the girl greeted the illumination with hilarious delight, 'Oh yes, Mr Charlie's wife that is me, Esmeralda Carter, a posh bird married to a *musungu* and living in a fine house in England. Drinking tea with English ladies and having servants, do this, do that, do the other. Thinking maybe I need an *askari* now that I am posh and sending for Adonis so that he work for me as my own personal policeman.' She was laughing loudly, slapping her knees in mirth and traipsing up and down to a gathering of villagers in a charade of mockery, imitating how she thought a posh bird would carry on in England. 'Oh Adonis, you would like that, working for me in England. Come work for me an' I might make you Sergeant. You would like that.'

In a warning tone through gritted teeth Adonis said, 'So smart and you a *shamba* girl with big ideas for yourself. One day, girl, you will go too far and I will arrest you and you will fear me then. You think no one knows that Mr Charlie took you to the Blue Post but I know because I know everything that goes on here. I have spies everywhere all reporting to Adonis.'

Following a small gasp of emotion, Esmeralda put her hands on her hips and dropping her head to one side, quizzically said, 'And so?'

Attaining again the moral high ground and replacing his shades squarely on the bridge of is nose, the corporal spoke not to Esmeralda but to a crowd that gathered around her in bemused silence: 'So Mr Charlie has survived a heart attack on the building site, so take the old man to a disco in Thika so that he might have a heart attack trying to keep up with a dancing chick.'

The eyes of the small crown shifted from Adonis to Esmeralda as she put a finger to her temple, the precise location of a good idea. She laughed. 'No I take Charlie disco dancing after I marry him not before. He must say "I do" before he die, you a policeman putting ideas like that in a young girl's head.' Her merriment was infectious, causing subdued laughter from the crowd which was growing bigger by the second; eyes shifting from one to the other they were gleeful at the obvious aggravation she was causing her detractor. 'Or maybe I get him to take me to the Nairobi Hilton so that I walk on a red carpet like the Queen of England. Oh Charlie will have a fine heart attack in the Nairobi Hilton when he gets the bill.'

The crowd now were clearly on the side of Esmeralda. Adonis was feared and for villagers to see him upstaged by a taunting girl was gratifying to them. He was sweating and now deeply regretting his instigation of the confrontation; he wasn't losing, he had lost. Waves of frustrated anger swept over him and he took a step down towards her and would have slapped her cheeky face if she had not seen what was coming and dodged behind members of the crowd. Rural Kenyan girls were supposed to be submissive and concerned with how they were viewed by the *wanachi* but this one wasn't. One day Adonis would have Esmeralda where he wanted her, preferably strapped to a chair in the police station, until then he would have to accept defeat. But he had one last ace to play. He hushed his voice: 'You know what the mamas say about you, they say Esmeralda is so cock-sure about herself that she will be the first girl around these parts to wear tight troosers, a *shamba* girl wearing tight troosers in the marketplace and bringing shame upon her parents. That is what the mamas are saying about you, girl.'

The girl fired up again, snorting, 'Phah, so that is what the mamas say, so when I get home today I will ask my mum to buy me troosers so tight the mamas will hide their eyes when they see me in them. Talk, talk, talk, tis this way, tis that way, tis this way. Me I bring this market down like Sodom and Gomorrah by wearing them.' There was a rumble of muted support from the crowd which had expanded further and in the distance the honking of a *matatu* seemed to ratify her resolution.

The corporal's voice faltered, 'What I say Esmeralda, and as a policeman it is my duty, all I say is you should behave in a more responsible manner and not have the mamas talking about you so much. Maybe you should think to marry a local boy and settle down and not have so much talk about you. That is all I say.'

Esmeralda sniffed. 'And maybe the local boy I should marry is Corporal Adonis Musyoka, because it's plenty of times he's asked me.'

Adonis had had enough. The crowd were laughing openly. Straightening his cap, he turned on his heel and stepped back up onto the porch to resume his earlier posture of high station. But in an attempt to have the last word as Esmeralda and the crowd were dispersing, he called, 'Bad time for an officer of the law to waste words on a jazzy *Kamba* chick who is too big for her boots.'

The *Kamba* chick called back, 'I'll be too big for my tight troosers too.'

For some time unseen behind a stall, Charlie Carter had observed the altercation. Too far away to hear what was being said but knowing from the body language of the protagonists that the discourse was heated and also that he was some way involved. To avoid looking furtive, he had feigned interest in a stall of stunted cauliflowers, compelled eventually to buy three in order to placate the stallholder. Shyly he emerged from hiding, pretending to catch sight of Esmeralda for the first time that day.

'Charlie,' the girl squealed, 'I thought you was in Nairobi.'

'I just got back. Freddie needed the truck.'

'Oh that Freddie, he always needs the truck. Even the times we go to Nairobi, we go by *matatu* 'cos Freddie has the truck. One weekend you should have it so that you can take me somewhere nice. I would like to be in that truck at some time so that I can wave to people. Freddie does not share, it is only you that share. In fact you don't share but always let him have his way.'

'He likes visiting new places each weekend, I don't mind.'

'But I do,' Esmeralda said.

'What was your quarrel about with Adonis?'

'That man is jealous, he says the people are talking,' she told him with a throaty laugh. 'Talk-talk-talk, let them talk is what I say.'

'About us?'

A pause ensued. 'He knows that you took me to Nairobi and the Blue Post. He says he has spies watching me. That man is very cruel, once he worked in a slaughter house and he says to watch out because that slaughter house is now transferred to Katamara police station. I hear he has ceiling hooks fastened in the wash house. He told me that he sometimes hangs men by the balls.'

'I think he is all talk and bluster,' Charlie said.

Looking suddenly wistful and twisting her fingers nervously, she said, 'Charlie do you think that one evening you might take me to the Nairobi Hilton? It would be nice if Adonis's spies could see me in the Nairobi Hilton then report it back to him.'

'Of course I'll take you to the Hilton,' Charlie answered succinctly.

Another pause. 'Charlie, I don't suppose you remembered,' she began uncertainly.

'I remembered,' he answered, smiling and taking from his pocket a small package.

'Oh you didn't,' she exclaimed. Her eyes were puppy-like, appealing. 'Oh Charlie, all my life. Oh Charlie it isn't, it isn't—'

'Don't open it here,' he said quickly. 'Don't let people see what I have bought you. Don't give them chance for more gossip, more talk.'

Ignoring his concern, she began to dance around him dizzily. 'Oh Charlie it isn't, it isn't—'

He nodded and said humbly, 'It is.'

'A watch,' she breathed, her whisper loud enough to reach as many ears as she could. 'Oh Charlie you are so kind to me, almost too kind in fact.'

'Please Esmeralda, don't make a fuss. Shhhh, look people are looking at us.'

At once, quiet and demure, 'I don't deserve such a gift,' she admitted graciously. 'I am just pulverized with gratitude. Is it gold?'

'Well no, it's not gold, but—' Charlie flustered.

Pulling the packaging apart, Esmeralda cooed over the little watch, kissed it then pressed to her bosom saying, 'Charlie I do hope you have a long life and pray that you continue to be good to me for all of it.'

Chapter Thirteen

*T*he night, after returning from a long weekend visit to the Maasai-Mara Game Reserve, Freddie Bristow regaled Charlie and Titus with tales of the abundance of wildlife he had seen. He talked of Tawny eagles, what an exhilarating spectacle they were. And the giraffe and the hyena; no, he didn't see a pride of lions but he saw a herd of elephants and white-backed vultures, high on thermals, scanning the earth beneath for the lame, the dying and the dead. He spoke, at length, of witnessing a gazelle brought down by a pack of wild-dogs and the feeding frenzy that followed. How the vultures homed in on the kill but had to wait their turn to scavenge on the carcass. Charlie talked of a disastrous weekend in Nairobi with Esmeralda.

Freddie now observed his co-worker, co-ordinator, house mate and fellow national with a brow furrowed in bewilderment and undisguised contempt. Not so much the bald, red bulb of a head, forever filmed with pink sweat, or the matching bulb of a belly, or was it a beach ball up his shirt? No, it was the feigned air of nonchalance he had brought with him on to site that morning. He had taken Esmeralda to Nairobi again and she had ditched him. It was Monday morning and she hadn't turned up for work, but he would show Freddie, the site-men and the world that he wasn't concerned. Charlie was not self-reliant; his penchant for continually seeking approval made him vulnerable to manipulation and right now he was a living, breathing absurdity in the hands of the arch manipulator of the mountain. How the hell did Charlie get this job in the first place? He had qualifications that's how; the only qualification worth a toss was proven ability. What worth written qualifications when measured against unschooled virtuosity and expertise? OK, Charlie had managed to oversee the digging of foundations but knew absolutely nothing about teaching third-world building techniques to untutored natives. Friendly and likeable yes, but what the hell was the agency re-cruiting office thinking of to employ him? Somehow they had been conned by qualifications.

Freddie was a cynic; he had volunteered with an ostensible motive therefore everyone else must have done so too. He even doubted the veracity of the agency. With its headquarters in Leeds, of all places, the East African Aid Agency was a government sponsored initiative, supposedly designed to wax the transition from a decidedly unfair occupation to the cultural and economic independence of a nation clearly not ready for such impelling autonomy; so why call it East African, when its operation, as far as Freddie could see, did not extend beyond the borders of Kenya? Was it pseudo goodwill by the government – see we haven't been kicked out, the Kenyan people still love us and need our help – or was the East Africa slant simply to avoid accusations of unwanted patronage? No one, once again as far as Freddie knew, had been sent to Ethiopia, Somalia or Tanzania.

Ok, he had no argument with its stated ethic. The agency was a non-profit-making provider of assistance in know-how as diverse as health-care to animal conservation with the vast majority of the volunteers involved in teaching. An organisation looking to engage experience in making sustainable improvement every-where it touched, fast-tracking ordinary working folk, generally good-natured souls, to make a positive difference where they could. But, using himself as a bench-mark, Freddie wondered was the Agency simply a vehicle for the temporarily disenchanted to pursue an agenda of their own? Freddie had found not an atom of missionary zeal or boundless idealism in any of the volunteers.

Notwithstanding their good works, he would wager that not one of them had left a contented or glamorous life in England to work for next to nothing in a backward, scorching foreign land. So why were they here? To travel, gain experience, have an overseas adventure, escape a lovelorn past, get a tan, or, as he strongly suspected of Charlie, come to Kenya with high hopes of getting laid? Esmeralda would not be back today. If she had wanted to come back, she would have come back with him in the truck, yesterday evening.

Charlie, his eyes were dull, his spirit remote, his mind far off, some-place else, an unhappy place. He said vaguely, 'Has everyone turned up today?' He was still trying to pretend he hadn't noticed that the only girl was missing from the workforce.

Freddie smiled inwardly, but shook his head in disgust. Charlie hadn't noticed, yet there he was now, standing, neck stretched, on a part-built stone wall, looking out jerkily north, south, east and west like a demented Meerkat. She hadn't turned up for work. Work! What a bloody joke. She hadn't turned up for her daily fashion parade, her flits around site like some glittering prima-donna; she hadn't turned up to feast herself on chicken and goat meat at Charlie's expense and she hadn't turned up to distract the men with her endless chatter, infuriatingly exclusive to their own *Kamba* tongue. Ever since the day she had arrived on site, looking like a Parisian model lost on her way to a photo shoot, Charlie had mooned around in a state of stupefied confusion, and to make matters worse he was now convinced their house was haunted by a girl called Shula. Poor Charlie, he had been warned about malaria and dengue fever and had been immunised against cholera and rabies yet no one had thought to remind him what non-existent ghosts and hopeless love can do to peace of mind. Charlie could be heading for a nervous breakdown.

As far as Freddie could gather from snippets of conversation, Charlie's third weekend with Esmeralda in Nairobi had been much like the first two; expensive. As before, they had spent two nights in a hotel, occupying separate rooms, but not the Hilton as Esmeralda had wanted and that had started her sulks. Charlie had tried to mollify her with a protracted shopping expedition, but when he refused to give her her own little plastic card instead of money, it was the last straw and she had walked off in a huff. That little plastic card was magic for buying things; much better than cash; she had never seen anything like it. But if he wouldn't give her one then that meant he didn't love her after all. She would have to leave him, and find a job as a mason to earn a crust. There were lots of building sites in Nairobi.

Charlie sidled up to him. 'Esmeralda hasn't turned up yet?' He looked at his watch: 'It's nearly eleven-o-clock.'

Freddie sneered, 'Charlie, you've been like a bloody jack-in-the-box since eight o clock this morning. And it won't make one ha'porth o' difference whether she turns up for work or not, because she doesn't do any. Good thing she's not here, we might get something done today. She won't share a bed with you, makes you get separate rooms, spends all your money then ditches you. She's taking you for a complete fool.'

'It's me that gets the separate rooms, it wouldn't be right, we're both single.' There was a whine in Charlie's voice. It spoke of exploitation and the complete lack of wherewithal to do anything about it.

On a ligger, Freddie moulded mortar with a trowel. The men had gathered around a heap of sand. A snake had laid eggs in the sand to incubate and they speculated on the type of snake. Freddie speared the mortar with his trowel. 'Charlie, sometimes I think you're not right in the head. You're certainly not right in the head, where that girl's concerned. I wouldn't put up with the way she treats you, no one would. She's taking the piss out of you for God's sake, can't you see it? Because I'm telling you now, everyone else can see it.'

Charlie was too emotionally bereft to argue; he was whining again. 'Truth is, Freddie, I'm not feeling well this morning.' Looking bleakly to the road by which Esmeralda would make her way to the site, he added, 'Didn't sleep too well last night.'

Freddie laughed shortly. 'Not that bloody knocking ghost again.'

'No, I just couldn't sleep.'

'This bloody knocking business has to stop. Half past two in the morning last time. And poor Titus, waking him up as well, and you know how he needs his sleep. I'm telling you, Charlie, things have got to change around here. I'm not going to be woken in the middle of the night to listen to non-existent knocking. And Titus, you don't spoil him, you bloody ruin him. He's supposed to be guarding us through the night. Only last week thugs smashed through the door of a house in Kusyokimanza, robbed the family and raped the daughter. The middle of the night, that's what they do, hurl a two hundredweight rock through the main door. That's what they do and that's what they'll do to us and there'll be our *askari* fast asleep He's a night-watchman for God's sake he's paid to guard us through the night. Did he hear knocking last night? Well no, of course not, he was fast asleep. It would take a two-hundredweight rock smashing through a bloody door to wake him up. It would be a bit too late for us then though, wouldn't it?' A cheer from the men at the sand pit, Paul, an authority on snake eggs, had identified the eggs as being laid by a black mamba.

Charlie wasn't really listening. Neck craned, eyes peeled, he had spotted a woman on the road approaching the site; she neared, it wasn't Esmeralda. Forlornly, his eyes turned back to Freddie.

'And I can't believe you bought him a camera. Here Titus, a reward for not waking us up with your snoring. Anyone in Katamara want a camera? Just take the piss out of Charlie.'

'A present, that's all,' Charlie answered wearily.

'And you got Esmeralda a watch. What the hell's the matter with you, Charlie?'

Charlie looked shaken. 'Who told you about the watch? That watch was supposed to be a secret.'

Freddie looked to the sky for deliverance. 'Who told me about the watch? A secret? Everyone north of Kilimanjaro knows about the watch. Esmeralda has been flashing it around, showing it off.

The bloody Queen of Katamara: that watch is the start of her very own collection of crown jewels.'

'Freddie, do you mind if I go back to the house? I'm tired and I definitely don't feel too well. I'll come back this afternoon.' Maybe he was going mad. The knocking, It wasn't muffled, neither was it frantic, it was like the grieving women knocking on the mortuary door, wanting attention. Was that what he was hearing? Next time he was in Nairobi he would visit the doctor. He hadn't seen Jennifer for over a week and now Esmeralda had not returned from Nairobi. Everything was getting on top of him. Too much sun.

'Take the truck. Take a couple of days off. We can manage,' Freddie said, not unkindly, his consideration relieving an incipient annoyance with the man's naivety, his stupidity. Letting him have the truck was like giving a bone to an irritating dog so that it would go away. 'You're not sleeping well because you're hearing things. That bloody scheming minx has scrambled your brains.'

'We have been getting on so well together;' the whine in his voice was back. 'It was just a silly row, and she walked off.'

'Because you wouldn't give her her very own credit card, didn't you explain what it was? Didn't you tell her that she needed money in her own bank account first, before she could have a credit card? For God's sake, Charlie, wake up to her.'

'I tried to tell her, but she didn't understand.'

'She didn't want to understand. Charlie, just go.'

Charlie went and Freddie listened intently to the tone of the engine, the change of gears. He shook his head. The truck hadn't crossed the bridge to start the climb to the house; it was heading through the village on its way to Uamani and Esmeralda's home, heading headlong to Uamani, and the home of a girl who was patently taking him for a fool. Did the natives take Charlie for the archetypal Englishman? If so, how could a race of Charlies colonise half the countries of the world, including their own? Freddie sighed; he asked Sammy to mix another batch of mortar then moved across the site to assist Caleb in the plumbing a rough stone pillar.

Charlie, who would have been happy with a crust, had landed a banquet and he didn't want to lose it. She was Esmeralda the gypsy girl from the streets of Paris; was he to be her hunchbacked dogsbody? It had all started with so much hope, a love so intense it was like a fever in his blood. Driving straight through Katamara, he picked up the dirt road through farmland and plantations, the shortest route to Uamani. Whenever he saw a distant figure on the road, his heart leaped in expectation, only to fall into a dispirited wasteland, when the figure turned out to be a lone woman carrying water from the Athi, or a herdsman on his way to tend his stock.

Victoria, Esmeralda's mother greeted him warmly. Esmeralda came home late last night by *matatu* but left for Nairobi this morning. No, she did not know where her daughter was staying but it was very likely it would be at her cousin's place. She had talked of trying to get a job as a mason.

'But Victoria, Esmeralda cannot be a mason, she hasn't learned enough.'

'She told me that she had watched you and Mr Freddie very closely, mortar, stone, mortar, stone and she's a very confident girl who can do the same. She said that every girl needs a chance. She said that someone will give her a chance.'

Suddenly Charlie was not so downcast. Esmeralda would be back in no time at all. He laughed emptily. 'Victoria, I promise you, no one in their right mind will employ Esmeralda as a mason.'

'You did,' Victoria said.

When he got back to the house, he was surprised to find that a letter had been pushed under the door. He read it twice, the first time in a sensation of numb disbelief, the second in a kind of glory. In haste, he sped in the truck to the project site. Taking Freddie to one side he handed him the letter. 'What do you think of this, Freddie?' he said breathlessly

The letter was written on three pages torn from a school exercise book, the handwriting neat and legible. Freddie read each word with a bemused incredulity.

My Dearest Charlie

Imagination no, a dream no, reality yes. I know Charlie that one day you will leave Esmeralda Ndete and go back to your Motherland to leave this African chick locked in by your love. Oh my darling when you go then please come back to our lovely Kenya, oh my honey please don't go forever. You will know this *Kamba* babe is crying for you, her tears will never dry. I will miss your tenderness, your smiling, laughing way, even your walking style. I sleep sleepless nights, knowing someday you will go and my heart has no comfort knowing I will be left alone in the wilderness. I am in love with you Charlie and wish I could kiss your head every day of my life. The people of the village say that you are an old guy but I call you Charlie the young guy. In fact I call you Moses who saved Israel from captivity just as you have saved me from the captivity of the guys around here who would have me locked in a *nyumba* for their entertainment. The first day I saw you I felt that one day you would be mine, it was a chemist's action that I had for you and always I will be faithful to you. It is my wish to say sorry for the silly row we had and would sooner have my Charlie than a bit of plastic card. That was a blissful time I had with you at the Blue Post and even though we were being watched by the spy of Adonis, the music will never leave my head. I pray to God for one more chance to be with you in Nairobi and to go to the Nairobi Hilton next time as it is my great dream in life for only God knows what awaits the chosen few. Charlie all my dreams are upon you and when I walk your vision is always upon me even sometimes I am affected by a periodic mental eclipse. You have driven me crazy and it seems we are made for each other until death us do part.

When I think of you, things start coiling and uncoiling in my sensitive zones and butterflies start flying about in my stomach. Always remember darling a *Kamba*, African chick who lives in dark corners of the world is crying for your company and your romantic love. It is because of this I feel I must leave you for a bit longer as absence makes the heart grow fonder. I have only come back to Katamara to deliver this letter and I am returning now to Nairobi immediately to look for work as a mason. Oh if only I had a camera to send you photos of me so you don't forget me. Maybe when I come home again I could borrow a camera from Titus as I heard that he had got one from you. Oh how much I would love a camera as sometimes I stand outside camera shops and weep. Oh my darling I know I will see you again before the world perish.

Yours Brim of Love Esmeralda.

'What do you make of that?' Charlie asked.

Freddie was shaking his head and chuckling silently. 'Let me get this right. You fell out with her in Nairobi yesterday and this was pushed under the door this morning. That means she's back.'

'Seems she's come back just to give me this letter then she's gone again.'

'I can't believe that you spent the weekend in separate rooms?' Not after reading a letter like this,'

'Yes, separate rooms.'

'Then when did you do it with her, because you must have done?'

'Do what?'

'For Christ's sake Charlie, you know well "what". She wouldn't send you a letter like this if you hadn't.'

'What?'

'Christ Charlie, you know what I'm talking about.'

'Kissed her? No, not yet.'

Chapter Fourteen

*A*lthough the hospital was open through the night as refuge and remedy for animal and human outrage, or, more likely, as a neutralizing haven for scorpion stings and snake bites, its clinic did not open until eight a.m. in the morning. By this time the lifting mountain mist would reveal groups of women and children gathered at its door, some would have set off walking in the middle of the night. The school for the disabled children did not start until nine a.m. and although most of the children who attended lived in at the hospital, there were many more able-bodied who had to travel miles. But, come the appointed time, rows of neatly dressed little students would be seated in class, eagerly awaiting the lessons of the day.

The hospital gave warmth to the community that did not come from the heat of fire or the sun but from the white hope of the stone building and its white-clad residents. This warmth radiated far beyond Katamara, its benign circulation reaching to Uamani in the east and around the curve of the mountain, westward to Kyeleni. It was a kind of glow felt more by the women, especially those that were pregnant. They laid their hands across their swollen bellies knowing their babies were being cared for, even before, with their first breaths, the babies had chance to complain about the strange world they hadn't asked to enter and hadn't known was there. The women knew that their living children were safer too for being born in the shadow of its walls. It was insurance against the ravages of dysentery and malaria and a sanctuary from the harmful beasts of the mountain and the reptiles that slithered at their feet. Men did not understand so well the subtle influence of the hospital but they sensed that their families felt secure, so they themselves felt stronger and less fearful of what each day would bring. It was the warmth of open arms, the unconditional helping hand and it was free to those without money to pay. It came from concord and not from a cold pocket wanting recompense. It was, simply, what the Missionary Sisters of the Precious Blood were giving to the people; the origin of that mysterious smile of theirs. And in such an environment there must be absolute trust.

Corporal Adonis had awakened with a feeling of well-being that morning and, still feeling mighty pleased with himself he approached the hospital with the aura of a mission accomplished, even though it hadn't started yet. He was laughing inside. He had heard that Esmeralda was in Nairobi seeking employment as a mason, well, long may she remain there. He could put her out of his mind as long as he didn't see her, for to even catch a glimpse of that girl filled his heart and head with an unhealthy mixture of desire and rage; a discomposing compound for any man, but drastic for a policeman. Although arrests increased dramatically with every sighting of her, and despite her working wonders for his monthly prosecution targets, his motives were untenable and his spirit unfulfilled. Another reason for his happy state of mind: men had started work on extending the electricity supply to the rest of the village.

Catching a nun's attention before she had chance to escape, the corporal said, in a voice melodious with pleasantry, 'Good morning, Sister Magdalene please may I speak with Mr Muinde, if he is available?'

Sister Magdalene was uncomfortable with Adonis at her side. 'You'll find him in his office,' she said without looking him in the eye.

'Oh, and Sister, I haven't seen too much of Nurse Collins lately.

Always I would see her in the market and shopping around but—' He shrugged.

'Nurse Collins is not too well lately,' the sister said abruptly.

Adonis looked at her intently. 'And what is ailing poor Nurse Collins?'

'Not too sure,' she answered and walked briskly off without giving him time to question her further.

Adonis grinned and let her go. Was it reprehensible to fantasize about nuns? If so, then, in Sister Magdalene's case, he was as guilty as hell; that impeachable beauty, that serenity. A slim figure beneath a sexless habit, what a waste of a woman, did she know how beautiful she was? No mirrors in the place, no one to tell her. What if he was to tell her and one day he would? What would be her reaction? She would be flattered of course, she was still a woman after all. Forever closeted in dogma, suffocated by faith. Did she know how much she had to give? He watched her grow smaller down the long corridor; beneath that shapeless habit, long slim legs, the subtle curve of buttocks and the gentle swelling of breasts. What was the point? A suit of armour cannot defy imagination. Adonis hoped for her sake that there was a hereafter and that one day she would meet the God that took her for his wife, a selfish God to keep such beauty to himself. Yes, one day he would do it. 'Sister Magdalene, have you any idea just how beautiful you are?' and, with thoughts marinated in self-conceit, he smiled as he made his way to rag-bag Muinde's office.

Mr Muinde groaned inwardly. His blank look was deliberate but he said, 'Good morning, Corporal, take a seat,' and they shook hands.

Adonis took a seat. 'It is good news, Mr Muinde. At last, electricity for the station – it will be installed soon. Even this time next week people will be seeing lights on all through the night knowing Corporal Adonis is hard at work and they are safe sleeping in their beds and be glad of it.' Swinging one leg over the other and clasping his hands behind his head with an aura of confidence, he continued, 'I don't know if you know it but, around here, bad men fear me a lot. It is good that they fear me and know what is in store for them if they are caught doing criminal acts. I have recently installed ceiling hooks in the washroom. An idea I brought with me from the slaughter house. Right now robbers and bandits are trembling all around the mountain at the thought of it.' Adonis was grinning from ear to ear.

Mr Muinde greeted this latest innovative deterrent with a faint smile and said thinly, 'Your policing techniques are legendary Adonis.' Could this buoyant braggart really hang a man from a ceiling hook and attach electrodes to his testicles? He regarded Adonis with mild contempt: yes, he could, do it with a smile on his face and boast about it afterwards. 'We just don't know how lucky we are to have you looking after us. And just what can I do for you?'

Adonis unhooked his legs, took his hands from behind his neck and flicking his tongue pleasurably about his lips, said, 'I am on a mission for Inspector Wamiru who rang me up only this morning and put me in charge of a very important event.'

Muinde shuffled some paperwork on his desk. 'I have to put a monthly report in on each child for the people in Nairobi. Got a bit behind, I'm afraid.'

Too full of himself to take the hint, Adonis said, 'As you know, me and the inspector have investigated a lot together and he admires me greatly. And you will have heard the name of Josiah Kariuki, or J.M. as he is known to many of the *wanachi*, who love him a lot.'

'Yes, of course I've heard of him. How is it I can help him?'

'Inspector Wamiru wants to use the hospital playing field as a place for J.M.'s political rally. J.M. is campaigning for re-election as I'm sure you know. The inspector was very impressed with everything he found here in Katamara and he was very happy about it. This is the place he wants and no other.'

Muinde did not respond but let the man continue.

'Inspector Sam Wamiru is J.M.'s good friend and is most always at his meetings. The inspector he will come to Katamara as a friend only and not as a policeman for he knows that I am in control here and ready to bang up any trouble-causers.'

'This rally—?' He left Adonis to finish the question and the answer.

Adonis had been well briefed. 'The rally, yes, I know J.M. wants to talk about people helping each other, all for one and one for all. I know from Inspector Sam that he wants to say good things about the *musungus* helping the sisters, and the volunteers of this village who are helping them in turn and the nations of the world being one happy family, free from bribery and corruption. The *wanachi*, they listen to J.M. He is more important.'

'He's the Member of Parliament for Nyandarua North, but not so important since he lost his position in the cabinet,' Muinde remarked dryly.

'But he is cheered very loudly by the people who love him, as you will see. So I can report back to Inspector Sam that it is OK?'

'A date,' the administrator mused, flicking the pages of a diary on his desk. 'Have to check that there's nothing else booked for the day he wants. Just when does he want to hold this meeting?'

'Inspector Wamiru told me to say it is when your very beautiful Jacaranda trees are in blossom. Sunday is the very best as the people are going to the market for the afternoon, and he can catch them on their way. It will be dinner time and in the hospital field there will be a feast of rice, *githeri, sukuma wiki* and goat meat so that people will remember the good times they had with J.M. and vote for him.'

'The jacaranda trees are due to blossom, how about a month this coming Sunday?' Although his mind was active with the possibility of a returned favour, Muinde's prudence with management and expenditure predominated: 'And who is responsible for providing food and paying for it all, and who's responsible for preparing it?'

Adonis answered quickly and proudly, 'It is me who is entrusted with arrangements. I will get women of the village to cook and serve the food and J.M.'s people will pay. A good time for every-one before they go to market and I will see to it.'

'Tell the inspector that I'll try to ensure that the Sunday is re-served. He must let me know soon if that day is not OK. Let me know in good time if there is any change of plan.' He made a note on an appropriate page in the diary.

Adonis smiled broadly. He had known everything would go well and it had. Inspector Wamiru would be impressed. Through Wamiru, he would make sure that J.M.'s people knew who had organised everything and Adonis Musyoka would be highly thought of. Surely he must be promoted to Sergeant soon. Sergeant Adonis Musyoka, he kept saying in his mind and liked the sound of it. 'Very fine, Mr Muinde, now I must make plans immediately. The first is to order two goats from my family in Tala which I will do this very day.'

Muinde looked up. 'Tala?' he queried.

'Tala, near Kangundo, my family have a *shamba* there. Tala is famous for having the very best goats. My family have the best goats in Tala, so I order now for them to be fattened up and then, when the time ripens, I will bring them to the hospital for the slaughter and I will do the slaughtering as I am as well trained in that department, as I am in many others.'

'The two whites, Charlie and Freddie, they come from a town called Tala in England. They will be pleased to know their town in England has a twin in Kenya.'

The corporal's face ignited with glee: 'I did not know of such a place as that in England.' He raised a leg and slapped his boot, 'This is most amazing, the three of us from Tala and we are brothers surely. That I am the brother of two *musungus* is such a laughing matter.' He left Muinde's office still chortling.

Mr Muinde had got rid of one unpleasantness but he had some-thing much more unpleasant to attend to. He followed Adonis out of the door and went looking for Nurse Collins.

Leaving the grounds of the hospital, Adonis encountered Ti-tus who was pushing the *piki* to the shack of the puncture *fundi*, located nearby. '*Jambo*, my good friend Titus,' he hailed, 'I must tell you the most amazing news, which is the shock of the year to me. You will not believe the name of the town in England where Mr Charlie and Mr Freddie come from. Do you know of it?'

'Yes, I know of it as Tala.'

Adonis could hardly contain his excitement: 'Tala,' he blurted and with his face flushed with the excitement, he expanded, 'They come from a town called Tala and me, I come from Tala near Kangundo. The three of us, we all come from Tala. Imagine, Titus, we are brothers.' Together the men's smiles blossomed into laughter and they began slapping each other's hands in ratification of the amazing coincidence.

'Most incredible,' Titus concurred, 'of course, Tala, but I never thought of it until this very minute.'

Adonis gloried, 'I never heard of a town in two different countries having the same name, it is a most outstanding achievement Almost I am thinking of writing to the *Daily Nation*.'

'Oh do it, do it,' Titus urged.

Adonis allowed his fervour to fade slowly, deliberately, then continued gravely, 'I am having a problem, which I am hoping Charlie will help me with. There is to be a political meeting in the hospital grounds. It is the great Josiah Kariuki, who will be talking to the people. There will be a celebration and a feast that day and I am to organise it by popular demand. Now Tala is on that side, and the hospital is on this side, and my problem is to get two goats from Tala on that side, to the hospital on this side so they may be slaughtered here and eaten fresh. Now, the last time I brought a goat from Tala it was on the *matatu,* and many people was angry with me when it began shitting on the floor with great abandon. Now as you know, Titus, I am a most important man around these parts with people looking up to me and I can never again have fingers pointed at me for transporting shitting goats. So Titus, if you can ask Charlie that I might accompany him in his truck to Tala on that side, and bring the goats back to the hospital on this side, then I will thank him fine for the proposition.'

'A shitting goat on a crowded bus is not good. I will ask him and I think it will be fine.'

They began walking together towards the *fundi's* shack, pushing the *piki*.

'Tell Charlie that I come from the same place as him, Tala, and that we are neighbours almost and brothers most certainly.'

'I will tell him, Adonis.'

'Are you footing back with that bike when it is mended?'

'Yes.'

'You are my good friend, Titus. So you will speak to Charlie today about my mission?'

'I am returning as soon as this bike is fixed and will tell Charlie. Mr Freddie is away to Kisii, and maybe to Lake Victoria, he is a very travelling man. Charlie is at the house, washing clothes. Soon I will be at my business of *askari* for the night, but when I return I think it will be OK as Charlie helps many people around these parts and although he is troubled just now I think he is in fair condition.'

'You are my good friend, Titus.'

Charlie was troubled and annoyed, troubled because he had been dreaming of a visitation by the Virgin Mary only to be awakened by knocking again, and troubled because Esmeralda had not returned as he had hoped. He was also annoyed because he had intended to travel to Nairobi for the day, only to find the *piki* had a puncture. Although laudable, Freddie's adventurous spirit and penchant for travel was becoming irksome. His commandeering of the truck most weekends had become the norm, so much so that Charlie had to pluck up courage to ask *if* on occasions, he might borrow the truck for himself. He had wanted it this weekend but, having found out that Freddie had made plans to visit Kisii, he didn't like to ask but vowed to assert himself in future.

Next weekend he would go to Nairobi. He would go early Friday morning to the main library and to the newspapers seeking archival information on Lord Delemere and the white settlers. The names of Johnnie and Clarissa Chance must be in there somewhere. Then, the Saturday and the Sunday, he would look for Esmeralda.

Huffing and puffing, the motor cycle almost as high as himself, Titus heaved the bike up the hill to where Charlie was hanging out wet clothes.

'That *fundi*, he found two punctures again,' Titus called sheepishly.

'Not two punctures again, not in the same wheel?'

'He swore that it was true. But that is his way with *musungus*, he knows the *piki* is yours, he knows I am your *askari*.'

'And he charged you for two.'

'He charge plenty saying "*Mbili, Mbili*" and I have no change left for you.'

This could not go on. The *fundi* might well hate the colonial British for what they had done to him but Charlie would have to start asserting himself, not only with Freddie and Esmeralda but with the cheating puncture *fundi* too.

Enough was enough.

There are no protracted twilights on the Kenyan equator, no resplendent sunsets; it is day then suddenly it is night, the end of one performance and the start of another; no curtain call. Jennifer Collins wandered the hospital grounds feeling sick. It wasn't the hospital sisters or Mr Muinde. It was some of the mothers. Not that Mr Muinde doubted her for a moment but from tomorrow she was not allowed to be alone with children. She must, at all times, have a nursery sister with her.

Chapter Fifteen

*H*aving been advised on etiquette during his induction course in Nairobi, Charlie now prided himself on discretion and tolerance; simple common sense was all that was required and very soon he had acquired the behavioural nuances necessary to socially integrate with the Kenyan people. The transient and street-wise people of the towns and cities that is; be very aware that the *wanachi*, in general, are not as well-off as the *musungu*, so don't make a show, not that Charlie had much wealth to show anyway. He didn't really like big cities, too much noise, too much ferment and no one should have to risk being trampled underfoot simply to buy a postage stamp. On his first few forays into the city he had given so much to pavement beggars, he was in danger of becoming one himself. Was that a show of wealth? Yes it was, he was learning.

But Charlie was not so confident with the people close to him, especially women. The biggest problem he had to overcome was how to conduct himself when invited to someone's rural *nyumba* for dinner. He simply would not allow a chicken to be slaughtered in his honour; a dozen chickens might be that family's entire wealth and on the first few occasions he had found himself, to his horror, involved in a chicken chase, the family trying to catch, kill and cook the chicken and Charlie trying to save it. The embarrassment came with the tug-of–war when the unfortunate bird was caught. He had thought long and hard about this before coming to a solution. As soon as he received an invitation to dinner he declared himself a vegetarian.

Far worse was the etiquette required when given honey-beer to drink, a favoured home-made brew of the village and mountain men. Honey-beer, he had found was a viciously potent ooze, the colour of – well – honey, impossible to swallow without eyes clamped shut and a face contorted in convulsion, agitations amusing and acceptable to the host with the most appealing to all being the spitting out of dead bees while drinking; now that was really amusing. And he couldn't handle the primary unfortunate side-effects of this brew either. After imbibing, it tended to cause the bottom half of the alimentary canal to operate like a pressurised hose-pipe. No bottle should ever be offered to a *musungu* without a mandatory ten-second warning on the label. Seated in the cosy ambience of an after-dinner *nyumba* a man might be regaling his hosts with talk of his cultural indiscretions and faux pas when the ten-second warning kicked in. That was ten seconds to enquire directions to the outside *choo*, politely ask to be excused, negotiate the family and the animals on the floor and so reach the *choo*, preferably unoccupied. Charlie, now, would never attend a *shamba* dinner without wearing a quick release belt and carrying his own toilet roll. And still it wasn't over. Having made the *choo* just in time and squatting above a hole in the ground, it was difficult to ignore the children who had followed, squinting through the slats and gleefully observing that white people did it just the same way they did. But he was trying and learning and laughing and the people liked him for his effort.

Often, in the evening of the day, Charlie would visit the village for groceries and hardware and sometimes he would stay behind, drinking in one of the bars. The people were always happy that he had joined them, for he was a cheerful man. A pleasing stream of conviviality flowed through him, unimpeded by the impasse of self-absorption and the locals compared him favourably with his compatriot, Freddie, who they considered to be a selfish man.

Freddie was the more assertive, more as they had always understood Englishmen to be; a true member of the colonial force which had swept across their land, treating it as their own exotic playground. Although Freddie never gave anyone cause to dislike him, they treated him courteously but uncertainly, noticing that when he passed children on the roadside in the truck, they not squeal for him to stop as they did with Charlie. The children would shrill and Charlie would stop and no royal retinue was ever so grand as those children were, as Charlie took them slowly through the villages to their homes. Freddie never stopped for children, why, it seemed almost as if he feared being suspected of something sinister; but how could that be?

Freddie played jokes and tricks but whereas the people enjoyed his tricks they often did not understand his jokes. They laughed because it was expected of them but he didn't make the people laugh as Charlie did, albeit often secretly among themselves. Freddie would never think of purchasing fruit and vegetables at one end of the market, only to gift them to a stall at the other end, then to reverse the procedure an hour later. To Charlie it was only a few Kenyan shillings creating commerce out of nothing and no one knew what he was doing, except that everyone knew what he was doing, and laughed at his madness but with fellow-feeling for his kindness nonetheless. Charlie made efforts that Freddie didn't. Charlie remembered key words from his language-orientation in Nairobi and would use them often: *Jambo, Habari, Azante* and *Kwaheri;* respectful greetings and farewells, and even though the people smiled at his mispronunciations, they respected his endeavour. And all were taken by the family photos of his home in England and still laughed at his mother's garden full of foolish flowers that would not be sold and how wild birds might be invited out of the sky to bathe and dine at tables. But they were utterly horrified by other tales that Charlie told. Politicians, even the Prime Minister mimicked and ridiculed on radio and television. No, it was impossible for them to believe that even the Royal Family, even the Queen of England herself were there to be lampooned.

Well – the British never did respect people, especially people from other lands. Now, all that was left for them was to parody each other. Such malicious libel and slander would never be permitted in Kenya. A tiny, crazy country called England who they might seek to imitate but would never understand.

But of late a change had come over Charlie and the people discussed it among themselves. They had heard rumours that he was troubled by missing girls. A missing girl called Shula, and he had started to question them about her. Over the years young girls had gone missing from the villages; one certainly taken by a crocodile while washing clothes in the Athi, and another taken by a German man who said he wanted her for his wife. Of Shula, a strange name for a *Kamba* girl, they professed ignorance and shook their heads. With Esmeralda, another strange name for a *Kamba* girl, they shook their heads too but also gave each other knowing and helpless looks. She was in Nairobi and could be doing anything. And now Nurse Collins was often missing too and the more Charlie defended her the more troubled he became. Rumour was rife in the village about the death of Kennedy. No doubt about it now, Jennifer Collins was being blamed.

Searching for knowledge of Shula, Charlie discreetly targeted the older people of the village, who spoke of a Lord William Northrup Macmillan, a Scot raised in St Louis Missouri and knighted by the King of England. Why, Lord William once owned Kilimambogo, yes, the entire mountain. And the same old people could remember the notorious Colonel Ewart Grogan, and talked of his wife-swapping, wild parties and riotous living. Some were sure that it was he who had once owned the *musungu* house on the mountain, but no one could remember a Johnnie Chance buying it from him. But surely someone must remember a dashing, debonair Johnnie Chance? What of his austere wife Clarissa: big Evangeline, two women, one day, with horses and carriage, could anyone remember them? Charlie was advised to consult with the puncture *fundi*, but he refused. That old man was a cheat and could not be trusted.

No one could remember the house being built, it was always there, always used as a hunting lodge right up to Independence. After Independence it was occupied for a while by a German family, who sold it to the Co-operative and moved back to the Fatherland. Although the Germans left in unseemly haste one early morning, even leaving all their furniture behind, there was no talk of a spectral girl or the Virgin Mary; no report of the sound of knocking in the night. Charlie found that history was not strong with the poor; history was the last time they had had a decent meal and posterity the day they might get their next one. The bats had gone because more people were moving about the house, the chimpanzee were curious and had come down from the mountain to view their new neighbour and finding little to concern them had moved back. As for Brownie, well there were some incidents of rabies reported around that time. Inspector Wamiru had not been able to come up with anything either but still Charlie was not convinced.

The people did not like to see Charlie in a preoccupied state of mind and they reassured him, and it is just possible that one of them contacted Esmeralda and asked her to come back just to make him happy again.

She returned late on the Sunday evening, the same weekend Charlie travelled to Nairobi in the truck to look for her. Over that long weekend he visited the archives of the *Daily Nation* and the historical section of the public library, and was astonished at the plethora of scandalous information surrounding the White Highlanders. It made him ashamed of his heritage, and amazed that the much abused nation of Kenya appeared to hold no grudges. Each name and biographical exploration he studied in depth. Baron Delemere, Jock Delves Broughton, Jossylin Hay, 22nd Earl of Erroll, Lady Idina Sackville, Alice De Janze, Frederic De Janze, Lady Diana Delves Broughton, Gilbert Colville, Hugh Dickenson, Jack Soames, Lady June Carberry, Junanita Carberry, Dickie Penbrook Broughton, Julian Lezzard and a host of other lesser lights, but no Johnnie Chance. But surely, Johnnie and Clarissa Chance must have fit in with that lot. Johnnie was one of the leaders, up there with Delemere. If there had been a cover-up, and there must have been, then the sophistry was matchless, the obliteration absolute. The Happy Valley set had two of its most prominent members missing from its history.

When he wasn't burrowing in newspapers and books, Charlie was visiting construction sites ostensibly gathering scholarship for a thesis he was doing on *The Provision of Adequate Shelter* for an Aid Agency he was involved in. In actuality, he was looking for a builder in a frock. Deep in his heart, he knew Esmeralda would not be found on a building site, but knowing the girl as he did, he couldn't take the chance.

Why had she not come back to him? He read her loving letter over and over. For sure, she was missing because she was looking for a job of some kind. She did not want to spend her life hungry, barefoot and pregnant and that was why she wasn't on site with him in Katamara. There was simply no paid work for a girl anywhere around the mountain. Thinking of Esmeralda and Jennifer made him unhappy, and thinking of Shula made him unhappier still.

Chapter Sixteen

C harlie met Titus as he arrived for his nightly duty.

'She's back,' Titus told him.

'Who's back?' Although he already knew, Charlie tried to sound blasé, but failed to keep the excitement from his voice.

'Esmeralda, I was speaking with her this morning.'

In truth Charlie, on his return from Nairobi the previous night, had already witnessed her arrival in the village. He was making his dismal way to one of the pubs, when he spotted her stepping down from a *matatu* outside the hospital. Unsure, he blinked repeatedly into the misty mangle of disembarking bodies thankfully separating on the roadside. His heart lurched with joy as they became identifiable; yes, it was her. She looked tired and a little forlorn, the plastic bags in each of her hands appeared heavy, and he had to quell an impulse to rush to her and relieve her of her burden. The bus did not travel to Uamani and it would become pitch dark on her way home. He could get the truck, just happen to be passing her on his way to her village; he could stop and give her a lift; tell her all the news, oh, and tell her about the camera he had bought for her. The camera was at the house, should they turn back and call to collect it; it was hers. It was hard for him to see her looking so doleful and with such a long way to go but he disciplined himself; Freddie was right, he simply had to stop being such a lap-dog. If she respected him she just might treat him better.

And with a sad heart he watched her set out on the darkening road towards her village.

Freddie joined them on the porch, and, resting his elbows on the hand rail said disdainfully, 'She's back then, wonder what the hell she's been up to.'

'She's been looking for work,' Charlie answered readily.

'As, a *mason*?' Disdain to derision in a word. Freddie continued in the same vein, 'It's no bloody wonder she's back then, is it? How could Esmeralda get a job as a mason? She's never laid a brick, never pointed one and she won't lift a stone for fear of damaging her fingernails. Does she know a mortar mix from a pudding mix? Does she hell. Just imagine Esmeralda, fifty feet up a scaffold with a hod of bricks over her shoulder tottering about in her high heels and mini skirt.' He began to act out a charade, lips pouting eyes flashing, bottom waddling, causing Charlie to frown and Titus to roar with laughter. 'For Christ's sake, Charlie, whatever she's been doing in Nairobi, it's not looking for work as a mason, she's much more likely to have been hustling herself down River Road. You've got to get a bloody grip. And the next time I see Esmeralda, I'll tell her to clear off and if she ever has the nerve to come back on site I'll stick her head-first in the bloody water barrel.'

'She's an employee, I employed her,' Charlie reminded curtly.

'She was telling me she needs a reference,' Titus broke in, defusing the burgeoning argument.

Freddie swung around on him: 'A what?' His voice was strangled in disbelief.

'When I was talking to her,' Titus explained, 'she told me she cannot get a job as a mason without a good reference from her last employer. She told me that she is back to seek a reference from Charlie.'

'I'll give her one,' Freddie volunteered, but with savage determination in his voice. 'That bloody girl's audacity knows no bounds.' He turned to Charlie: 'I'll see she gets a bloody reference.'

Charlie upset at Freddie's denigration of his girl-friend, protested, 'You won't, you'll leave her alone.' The girl he loved had
come back to him, she needed him and how he needed her.
Freddie, with his cynicism and sly trickery, must not be allowed
to jeopardise what they had. Charlie had loved before, but from
afar and always unrequited, but never had he felt the way he felt
for Esmeralda. The love he had known before was a nervous,
secret yearning for the unobtainable: the love that he had had
for Jennifer Collins, the girl at the social hall who refused him
every dance and poked fun at his premature baldness. The buxom
barmaid who wouldn't give him a second glance no matter how
many halves of beer he bought her and the secretary at the office
who consistently spurned his gauche and tentative advances
until eventually telling him, to his face, to 'bugger off', he was
boring her. But now, for the first time, he was 'in' love. 'To' love
is humiliating and destructive of self-esteem but to be 'in' love is
the most beautiful feeling in the world. He loved Esmeralda and
she loved him and he had her cherished letter as proof. No one
could write a letter such as that without it being an expression
of sincere love. 'I'll write her a good reference if that is what she
wants.' Secretly Charlie wanted her back on the site and secretly
he would pay her a wage out of his own subsistence allowance.

Freddie grinned. His grin was leery, reflecting a mind absorbed
with plot and the likely outcome. 'She can have one each from
us,' he said and turned to go inside.

Now that Esmeralda was back, Charlie had to get in quick.
'Could I have the truck this weekend, Freddie, I've some things
to get from Thika.' Esmeralda may or may not come back on site
but if he had the truck he could visit her in Uamani, he could take
her to Nairobi. He could open a bank account for her; get her the
credit card that she coveted so much.

Considering Freddie's selfishness with the truck, Charlie was
surprised at the absence of any argument. Freddie wasn't thinking of the truck for next weekend, his mind was occupied in a
malicious marshalling of intent. He went to his room. He would

write Esmeralda a reference without delay and he did so while irony and farce were cardinal in his mind. Using a typewriter supplied by the Agency and assisted by some fashion ads in an old magazine, Freddie typed the reference that same night, signed it 'Love Charlie', sealed it, then, having driven to Uamani later that night, pushed it under Esmeralda's door.

'I delivered it,' he told Charlie, 'on site the following morning.'

'Delivered what?'

'Esmeralda's reference.'

Charlie's choked at the audacity. 'That was my job,' he snapped angrily, Very seldom did Charlie stand up to Freddie but this was too much of a liberty, even for him. 'The reference had nothing to do with you, you had no bloody right.'

Freddie snorted, 'But I told you that I was going to do one. It'll save you the trouble. It's a good one, I signed it "Love Charlie." She'll think it's from you.'

Charlie paled: 'Without me seeing it first, you signed it without letting me read it first? You had no right to do that, Freddie.' With trembling lips he fought to control his breathing. This was Bristow at his worst: the derisive, cock-sure Freddie belittling those he considered beneath him, which was everyone. He faced Freddie squarely, menacingly, forcing the bigger man to take a backward step, straighten up and widen his shoulders. 'I needed to see it. If you signed it from me then, at least, I needed to see it before it was given to her. You don't like her, you've no time for her, you hate her in fact, and hate what Esmeralda and I have got between us. You don't want her to be back on site. You had no right to sign that reference in my name. I don't know who the hell you think you are. I can't imagine what you put in that letter, I can't —'

Muscular Freddie did not answer immediately, he was not contrite but he had wariness in his eyes. Charlie's mouth was distorted in a snarl and his eyes were bulging. Everyone on site had stopped working. All were looking at the ground in embarrassment. The atmosphere was electrified; were two *musungus* about to start fighting? Freddie held his hand up defensively, protectively, and took another step backwards: 'Charlie, it's a joke letter. I know that girl, believe me I know her better than you think. I've met girls like her before. She doesn't want to be told that she's a hairy-arsed brickie, she wants to be told that she's beautiful, and she is beautiful, I'll grant her that. Charlie, it's an OK reference she might not understand the joke but she'll love the letter nonetheless, and it's from you.'

All blood had drained from Charlie's face. Freddie was playing with something of towering importance. Charlie's all-consuming love for Esmeralda was not something to be trivially distorted.

'You'd better have kept a copy for me to read,' he growled ominously.

Freddie's face was bloodless too. He did have a copy but it was back at the house.

The men on site looked up now but shuffled uncomfortably. Even Mama Mary, perplexed by the tension, did not step outside but peeped out from the kitchen hut. The copy reference would hopefully restore the status quo, they waited in expectant silence. Freddie said, 'I haven't got the copy with me here but there's nothing nasty in it, Charlie, I wouldn't do that to you. It's only a joke.'

The site held its breath.

Charlie ran a dry tongue along his dry lips. Anger had tightened the contours of his face and the skin of his toes and scrotum had tightened too. He didn't have to read it. The reference would have the stamp of Freddie's humour, bathetic and derisory and how insensitive and insulting to put his name to it without consulting him. The indignity of being unwittingly associated in ridicule towards the girl he loved and cherished more than life itself. Freddie was on the back foot. Charlie seized the initiative. 'Go get that copy now.'

'OK, OK,' Freddie acquiesced readily, then continued, 'Honestly Charlie, was you going to write and tell some poor unsuspecting site manager that Esmeralda was a mason. What would he have thought of you, of the agency, if he had been stupid enough to give her a job?'

'I expected you to mind your own bloody business,' Charlie retorted strongly. 'Whatever rubbish you've written you had no right to put my name to it.' He knew the *Kamba* people a lot better than Freddie; he had been with them longer, integrated with them, Freddie hadn't. They didn't understand British humour. Give them a banana skin and some slapstick and they'll bring a cinema house down in laughter. British humour is cutting and hurtful and the crueller it is the more the British find it funny, bathos, irony and farce are completely lost on the *Kamba*. 'I don't know what the hell Esmeralda is going to think of me.'

'You can ask her what she thinks 'cos she's here now,' Freddie said grimly, casting his eyes along the road.

Charlie's heart flipped so quickly, he almost tumbled over. Entering the site, Esmeralda was smiling and waving some sheets of paper above her head. Charlie reached her before anyone else could even greet her. 'Esmeralda, I didn't write that reference.'

The girl stopped as if checked by reins. 'You didn't write it, yet it has your name on it, Charlie,' she said incredulously.

'Freddie wrote it. Ask him.'

The girl puzzled a moment before her face became mobile with joyous emotion again. Ignoring Charlie she sprang to Freddie's side. 'Oh Freddie this is wonderful, wonderful. In all my life no one has ever written such magical stuff about me. And I swear to God it's absolutely true. Freddie I didn't think you liked me,' and flinging her arms around his neck she tried to kiss him. Freddie, embarrassed, averted his face. 'Come, come,' she cried, summoning the site men to gather around her. 'I will read this reference to all of you so that you can see what Freddie Bristow really thinks of me.'

She began –

'TO WHOM IT MAY CONCERN
The Reference of Esmeralda Ndete for Employment as a
Stone Mason and Associated Trades.

My name is Charles Carter and I am currently engaged,
with local volunteers, on an accommodation project for
the Missionary Sisters of the Precious Blood, at the village
of Katamara. The work includes the understanding, and
implementation, of work to scale drawings, the laying
of foundations and drains, stone masonry, bricklaying,
plastering, carpentry and roofing. In addition we are
also constructing pit latrines and static water tanks. We
manufacture our own bricks by use of a device known
as a cinva-ram and our own roofing tiles, using a sisal-
cement technique as an alternative to *mabati* and other
traditional methods, in every case employing alternative
technology and maximising local elements of construction.

During the early stages of the project we were joined on
site by the delightful and attractive, above named, volunteer. This girl immediately adopted a hands-on approach
to every aspect of construction work and proved to be a
real asset to the project, with photographs of her versatil-
ity and expertise available on request. One photograph
in particular is outstanding, showing Esmeralda to her
best advantage. She is seen examining the specifications
for a pit latrine, whilst wearing a skinny, denim pencil-
skirt, complemented by a no-fuss, U neck sweater and
elegant black-and-white patent wedges, all from *B.A.T.A.*
of Nairobi. In another shot she is shown handing a sta-
bilised soil-block to a fellow volunteer, whilst wearing a
simple, smooth-shape pure cotton dress from *Pepper* with,
draped over one arm, a flattering fully-lined pac-a-mac
which, as you will know from your own experience of
site-work, is indispensable for those rainy days.

Many more photographs of the glamorous and seductive Esmeralda are available in a portfolio entitled 'Esmeralda at Work on a Building Site' and can be delivered in a plain, brown envelope on request. My own favourite, which I have framed above my bed, is of the lovely girl holding what initially appears to be sisal-cement ridge tile but on further inspection turns out to be a print-design woven handbag with leather tassels and a tribal *Kamba* motif. In this bag, obtainable from *Forever Mine* of Thika she carries her site-tools each day, i.e. combs, powder, lipstick and a nail file in the unlikely event of her ever breaking one. As a stone-mason and all-purpose tradeswoman I have no hesitation in recommending this teen-queen to any construction site manager for employment as an alluring photographic model.

Yours sincerely

Charles Carter
Project Co-ordinator

Charlie stepped forward hurriedly and bleated, 'Esmeralda, you know the camera you wanted well I've bought one for you, it's a lovely one, better than Titus', it's at the house.' But Esmeralda wasn't listening.

Chapter Seventeen

*I*t was the box from upstairs, the one propped against the wall, but now it was laid on the floor, caked in dust and dotted grotesquely with the tiny detritus of disuse. Charlie crawled towards it. He could see blurred letters beneath the dust. He rubbed at the dust until, one by one, the letters slowly appeared. They spelled out JOHNNIE. Of course, it was Johnnie's box. What was it doing in the mortuary aisle? Who had carried that big box down the rickety stairway and all the way to Thika? From inside the box, the sound of knocking, it would be Shula, of course, she wanted to get out. She was knocking for Charlie to open the lid. Charlie opened the lid but it wasn't Shula, it was Titus. His eyes were wide open and he was grinning broadly but he was dead. He was more than dead, he was decomposing. Charlie tried to scream but his scream was silent and as he tried to crawl away he found his limbs were paralysed. Then he was at the mortuary door and he was frantically knocking but the door wouldn't open. Hammering, hammering but the door wouldn't open. He had to get out because corpses were gathering in the aisle, and, led by Titus, they were moving inexorably towards him. Titus' eyes were still wide open and he was still grinning. Of course the door opened inwards.

Charlie sat bolt upright in bed and began fumbling for matches to light the lamp, his nerves electrified. It had been a dream, a nightmare, and it was over except for the knocking; not loud, or frantic now but a tap tap, tapping and impossible to determine where it was coming from, the ceiling, the window, the floor, inside his head. It was the same knocking that no one else could hear. It would stop soon, it always did; knock, knock then silence for ten minutes, twenty minutes, then it might start again then stop again. It was very much like the sound the women had made that day at the mortuary doors, not exasperated, not even impatient, just a communication for attention.

He slumped back under his bed covers, praying for silence and peace. But it had not stopped, tap, tap, tap as before. There were times when he could not get back to sleep at all but the knocking would never be heard beyond the crowing of the cock; the advent of filtering dawn. It was a thing that feared the deliverance of day. Weeks of nightly peace would pass and then it would start again. The box was in the room upstairs propped against a wall. One bright sunny day he would clean the windows and take Titus to the room and they would open it, let Shula free and then the knocking would stop forever. He listened, it had stopped. Was it more prevalent when he was unhappy and disturbed, he thought that it was triggered by the emotional affliction that he had been taking to bed with him of late.

Esmeralda was back on site but she had noticeably cooled towards him; and the grief and loss was eating his soul. He would pay her a wage and would broach the subject with her the moment her attitude towards him became more loving, friendly even. He couldn't talk about giving her money while she was ignoring him. He couldn't pay for her love so blatantly, not even Charlie could do that. He blamed Freddie's testimonial. If anything Freddie was more caustic towards her than ever. The dynamics of the three respective relationships had changed and Charlie was at a loss to know how to change them back. Could he get to sleep and ease his troubled mind? He was about to turn off the wick of the lamp when he heard a shriek and saw, or thought he saw, something far more fearful than the sound of knocking. What the hell was pooling beneath his bedroom door?

Was it blood, it looked like blood? From outside on the porch, another shriek of alarm; a tumid crescent was seeping beneath his door, its relentless expansion silent and terrifying; it would soon maroon him in his bed. He must get out; he must paddle through the blood. He lurched down to reach his shoes and in doing so knocked the lamp. The flame went out. In inky darkness he tried to find his shoes; he couldn't. He paddled in bare feet and opened the door from his room. At once his feet were ablaze; he was paddling through blazing blood. He bumped into a floundering, cursing Freddie at the doorway to the porch and they tumbled out into moonlight.

Soundless and terrorizing, the moon-washed landscape was undulating with a lake of fire ants.

Alerted by a warning from Titus, Freddie had been able to get his shoes and clothes on whereas, apart from shorts, Charlie was naked and being eaten alive, the ants were starting at his feet and working inexorably upwards. Hopping from one foot to another he was trying to swipe them off. But it was futile: he was standing on a living carpet that was swallowing the porch, the house, the terrain, him. 'For God's sake Titus, get in there quick and get me some bloody shoes,' he squealed at the *askari* who was ineffectually attempting to sweep the invasion from the porch with a yard-brush. Titus crunched past him to return seconds later, with shoes. The three men then made it to a patch of higher ground free from the burning lake.

Freddie turned on Titus barking angrily, 'We should have been warned earlier. You should have seen this coming. You're supposed to be a bloody *askari*, we don't want a bloody soldier, just a watchman. It's not a bloody bow and arrow you need, it's an alarm clock. It's what you're being paid for. I'm telling you, Titus, from tonight that bloody chair goes.' He turned on Charlie: 'It's your fault, for Christ's sake. An early warning and we could have done something about it. There's are buckets of sisal ash in there, cartons of doom powder that would of kept them out if we'd been warned, if Titus hadn't been asleep.'

'I somehow missed them coming,' Titus admitted sheepishly, flicking at ants that had discovered their unaffected haven and were encroaching quickly.

'Somehow missed them coming,' Freddie mocked. 'You make it sound like a cute little family of ants from under a stone on a friendly visit. It's an acre of them: a bloody square acre of fire ants, hell bent on eating us alive and you somehow missed 'em coming. I'll tell you why you missed 'em coming Titus, because, same as every night, you were fast asleep.' He swung around on Charlie, 'From now on, no more chair and blankets. From now on, he does the job he's getting paid for or he goes. Understand?'

Charlie's legs were still covered in ants and, as he swiped at them, it felt as if each one had bitten him a dozen times. Freddie's anger irritated him but he was in too much pain to respond. Freddie was furious, and it was only the frustration and discomfort of their situation that was preventing a far more virulent tide of abuse from being released upon them. Titus, resting on his hams, was squashing individual ants with his thumbs while maintaining a gung-ho expression of resolve to make amends for his neglect of duty. 'The ant has been known to kill a buffalo,' he attested, gravely crushing a specimen with such purpose as to suggest that he had found the very one responsible.

What an unbelievable sight this monster made. Open-mouthed in wonder, Charlie and Freddie watched the boiling blood-red phalanx converging relentlessly upon their home, one body one mind, inexorable and all-consuming: untold millions yet a single heart that pulsed more strongly than that of a great whale. Clinging together they could ford a river, devour a buffalo yet had Titus been alert, they could have been prevented from encroaching on the house with powder. Titus had seen such an incursion many times before and was greatly embarrassed but not as awe-struck as the whites.

'Very dangerous,' he kept repeating, inciting Freddie even more.

Now relatively free of the creatures, Charlie straightened and in the sharp night air realized for the first time just how cold he was.

'Titus please go inside and get my coat, it's hanging on the back of my door. I'm bloody freezing.'

Tucking the bottom of his trouser legs into his socks, Titus shaking ants from the coat, was back in seconds.

'What's it like in there?' Freddie asked, his inner fury in no way diminished and needing only a provocative word or action to ignite the touch-paper of its force. Could he lose his home and his possessions to this creeping monster? Freddie observed Charlie shivering as he put on his coat. He blamed Charlie more than Titus; his undue consideration, his stupid magnanimity, that innate, misplaced benevolence which unchecked would have them killed. 'What's it like in there?' he asked again.

'It is like those things are about to carry away the house,' Titus answered, ruefully brushing at his legs. 'I am sorry, no doubt I was neglectful.'

'Will they have got rid of the cockroaches?' Charlie asked hopefully, trying to glean something positive from the night's wretched disturbance.

'Yes,' Titus answered readily, then cautiously, 'but maybe not the mother.'

'The mother?'

Titus said gravely. 'Somewhere in that kitchen there will be a big mother.'

'How big?'

'Big.'

I've never seen her – this mother.'

'You won't. But she is in there somewhere and day and night she is making little ones, little cockroaches. She is as big as a baby's foot.'

'Then why won't the ants get her?'

Titus shrugged. 'Either she will hide so well that even the ants can't find her, or else she will have known that they were coming and escaped but she will be back when they are gone. Always, somehow, the mother is back.'

Charlie shuddered at the thought. A mother, what other unseen aberrations were undercover in this house?

Time passed and the moon was wasting in the west and in the east the earth was shading lighter by degree, the ground around them was lighter too, the ant army was passing. Charlie's spirits rose with coming day. He spoke again to Titus, 'I was having that bloody awful dream again, it woke me up, and I could hear knocking again. Then I saw the ants spreading beneath my door and I heard you calling out.'

'The ants will not enter the house again. From tonight I remain more vigilant,' Titus assured.

'You can count on that,' Freddie said through gritted teeth.

Charlie said, 'The knocking that I hear, it's hard to describe, I can't tell where it's coming from. It is as if it's trying to alert me to something.'

'For Christ's sake, shut up Charlie,' Freddie said nastily, 'alerting you is it ? I'll tell you who it isn't alerting,' he levelled at Titus, 'it isn't alerting you, is it, chum?'

'Mr Freddie, it is my shame, I should have been more vigilant,' Titus said.

Freddie swung from Titus back to Charlie. 'Best thing you can do is go back home to England.' Deliberately confrontational, Freddie thrust his face into Charlie's. Charlie backed away. 'Go back to England while you can, while you've still got a brain cell left.'

Charlie wanted to answer back but words failed. Things between him and Freddie would never be the same again. He had not forgiven Freddie for his stupid reference, and the cooling of relations with his beloved girl. Now Freddie was telling him to go back to England. Charlie had been the first in Katamara. He was the project co-ordinator, Freddie had over-stepped the mark once again. Charlie looked to Titus for support.

But Titus was subdued and apprehensive. He looked at the two men uncertainly, each of whom he cherished, not wanting them to quarrel, to disturb a co-existence that he and his family depended on. His wife and children were eating because of these two men and his children could go to school. He stood as tall as he was able and said bravely, 'It is I who am to blame. It is a very poor *askari* who sleeps on the job. I know it, and I am ashamed. One day you will be proud of me, and by the will of God, I will again be proud of myself.'

Charlie's throat was dry, he was still cold and his legs were burning from ant bites. A mist was coming with the dawn, beneath his coat mist clung to his bare flesh like the dead, wet leaves of autumn. He wanted to defend himself, speak up for Titus, but Freddie was right. He was right about the reference. He was right about Titus and the ants. Freddie was always right. Maybe he should go back to England.

Freddie was still very angry: 'When those ants have cleared I'm going to pick up some stuff, some money and set off, away from sleeping *askaris,* ants and bloody knocking ghosts. And I'm getting sick of this bloody country altogether. And I'm telling you Charlie, by the look of your legs, you'd better get yourself to hospital.'

'I'll be there when it opens,' Charlie mumbled resignedly, then remembered, 'Freddie, you promised I could have the truck this weekend.' Esmeralda had cooled towards him but if he had the truck, all sorts of possibilities would open up for him. He would take her anywhere she wanted. Buy her anything she wanted too.

Freddie remembered and groaned, 'Yeah, OK, I'll take the motor-bike.'

Averting blameworthy eyes from the two men, Titus said, 'When I get home this morning I will gather my family and tell them that I have shamed them. My children must know of their father's failings. I have four children and, in order to do God's work must have many more. In the book of Genesis it say "*be fruitful and fill the earth*". It is what I tell my wife Josephine, but she say we have been fruitful and filled the earth enough, but I tell her that God will always provide. Today when I get home I will tell them all that I will have no more children, they will have no more brothers and sisters until I am a man again. I am ashamed and feel that I have caused trouble between my good friends.'

Later that morning, still smarting over the events of the night before, and cursing Titus and Charlie, Freddie arrived in Nairobi. He hated using the *piki*; the crash helmet, that the agency insisted was mandatory, ruined his hair. Cursing himself too; he had forgotten that he had promised the truck to Charlie. Esmeralda would not take kindly to being taken to the Nairobi Hilton on the back of a motor-bike.

Chapter Eighteen

*T*he cloud that hung over Katamara did not drift down, dew-filled from the mountain nor did it break up into cloudlets when it settled on the gritty streets. It could not be shifted by wind or brightened by sunlight; it did not cool and did not give shade but it was a cloud nonetheless and suffocating in its merciless purulence.

These clouds are many, they exist everywhere: in homes, in villages, in towns and cities and are unique in that they are invisible. They are also man-made. One of these pernicious clouds had been made for Jennifer Collins.

She had been aware of its formation and had tried to avoid its malignancy. She was wild-eyed with desperation as it enfolded her forcing her to seek the relief of a smile or a handshake anywhere, with anyone, any small deliverance from the degradation of the spite surrounding her; what worth all the good that she had done in her life if she was now dishonoured? She could feel her dignity evaporating and when dignity goes, all else follows.

No one had ever suggested it; his name was never mentioned but his saviour image, wraith-like, hovered over Katamara inviting the dispirited to come to him. And no one was more irresolute and dispirited than Jennifer Collins but Corporal Adonis was not her saviour. He couldn't be. She couldn't prostrate herself at the feet of the corporal and yet, there was no one else. All she knew for certain was that she was innocent but that was not nearly enough and one day she found herself walking to the police station for deliverance but something stopped her.

Her life now was going through the motions; she could only pretend to enjoy herself. Her laughter was a mime, and empty of mirth. Nothing tasted good, she didn't sleep: her work with the children was a chore. Their little games no longer appealed to her; good God, they were being supervised. All sociability was nervy and fidgety. She felt that even the sisters had begun to wonder. Her uncharacteristic behaviour was something to do with insatiable, swollen, brutish words sisters didn't use: too awful to contemplate, to sinful to conceive, those words forever thrusting into the warm gulch of their own forbidden fruit. Disavowed in themselves, they were titillated to think that such unvoiced dynamism had been manifested on their own doorstep. They could not admit their thoughts or talk of them to others but the thoughts squatted in their psyche and refused to budge and like all unknowns it was a wonder. Holy Sisters are not immune from gossip and a dead child, and Sam Wamiru's name kept cropping up.

Early Saturday morning and standing forlornly by the entrance to the hospital playing field, where a *harambee* was due to take place later that day, was one face she could trust. No handshaking, no small talk. 'Charlie, you know I'm innocent,' she petitioned. 'There are people in this village who think I killed those children. Even Mr Muinde and the Sisters are beginning to have their doubts.'

Charlie began to stutter repudiation.

She gripped his upper arm. 'Charlie, I'm no longer allowed to be alone with the children. Inspector Wamiru declared me innocent. And *I am* innocent, Charlie, I love it here at the hospital and I don't want to leave. If I leave then everyone will think I'm guilty, no one will ever know the truth.'

'Of course you're innocent, Jennifer. Everyone knows your innocent, Inspector Wamiru told you, told everyone. You were never arrested, never charged. It was even in The *Daily Nation* – accidental death.'

He was sure to see Esmeralda later, so Charlie went to the hospital playing field hoping to see Jennifer who had been missing too, Surely Jennifer must turn up at the *harambee*, it was she who organised them. He found her standing alone and, putting aside his own troubles, he tried to reassure her. He couldn't understand what the nurse was going through, his profile in life had never been, and never would be, high enough to invite such slander.

'Then, Charlie, who or what is making me feel so guilty?' And she gestured helplessly.

Charlie was about to put a reassuring arm around the nurse; it was his best opportunity yet but, at the last moment, his courage failed him again and as a diversionary tactic, he showed her what the ants had done to his legs. From his sandaled feet to his bare knees, his flesh was red and swollen; his feet unrecognisable balls of burning pain.

'That is why they are called fire ants,' the nursing sister at the clinic had told him, 'it's the burning sensation that they leave behind.'

Such was the swelling of his feet that early that morning, as Freddie, still in high dudgeon, had set off to Nairobi on the *piki*, he and Titus were carefully tweaking live and dead ants from between his toes with twigs. Savage irony, he had the truck for the weekend but his feet were too sore to use it.

Charlie had been at the clinic as the doors had opened and had been prescribed pills and an antihistamine lotion which he had liberally applied. Immediately afterwards he began to look around for Esmeralda, he wanted to show her his ravaged legs, if not love, then surely he may receive a little sympathy.

'Don't scratch,' the nursing sister had warned but such was the intolerable irritation, she might as well have told him not to breathe.

Mr Muinde watched through a window as preparations were taking place. The jacaranda had begun to bloom and would be in full bloom in time for J.M.'s booking of the playing field. He felt satisfied that he need not concern himself with the politician engagement. Adonis, the policeman was seeing to all of that.

He watched Nurse Collins talking to Charlie Carter as the nurse' attendant nun began to marshal the children in their care. He didn't like what he had done but rumours throughout the village were rife and the women who had approached him with their concern paid money for their children to be schooled and cared for at the hospital. Yes, Nurse Collins had been exonerated but too much doubt remained. And it was clearly obvious by the change in her personality that she had not yet got over the trauma of finding Kennedy strung up from the window cord. What he had done smacked of expediency but he had a hospital to run and bills to pay and lately Nurse Collins had been so preoccupied, she was making uncharacteristic mistakes. He couldn't take the chance on another child having an accident; really, he hadn't had much of an alternative.

He saw Adonis striding towards Charlie and the two women and he smiled as the women turned on their heels to avoid him. The two men shook hands and began talking. Mr Muinde was too far away to hear any of the conversation that then took place between them.

'*Jambo*, Adonis.'

'*Habari*, Charlie.'

Charlie displayed his legs and after some compassion was compelled to listen to Adonis elucidate on ants, especially fire ants until he could not bear to hear another word more about the confounded pests. 'Titus tells me that you are very happy to take me to Tala in your truck,' Adonis said when his knowledge of the ants of Africa was exhausted.

'For the goats, yes, when is it?'

'It is three weeks from today. I will be at your house at eight o' clock in the morning and together we will then go to Tala. There you will meet with members of my family and see how well they are pushing on with life.'

Charlie's assertiveness hadn't lasted long. He needed the truck again. Freddie wouldn't take kindly to that. He shouldn't feel anxious about an advance booking, but he did. 'Ok, I'll try and book the truck again,' he said wearily.

For some time they talked of the proposed journey to Adonis' village, his family and farm, how they would collect the goats and the problems of their confinement on the way back. Then Adonis said suddenly, a little too suddenly Charlie thought, 'Imagine, I heard that Esmeralda was seen boarding a *matatu* to Nairobi early this morning.'

As if Charlie didn't feel bad enough.

'That Esmeralda, she is too much, she is this way, she is that way, she is here and then she isn't. Me I am thinking she is with Charlie again and everything is fine then lo and behold she is away to Nairobi on a bus.'

To Charlie the news was devastating. She had just returned from Nairobi and he was counting on this weekend to win her back again. 'Yes, she told me she had to go back to Nairobi this morning,' he lied nonchalantly, attempting to sound as if the girl's absence didn't matter to him one way or another. 'She didn't say much. Maybe she has not gone to Nairobi, maybe she will be back tomorrow.

'At Muka Tano where she caught the bus, the bag she had with her was big, a Nairobi bag surely, almost as if she was intending to stay there for some time.'

Charlie swallowed hard. What could be so compelling in a city she had just left? She had told Charlie nothing; she hadn't said much of anything to him at all since glowing excitedly over Freddie's reference.

'You know Charlie one day that girl will disgrace herself. She will one day be seen in the market wearing tight troosers, mark my words on that. The mamas know it and so do I. It is a disgrace, but not an offence because I looked it up in the law books and, under Kenyan law, nothing can be done against girls wearing tight troosers. I think it is indecent and there should be laws preventing it. One day I might be in a position to do something about it.'

'I'm sure you will,' Charlie grunted.

'She is here and she is there, she is this way and she is that way. The *wanachi*, they talk about her a lot. Esmeralda, she is a fine girl and should marry.' The corporal's voice strained to be benevolent, but had nuances of exasperation in its tone.

The name Esmeralda on the corporal's lips simultaneously electrified Charlie's senses and numbed his soul. Having read Freddie's testimony to the site men, the girl had reprimanded him for not being the author then danced off into the village to spread the word. The camera he had bought her was still at the house, she didn't seem to want it anymore. Oh, Esmeralda, it was like falling in love with the wind. 'She is young and is wilful,' Charlie said.

'Yes, but sometimes she is bad and when she marries, her husband must take her into hand and get the devil out of her,' Adonis declared bumptiously.

Charlie grunted again

'Did you know that Mr Freddie has a wife and children at home in England?' Adonis asked suddenly, with a face full of well-rounded duplicity; as if Esmeralda's absence and Freddie's marital status could have some particular significance.

Charlie was shocked but pretended not to be. 'Freddie tells everyone that he is divorced.'

'As policeman around this place, it is my duty to know many things. His wife, she writes to him a lot. He picks her letters up from the P.O. Box in Katamara.'

Charlie felt sick, all he wanted to do was go home and nurse his legs.

'So I've been told,' Adonis added.

Chapter Nineteen

*F*reddie Bristow could not believe what had happened. Esmeralda hadn't turned up. This was a *first* for Freddie. Girls always turned up for Bumble Bristow. Had she changed her mind and gone to the *harambee* instead?

Having waited for hours, he had spent the rest of the boring day hiking and biking around the city, Freddie not only chained the *piki* to a lamp post outside the small hotel, he also chose one with an all-night duty man posted in the foyer. Not to take such extravagant precautions was to ensure the wheels would be missing in the morning. It was a cheap hotel at the rear of Lagos Road, the only cheap hotel in that area of the city. He was tired, and irritable and couldn't forgive an impotent *askari* for allowing an army of ants the size of a football field to overrun his home while fast asleep, neither could he forgive an idiot house-mate who not only permitted such irresponsibility, but actively encouraged it. And he certainly couldn't forgive Esmeralda. He would return to Katamara in the morning.

An unctuous porter showed him to an upstairs room, which stank of stale cigarette smoke and sweat. 'I would like a room with a window,' Freddie asked tiredly. The porter happily took him across the corridor to a room which boasted a large window, but which also stank of stale smoke and sweat. Freddie tried the window, it was permanently sealed. 'Preferably one that opens,' he suggested sourly. The hotel had lots of rooms, all with windows, but unfortunately none that opened. 'What about a fire?'

'It is very hot at night, you won't need a fire, sir, but you can have an extra blanket, even two,' the porter anxiously explained.

'Oh forget it, this'll do,' Freddie said despairingly, too tired to negotiate, not even with his life. With the porter gone, he whipped back the unsavoury bed sheets; quick enough, so he had been told, and bed bugs could be caught unawares. The sheets were clear as far as he could see, and undressing quickly he flopped on the bed, eager to put a depressing day behind him. In the darkness of his airless room, he reflected on the folly of filling a building with highly flammable commodities and materials: creating a veritable bonfire then blithely climbing up to sleep on top of it. However did his species manage to escape from caves?

Still suffering the pain and itching of ant bites, he had listlessly wandered the main shopping centres taking in the sights and sounds of a city so divorced in style and substance from those he was accustomed to that every perception was a distasteful cultural education. Not once did he think of visiting a building site. Sapped of vitality, he pictured the brisk sequence of events that had led him to this fruitless expedition. It was Freddie, not Charlie, who had written that lovely testimony to a girl's spirited disposition. How mean of Charlie to say it was a joke when it was a valid attestation of a delicious, earthy, potential fashion model and the start of a personal curriculum vitae. It was Freddie who would have her love, Charlie did not deserve it. She had loved Charlie, yes, but he had let her down; now it was Freddie's turn. Well, he would meet her in Kamathi Lane at ten o' clock on Saturday morning and yes, just maybe he would take her to the Nairobi Hilton that night, which despite his promises, Charlie had failed to do. On the Friday, Freddie would get a good night's sleep as with the promise of a Saturday night with Esmeralda; he reckoned he would need it. 'The Best Laid Plans of Mice and Men,' he thought miserably as he lay on his bed thinking of the ant invasion and the non-appearance of his mercurial date.

Thankfully, uneaten by bed-bugs, he got up early Sunday morning and, after a breakfast of tea and toast, packed his bag and left the hotel to find Esmeralda in a dreamy mood, sitting astride his motor-bike.

He felt joy and shock in equal measure to see her sitting there, but she had badly let him down and it would be a mistake to let her know how pleased he was to see her. He was no Charlie Carter, prostrate and submissive; either slobbering over her or begging for a crumb of comfort. 'Where the hell have you been?' he demanded, his eyes squinting, his manner suspicious. He eyed her curiously, she was somehow different, her face bereft of makeup. The beads from her neck and wrists were gone, and so were the braids from her hair. And her customary chic clothes had been replaced by a plain white blouse, buttoned to the neck, and a plain skirt hanging below her knees. She was barefoot, and for the first time, completely divest of glamour.

She did not leap from the *piki* seat to greet him. She didn't even smile but with dreamy eyes slid towards him, swaying, as if responding to slow and moving music, 'Oh Freddie something wonderful has happened to me. I am saved.'

Was she drunk? No she was gliding, not staggering, and her speech was sensuous not slurred. 'Saved, saved from what?'

Lacing her fingers beneath her chin in a gesture of supplication, she looked upwards to the morning sky and said, 'Saved by the Holy Ghost from the road to hell.'

Freddie felt a vague unease and dropped his overnight bag on the hotel steps. Had he seen, momentarily, in her eye, the fanatical spark of a zealot? Had something happened to her? Had she been transformed into something he didn't understand? He did not want Esmeralda saved by the Holy Ghost, or anyone else in the Holy Trinity. A girl in a state of grace was no good for what he had in mind. It was the devil that gave this girl her potency. 'And just where was it that you got saved?' he asked tonelessly, stubbornly disregarding her supposed salvation.

The answer was written in the sky above, she read the words

in rapture. 'In the church I was invited to. Almost as I stepped off the *matatu* yesterday I heard the voice of a holy man calling to me, "Come to me, sister, that I may save your immortal soul." It was as if the good Lord Himself was bidding me to His side.'

'Save your immortal soul from what?' Freddie was refusing to humour her.

Theatrically, Esmeralda threw out her arms and grasped his hands: 'From itself, from the path to hell that it was taking. There is a devil inside us all and must be driven out. This holy man promised me that he would drive the devil out of me and let the Good Lord in. Oh, and he did, he did. And to fulfil my own spiritual destiny I was given my very own angel to guide me through my life.'

'And who might he be?' Freddie asked suspiciously.

'Raphael.'

'I've never heard of the Angel Raphael.'

'Yes, the Angel of financial security.'

'Of course, who else?' Freddie wondered laconically.

Dropping his hands and throwing her eyes and arms to the sky she called, 'Oh Freddie, open your heart to Jesus and let his light illuminate your soul. Come in, Jesus, my heart is ever open unto you.'

Freddie was shaking his head in disbelief while behind him, standing in the doorway of the hotel, the porter, was open-mouthed in awe. 'Just a minute,' Freddie said sternly, 'stop these antics. Just where the hell have you been and who with?'

'With a holy man who was prodding and poking at the demons inside of me, oh Freddie, I declare he said that he had never seen so many demons in one person in all his holy life. It is a fact he chased them out of the open door like a herd of horned beasts.'

Freddie did not like the sound of this. If there was to be any prodding and poking of Esmeralda this weekend, it was he that had plans to do it. 'And where the hell did you get those cheap clothes from, where are your own nice clothes? Those clothes don't even fit you properly.'

'In the Church of the Ever Open Door we must all disrobe the trappings of sin. We were all throwing off our devil clothes and crying Halleluiah, Halleluiah.' She was enacting the divestiture of sinful attire, aping the holy man's extravagant gestures, 'Sister, remove those braids and brazen beads. Sister in Christ, rid yourself of the harlot hair and those clarted lips forever pouting at the devil.'

Irritation with the girl had given way to bemusement, admiration and suspicion: a potent mix of bewilderment. In the hotel doorway the porter appeared mesmerised and across the street a small crowd had gathered: was it street theatre they were experiencing or the antics of a mad woman? She was now dancing up and down the pavement outside the hotel, seemingly oblivious to the attention and chanting 'Halleluiah, Halleluiah' to the stamping of her feet and the clapping of her hands and Freddie started laughing. Was the girl unhinged, acting a role, or was she really imbued with the Holy Spirit? Whatever it was, he couldn't help but feel an overwhelming warmth for the outrageous girl.

She stopped her dance and clutched his hands again as if suddenly remembering something of the utmost importance, said, 'Oh Freddie there was this boy there, this lovely boy, and we supported each other as the demons were being driven out of both of us. Oh how we danced, no, not the disco dancing of the devil but a clapping and a stomping and a hopping to the glory of God. And when it was over we knew that we were saved. Oh that saved boy, when I think of him, it makes me want to cry.'

Persuading her back to the seat of the motor-bike, Freddie calmed her down. 'This church, was it an official church, was the holy man a priest or something?'

'The Church of the Ever Open Door,' she answered soberly.

'And where is this church?

'I think it is in Latema Road, off Tom Mboya Street.'

'You think?'

'Oh, my head was spinning so much, I was this way in heaven and that way in hell, then this way in heaven when, in fact, I think I was in Latema Road, off Tom Mboya Street.'

Freddie didn't like the sound of the Church of the Ever Open Door either and his emotions were changing by the second. She had been in the hands of a charlatan, she had been given hallucinatory drugs, her expensive clothes had been swapped for cheap ones, yet Esmeralda was anything but stupid. 'And this saved boy, how close did you get to him?' he asked, warily.

'Very close. You know the holy man told me I had such a beautiful smile that it must have been given to me by the devil. He said I must be the devil's soldier to have been given a smile like mine, and that saved boy argued with him, said that he was wrong, and that my smile had been given to me by Raphael my guardian angel to help me gain treasures throughout my life when in fact, they were both wrong for my smile was given to me by the sun. When I was a child and lost a tooth I would awaken at dawn and go cast the tooth to the rising sun. I would call out "Oh golden one I give you this tooth so that you may replace it with one that shines as bright as you." '

Captivated, Freddie felt a flush of love for the girl and did not care if she was playing a role or not. And then the little public drama was over, the porter was back inside the hotel leering at someone in reception and the small crowd had dispersed. 'Well the sun has done a wonderful job. Esmeralda,' he continued kindly, 'you've been conned. This holy man, whoever he is, has taken you for a ride. He's nicked your nice clothes and given you rubbish in return.' He tweaked the fabric of her thin blouse, 'I think we should go to the Church of the Ever Open Door and get your clothes back, that's if his wife has not already sold them in the market.'

'But Freddie I am saved. It is my joy to be saved.'

'But I don't want you to be saved. I liked you the way you were before.'

'But I am now so free from the devil and all his works.'

'You look tired out. Sounds to me as if you were there all day Saturday and Saturday night, hopping around, what time did you leave that place?'

'I think when everyone was exhausted.'

'Are you hungry?'

'Well, I am somewhat.'

'How did you know where to find me?'

'I heard you tell Charlie that when you stayed in Nairobi, you sometimes stayed at hotels near to Lagos Road. I looked for the truck but found the motor-bike instead. I thought it must be Charlie. I asked the watchman in the hotel who's the *piki* was? And when he described you I knew it wasn't Charlie. He said a good-looking *musungu* with curly black hair.' She laughed, 'Dear God, I knew it wasn't Charlie. But to be truthful I was disappointed that you were not in the truck.'

'I told Charlie he could have it this weekend, I'd forgotten. Friday night we got attacked by ants, I'll show you my legs. Esmeralda, I'll take you for something to eat.'

'But Freddie I really am saved. We were all saved, but me and that saved boy, we were saved the most. The holy man said that he had never seen anyone quite so saved as us. And he taught me so much. No longer do I want to be wearing the trappings of sin, material things of life are worthless. I am now a new girl and have no wish to be like the serpent and be cursed above cattle so as to be on my belly and made to eat dust all the days of my life.'

'They won't let you into the Nairobi Hilton wearing clothes like that and with no shoes.'

She frowned as his words registered.

Freddie shook his head, 'Esmeralda I was so worried about you – yesterday I waited hours for you and then looked for you all day. I must have visited every clothes and shoe shop in Nairobi.'

She touched his arm suggestively, 'And I hope you bought me something nice?'

Chapter Twenty

*H*arambee is a Swahili word for 'all pull together', a Kenyan tradition of fundraising and self-help for the community. In 1963, following independence from Britain, Jomo Kenyatta adopted this concept of cohesion and harmony in order to underpin the country and galvanize its people to row in the same direction. If a city wanted funds for some large industrial project then it would use the media to rally the people and when the shillings of each person were gathered and accumulated, then the project was completed. Similarly, the parents of a sick child needing prolonged hospital treatment, might, through word of mouth, organize a *harambee* in their own backyard and when the shillings were gathered up from friends and neighbours, the hospital bill was paid. This concept feeds on the positive elements of society: community, compassion and generosity and is the backbone of the Kenyan nation.

The hospital in Katamara often held these events: a crippled child requiring specialist equipment, the schoolroom, new benches and desks, the clinic, a new roof. And if it wasn't for *harambee* funds collected over many years, the new accommodation block, currently being constructed by the *musungus*, and their voluntary labour, would never have got started.

The *harambee* about to take place on this beautiful sunlit Saturday at the hospital in Katamara was in aid of a child's heart and lung operation in Nairobi and by the number of early patrons streaming through the gates, it was going to be well attended. An entry fee of five Kenyan shillings was charged at the gate for those who could afford to pay but the gatekeeper knew those that couldn't afford to pay and they would be waved in free of charge. Families mingled and integrated until they appeared as one huge family, getting bigger all the time. This family moved with a common aim, the healthy salvation of its most vulnerable member

Harambee dates were set months earlier, usually for a Saturday afternoon, or a Sunday morning, never Sunday afternoon; Sunday afternoon was market day and no occasion was allowed to usurp the grandeur of that iconic event. A committee was responsible for choosing the date and for the organisation and usually consisted of Nurse Collins and two or three sisters, those of a more convivial persuasion. Time, patience and management were asked for and each event was advertised and promoted well in advance.

Food products from neighbouring *shambas* were collected for sale and displayed on tables, with a proportion of the funds going to the organisation coffers and the remainder, welcome revenue to the dirt-poor smallholders who had supplied them.

Volunteer helpers were always plentiful, usually the parents of the hospital children, privileged to be seen assisting the nuns. Cupboards, drawers and boxes had been ransacked, for the sale of what was worthless and obsolete to one family was a treasure to another. And when the people had sifted and rummaged through the goods they would likely retire to the tea-house to talk and laugh about the bargains they had made and await, with anticipation, the heralded sports events.

Each child would revel in an exhibitionist moment in the sun and every parent knew it and triumphed in their approbation. Great emphasis was placed on the physical and mental competence of each participating child and allowances made but competition and excellence was expected and promoted and with gusto a crippled child would chuck a ball or wang a welly with the best. They would be rewarded too for each was certain of prize or a trophy by the end of the day.

There was a gasp from the crowd when Paulina, who had been collected from Kangundo that morning, lined up with able bodied girls for the 50 yard dash; followed by a roar of approval when she summersaulted down the track to finish last. Then able-bodied children raced each other as if their lives depended on it and they were clapped and cheered in the glory of their achievements. These were the Kenyan children who would one day race the world and give credit to their nation.

The *harambee* was over and the next one planned for Christmas and all that remained on the playing field was the debris of the long afternoon. As the sun reddened the earth and the shadows of the jacaranda lengthened, the people were leaving by the gate. It had been a good day; the *harambee* a great success and the main topics of conversation as they left, were Paulina, the girl with no legs who had certified the day and Nurse Collins.

The nurse, she is not well. She was so friendly, now she has nothing to say. Have you noticed that she doesn't look you in the eye anymore? Always that woman ran the sports, sounded the starting gun, gave out the prizes. Nurse Collins selling cakes, what was she doing selling cakes? And she didn't sell too many. Seems she wasn't trying. She didn't sell any of mine and I took a long time making those cakes. I was nice to her, wanting to talk but she turned away. Seems she doesn't trust me anymore. She told someone she couldn't sleep. That will be true for nowadays she has dark rings beneath her eyes. I saw them. You couldn't miss them. And her eyes are red nowadays, seems she is crying a lot. I was talking to friends and when I came to her table to buy a cake, she thought that we had been talking about her. Of course we were not, can't remember now what we were talking about but it wasn't her. Oh yes, we were talking about Paulina, she lives in Kangundo now. Remember her mother Elizabeth, dead now some weeks ago. Have you noticed that when the nurse talks nowadays, her voice is different, somewhat, high pitched, almost hysterical. Of course all this has happened since she found poor Kennedy hanging from a cord. Oh imagine that. Kennedy's mother was here, did you see her, she looked so sad? And the nurse to be under suspicion for such a horrible death, is it any wonder she is feeling bad? But ask her how she is and she tells you she's OK. The inspector with the one arm, he cleared her. Cleared her, then they were seen in his car going to Nairobi. That was the day the *matatus* couldn't make it for the rain. The *matatus* couldn't make it but that inspector and that nurse they could make it very OK. Imagine trying to drive that road in that rain with two arms. That inspector, he did it with one. How keen they were to get away together. Came back very OK too and happy with themselves on the Sunday evening, they were seen.

Oh yes, they didn't think that they'd be seen but they were. Well they're both single but look at her now. She's pale, she's tired, she's fidgety, she's sick. She's guilty.

The same great family that can bond together in benevolence to save one of its kind can also bond to destroy another. Jennifer Collins hurried from the playing field to the hospital and threw herself upon a bed which shook with tears.

Chapter Twenty-One

*I*n the stylish ambience of the Nairobi Hilton hotel three wait-ers were gleefully occupied in trying to determine Esmeralda's tribe. Which tribe could possibly take credit for producing such a beautiful girl? It couldn't be said that they were neglecting the requirements of the rest of the patrons, but this girl's ethnic origins were definitely taking precedence above routine catering commitments.

'She is not *Maasai* or *Kikuyu*,' the head waiter told his attend-ants, with the assurance of office. 'But she could be *Samburu*.'

'No, she is *Luo*,' the youngest of three judiciously declared.

Smiling, Freddie Bristow shook his head at the overt exhibi-tionism of his date for the night. Her naturally vivacious nature flourishing unbridled with the attention she was getting, a girl preening herself, thrusting her jaw forward and slowly rotating her face so that it could be examined from all sides. Other patrons in the lounge were watching too, their expressions a mixture of bemusement and good humour, with no chagrin at all at their relative neglect. Freddie was mightily proud that she was being seen to be his. She was a phenomenon, her attraction to others immediate, her birth-right centre stage; her God-given charisma indisputable.

'The girl is *Kamba*,' a small, fat avuncular waiter proclaimed, as if assessing a fine piece of china. And when Esmeralda con-gratulated him on his astute denouement, all three men crumpled into laughter and danced a most undignified jig, considering the primness of their surroundings.

Freddie had not had a particularly fruitful day but the night promised to be a lot better. Not all the fashionable clothes shops were open on a Sunday in Nairobi, but Freddie, on his motor-bike, had taken the girl on a tour of the city to find those that were; just his luck they were the most expensive ones and by late afternoon she had emerged from the trip in possession of as much chic as his credit card allowed. The card was a different colour to Charlie's but, as she had observed studiously, just as effective. Before embarking on their shopping trip they had gone to Latema Road to try and get her own clothes back, but no one had ever heard of The Church of the Ever Open Door. Esmeralda explained that, such was her state of ecstasy at the time, the church could well be anywhere in Nairobi. After the clothing expedition he had then taken her to her cousin's place so that she could prepare herself for a night out at the Hilton. Charlie had promised her such a night at such a place but had never got around to it; Charlie had never experienced such a salubrious environ and was far more overawed by its grand reputation than Esmeralda was. Freddie had parked and secured the bike some half-mile away, outside another hotel, once again with a porter in night attendance. There was no way Esmeralda was going to be seen arriving at the grand doors of the Hotel Hilton on the back of a *piki*.

Freddie was drinking Tusker beer moderately and Esmeralda, her very first gin and tonic with an alacrity that had the three waiters jostling to be the first to fetch her a second.

'That drink is too much,' she said, felicitously smacking her lips.

Now Freddie was accustomed to plying young girls with strong drink but, by and large, these girls were seasoned drinkers and the assignment generally took some time and cost money without always being fruitful. With Esmeralda there was a quandary. Although, she assured him, she had, many times, drunk large amounts of strong home-brewed *changaa* beer – without ill effect – this was the first time she had ever tasted spirits. And she liked the taste; it made her giggly and warm inside. From the first sip she had found an immediate and voracious appetite for the stuff and far from plying, Freddie knew he would find himself having to curtail her consumption. It wasn't that he was trying to get the girl to lose her inhibitions, she didn't have any. He wanted her just malleable enough to get her upstairs and into bed without being drunk and incapable. After her fourth gin and tonic, he looked at her closely but the drink appeared to be having no affect at all; her eyes were still clear and her speech was not slurred; of course not: the girl had been weaned on *changaa*.

The three waiters had dispersed in answer to other demands, and they were left alone. Now Freddie could get down to the real business of the night. It was nothing new to him: the seductive milieu of a hotel lounge, the lazily drifting cigarette and cigar smoke, the relaxing warmth of alcohol flowing through the blood; the closeness, the intimacy, now for the introduction of salacious subjects, the prelude to sexual abandonment.

Like so much about the beautiful girl sitting next to him, her sexuality was a contradiction. He had been told by another volunteer at the language school that Kenyan girls were promiscuous by inclination, carnal by nature, but was this true? Although Esmeralda flirted outrageously her psychic demeanour was virginal. She was circumspect in volunteering sexual enlightenment about herself but could chatter endlessly about sex as a subject, and the sexual predilections of others she found positively engrossing. To Freddie's mind, if ever there was a girl who deserved a good shagging, it was her. She was now in full flow about the promiscuity of her auntie's kid.

'But how old is she?' Freddie asked.

'Twelve.'

'Twelve,' Freddie echoed, 'a promiscuous twelve-year-old. She isn't even old enough to be having sex.'

'She must be.'

'No she isn't.'

'She's having a baby.'

Freddie choked, 'She's simply not old enough.'

Esmeralda shrugged, 'How could she be expecting a baby if she wasn't old enough?'

The lucidity of her argument silenced him. Of course, at twelve, a girl is old enough to conceive. Nature does not conform to the mores of society and certainly not Western society. These were not the leafy avenues of suburbia but the untrammelled wild-lands of the bush where animals mate as soon as they are old enough. This was the third world, a convenient Western euphemism for the untamed world, the wayward world. Why not call it the starving world, Freddie thought grimly, maybe, then, the West might be less inclined to pontificate their neat moral values from atop of their food mountains. He smiled to himself: these thoughts entering his head while lounging in the hedonistic environs of the Hilton Hotel, planning the seduction of a girl young enough to be his daughter. The irony did not escape him.

'Where I come from the father would be jailed,' Freddie said.

'The father's probably twelve too.'

There was an argument of course but Freddie couldn't find it; couldn't be bothered to look for it. 'Well what's underage over here then?' he asked lamely.

'Underage is when it is impossible for a girl to have a baby, because she's too young,' Esmeralda answered elementarily. To her there was no argument, just common sense and she endorsed the credence by standing up abruptly, tossing her head and making her way, with serpentine grace, across the lounge to the toilet lobby.

Freddie regarded her progress attentively. She had consumed four gin and tonics in quick succession. Esmeralda was unrestrained in her eating and drinking habits; he had watched her closely many times on site at lunchtime. Her appetite was abandoned and rapacious, and he knew that once they got down to it, her sexual propensity would be the same. But he did not want her drunk, he didn't want her incapable; he didn't want a night's pleasure deferred and all the money he had spent on her new clothes wasted. He satisfied himself that she wasn't drunk, she wasn't even tipsy. Even in four-inch high heels she didn't put a foot wrong, walking erect and assured, hips swinging in accord to the tensile movement of her muscular calves, her ample buttocks heaving through a tight, white dress. He would have no more beer himself, it might inhibit his performance but with Esmeralda he wasn't sure. She appeared stone-cold sober; she could continue to enjoy herself a while longer yet; he would happy to pay for the privilege but diligently monitor her behaviour.

In her absence he went to reception and booked a double room for one night, unconscious that his face told the story of a lust-filled life, full of short pleasures awaiting long sorrows, but too self-indulgent and voluptuous to change. The receptionist, a well-kept lady with impeccable English did not raise an eyebrow: a *musungu* sharing a room with a beautiful young Kenyan girl was nothing new to her and she twitched her nose in recognition of the unmistakeable redolence of middle-aged testosterone.

Well, in Kenya, he didn't have to worry about the judgemental speculation of hotel staff as he would back home, but he did have to worry about a credit card debt that was racking through the roof. He was back in his seat as Esmeralda was returning from the toilet block and he observed her as lasciviously as before. Fan-like the waiters gathered about her, again chiding her. Irrepressible, she responded with vivaciousness, still not slurring her words, answering the waiters teasing by laughing at herself. How refreshing, thought Freddie, far from laughing at themselves most of the white women he knew, couldn't even grin. Yes, she was OK for at least one more drink, but no more. Definitely no more.

On his way back from reception he had picked up a copy of the current *Daily Nation* with a front page giving prominence to a multiple rape case in Nairobi. Not the most conducive subject to precede a night of tender loving but expeditiously placed on the table in front of them it served as a subliminal reminder of what this night was all about.

Sitting down, Esmeralda took the bait immediately, saying

gravely, 'Those guys was too much, can you believe it, even threatening to murder the girls if they didn't do what they wanted.'

A little smugly, Freddie said, 'Well, I will say one thing; rape is as serious here as it is in my country.'

Esmeralda turned to him sombrely. 'Here it is a hanging crime.'

Without invitation, the head waiter appeared at their side with a tray bearing a bottle of Tusker, and another glass of what appeared to be gin, accompanied by a small bottle of tonic. 'On the house,' he beamed with a surreptitious wink at Freddie, inferring that the 'house' belonged to the combined generosity of an empathetic male waiting staff, and that the gin could well be doubled. Well, OK, Freddie would allow himself one more Tusker and the girl was still in full control so he winked back, after all, men were men the whole world over and women the whole world over were there to be exploited. 'Very kind of you,' he said with a second wink.

Topping the gin with tonic, Esmeralda tossed half of the contents down in one gulp, and smiling happily, she gestured to the newspaper article, saying, 'Around the villages, when the guys have been drinking *changaa*, they follow me saying, "Sister, sister we will rape you tonight."'

'Then why don't you report them to the police and have them arrested immediately?' Freddie asked indignantly.

Esmeralda pointed to the newspaper and said adroitly, 'Those guys were police, one was a sergeant.'

'Well they should be reported to someone.'

Laughing uproariously, Esmeralda responded, 'Talk, talk, talk, talk 'tis this way, 'tis that way, 'tis this way. Those guys are all talk, talk, talk. Not them talking, but the *changaa* they have been drinking. Nothing like *changaa* for making little men talk big.'

'Well thank God for talk,' Freddie said, picking up the newspaper and scanning the text.

'Those guys in the villages, pwah,' she scorned.

Her frivolity at the concept of rape intrigued him, a case of words being infinitely better than deeds. 'But what if, one night, one of those guys carried out the threat?' he queried, putting down the newspaper.

Another frivolous question to be answered with stifled mirth: 'So I close my eyes and have it with someone I don't like, so what? I know many wives who don't like their husbands, but are made to have sex every night, what's the difference? Maybe, if I don't give the guy what he wants, so he murder me outright. Better to have it with someone I don't like than be killed and lay like a fish on a slab on a stall.' She drained her glass, her tongue, wanting more, probed her lips for the last vestiges of liquor and her candid eyes began searching meaningfully for a waiter.

Once again, Freddie was stumped for an argument. What was the use in raising issues of brutish dominance, humiliation and violent sexual assault? This girl had given the concept of rape some thought, she would rather be forcibly intimate with a man, however much she disliked or hated him, than be murdered. This wasn't a disturbed mind at work, it was pragmatism. If Esmeralda was to be raped, she wouldn't suffer psychological trauma, she would just pull her pants up and get on with her life.

'I think you've had enough to drink now,' Freddie advised.

The waiter who had guessed her tribe as *Kamba* answered her eyes. Freddie waved him away. Esmeralda called plaintively, 'Just one more.' The waiter looked at Freddie, his expression creasing with uncertainty. Esmeralda nodded her head vigorously, pecked Freddie on the cheek, squeezed his hand and made him give in.

'OK, just one more,' Freddie stood up and stretched his legs. On a nearby table was a bowl of salted nuts. He palmed a handful into his mouth, then wished he hadn't as they gummed his teeth. 'That is your last drink tonight, Esmeralda,' he spluttered unconvincingly.

She smiled up at him. Her skin was golden and without blemish, her teeth brilliant white in the soft flush of the subdued lighting, and he smiled back at her, knowing his smile was fatherly even if his intentions were not. Freddie finished his drink and sat down again, this time facing her. He watched her as she delicately pursed her lips and flicked the tip of her tongue around the rim of her glass teasingly. She knew that this was her last drink and she would not hurry to finish it. Leaning forward, she slipped her hand to his knee and said huskily, 'You know, Freddie, I have always thought it nice to see a man run his fingers through a girl's hair. A man cannot run his fingers through a black girl's hair. I would love to toss my hair back and forth like white girls do. I regret that in my life.' She nuzzled his neck, 'I want you to tell me something, Freddie. It is something that I have heard, in fact I have heard it many times but, oh, I do not believe it, it is too ridiculous to be true.'

'What is it?' he asked tautly. Her speech was starting to slur, and yes, her eyes were finally glazing over. He had ignored his own reservations and might well have given himself a needless problem. He must now get her up to bed quickly and he didn't want to be seen carrying her to the lift or up the stairs.

She laughed shrilly then bent to his ear again, 'I have heard that in your country, when a woman is having sex with her man, she sometimes shouts and screams with delight, at the top of her voice. Is that true, for surely it cannot be?'

For a moment Freddie looked dumbfounded then, preoccupied with signs of her inebriation, he chose to ignore her question.

'But Freddie, is it true?' she insisted.

'Yes, it is true, sometimes.'

She put her slender fingers to her mouth to stifle a little gasp, and whispered, 'Oh my God, so it is true. It seems so strange to me. What is there to shout and scream about? What is so delightful, to make your Western woman want to inform the *wanachi* all around about the good time they are having. The women of your country must be mad to carry on like that. Is it so too in America?'

'Probably worse, louder, in America.'

The smile on her face was fixed and her expression vacant as her confused brain wrestled to absorb yet another absurdity of Western life. All those graceful, white magazine models, did they caterwaul like crazy with a man between their legs? 'Seems so strange to me,' she repeated to herself.

Freddie couldn't resist, 'Some even shout and scream obscenities.'

He felt her hand fall from his knee, and he saw that her eyes were closed and she was rocking to and fro in contemplation. 'That would never happen here in Kenya then?' he asked.

Her eyes opened wide and her mouth opened wider. 'Oh my God no, it would wake the kids and the grandparents with such going on. They would think a lady was being murdered in her bed. Women in our little houses would make no noise at all, but only whisper for her man to proceed on,' then inexplicably her eyes filled with tears, and she began to cry softly. She was drunk and Freddie was now very worried.

'Esmeralda, please pull yourself together. I knew you were drinking too much, I bloody knew it. I've booked a room here for the night. Esmeralda, are you listening to me? Oh God, what a fool I've been to let you drink so much. What the hell are you crying for?' He stood up and tried to pull her to her feet, but she resisted. 'What the hell's the matter with you?'

She raised herself and yielded to his arms, resting her tearful cheek in his neck. 'Women in our little houses would make no noise at all. They would only say "proceed on".'

The lounge floor yawned in front of them, like a richly carpeted highway. The three waiters were grouped together, worriedly watching. Clientele in the vicinity were watching too.

'Proceed on,' she sniffled, 'they would only tell their man to proceed on.'

Freddie was angry with himself. He would do well to get her past reception, never mind upstairs to bed. 'Esmeralda, stop crying, what are you crying for? What I've just told you about Western women, why has it made you cry?'

'I was thinking about that saved boy.'

'Where the hell has he come from all of a sudden?'

'Oh but I left him behind.'

182

Freddie groaned. He did not want sentiment and nostalgia, not at this time; these emotions were not congruent with the unbridled passion he was hoping for. A pissed-up teenager crying for another man: the night no longer boded well for him. Holding her upright, he began to guide her forward to reception. She was unsteady but she wasn't staggering. There was hope. The well-kept receptionist regarded them quizzically.

'We were saved, you know,' she slurred sadly.

'Key to our room,' Freddie demanded of the receptionist with an authority he knew he didn't have. The entrance doors opened to a porter carrying bags. Cold night air entered with him. Esmeralda's knees buckled and he caught her in his arms. 'A little too much I think,' he told the receptionist with a sickly smile. 'Oh Christ,' he groaned, as Esmeralda slipped through his arms to the floor. 'I'm going to need a hand with her,' he pleaded, all semblance of authority gone from his tone.

Unfazed, the reception woman glanced over the counter at the stricken girl and said, in perfect English, 'I'm afraid that that young lady is not staying here tonight.'

'But I've paid for a double room,' Freddie protested.

'I know you have, but she's not staying here,' she confirmed with a tone of authority that was unassailable.

'Then what about the money I've paid for a double room?'

'You paid with your credit card. Come back later in the week, you might get a refund.'

He had a wreck on his hands. 'Esmeralda, please stand up,' he pleaded. She answered by projectile vomiting over his trousers and his shoes. 'What the hell am I going to do with her?' he implored.

'Get a taxi but not until you've cleaned that sick up.'

'I haven't got the money for a taxi.'

'Tough.' The woman's English was so perfect she could put its infuriating vernacular to devastating use.

PART THREE

Aisha

Chapter Twenty-Two

*E*xtract from a letter from Charlie Carter to his mother dated sometime November 1974.

> *Esmeralda and I have not got back together and I've told her that there is no chance we will. She is still terribly upset. Yes Mother, she knows that you would make her welcome over there and I know too. And yes, we could live with you until we got a place of our own. It's not that at all. It's the age difference. She just has to accept that at about nineteen she was far too young for me. Thankfully, I think that at long last she's finally coming to terms with reality.*
>
> *On the bright side, you will be pleased to know that I'm back with Jennifer, the Irish nurse (who I know, was your preference) but don't get excited, we're not quite an item again as we were before, but we're very close. There's also been a Kenyan lady called Lucy but I don't think anything will come of this one as she's not quite my type.*
>
> *Another girl called Aisha has come into my life (and believe it or not) she is every bit as beautiful as Esmeralda. Can't say too much about her-us, at the moment but any developments and you will be the first to know.*

Freddie was in a foul mood when he returned to Katamara. It was Monday noon when he paid a cursory visit to the site to report that he was back, and was surprised to find that Charlie had taken the truck into Nairobi on some business and would stay the night. Business and Charlie – the words were not synonymous. Before going home, Freddie complained of exhaustion and when questioned by the men on site and later by Charlie, he refused to speak about his weekend but it was evident that it had been one of wretchedness.

After a miserable weekend and a frustrating Monday morning in Nairobi, Charlie returned home, also refusing to speak to anyone about his business trip. It had been fruitless. In a last-ditch attempt to win Esmeralda back, he had tried to open a bank account for her so that he could present her with her very own credit card when she returned. 'But the lady has to be here at the bank in person with her identity card. Not only that, she also has to have two witnesses present to verify her identity.' What nonsense; Charlie was trying to put money into a bank, not take it out. 'You must understand sir, we can't be too careful,' the bank teller told him ambiguously. Charlie thanked the teller for her trouble and, scratching his head in bewilderment, went to two other banks and was confronted by protocol, much the same.

Charlie's bank account, in spite of Esmeralda, was still in the black, but only just. Ever since his arrival, he had attempted to live off his meagre, volunteer salary, and would continue to do so. Avoiding the better class hotels and guest houses of the inner city, he was happy to suffer the bed-bug indignities of cheaper lodgings on the seedier sides of town. Like the Hotel Splendid at the bottom of River Road. River Road; not a street for the faint-hearted: a seething scramble of crazy traffic and crazy people; chaotic, like ants on a strip of sweet-cake, all hell-bent on doing something, but seemingly creating nothing but noise and refuse. What nerve for a *musungu* to venture alone down River Road, a babel bedlam of bars, brothels and beggars.

It was the chalked sign on a blackboard that had attracted his attention. It read – *The Hotel Splendid is a posh place that remains Exclusive and Classy. Our Barbequed Restaurant with its Rioting Dishes must be experienced.* This was an invitation he could not resist and he was greeted warmly at reception. The room he was given was very reasonably priced; it was also infested with cockroaches, so much so, that he immediately demanded another. The manager himself dealt with the issue, apologising profusely and berating the shame-faced receptionist for providing a *musungu* gentleman with a room so close to the kitchen. Charlie declined breakfast and, supported by his ant-ravaged legs, had set off to another bank.

Charlie had spent the day of the *harambee* getting steadily drunk, going from one bar to another loquaciously rambling on about the ant attack and showing off his legs. Esmeralda didn't turn up for the event either, just as he knew she wouldn't. She didn't turn up in the village that evening and was not at the market on Sunday. What was she doing in Nairobi?

He was a broken man whose sore, blistered and itching legs were trifling compared to his emotional wounds: wounds that would never heal; old wounds inflicted by every desirable woman who, by accident or otherwise, had strayed into the coral of his wishful thinking only to escape the moment he failed to come anywhere near their expectations. The wounds were opened up again, fresh, raw and incurable. Esmeralda. Would he ever get over her? She was rooted in his soul, her voice, her laughter, her spirit. She was exalted in his mind and every night she shared his bed but only in his dreams.

Darkness clumped on Katamara like a sack of coal. Charlie was drunk in the village and with blistered, itching, aching legs, he was without a truck or a motor-bike. He would have to walk home, alone and adrift in uncharted night. Soon he would stagger into blackness and a terrain of night-stalking predators but before he reached the bridge a sudden scream of pain split the darkness into atoms and Charlie froze. He was outside the police station. A prolonged, almost porcine shriek; it was coming from the direction of the ablution block where Adonis had his hooks. Doubting his ears, Charlie clutched at the rough stone wall of the building; was it male or female? Adonis had arrested a couple earlier that day for pilfering from one of the stalls. It was an animalistic howl of torment; surely such punishment didn't fit the crime. Paralyzed with shock, Charlie prayed that it was not a woman; surely even Adonis would not subject a woman to the anguish manifested in that God-forsaken sound. But how often had the policeman crowed of bringing with him to Katamara the quintessence of the abattoir; it was true, it hadn't been an empty boast. Charlie's blood unfroze as a second anathema rent the night. Closing his ears to the sound, he stumbled onwards towards the bridge, across the bridge and into the pitch-black featureless bush.

Jerking his head from side to side, he felt he was being watched, and of course he was. Unseen bodies brushed against him and his nostrils filled with the rank odour of the carnivore and his staggering feet dreaded the spongy, fatal step upon a reptile. But he made it home and Titus was on the porch to welcome him. Charlie fell into his arms. 'Titus, I think Adonis is torturing someone in the cells and it could be a woman. I'm thinking Jennifer Collins. God it was awful, awful. We must go back. Try to save her.'

'Sometimes, that Adonis Musyoka is too much, Charlie. Me, I have heard such things before. Often on a weekend night do people hear those screams. Bad men fear him greatly but what he does is not good, not right. People think that Adonis is all talk, talk, talk but he is a truly fearful man although I know he would not torture a *musungu* woman, even Adonis would not dare touch Nurse Collins. It is not Nurse Collins that is hanging by her balls.'

'She was screaming, Titus, screaming.' Leaving his *askari* on the porch, Charlie lurched past him in torment and with his courage bolstered by White Cap beer, he climbed the creaky staircase to the decomposing room above. He must save a woman. If Shula was anywhere she was in this upstairs room. He slumped down and picking up a torch by the doorway he played its beam about the room; in one corner its light rested on the upright box; it was the mortuary box of his ant-night dream. It should have 'Johnnie'

190

written on the side. Assisted by the door jambs, he pulled himself to his feet. In his dream it was Titus in the box, but he was downstairs on the porch. A strange horror overcame him, advancing to his limbs until he couldn't move. That was what the knocking was: she was in that box, as he had always suspected and only he could get her out. There was a creaking and then a touch to his shoulder and a voice, 'You OK, Charlie?'

'Jesus Christ, Titus. You nearly gave me a bloody heart attack.'

'You OK up here, Charlie? What you doing?'

'Shula, I think she's in that box,' Charlie slurred.

'Please Charlie you have had too much drink, come back down the stairs. Please don't be messing with stuff like this. Please Charlie, it is black magic. It is witch-doctor stuff.'

'I dreamt about the mortuary in Thika and there's the box that was in my dream.' Charlie found it with the beam of his torch again, 'Titus, you go see, there will be the word "Johnnie" written on the side and I'm sure that Shula is inside, it's her, the knocking that I hear. We must release her.'

Titus's voice now came from the bottom of the stairs. 'Charlie, I think that you have drunk a lot too much. I will make you a cup of coffee.'

'When I had that dream Titus, it was you in the box,' Charlie called. 'Titus you and me, we'll do this together – Titus—'

'I am fearing we will be visited by ants again this night,' Titus' voice, this time from a distance, coming from the porch.

Without his *askari* by his side, Charlie's courage dissipated. He needed more alcohol. Carefully, he backed down the stair but did not join Titus on the porch. He went to his room and opened a can of beer.

'Freddie returned to site-work on the Tuesday morning to remain sullen and uncommunicative for the whole of the week. He worked as hard and conscientiously as ever but his feet dragged a little, and his flow of joking banter was missing from the site. He was impatient with trivial things that wouldn't normally bother him, like mortar being too soft or too rich with cement. He gave no indication whatsoever for the cause of his bad mood and he hardly spoke a word to Charlie, his longest conversation being to reserve the truck for the coming weekend.

'OK, but I need it two weekends after to collect the goats,' Charlie said.

The accommodation block was now taking shape. A chimney stack, incorporating two fireplaces to a common flue, had risen at both gables and stood against the sky, facing each other in stark reminder of the effort that had jointly taken place, and the differences that had come between them. External walls were now at pan height, waiting to support sisal roof trusses, and internal stabilized soil-block walls were all at joist height. At this stage, Freddie, who now, in everything but appointment, was in charge, had temporarily abandoned the construction of the accommodation block so that he could work on his own. He was concentrating on latrine pits inside an attached annexe. Isolation now appeared to be his choice. In his absence, the men talked about this uncharacteristic churlishness and figured it was the heat. Now the men looked at him the way they sometimes looked at Charlie – much as a mother may look at a backward child – and they could not understand why Freddie sometimes jerked his eyes hopefully towards the road, especially with any sudden peripheral flash of colour.

They saw how the two men had got on well at first but how things had slowly changed, Freddie now looking upon Charlie with a mix of distaste and contempt. Charlie no longer made decisions on site; a responsibility he had begun to relinquish from the day of Freddie's arrival. Charlie, even now, as he helped Sammy to construct a concrete lintel, didn't make a move without looking to Freddie for approval first. But they knew that Charlie didn't like Freddie anymore because he made it clear, speaking of his dark and handsome narcissism, his over-confident and arrogance but would never deny his outstanding ability. They worked together because fate, in her mischief, had put them together, a union that neither would have chosen. They lived together too, but hardly ever now entered the dynamics of co-existence, they occupied separate rooms, never ate together, never shared a few beers on an evening and conversation, when they had one, was confined to work. Two Englishmen from the same town, living and working together and although the site men guessed what the matter was, no one spoke of it; the only thing the two men had in common now was what was driving them apart, Esmeralda.

The men on site were not happy with the fall-out. They had laughed at Charlie and with Freddie, and had laughed among themselves, but there wasn't laughter anymore on site, only hard work and *ugali and githeri at* dinner time; chicken and goat meat were off the menu when Esmeralda wasn't there. Dejection had fallen on the site and some of them even wished they hadn't volunteered.

Freddie watched Charlie struggle with the lintel: project co-ordinator, what a joke. He cleared his throat and spat on the ground; phlegm like a living thing, curling in a dusty ball at his feet. Charlie Carter, inept, never able to pass a scheming child or beggar without resisting the weak-kneed impulse to empty his pocket into dirt-encrusted hands, stumbling through life, never daring to look to the dizzy heights of mediocrity, knowing he could never make it. People with low-esteem usually replace it with ego, but Charlie didn't have either – just the compulsion to be a calamitous do-gooder, investing in a kind of anti-post gamble, that what had been denied him in this life would be dealt in spades in the next. No doubt, what people saw in Charlie they got, but God knows it wasn't much. Could it be that Esmeralda was treating him, Freddie Bristow, the same way that she had treated Charlie? Never. Oh where was she? She was not at her cousin's place when he had gone back for her. She had not come home. She had not come back on site. She had made a spectacle of herself at the Hilton Hotel, was she too ashamed to face him? Come home, Esmeralda, Freddie has forgiven you. This treatment was identical to how she had treated Charlie. But it couldn't be happening to him, it couldn't. Freddie Bristow was not a Charlie Carter.

Work was over for the day and Freddie brooded. The building wasn't progressing, it was just unfinished. Would it ever be finished? He sat on a hard, bare rock watching geckos teasing the last rays of sunlight to spot them on the baking stones. The project wasn't calling to him anymore, only Esmeralda. The week was coming to an end and she still wasn't back. He had the truck for the weekend. He would visit Kitui; he told everyone how he had intended, for quite some time, to visit Kitui. What he hadn't told anyone was that he had no intention of visiting Kitui. First he would visit Uamani, and then her cousin's place in Nairobi, and if she wasn't there he would try, again to find the Church of the Ever Open Door. The thought of her with 'that saved boy' was driving him insane. If he found her, he would take her shopping and buy her something that Charlie Carter could never afford. He would buy her anything she wanted. He would even take her to the Hotel Hilton again but without the gin and tonics. And if he did not find her, he would return to Katamara, tell everyone about the wonders of Kitui, then sit and watch the geckos again.

Chapter Twenty-Three

*I*s there anything on earth as irredeemably miserable as lost love? It was early Sunday morning and Charlie hadn't slept well again, tossing and turning, his mind absorbed with Esmeralda. Where was she? Surely she must attend J.M.'s meeting. Unlike the *harambees* this was a huge event for the village with important people sure to attend. Esmeralda could be relied upon not to miss this event; if J.M. was the main attraction, this girl's spirited nature and outstanding looks would give her second billing. What could be more compelling in Nairobi or wherever else she was?

He had risen early because she just might arrive early, and he would be last to leave, in case she might arrive late. He was one of the first to enter the hospital grounds and as he trod the crisp, misty grass of the playing field, desolation trailed his wake in bleak despair. No one in the village that morning was more laden down with woe than Charlie, except maybe Freddie speeding towards Uamani.

Last evening there had been a stronger wind than usual and the green field was patched blue with fallen blossom and the sun, balancing on the horizon, cast long shadows through the trees, so that the blue was segmented in long freckled stripes: lavender then purple then lavender again. At any other time, Charlie might have rejoiced at such a lovely scene, but not with a fog upon his life. Ever since Esmeralda had turned up that day on site, his world had vaulted to unimaginable heights only to spiral downwards into grief. Moments of euphoria, experiencing inexplicable ecstasy sweeping his loving heart into paradise with a look, a word, a touch, but these emotional bonanzas were fleeting so that when the experience was over, the world dipped so deep it reached the bottom of his soul. She was a drug and he was desperate and dependant, and would discard the last vestiges of his self-esteem to regain, just one more time, the high she gave him when she was nice to him. He did not blame the girl for his misery; how can anyone be blamed for being themselves? He blamed himself. How could he have been so naïve, so stupid; so besotted as to believe that a girl like Esmeralda could love him; Charlie Carter, who had never had a proper girl-friend in his life? OK, that letter she sent him was so full of instinctive passion it could not be false, no one could fake the ardour imbued in every line. But she was young, and carefree, and fickle, like all girls of her age. He had been a fool. He had never even known an ordinary girl, a plain one, so how could he have hoped to know an Esmeralda? The terrible cruelty of an uncaring girl, an exploitative, laughing girl; where was that protective cloak of caution he wore when he encountered one? Where was it the day that Esmeralda stepped from the vibrant streets of Paris, and into his unacknowledged life? Was this his last chance? Was Josiah Kariuki's rally his last and only hope? Oh, he would sell his soul to see her skipping through the blue blossom, with her hands outstretched towards him. If only he could feel once more her hand in his, her damp lips pressing upon his own. Yes, that had happened once, and also once, the time she had put her hands behind his head and plunged his face between her breasts. Oh to experience such a thrill again. Oh Esmeralda, please come back today.

He had made his mind up. If she did not return today, he would spend Christmas in Katamara, then go back home to his mother in Tala. He wouldn't be letting anybody down. He had tried and failed, but at least he had tried. Freddie Bristow could more than manage the project on his own, and who would miss him but the little children? Miss his chocolate and sweets and their free rides on the truck. Yes, back to his old life, his old job, his mother nattering at him to get a wife and settle down. He would be just in time for her garden too and the daffodils that so puzzled and enchanted his new friends. Back to his old friends and the pub, but at least he would have some good stories to tell, like the ghost of Shula who haunted his home and the day he took the weeping women to the mortuary in Thika. Yes, and the night an army of ants squatted in his house and turned his legs into red hot swollen pokers. He stopped at a beer stall and asked what time it opened.

Homes were emptying and the field was filling up. From somewhere in the hospital complex, the aroma of cooking alerted taste buds to expectancy and already children were being shooed away from tables. People shook Charlie's hand and passed the time of day and rejoiced at the improvement in his legs. Children, knowing they would have to wait for food, gathered around him chanting, 'Charleee, Charleee, chocolat, chocolat.' They would have to be patient, it was going to be too hot to sell chocolate from the stalls, but there were shops now with refrigeration. Charlie made a mental note of the number of children pestering him and knew he was going to have an expensive morning.

At the field entrance Corporal Adonis was talking earnestly to Mr Muinde the hospital administrator; they returned Charlie's wave of greeting.

Driven slowly, a police car came through the entrance to stop on a hard standing, causing Adonis to spring to attention and salute. Instantly recognisable, Inspector Sam Wamiru got out, and while his driver stayed to talk to the two men, Wamiru made his way towards Charlie, smiling and holding out his hand. 'Charlie Carter.'

The senior policeman bore himself with confidence, his flaccid jacket sleeve a badge of honour. Shaking hands, Charlie felt inferior, but then he always did. He flung his arm far too grandly around the playing field, saying, 'There's going to be a big crowd for J.M.'s meeting today, Inspector, and what a truly lovely day it is.'

'It is. J.M. and his team should be here about 10-30.' The jacaranda, how beautiful they are, Wamiru thought as he breathed in
the full-blown enchantment of the trees. Over Charlie's shoulder
children played among the fallen petals, stirring blue flakes about
their lawless feet. Could anything compare with the brilliant,
scarlet clusters of the flame trees? Yes, the jacaranda.

People were arriving, women and girls, as always, adding to
the colour. Wamiru put his hand on Charlie's shoulder and said,
'Some months ago, when I was here investigating that little boy's
death you were writing something or other for your agency and
you asked me to check archives at HQ for any information on
your house. I checked, as you know, but found nothing. I told
Adonis to tell you, I hope he did.'

'He did, sir, yes.'

I suppose you're finished your article, or thesis, or whatever by
now but knowing I was here in Katamara, today I thought I'd look
you up and tell you what I heard. I should say overheard, because
it involved a little eavesdropping.' He laughed and Charlie, for the
first time, looked closely into the man's face. He liked what he saw;
the high bronzed forehead, the honest light brown eyes, kind eyes.

'The Provision of Adequate Shelter,' Charlie remembered.

'A few weeks ago there was a retirement function at HQ a
Deputy Chief. Strictly for senior policemen and for government
high ups, I was the lowest rank there. Don't know how I came to
be invited,' he laughed. 'I heard two guys talking at the bar, they
were not police, they were government men, one of them I recognised from the newspapers. They were talking about sensitive files
left over from British rule. I heard them talk about Katamara, and,
because of you, I bent my ear towards them. They were talking
about a house on the mountain, and about something happening
years ago that was hushed up. Apparently, following independence, there were a lot of secret files that were supposed to be sent
back to the UK or burnt, or destroyed but some remained. I don't
think they are quite so secret now, but you still can't get at them
without a court order.'

Charlie cut in, 'There are other houses on the mountain but the only one close to Katamara is ours.'

'Yes, I could understand that from their conversation. Anyway, from what I could gather, something criminal happened that caused a prominent family to flee back to England, with every record of them ever being here wiped out. It was obviously something very serious and I wanted to know more. I moved real close to them, but some other guy started talking to them and they changed the subject. Pity.'

'Were any names mentioned?' Charlie breathed.

'I couldn't hear too clearly. Easy for the Brits to do something like that in those days, people were either threatened or paid off,' he laughed ruefully. 'Still goes on, I can tell you. Does it mean anything, what I've just told you?'

'Were any names mentioned?' Charlie asked again.

'I think so but I can't remember any names. Does what I've told you mean anything?'

It meant everything. It meant that he was right all along and Freddie was wrong. It meant that Shula was sadistically killed by Clarissa Chance and big Evangeline, and although he didn't trust him, it was just as the old *mzee* had said it was. And it meant that Shula, mistaken by Esmeralda for the Virgin Mary, had never left the house. 'Yes, it does mean something, Inspector. It confirms something to me about the history of the house. A murder close on seventy years ago, far too long ago now to do anything about, but thanks, Inspector, I can amend the article now. It's the one piece of information that was missing.'

Charlie felt the urge to tell Wamiru all he knew, but resisted. He was shaken. She was there in his house and would be waiting for him, listening for him. His bond with the dead girl was even greater now. For seventy years she had been waiting to let some-one know what had happened to her. She had chosen Charlie. It was why he was here; all along it had been his destiny. 'Thanks again, Inspector, I'm really grateful.'

Wamiru looked over Charlie's shoulder again. 'I know J.M.

will be happy with this set-up.' The tone of his voice lowered, more serious, 'Now, I know he's going to talk about what the *musungus* are doing here. His theme is going to be self-help in the community, *harambees* and volunteer work. You are here, Charlie, but it would be better if the other guy could have been here too.'

Adonis who had been hovering jumped in quickly and, standing to attention, said, 'His name is Freddie Bristow, sir, and although I told him to be here and that J.M. expected him to be here, he sped off early this morning in his truck. I have men about this village who inform me of such things but as I was not informed in time, I was unable to apprehend him. This organisation is something I think the great J.M. should know about.'

Wamiru looked to Charlie for confirmation. Charlie nodded and Wamiru nodded in mute affirmation of the corporal's proposal. Satisfied, he raised his nose to the air and addressed Charlie, 'Something smells nice.'

'That smell, sir, it is the goats cooking,' Adonis jumped in again. 'The goats I got from Tala yesterday. Me and Charlie, we brought the goats from that side to this side in the truck. I then slaughtered them with my own bare hands last night and now they are cooking and smelling good enough to eat.'

'You have done well here today, Corporal,' the inspector allowed.

And he would do better. Today was a fateful day, his opportunity to finally get recognised. 'Everything is becoming so ready, sir. The goats is in the pot with many vegetables and there is rice and chapatti and the women are working hard to do my bidding. We all hope there will be enough to go around. J.M.'s party will eat first and then the children and then the women and then the men, and me and my men will only eat if there is food left over as it is my wish to set a good example. There is plastic bowls and spoons and lots of salt that I have provided from my own pocket, and if drunks cause trouble they will arrested by my men and kicked in the bollocks.'

Wamiru said, 'Yes, I see you have support staff here, Corporal?'

'Yes sir, although I police this town successfully on my own, two men from Mavaloni have been instructed to post themselves at the gate when J.M. arrives, and there is one other in plain clothes who will jump into action at the snap of my fingers. I wonder if J.M. will ever know who is responsible for all this good work.'

'I'll see that he gets to know, Corporal,' Wamiru assured wearily.

'Please sir, it is only my wish, that you mention my full name which is Adonis Musyoka, and for J.M. to see that everything is very fine in Katamara and for him to know who is responsible for all of it.' Taking off his shades and pocketing them, he humbly looked his superior in the eye to endorse his veracity.

Adonis was behaving as expected but Wamiru looked around for Mr Muinde, he must thank him personally. Adonis was seeking compliments, boasting, shifting his feet, casting his eyes expectantly about the gathering crowd. Adonis had done a good enough job but there was something else on his mind, he could tell.

He did not have long to wait. Narrowing his brows and taking advantage of Charlie's earnest conversation with a bar-tender, Adonis began speaking softly in his best English. 'Perhaps you have noticed, sir, that Jennifer Collins is not here?'

Noticed! Jennifer Collins was the reason the hospital had been chosen for the meeting. Wamiru could have chosen any one of a dozen venues. What had she seen of him so far? An archetypal, morally upright, hard-boiled cop who had surely lost his arm in some drug-den in Kibera, unmoved by tears, relentless in pursuit of justice. She needed to see more of the other side of Sam, the side she had seen the day he took her to see Elizabeth. 'No, I hadn't noticed,' he lied. 'Why, is she ill?'

'More perhaps – troubled, sir,' Adonis answered, his face screwing with compassion.

'Why troubled?'

Adonis paused, picking his words carefully. 'There is a lot of talk in the village sir, I have heard it myself. About Kennedy's death, I have told the people – Coroner's verdict – Accidental Death – and everything is fine and above board in accordance with the laws of this land, seems the nurse has been acting very strange.'

Wamiru was intrigued and more than a little suspicious. He raised an eyebrow in invitation for the corporal to carry on.

'Maybe people are thinking—' The corporal left the supposition unfinished.

Wamiru stiffened noticeably. He fixed his eyes on the corporal's face and saw the man gulp. This man was way overstepping his mark. He had been a nuisance during the investigation. What arrant bombast was he about to come out with now? Or did he know something new? If so, then Wamiru's own investigation was deeply flawed, his conclusions wrong and his reputation in trouble. 'Just what exactly are you implying, Corporal?' The inspector's eyes screwed menacingly.

The corporal gulped again, that emasculating gulp of his. 'Not implying, sir, but as you know I am most familiar with what goes on in Katamara and you did ask me about Nurse Collins.'

Wamiru replied irritably through gritted teeth, 'I didn't ask you about Miss Collins, you volunteered the information. Listen, Corporal, I'll tell you for the last time, Nurse Collins had nothing to do with that little boy's death.'

Adonis' voice was edged with panic: 'Oh I know, sir. All I was—'

This buffoon of a corporal was out of his depth. Adonis Musyoka, more semblance than substance, could not be permitted to blunder and bluster his way back into a case that Wamiru had solved himself to everyone's satisfaction. Adonis was what the English call a jobsworth and the Americans call a jerk. How much mayhem is caused when a self-important travesty of a corporal is dressed up in a uniform? A posturing parody, who somehow did his job. Wamiru's subordinate had reached the threshold of his tolerance. 'Corporal, I think you had better explain what the hell you're talking about before you get yourself into serious trouble.'

The face of Adonis sagged visibly. It was grossly unfair of the inspector to impute suggestion that he was biased against the nurse. Far from it, he could like the nurse, could be very fond of her in fact, if only she would let him. That wasn't much to ask. Killers are often known to have interpersonal skills and to be brilliant at deception. He had read that recently in a manual, and it fitted the nurse perfectly, lots of other people thought it fitted her too. On top of that she was now looking and acting guilty. But if she was nice to him he wouldn't have the need to express his doubts. What was happening to her was her own fault; all she had to do was show him a little fear.

Chapter Twenty-Four

*L*oud cheering and commotion signalled the arrival of Josiah Kariuki and his entourage and Wamiru observed the unfolding scene before him with satisfaction. Was there ever a re-election site more colourful than this he wondered as he took up his customary position, directly in front of the rostrum where his friend could clearly see him, they acknowledged each other with a quick smile.

Although, on occasions, J.M. often asked Wamiru to choose a venue, it wasn't necessarily the inspector's choice to attend, but he was often assigned to do so by his superiors in Nairobi because he couldn't be in a better position to do what they had in mind. Chauvinism was not expected, it was demanded, and Sam Wamiru was no exception. J.M. had to be watched; who better to watch him than his trusted friend? And although he did his job as a policeman as well as he was able, he was not in thrall to the oligarchy that controlled him. His was intelligence surveillance with a difference. He let J.M. know that he was spying on him. He knew what the executive ring-masters were looking for, and he tipped his friend off accordingly. Far from being an informer he was an umpire, an emollient moderator between the forces of greed and corruption, and their would-be nemesis. Whenever he thought his friend was being too provocative, easy to do with a crowd urging him on, he would give a nod or a wink in his direction and J.M. would answer with a grim smile, although not always with prudence. Wamiru knew that he was treading on thin ice, but everything would be fine as long as J.M. didn't go too far.

The crowd were silenced and stilled as the politician mounted the steps to the rostrum with the relaxed, self-contained assurance of the consummate professional. An undeniably handsome man, the bone structure of his face was well balanced, his eyes calm and wide set and a Clark Gable moustache emphasized the row of even white teeth, ever ready with an easy smile. An elected member of parliament, so potent in his appeal to the *wanachi* that the government were pulling out all stops to prevent his re-election, but what can be done to negate a man's appeal when the people love him? How many politicians can command a full-house in every village and town that they attend? The people of Katamara had turned out in force to listen to him rail against the widening gap between the rich and the poor, the unfair distribution of land, and they would not be denied. Of course J.M. would be re-elected, did he not represent the independence the poor people had fought so hard for? The rich had fought for independence too, but what they had fought for without quite knowing it, was independence from the poor. And they had it and didn't want to lose it. The rich didn't understand that in a democracy the concerns of poor people had to be taken into account as well. This is what the much-loved Kariuki was advocating. A man like Kariuki must not be re-elected.

Wamiru's trained eye scanned the crowd as the politician began his speech. The two uniformed policemen from Mavaloni stood at the main entrance as Adonis had promised, he couldn't find the plain-clothed one. Charlie Carter, whom he liked, appeared to be mildly drunk already and looked a little sad. Mr Muinde and nuns were among the crowd, all of whom he recognised, many of whom he could name and there were others from the village that he knew by sight. He looked around for Freddie Bristow, hoping he had arrived late but could not see another white male and for J.M.'s sake was mildly disappointed. There was only one person, conspicuous by her absence.

He sniffed the air for trouble, which usually came from hecklers, government men especially planted in the crowd but he could not see any likely candidates. There was growing excitement in the air, a quiet rumbling of agreement which seemed to come from the bellies of the people, a buzz of expectation. J.M. was at his best. He was the helmsman, trying to steer the mighty ship of independence in a new direction; the roars of the crowd a following wind of support.

It was hot. The sun was high in the sky, and the shadows of the trees had shrunk to deep purple patches, shades on which brightly coloured *kangas* lay ready to be occupied by families when the food was served. J.M. had been talking for some time, the crowd now in abeyance, stilled by the hypnotic eloquence of nationalistic rhetoric. The evocation of the trials and bloodshed of their fathers and the light of new horizons, Wamiru had heard it all before, it was building to a climax. Soon the people would be ecstatic in their approval. A sudden storm of accordance, the *wanachi* were jumping up and down and waving their hands. He blinked away his introspection; he had been preoccupied with the crowd. He looked up to the rostrum; he was supposed to be listening intently to every word being said. Had he missed a repudiation of unbalanced and elitist doctrines, an urging of rebellion against the state? Surely not, but he was listening intently now.

'It is greed that will put this country in chaos, let me state here and now that this greedy attitude among leaders is going to ruin this country.'

Again the crowd roared. The quiet belly-rumble of approval was now full-throated, and hands had closed to fists and were raised in unison. The *wanachi* had one ear, one voice and most importantly to J.M., one vote – his. Their leader, their spokesman, was talking about persons who were using their position to amass colossal wealth by means of corruption. In Wamiru an alarm had started, his friend was in danger of being carried away by his own rhetoric, and the swell of support his words engendered. He began nodding his head violently, not in agreement but in warning, which J.M. acknowledged with a quick wry smile.

But he continued, '*Did our nation really fight tooth and nail, suffer, leave behind countless widows and orphans for what we have now, a nation of ten millionaires and ten million beggars?*'

The people were ready to ignite. A few more incendiary words from J.M. and they could be marching to the barricades. Wamiru once again caught J.M.'s eye in warning, and just as easily as the tenor of the crowd had been raised, J.M. calmed it down. His tame theme now was the spirit of self-sacrifice. *Expressive giving* he called it; each man, woman and child giving of themselves to something bigger than themselves; a nation, a nation where everyone had a common aim, a massive move towards self-sufficiency. It was at this point that he addressed the contribution of Charlie Carter and his colleague Freddie Bristow, and the local volunteers, in what they were doing unconditionally for the Holy Sisters of the hospital in Katamara. Wamiru smiled as he turned and saw Charlie with a bottle of beer in his hand, blushing to his roots. Josiah Kariuki had brought the meeting to a close. The area chief and other local dignitaries were shaking his hand and people were dispersing, muttering their endorsement. This meeting was to be J.M.'s last before the forthcoming general election and it had been a rousing success, typical and, to Wamiru, no more seditious than usual. A rich smell permeated the playing field and children began to rattle spoons and bowls in anticipation as the splintering crowd moved towards the food tent.

Wamiru did not want to eat. The sisters didn't want to eat either or maybe they were just hanging back through selflessness. Wamiru studied the sisters until one of them smiled at him. It was Sister Teresa. Adonis was latched on to the trail of dignitaries, trying to get noticed and Mr Muinde was heading back to the hospital. After detaching her from the group, Wamiru started to make small talk with Sister Teresa: the crowd, J.M.'s rousing speech, the response, the smell of food. 'Thought I might see Nurse Collins here this morning, Sister,' he said casually.

'She has her duties with the children,' was all the sister would say.

Wamiru pulled at his earlobe uncertainly. 'Will she be in class?'

The Sister smiled. 'Not on a Sunday morning.'

Wamiru felt himself flush a little with embarrassment. 'Would it be OK, Sister, if I was to pay her a short visit? It's not official or anything – just – I know she's been through a lot.'

'It is true. Nurse Collins is not well just now. Yes of course, Inspector, everyone knows who you are. You will find her with the children somewhere, probably in the garden.'

Wamiru must call on Mr Muinde first, thank him for his co-operation. The unvarnished hospital administrator, with his loose tie and grubby collar, an easy man to deal with; he would thank him unreservedly. Making his way along the corridor to Muinde's office, he passed Anthony of Padua; his absence over the past weeks did not appear to have made the Saint's stone heart any fonder. The Franciscan didn't seem to glower at anyone else, only Wamiru. The inspector glowered back. Through an open window, Jennifer Collins and another sister with children; he stopped; the nurse looked up and briefly caught his eye. Her head jerked like a hooked fish. She didn't want to see him, acknowledge him, he could tell. She did not resemble Clara, how could he have thought she looked like Clara? She looked more like one of the children in her care.

Wamiru was puzzled and disappointed. He turned back along the corridor. He would thank Mr Muinde by telephone.

Chapter Twenty-Five

*I*t seemed to Charlie that every time Freddie had the truck for the weekend, the *piki* had a puncture. It was usually in the front wheel, this time it was the back, but sick of being ripped off by the *fundi*, he was prepared; this time; he had his own puncture outfit. And so he set to work.

He had an indelible pencil, glass-paper, an abrasive stick, rubber solution, a selection of patches, French chalk and tyre levers; and as with his site work, the only thing he didn't have was expertise. With the tyre off, he tested the tube in a bowl of water and, lo and behold, one puncture, one tiny hole erupting interminable bubbles of water, and, following the puncture outfit instructions to the letter, it was repaired. Now to put the *piki* back together: but how had the wheel become loose, how had the tube, the tyre and the webbing tape become inextricably entangled with the chain, and what were ball bearings doing littering the ground? And how had the patch become loose? Ripping the patch off the tube in frustration and saturated in oil and sweat, Charlie reassembled the bike, in a fashion, and half-wheeled, half-carried it to the *fundi*.

'Please put the bike together again but back wheel, one puncture,' he enunciated politely but loudly, to the supposed non-English speaker. 'I know you understand English and I know why you pretend not to. Well that's OK with me but this time, one puncture, one only, I've already tested the tube, you understand, only one.' Charlie's rigid index finger reciprocated only inches from the man's pock-marked nose.

The *fundi* answered Charlie with a prolonged glowering frown of misunderstanding.

It was Sunday afternoon in the market and the *motor-bike* was surely fixed by now. Anxious about confronting the *fundi* and terrified that he might have to deal with a two-puncture issue again, Charlie spotted Titus in the marketplace with his wife and children. 'Titus, please call and collect the *piki* from the *fundi*, and if he says he's found two punctures again, he is most definitely a liar. I've checked the tube myself and there is only one.' He gave Titus fifty Kenyan shillings which should be more than enough to cover the costs. 'He will certainly charge for putting the bike back together and that's fine with me, but if he says he's had to repair two punctures, pay him for the bike repair only but leave the bike with him and come back to me. I'll have it out with him once and for all.'

'I will do it,' Titus agreed, and Charlie took care of his children, taking them to the bar for a soda pop whilst Josephine exchanged topics of the day with a mama at a nearby stall.

Sitting on bar stools, the children vied with each other to be the first to drink their pop through slender straws whilst Charlie sat below them, alone at a table, gathering his wrath, nursing it, indulging it until it became incendiary. If the *fundi* had the sheer audacity to claim repair to a second puncture then he would see another side to Charlie Carter. But surely he would not try and cheat him again? The gloomy face of Titus, returning through the doorway, told a story that he would.

Enraged, Charlie stood to his feet. 'Not again?'

Titus shook his head despairingly, 'That *fundi*, he took the full fifty shillings for putting the *piki* back together but he found two punctures in the same tyre again. "*Mbili, mbili*" he kept saying. Charlie, I have left the bike as you said but once again you owe him for two punctures.'

Charlie was overcome with the seething fury reserved for the hapless in the face of gross injustice; a rage genuine and justified. This time he would smite this conniving swindler with unbridled vengeance. He would see that the *fundi* had his licence to trade revoked. 'No Titus, not this time I don't.'

Titus called Josephine to look after the children, then trotted behind Charlie as he strode purposefully towards the puncture shed. They found the man smoking his pipe, unfazed by the manifestation of rank disservice confronting him. There was no greeting this time, and the *fundi* was sufficiently circumspect not to offer the customary handshake to either man. Charlie would show him who was hapless. He gripped Titus by the arm.

'Titus, I am not going to talk to him. I refuse to talk to him but make this clear. There was only one puncture because I tested the tube myself. Tell him he's a liar and a cheat. Tell him he will be paid for the one puncture only and I want my bike back. Make it clear.'

Titus made it clear.

'What did he say?'

'He said he found two punctures and it is the law that he must be paid for two.'

The incendiary ignited in Charlie's toes and moved instantly through his veins to reach his fevered brain. Steaming words spluttered snarling through his mouth, 'Titus, tell him he's a cheating bastard. Every time I bring my bike to him, in good faith, for a puncture to be mended he finds two. Does he take me for a fool?' Charlie turned his face from Titus and thrust it so far forward that the *fundi* had to quickly remove the pipe from his mouth, but he still remained unfazed. 'In future I will take my bike to Thika and will never do business with him again. Tell him, Titus.'

Titus told him.

'What did he say?'

'He said he found two punctures.'

'*Mbili, mbili,*' the *fundi* muttered along the stem of his pipe.

'I'll give him fucking *mbili,*' Charlie raged.

'*Mbili*,' the *fundi* insisted waving two fingers the wrong way round which incensed Charlie even further.

OK, obviously rage had no effect. When temper is used as a last resort and fails, a man can look a fool. Charlie stepped back a pace and calmed himself. He then began speaking quietly to Titus, 'Tell him to keep the bike. Tell him I'm now going to see the Chief for the area, and the Chairman of the Co-operative, they are both friends of mine, and I will see he has his licence to work removed. I know all *fundis* must have a licence to operate and no tradesman is allowed to carry on working and do business with the public without a licence. Tell him that I am now going to report him as a thief and a disgrace to the village of Katamara. On no account will I pay for two punctures when, this time, I know, for certain, that there was only one.'

'I will tell him,' Titus answered gravely.

With contrived dignity Charlie turned on his heel and set off in the direction of the chairman's office, leaving behind him an earnest and unintelligible exchange between the two Kenyans. Charlie wasn't bluffing; unless he received satisfaction he would, this day, see both the chairman and the chief and register strong complaint.

He was aware of Titus hurrying to catch up with him. 'Charlie, you must come back and collect your *piki*. It is ready.'

'And the two punctures?'

'Yes two punctures but the *mzee*, he promise, next time there will only be one.'

In Nairobi, at Esmeralda's cousin's place, Freddie was recognised immediately as the man who cleaned the sick up and was told that Esmeralda had found a job as a maid.

'It's not at the Church of the Ever Open Door is it?'

'No, it is at a hotel in Busia. She is to return for her stuff in a few days, I will ask her,' the cousin explained.

'Will you tell her Freddie called and he needs to see her as soon as possible?'

'I will tell her.'

'She didn't happen to be with 'a saved boy' did she?'

Returning to Katamara, Freddie collected his mail from the P.O. box. There were two letters from his wife, which he expected, and another which he hardly dared to open. He opened this one first.

My Darling Freddie

It is with much respect and pleasure that I dedicate to you this significant document. I am lonely and lost without you in Busia and the smudges on this letter are my teardrops which have been flowing like the Fourteen Falls during the long rain periods of March and April. Just now the smile is missing from my face but when I think of you it comes back like magic and everything is well and wonderful again, thinking of you makes me shine inside so much I think I might have yawned and swallowed the sun.

Oh my dear I am unhappy working at this hotel in Busia as the owner's wife is cruel to me and sometimes threatens to beat me with a stick but I must stay with them and work for money or have nothing but a life of empty despair. Sometimes I dream that you have come to save me.

First of all my cousin tells me that when we got back to her place I had been so sick in the taxi that she sends her congratulations to you for cleaning it up. Also I admire to convey my own thanks for cleaning it up and also in the hotel where you did a lot of cleaning too. And we both think that it was bad of the taxi man to make you pay for extra cleaning even after you had been cleaning it up but God bless you a lot for cleaning it up. But whatever I still had a blissful time with you in Nairobi and at the

Hilton Hotel with those waiter guys trying to guess my tribe and one guy saying *Kamba* and another guy saying Sheba. I said I never heard of the tribe of Sheba and he said there must be such a tribe because he had found the Queen of it. It was me, imagine. Always when I think of that night at the Hilton I think of such a wonder as I never knew existed in the world. It makes me think of my place in Uamani in the kitchen with the open fire on the floor and children around the fire and cats and dogs and chickens and even goats sometimes, looking through the door and smoke hanging in the roof so it just might be like the stable in Bethlehem And now that I am part of both those worlds, I think I like the Hilton best.

Oh my beloved one this *Kamba* chick is thinking of you every night and I take my pillow in Busia and lying against it pretend that it is you and I feel I am in heaven and when I see you again my heart will sing and I will be well and wonderful again. Oh my honey how I long for one more chance to go back to the Hotel Hilton and be a posh bird again. It would be nice to see those waiter guys again but not to drink gin and tonics anymore as for many days afterwards I thought I must be dead.

Maybe you will come and find me in Busia and rescue me. It might help if you bring that plastic thing to help me with my dilemmas. But until then I know my life must go on until the day I die and I hope that you will not grow so old as to walk with sticks and forget who I am when you see me. Congratulations again for cleaning up the sick and I hope you are as fine as a heartbeat which never stops until oneself has kicked the bucket.

From an African chick who is dying for your love.

Esmeralda

Chapter Twenty-Six

Charlie might well return home to England in the new year but he wanted to spend Christmas with a woman This was nothing new to him, since pubescence he had wanted a woman, and never more so than at Christmas. Twice, lately, he had taken Lucy, a local widow, for a drink at the Taifa Bar in Donya Sabuk; week-day nights, when he could wrest the truck from Freddie. She was a widow in her early forties, and like most *Kamba* women of her age, she was plump and fighting a losing battle with the onset of fat. But she was nice and friendly and well-mannered; he, in turn, felt that he bored her but he was always polite; and although he felt that his conversation was ever banal, he was careful never to use expletives to keep it afloat. But Charlie could not fall madly in love with Lucy as he wanted to. Having once experienced the exquisite emotion of falling in love, as he had with Esmeralda, he wanted to sample the sensation again. He knew that he was a simple man who should never have dived head-first into the pool of promise that women make for men, he should have stayed forever at its edge. He could have tested the water, dipped a finger to see how hot and genuine it was. Trailed a finger through edges rippling with seduction, flattery and tenderness; weighed up sincerity, and more importantly, insincerity. But he should never, ever, have precipitated himself into the fathomless mystery that is a woman, not Charlie. He and Lucy had drifted together and then, without causing a stir in the flowing flotsam of aimless interaction, they had drifted apart. Floating by were other women too, but were they after a watch or a camera or new clothes or shoes from BATA? Had they been talking to Esmeralda he wondered bitterly? Life had been unfair to Charlie. He loved women so much that sometimes he felt his heart would burst from having so much love and nothing or no one on which it could be lavished. This was his life; it had always been this way; in Tala and now in Katamara and then back to much the same in Tala when he returned

How he wished he could be more like Freddie Bristow. How he envied Freddie's looks, stature, personality and confidence with women. He had charisma, that indefinable quality of radiance, the one pearl so bright among others, so prized but so incredibly elusive. One cannot learn charisma; it is neither physical nor spiritual but metaphysical, an inner core bestowed some time in lineage, designed for the future to blossom in a chosen one. Freddie had charisma and so had Esmeralda; which one would be swallowed by the bigger? Charlie had heard the rumour that Freddie was visiting her in Busia. Freddie had gone there the last two weekends; why else would he go to Busia? Everybody was gossiping about this new romance. Everyone knew because Adonis knew. But they didn't know why Freddie had returned on the two consecutive Sunday nights increasingly miserable. Charlie had a good idea why, because the same thing had happened to him. Anyway, Freddie could have her. The girl was a lost cause to him now and he was coming to terms with life without her. Charlie wondered about this new liaison. Freddie had so much more pride than he, Freddie had a history of triumph over women, Freddie, with too much drink in him, had, one night, talked of bedposts, back home in England, that couldn't hold the notches. And a married man with children too. Freddie must be terribly frustrated because he wasn't a man to chase lost causes.

Freddie and Esmeralda; they deserved each other. Charlie had another woman in mind. Jennifer Collins was so vulnerable now she even made Charlie feel confident. She seldom ventured into the marketplace and when she did, she was withdrawn. It was obvious; she hadn't got over the death of Kennedy.

Yes, he feared making the same mistake with Jennifer as he had made with Esmeralda. Jennifer had been his first love, but having never declared it, she had never known. Charlie knew that he could fall in love with Jennifer again, and with the same passion; he also knew that, this time, he had a chance for, no longer, was she quite so unattainable. She used to be so nice to talk to, friendly, so nice to listen to, that purring enunciation that she had brought with her from her lyric land. It had gone now but could Charlie bring it back? There were rumours abounding in the village that Kennedy's death was not an accident. No one accused Jennifer outright of being a murderess but the implication could be seen weighing on her like a millstone. So heavy was her burden, she could barely raise her eyes from the ground. There were occasions when Charlie had got angry. The verdict was accidental death and to suggest otherwise was a vile, malicious defamation of character. Was it any wonder that the nurse's visits to the village were now infrequent and often early in the morning when there was hardly anyone to look at her.

Charlie was wise to her new routine and he was still able to bump into her on her brief shopping trips, or again, by happenstance, meet her as she was leaving the hospital, and how before every coincidental meeting, he would have the words ready on the tip of his tongue to ask her, if one evening, just as friends, they might go for a meal or a drink somewhere, and how, after every coincidental meeting, he would curse himself for cowardice.

Early morning and it was a week since he had last seen her. They met at a market stall and she was choosing fruit. Words slipped from his tongue of their own volition; they had waited so long that the wariness that restrained them simply gave way beneath the weight of procrastination. 'Jennifer, would you like to have a drink with me one evening?'

She was handling a pineapple, big and ripe and yellow. She said, 'That would be nice.'

Struck dumb by the immediacy of her acceptance, he had no idea what to say. Had he heard her correctly? Had she said 'that would be nice'? Was she talking about his proposal or about the ripe and yellow pineapple she held in her hands? He felt awkward and flustered and he felt himself blushing.

She saw his distress and rescued him by placing her fingers gently on his wrist and saying, 'That would be nice, Charlie. Really Charlie – yes – I need to get out. Let me know when it suits you. Really, any evening at all is fine with me. I'll look forward to it.'

Tonight, tonight, Charlie's brain was screaming. Oh blissful day, where had his courage come from? Fortune does, indeed, favour the brave and he was brave, and who was Esmeralda but a capricious adolescent, paling to inconsequence beside a real woman. She would be his woman for the evening, and he would be so proud to be seen with her, and her lovely words, like poetry, would be addressed to him and he would pick a busy place so that there would people there who would look at them and envy him.

'Not in Katamara, maybe somewhere else,' she prompted.

No not this evening, this evening was reserved for luxurious thought, plans. He was a giant now, ten feet tall he was. He hooked a thumb in his belt and held her gaze. 'I was thinking perhaps one evening this week. Oh Jennifer, we will be fine in Katamara.' He wanted to show her off in his own village. Make other women envious. Maybe even Esmeralda would get to know of it. 'Another time we could have a drink in Donya Sabuk. Anywhere, I'll have the truck, Thika if you like, anywhere. But please, the first time here in Katamara.' He wanted to show his support for her, restore the loving status she once had. Charlie was the man to do it. Oh how grateful would she be?

Picking up a hand of bananas, she examined them closely before giving them to be wrapped by the cherubic lady minding the stall. 'Charlie, I'm not happy in Katamara anymore.'

'Please trust me, Jennifer.'

She did.

Giddy with courage and accomplishment, he walked homeward

as if on air, and the stirrings in the deep bush at either side of him were the small and the defenceless and the hunted, he was one of them and they had gathered to honour him. The iridescence of superb starlings dazzled him: two black and white butterflies, like dominoes, tumbled above his head along the path. And the trees were full of chimpanzee again, they had come down from the mountain to applaud him. How beautiful this mountain path with all its wonders. All that evening he wandered the house, joy coursing through his blood, enlivening his senses and he grasped greedily at every sound and sight because all were pleasing to him. In the air, a change of fortune, no longer ephemeral; Nurse Jennifer Collins was more than mere promise.

Titus arrived, and was without his smile. He entered the house trailing gloom. Lamplight fell faintly on a small stack of photographs which he put on the table for Charlie's attention; they bore testimony to the life of his father, suddenly and unexpectedly dead. Charlie fiddled with the knob until the flame was maximized; and complete blackness fell outside the orb of light. Within the orb, Titus talked of his father, a man of quiet life and quiet loves and of the *shamba* where he sired his children. The orb was melancholy with remembrance as Titus dwelt on that dominion of the dead to which his father had gone with such little notice, and his eyes dimmed in sorrow at the insurmountable distance between the earth of the son and the heaven of his father. 'He had a pain and went to bed with his pain, and suddenly the pain was gone but he was gone with it and was no more. November is a bad month, my mother passed on in November. December is the happy month and I do wish Decembers would come around more often. Tomorrow we will take him to his Mavaloni home and he will be buried next to my mother, who has resided there for many Novembers. There are orange trees at the bottom of the *shamba* and many of my family lie in that quiet place, so he will not be lonely with company that he knows well.'

Leafing through the photographs, he handed one to Charlie. It was of himself as a young boy, standing with an older man against a back-drop of burgeoning crops. The older man, his father, was wearing a checked shirt and baggy trousers and was only slightly bigger than his son. A pale sky embraced a tender, but unsmiling face of the father, as, with legs astride, he stood on ground lush green with achievement and his small fists were clenched against the vagaries of nature.

'My father was very hard working and very wise,' Titus told Charlie proudly. 'Working hard to keep hunger from our home. "Always work hard in your *shamba*, Titus," he would say to me, "for when the rains don't come, you will see that the people who are able become less able and then poor, and poor people become even poorer, to become very poor. And those that were very poor before the bad times, with no rain, are no longer very poor because, they are dead from starvation." Those words of my father are very wise, Charlie.'

'They are very wise,' Charlie answered as he began fingering through the photographs on the table.

Even though Charlie knew well his wife and children, Titus pointed them out, extoling innumerable talents and virtues with which they had been blessed.

'Why do Kenyans never smile on photographs, why does everyone always look so solemn?' Charlie wondered aloud but didn't await an answer. He had come to half a dozen photos of his own house on the mountain, taken from different angles. Stunned, he inspected one taken from the path below. He held it close to the light. 'Jesus Christ,' he gasped. Titus leaned forward closer, to the light, to see what had provoked the blasphemy. 'When was this taken?'

Titus shook his head. 'I don't know. I have taken many photos of this house, many times.'

'Have you seen this?'

Titus took the photograph from Charlie's hand and turned it over to see if anything was written on the back, nothing was. He examined it. 'I cannot see anything,' he croaked, disturbed by the agitation in Charlie's voice. 'What is it that you see?'

The luxurious conception of Jennifer Collins inhabiting his heart and soul was gone, replaced by a large spider crawling up his back, its hairy legs astride his spine. It was tickling at the nape of his neck. This spider had fangs. They drove into the nape of his neck as he pointed a finger at the house. 'Look:' his finger trembled.

Titus tilted the photograph further under the light, tipping a shape towards the upstairs window of the house. He took a shallow breath and put a finger to his mouth: 'Never have I seen that thing before now.'

The two men's eyes fixed upon a shape in the window. It was as if an artist had let his brush fall against the glass, a cloudy female form was crouched towards the window, a featureless form of bluish white, insubstantial in reflection of the trees. There was nothing strange about the print; above the house the sky was pale, a few small clouds rimmed yellow in the sunlight, gentle shadows on the porch. The shape seemed to be moving towards the window as if to call to someone. Both men were visibly shaken.

'It is—' Titus ventured.

'It is the same girl I saw in the window the day that Freddie came,' Charlie breathed.

Chapter Twenty-Seven

*T*he Habari Hotel where Esmeralda was a chamber maid was on the outskirts of Busia and Freddie was irritated that, not once, had he been invited to step inside. She had never properly explained how she had come to land the job, a friend of a friend who knew someone of influence: that kind of correlation, but the proprietors, black of face and grey of manner, had nothing to do with the unbridled evangelism of the Church of the Ever Open Door. Freddie, in reality, was past irritation and had become bitter. Nowadays, and uncharacteristically, he carried the air of a man uncertain of himself, quick to argue and quick to agree, appeasing and prone to answering his own questions. He often found himself staring abstractly into space, or being inordinately angry with native serving staff, these unwanted peculiarities he tried to ascribe to overwork and heat but he knew what really caused them, it was the girl. He had invested a lot of money in this girl, and was no nearer to bedding her than he was those months ago when she first wantonly appeared on the building site. He hadn't taken her back to the Nairobi Hilton because she hadn't asked him to. She seemed content, for now at least, to trail him and his credit card around the shops of Busia, still unable to understand, and patently not wanting to, exactly, how such transactions worked. What definitely wasn't working anymore was Freddie's tried and trusted seduction techniques.

The scorching heat of the afternoon nourished globes of sweat on his brow, until they were plump enough to bowl down and scald his eyes. The sweat and the heat fogged his vision and he drove slowly. The wind through the open windows offered some relief, but it was sharp and dusty and carried the excreta of the town. He hated his feeling of bitterness that was growing more astringent daily but he was careful not to upset the delicate balance of amiability that he had managed to restore.

He attempted to lift his spirits. 'The letter you wrote to me, it was quite beautiful. I have never read a letter quite like it well, yes I have, once before, the letter you wrote to Charlie, I suppose, was much the same.'

With a native immunity to equatorial grilling, Esmeralda was sitting comparatively cool and composed beside him. She seemed as if she was about to answer, but instead chuckled sheepishly and bit into her bottom lip. Composing thoughts, she allowed a few moments to pass in silence before slapping her knee and saying with a laugh, 'Imagine, I stepped out of the streets of Paris onto Charlie and with you Freddie I became the Queen of Sheba, really it is quite sensitizing to me to know where I will end up next. But oh my God but I do say funny things in letters. I really do, and afterwards I think, Oh, my God, what have I said? God help me but I must be going mad to say such funny things, I think it is because half of the time I don't know where I am – Katamara – Nairobi – Busia – Paris—'

'So you don't mean what you say?'

'Oh Freddie, I always mean what I say at the time of writing, as I always write with my heart. And it feels good to write such letters as it lubricates my senses.'

'But the words are meaningless if you don't mean what you say.'

Turning in her seat, she lifted her eyebrows and provocatively poked out her tongue at him. 'Freddie, you know I have a sincere heart.'

'I don't know you at all,' he answered sourly.

She regarded him patiently, reading his thoughts. Presently she said, 'Freddie I know what is making you grumpy but I can't invite you into that place as those owners are very strict. The lady, she is cruel to me, and makes me frightened, but they pay me a wage each week so that I may help my family.'

'Cruel,' Freddie snorted. 'I don't see any bruises.'

'So far, the bruises are to my heart and to my soul.'

'I don't believe that you have been strictly forbidden to have a man visit you in your room. It's a hotel, for God's sake, there are people going in and out all day long.'

She was slow to answer, then, 'Men come to my door like children come to Charlie's door for chocolate. "Esmeralda do this, Esmeralda do that, Esmeralda I would like a cup of tea." But they are guests, and I must be nice to them, but a man of my own, never. Freddie I do not want to be beaten with a stick, which I feel in the waters of my being, would happen if I was to invite you in.'

The thoughts of her flirting with male guests boiled inside of him. He could see her tempting them, flashing her eyes and poking out her tongue as she did with him, her lips pink and wet and parted, she would drop keys on the floor and bend to pick them up and her skirt would ride up on her thighs and she would remain bending longer than she needed to, just as she did on site. He saw her at the door of her room, inviting men inside but equally, he saw the door shutting in their faces as they rose to the bait.

He knew the town well by now, and parked the truck close to its centre. It was surely the hottest day that he had ever known, the sun an angry glowing ball dissolving the earth, frying the sky; a few white clouds frizzled in the heat. He slumped out of the cab onto the pavement, and sweat that had gathered in the folds of his neck trickled down his spine. By contrast, Esmeralda vaulted from her seat and with steps so much lighter, more carefree than his, headed towards the clothes shop on a mission for new shoes for a wedding. He followed dismally, his mission to pay for them. He caught up with her and with drooping eyelids, she held his gaze before tossing her head to one side. 'Oh Freddie, you are sulking today, but one day soon everything will be perfect for us. I see a quiet place somewhere. Romance is only round the corner and we will turn that corner soon. For I am sure it is written in the heavens.'

A storm-cloud fell upon his soul and he felt his face flush with rage. Freddie Bristow was in the grip of promise. She had never refused his advances, but never permitted consummation. It had never quite been the right place or time: it was too hot, too cold, too wet, too dry, and she was the only girl he had ever known to have inconvenient visitations twice each month. His own lack of resolve, he put down to her being so much younger, kidding himself with recognition of a moral rectitude he knew did not exist; a drowning man, clutching at a promise being offered, fulfilment in easy reach, but impossible to grasp. What had happened to Bumble Bristow?

'I think it is that you have not forgiven me for being so sick,' she said, almost absently.

'I don't want to talk about that night.'

'Oh, it was a lovely night, until you got me sick.'

His anger could no longer be held in check. 'It wasn't me that got you sick, 'he spat out savagely. 'It was you, boasting how you were bloody weaned on *changaa*. You got yourself sick asking for more gin. I never told you this, but after I cleaned your vomit up, I gave the bloody taxi driver every cent I had, then leaving your cousin's place, it took me two hours to walk back to where I'd left the motor-bike, only to find that some thieving bastard, probably the porter, had syphoned the petrol tank. Then I had to wait for the agency to open up and borrow money to get back home.'

'I'm thinking that it must have been a punishment from God.'

'God?'

She put a finger to her mouth to suppress a giggle. 'God, paying you back for getting me drunk and making me sick.'

'I didn't make you drunk, I didn't make you sick.' He clenched his fist in livid rage and for the first time in his life, he almost struck a woman. 'You made yourself sick with being so bloody greedy.'

Oblivious to the level of his anger, Esmeralda said, 'It all began the day before, when I got called into the Church of the Ever Open Door and that saved boy came to me—'

Freddie cut in furiously, 'I'm sick to death of hearing about that bloody church. I don't know where you were that day, that night. I don't believe that there is such a church. I think you were screwing that saved boy.'

She laughed disarmingly. 'There is such a church and its door is ever open, Freddie.'

'What use is an ever open door if you can't find the fucking church? And that fucking saved boy. Stop calling him "that saved boy". He must have a name, for Christ's sake. He wasn't christened "That Saved Boy". What do they call him?'

'John.'

'Then for Christ's sake call him John. "That saved boy": it doesn't make sense. Saved from what, for God's sake?'

'Same as me, Freddie, saved from the evil inside of him just as I was. As I was passing the door I heard a voice calling to me "sister- sister".'

Freddie stopped her and swung her around to face him: 'Listen, The Church of the Ever Open fucking Door stripped you of your decent clothes and gave you rags in return, then conveniently vanished off the face of the earth. And that saved bloody boy, he's done a lot for you, hasn't he? Who was it bought you new clothes so that you could act the posh bird in the Hilton? Me, it's me that's done everything for you, not that bloody church, so don't mention it again to me and if ever I catch up with that saved boy I'll screw his bloody head off. Understand?' They were walking again.

'Ooooooo,' she cried in alarm then, with a little arresting skip of delight, she added, 'So much chatter and we almost passed the shop.'

'I'm waiting out here,' Freddie was so angry He felt he might explode.

'But I'm going to need you, Freddie,' Esmeralda said, with eyes like a wounded fawn.

'Of course you're going to need me. Who else is going to pay?'

She stood in the doorway one hand resting on the jamb, behind her. A young male assistant hovered expectantly.

'Oh Freddie, I don't like to see you looking so cross.' She pulled a sour face in imitation, to which he refused to respond. 'These shoes are for a special occasion and it might take some time.'

'I'll wait half an hour and not a minute more.'

'Half an hour,' she expostulated, 'these shoes are for the wedding of my auntie's kid. It will take me half an hour to decide what colour I want.'

'Half an hour, and that's it.' Freddie put his head close to hers so that the assistant couldn't overhear him. 'I'll pay for these shoes, Esmeralda, and then that's it. You'll get nothing more from me ever, it's over.'

'Oh Freddie please don't be so cross.'

'I do everything for you. It's time that you did something for me.'

She pulled her head backwards in alarm. 'What do you want from me that I don't give you?'

'I don't get anything from you. That's just it.'

'But you get love and affection, Freddie, and my company.'

He followed her with his face. 'You know only too well what I want from you.'

The girl had no idea what he was talking about and arched her eyebrows questioningly.

'You've messed me about long enough, Esmeralda. What I want from you is—'

'What?'

'You know what – you must know what.'

'Oh, that. But there's a problem.'

'What's the problem?'

'Your wife.'

He was stunned. She was inside the shop and already the assistant was fawning over her, conviviality between the two immediate. He had told everyone he was divorced. She knew he was married. Who else knew he was married? All his letters were delivered to the post office box in Katamara; he collected them himself and he had never told anyone he was married. The agency knew but it was their policy of confidentiality not to disclose an individual's personal circumstances to anyone outside the office. Moreover, if morality was an issue, she should have said so and saved him a lot of money. If adultery was a deadly sin then so was avarice. He stepped deeper into the shade.

Only yards away a small donkey pulling a cartload of timber, struggled through the heat, a bedraggled boy coaxing it along. The donkey's legs were trembling, its nose so low it almost touched the ground. Nothing was as it seemed. The leaves of trees hung limp beneath a suffocating sky, and the sky slumped helplessly on top of drooping buildings, and the drooping buildings melted into roads and littered paths, everywhere he looked a shimmering, sweltering melange.

Through gritted teeth he sucked in air. It was time to end this debacle of a romance. He looked through the window, Esmeralda was seated, the assistant was at her feet, and already shoe boxes were piling up around them. A man at her feet, men at her feet, who the hell did the deluded creature think she was, she really did imagine herself as the bloody Queen of Sheba? And who was the underling at her feet? Of course, a footman, a stooge, a Charlie Carter, but no more a Freddie Bristow. She wouldn't even get the half an hour he had promised. There might be rumour afoot but no one could know for sure that he was seeing Esmeralda and no one could possibly know how she belittled him. He would get out while he could, get out while he had an atom of self-esteem left in him. He glanced in the window again. The assistant was still at her mercy, the pile of boxes getting higher, he was on all fours, like a puppy soon to grow into a snarling cur when he found out she couldn't pay. It was Freddie's turn, big embarrassment for the Queen of Sheba, thrown out of the shop and how inconvenient would be a four-mile walk back to the Habari Hotel on a day that threatened to melt the earth. She would be late; what he would give for the proprietor's wife to be waiting for her with a stick. He had once heard it said that those who bite the hand that feeds them are sure to lick the boot that kicks them. He would put that adage to the test. Let the bitch come running after him.

He left, as he promised himself he would and he didn't look back.

'I think he's gone,' Esmeralda said and laughed. 'And he says I'm not allowed to call you "That Saved Boy" anymore.'

Chapter Twenty-Eight

*I*nspector Wamiru was sitting at his desk, painfully contemplating the stacks of paperwork in front of him. He groaned; at least seventy-five per cent of it was irrelevant. It was how masters controlled their minions nowadays, not with whips and chains but with scribble and script. It was much as the commandants of concentration camps controlled their inmates. Wamiru wasn't being compelled, day after day, to heave huge rocks from one end of a camp to the other and back again until debilitated by despair and exhaustion. No, his was to shift paperwork around his desk but the end result was just the same. He got up from his desk and went to the window, viewing with tired resignation, the towering skyline and the tumult of activity beneath; nothing inspired him. Back at his desk, he switched his thoughts to Jennifer Collins – he had been thinking about her a lot lately – and more so since she had avoided his eye at the window. Yes, he had given her a hard time: questioned her relentlessly, but he had exonerated her, befriended her. He was genuine in his belief in her but he knew that no longer did she trust him. She was an unusual woman. She was driven. In his experience, driven people were either very good or very bad. They were ordinary people nonetheless, the significance being in what or who was driving them. He decided that, in Jennifer's case, it was something good.

The ring of the telephone startled him. He snatched the receiver. It was Charlie Carter. Wamiru was pleased to hear his voice; a relief from paperwork. They exchanged pleasantries but Charlie's voice was weighted with gravity. 'Inspector, something happened last night in Katamara and I've been awake all night worrying about it and wondering who I could turn to. It was something that shocked me. I couldn't handle it. Something has to be done but I don't know what. I was with Jennifer Collins, just a quiet drink in the Jaffa bar. She has not been well, ever since—'

Wamiru was doodling; a little unsmiling, oval face. 'Since the boy died, since the investigation,' he finished.

Charlie began speaking again, his words rushed. 'Jennifer agreed to go for a drink with me but she didn't want to go in the village, not Katamara. Even though you have given her the all-clear there are still rumours, heard them myself, some people in the village believe that Jennifer—' He paused. 'Last night she told me, how uneasy she was. It was why she hasn't been seen in the village too often lately. She feels that everyone is accusing her. I told her not to be silly, it was only her imagination. I told her that nobody thought that she had anything to do with that little boy's death. Seems I was wrong. Anyway, I persuaded her to go with me to one of the bars. Selfish of me, I wanted to be seen with her—' He hesitated, wanting a response.

Wamiru's stomach had twisted in a knot. He had doodled many oval faces. He began to ink them in, leaving two untouched. He didn't like what he was hearing. He didn't want to think of Charlie and Jennifer drinking together in a bar. Charlie and Jennifer – surely not; he had had the opportunity and had missed it. He couldn't lose out to Charlie Carter. 'OK Charlie, I'm listening.'

'We went to the Jaffa Bar, one of the bars in the market. Things were OK at first. There were a few people in the bar, regulars, maybe half a dozen men and one woman. Know her by sight, don't know her name. They spoke to me but I noticed that no-one spoke to Jennifer. Noticed there was an atmosphere, a really awful atmosphere. These people were talking among themselves but quiet like, whispering. Jennifer was getting agitated. I looked at the bar-man, Pius, don't know if you know him. Pius was looking uncomfortable. One of the men was a bit drunk, not falling about or anything, but he was louder than the rest. It was him that started it. He made a remark about the type of people that Pius was letting in to his place. He looked directly at Jennifer, no question who he was talking about. I asked him what he meant by a remark like that and he couldn't answer, just shrugged and kind of laughed it off. Jennifer had had enough, she stood up. "Charlie," she said, "just let's go, you see what I mean, please just let's go." I stood up and I said, "We're not going anywhere." Then the woman got really nasty. "Two kids," she kept saying, "two kids, two little black kids." She didn't accuse Jennifer of anything, no one said anything outright but no doubt about it, they were trying to drive us out of that bar. We had done nothing, we were just sitting there. We'd hardly got into conversation our-selves when it started. Pius was helpless, he didn't say anything, didn't take sides, just looked helpless. That group of people, they shouldn't be allowed to make accusations like that, something should be done.'

Whispers, so insubstantial they can't be challenged; above the law and free to roam at will. What chance innocence against such adversity, insidiously devastating, as malignant as any cancer. Wamiru sighed. 'They didn't make accusations, Charlie, not a lot can be done. They believe the rumours. They believe them to be true. They – want them to be true.'

Charlie cut in: 'Jennifer started crying. We got up to leave. I was absolutely furious. I turned on them. I was going to have a go at them, especially the loud bastard. Jennifer pulled me away. I was really looking forward to having a drink with her and those bastards ruined it. I had to take her straight back to the hospital. An innocent person should not be treated like that. On the way back to the hospital, she told me that she had been through something like this before and she couldn't stand it, she couldn't stand to go through it again. She said she would want to die first.'

Wamiru said, 'Everyone has something in their lives that they never want repeated.' He felt the need to defend himself. 'Charlie,

I made it clear to everyone that there was not a shred of evidence against Nurse Collins. Headlines in the nationals – Katamara – Nurse Jennifer Collins – Innocent – Accident- I was behind that. You can't stop people believing in something, even if we know that they are wrong.'

'And to call her racist, that was the final straw. Never have I—'

'Racist?' Wamiru interrupted.

'As we were going out the door, the woman it was, 'Racist,' she mumbled. She may have been aiming it at me, but I don't think so, it was aimed at Jennifer. For sure Jennifer knew that it was aimed at her.'

The quietude of Wamiru's office had been energised by a single word. There might be enough conjecture in the marketplace of Katamara to imply that the woman might be a murderess but none at all to suggest she was a racist. He noticed that he had inadvertently scribbled out his oval faces, leaving only one untouched. 'Charlie, I can't promise anything, but if I can do something about it, I will.'

Chapter Twenty-Nine

*A*bsence did not make her heart grow any fonder and adages did not apply to Esmeralda. No doubt, she had a tendency to bite hands that fed her but it didn't follow that she would lick boots, any boots, and certainly not Freddie's. For Freddie, this indifference was hard to bear. Contrary to his expectations, he had not seen or heard from her since the afternoon he had unceremoniously dumped her in the shoe shop in Busia. He had hoped to find her looking sheepish at his door, or at least to receive one of her bizarrely eloquent letters. Why had he left her? What had she done? The man in the shoe shop had been so angry. She had to walk all the way back to the hotel where she got beaten with a stick. Oh what she would do for one last chance. Oh Freddie, Freddie please forgive her. No way. No, he had no illusions about her now. The girl was unequivocally mercenary and the most fickle creature that he had ever met. The problem was, he was still in love with her. The eye he turned away from her peccadillos was not blind, but admissible. That's what love does to even the biggest cynic.

He knew that he was expending too much concentration, far too much energy and far, far too much money on the girl; his conduct was bordering on the obsessive. One of his abiding maxims on life, had been, hitherto – Don't fight too hard for something not worth winning – too frustrating, too exhausting. Yes, he did love her but the inescapable truth was something more important than love, Freddie wanted back his self-esteem; one last chance of another notch on a bedpost, He must return home to England in triumph, but he'd never met before a bedpost notch like this one.

And so, having given up on reverse psychology, he set off to Busia again, full of wishful thinking and smouldering discontent. He deeply resented all the money he had spent on her without reward, and he felt guilty too. His wife had been working full-time in Tala for the upkeep of the family, while Esmeralda had been spending all his money. Really, the girl had a lot to answer for. He glanced at his sullen face in the rear-view mirror, feeling inadequate; he couldn't rehearse what he would say to her without knowing her reaction to his return. How he had despised Charlie Carter for the way he had allowed himself to be treated, but he had a grudging respect for the man now at how he had got over the girl so quickly, notwithstanding the bigger fool he was about to make of himself with Jennifer Collins. He tried to reassure himself; there was not a woman living that could turn him into a Charlie Carter. Maybe she would respond to him warmly, he hoped so. He would rebuff her of course, but not for long, her slightest show of contrition and she would be in his arms again.

The Habari Hotel was a two storey, block-built building of considerable proportions, and although he had never been per-mitted to cross the threshold, the entrance door had always been ajar. Today it was wide open. He peered inside the empty lobby and called, 'Helloooo.'

He kept calling until a huge breasted servant lady, with the blackest skin that he had ever seen, materialised before him. He had expected one of the allegedly grim proprietors, so it was a pleasant surprise to find this woman, with eyebrows raised in expectation, grinning broadly. Freddie smiled and raised his eyebrows too.

'Do you think I could speak with Esmeralda?' he enquired.

The lady's smile faded, her eyebrows plummeted and her mountainous twins fulminated in reproof. 'She is no longer here at this place. She is a bad girl and the owners are not happy with that girl.'

Freddie's smile disappeared. He waited for further explanation, none forthcoming. 'When did she go?' he asked.

'A few days ago, one day she is here and the next day, she is gone. She is paid her wage and then she is gone, leaving the hotel in a big fix. She was treated well here but no goodbye, just gone with all her stuff.'

'Do you know where she went?'

The lady shrugged her heavy shoulders and her breasts shuddered in correlation. 'No one knows, and it does not look good for the owners of this place that a servant girl, she go so quickly without an explanation.' There was no smiling now, the thought of Esmeralda's fallaciousness souring a natural effervescence.

'Do you know if she left with anyone, a boy perhaps?'

'I think she must have left with someone, for I never saw a girl with so much stuff.'

'Yes, she has a lot of stuff, I bought most of it.'

He thanked the lady kindly. Wilful and inconsiderate Esmeralda would have acted on impulse, without a thought to consequence. She would not think of herself as selfish, her life was her own, and come what may, she was determined to make the best of it. How she would deal with the inevitability of consequence was what made her so unique, it was what gave her that indefinable quality.

So, immersed in vexation and souring the air he breathed, it was back to Nairobi, and her cousin's place.

'Oh it's the man who cleaned the sick up again. I told her you had called. She left here with a boy,' her cousin told him.

'Thanks.'

'She remembered you.'

'She remembered me! Well aren't I the lucky one? This boy, was it a saved boy?'

Esmeralda's cousin did not recognise sarcasm. 'A boy she is deeply in love with.'

'Called John?'

'Yes, they are to be married and live a happy life. I think they have gone to Embu where his family comes from.'

'Did she leave a message for me?'

She eyed him closely. 'No, but I know she is grateful to you.'

'For cleaning her sick up?'

So what had never truly begun was over, his legacy: the man who cleaned the sick up. Could he deal with a failed relationship as Esmeralda would, with all the emotional sensibility of a blood-axe? Christmas was getting close and there was no way he was spending Christmas with Charlie Carter. Silly Charlie, now fawning over another lost cause; Charlie had more chance of success with his bloody ghost than he had with Jennifer Collins. Well, he would take one leaf from Charlie's book: cast Esmeralda aside. He doubted that she had gone to Embu, there was nothing for Esmeralda in Embu.

There was plenty of street-meat in Nairobi. And he wondered if he could find Aisha again. He had a better chance of finding Aisha than he had of finding Esmeralda.

Where was Esmeralda? She had already returned to Uamani to spend Christmas with her family. As soon as she had found out that her beloved saved boy was expected to give half of his earnings to The Church of the Ever Open Door, the romance was over.

Chapter Thirty

*T*he late afternoon was very hot. As the sun was sinking, so its heat increased, sending strobes of firelight through the branches of the trees, viciously intolerant of anything in haste beneath its glare, even thermals dared not raise their wings from the base of the desiccated mountain.

Wamiru sat at a table outside a bar, drinking a coke and watching the police station. He was waiting for Adonis to return. He was surprised to find that he did not feel anger and was pleased; he dealt with difficult issues better when he wasn't angry. Why get angry at the frailties of human nature: jealousy, falsehood, malpractice, baseness, culpability, dishonour. Moral deficiency, which everyone is heir to? But there is also truth with its ever present attendant, humour; human nature has that too. Men can play with truth, distort it, twist it to their own advantage, infuse it with untruth until it is barely recognisable, deny its existence but when all equivocations are unravelled, truth will remain unassailable and indisputable, making life congenial and blessed. But with some people a little duplicity is necessary to winkle truth out of a shell of lies.

Whatever Wamiru thought of Adonis, he had to take his hat off to him as far as crime prevention and local intelligence was concerned. He had looked it up. Yes, Katamara had the best crime prevention record in the area. Wamiru didn't like the corporal, doubted the fidelity of his methodology but had to admit, it seemed to work.

He swept his eyes across a field of vision containing people going about their daily tasks. Children, in defiance of the sun, ran squealing through the jacaranda blossom, their feet dusting their playing ground in different hues of blue and purple. Adonis in uniform strolled along the street towards him. He was wearing shades and had an unlit cigarette in the corner of his mouth. He was an imposing sight and Wamiru could understand how the *wanachi* of the village were in awe of him; his persona, undoubtedly inherited from some American movie, a cop movie or a Western. He was supplied with a gun, but only permitted to wear it when specific occasions demanded. Wamiru imagined the regret with which Adonis donned his uniform each day without a six-gun fastened to his hip.

Did Adonis have an Achilles heel? Yes, a big one, his ruinous vanity. Across the street, their eyes met and Adonis jolted to a stop and spat his unlit cigarette to the ground. Wamiru waited for the corporal to march across the street to greet him.

They shook hands and Adonis sat at the table facing his superior. 'I have been about my business, sir. Each day I am on duty I patrol every corner of this place, always watching, always listening. The *wanachi*, they feel safe knowing I'm around.'

'Corporal Adonis, I have been looking up the records and Katamara, without doubt, is the most crime-free village in the area. And I know that you run this village unaided. This is very much to your credit.'

Adonis' face hung humbly and his eyes rested on his fingers. He studied them regretfully as if each one characterised a calibre of duty; he appeared disheartened that there wasn't more than ten. 'But of course, sir. It is my only wish that the people of Katamara can rest safely in their beds knowing that Corporal Adonis is ever watchful over them.'

Wamiru replied readily, 'I think it is somewhat unfair that you have not been promoted. This is a big village. Its population—'

Adonis cut in. 'Almost a town.'

'I'm thinking that perhaps you were right about some things

239

and I should have listened to you during our investigation. There is much talk at HQ right now.'

The corporal raised his eyes from his fingers. He was right about everything, just what rectitude of his was the inspector referring to? 'Sir, if it is to do with Katamara, then you can be sure of it.'

Wamiru was thoughtful. 'Rumours are very strong about Nurse Collins.'

'That woman, Inspector, she is suffering much just now. Hardly dare she show her nose out of the hospital door. No longer does she swan about the market. No longer does she look down her nose at people. I know people are saying that maybe she did kill that kid. Me, I tell them, no, Inspector Wamiru found that last kid's death to be an accident. But it is good that she knows her place. It is good that the people of this village no longer bow to a *musungu* woman.'

Wamiru stroked his jaw. 'Yes, you spoke to me about this before, but she is a good woman.'

'But people must look up to the law.'

Wamiru said, 'It is maybe a good thing that she's fallen somewhat from grace. How we fought to get rid of the whites, yet we are giving them important positions in the community. Now don't misunderstand me, Corporal, I like Miss Collins. She does a fine job at the hospital but it isn't right that a white should have so much influence.'

Adonis laughed. 'That woman, she hasn't got so much influence now, Inspector. I think she is a good woman too. And if only she feared me a little, then all things could be different. But I think she is fearing me much just now.'

'The law must come first, Adonis,' Wamiru conceded gravely.

Adonis tapped his nose. 'I know my people, Inspector, they listen to Adonis and they fear me a lot. How is it that I keep this place so well-kept?' A man cruelly carrying half a dozen live chickens, upside down with a noose around their collective legs slowed and saluted the two men with his free hand. 'Cuckoos for sale,' he explained in a sing-song voice. He passed them by.

'That man Joseph Odinga, he fears me a lot and gives me cuckoos free.' Adonis said, taking off his shades and inspecting his reflection. 'I wonder, Inspector, when you are back at HQ if it would be a good idea to tell higher-ups about my running of this place and how right I am about things.'

The heat flailed. Adonis took off his cap and wiped his brow with the back of his hand. 'That is exactly what I'm here to see you about,' Wamiru said. He lapsed into deep thought, long enough to see a puzzled look cloud the corporal's face. Then he continued worriedly, 'I was at a meeting of senior officers, a seminar they call it, and the issue of crime prevention was raised. I brought up Katamara and the way you ran it as an example. But I got—'

'It is good sir that you spread that news,' Adonis interrupted.

'Shot down,' Wamiru finished.

'You got shot down?' Adonis puzzled.

'They were laughing at me, laughing at Katamara, laughing at us.' Wamiru leaned across the table and gripped the man's arm in a show of victimized consolation.

Adonis put his shades back on his nose, not this time for effect but to hide his eyes and fumbled a cigarette from a packet on the table. The bar-man came to their table questioningly. Wamiru shook his head, waved him away and gestured Adonis to his feet. Flies started to bother them. They began to walk slowly towards the hospital playing field. The ground was hot through the soles of their shoes. 'I don't understand, sir,' Adonis said.

Wamiru began to speak very softly, almost inaudible, so that Adonis had to tilt his ear so close to his superior that their heads almost touched. 'I think there is a big problem in Katamara and it is beginning to affect me greatly,' he began.

Adonis chewed the end of his cigarette.

'Someone in your town is spreading false rumours about Nurse Collins.'

Adonis tried to spit out his cigarette but his mouth was dry, the paper stuck to his lips. 'That cannot be, sir, surely I would know of it.'

Wamiru continued, the tenor of his voice still very low. 'Because of all this talk about Nurse Collins, gossip has spread all around the mountain, the story is in Nairobi, even the national newspapers are getting interested. It's all over HQ and my superiors are now doubting my judgement.' Flies had followed them, buzzing at their faces. The men swiped at them in turn. 'Word is going around that the nurse is guilty after all and I am beginning to look a fool.' To rid themselves of flies, they increased their pace. The flies moved with them. 'When I tried to praise you and your running of Katamara they laughed at me.'

Adonis gulped. 'But that should not be – it should—'

Wamiru sucked his teeth and shook his head slowly. 'These rumours must be stopped.'

Adonis shook his head slowly too. 'Then I will find this man, sir, and I will stop it. Maybe this guy did not intend for the rumours to go beyond Katamara.'

'That is likely, Adonis, but once someone decides to spread something, how does he stop it spreading? I'm losing credibility daily. There is talk of re-opening the investigation and putting someone else in charge. How can I put a good word in about anybody with higher-ups if I have lost my credibility?'

Adonis' lips were dry, his throat was dry; the sun was merciless. Beads of sweat were forming on his brow. Flies were landing on his face. The men entered the playing field and sheltered beneath a heavily blossomed jacaranda tree. Flies sheltered with them. He stared out over the playing field and his face screwed up in consternation.

Knowing that a man's great strength is also his biggest weakness, especially when it is not entirely bona fide, Wamiru raised the preventative methods of the corporal's administration. 'Because of all this gossip, I know that right now that there is a chief superintendent at HQ looking closely at what is going on in the village of Katamara.'

'About Nurse Collins?' Adonis gurgled.

'That yes, but once rumour gets a hold, it knows no boundaries. There is now much talk about torture.'

'Torture!' The corporal began to splutter denials. Torture! In Katamara? How could such a thought ever enter the head of any policeman, much less the head of Adonis Musyoka? Do not men and women have rights entrenched in human dignity? Was not a policeman entrusted by the *wanachi* to uphold the law of the land? Was not torture an abhorrent evil to every right thinking man? Katamara village, of which Corporal Musyoka was in charge, was a torture-free zone, an illuminative example of wholesome co-existence. 'I never tortured no one, sir. This is all very untrue.'

'But I've heard you talk of it, Corporal. Even boast of it.'

'Talk, talk, sir, it is to make men fear me,' Adonis gulped.

'All this talk must stop, it is not good for either of us but I just don't know how to do it, how to turn it around.' Wamiru sounded defeated.

'I think I know what must be done, sir. Rumour about torture and Miss Collins must be stopped.'

The inspector could not keep admiration from his eyes, his voice. 'You do?' The flies had gone and Adonis, after bidding his superior an ingratiating farewell, was worriedly hurrying towards the village

Ubiquity is the nature of the conscientious policeman and that night it was reported that Corporal Adonis was moving about the village and talking to people as if he was on some kind of mission.

A week later, Wamiru called at the hospital, met with Jennifer Collins and persuaded her to come for a drink with him. She appeared much more contented with herself and agreed. But not the Jaffa Bar. But Wamiru insisted and the Jaffa Bar it was. They had a good night, the best that both had had for a long time. It was on their way back to the hospital that Jennifer asked him if he was married.

Chapter Thirty-One

*I*t was early December and the rain of the short season, which had begun drizzling in October was now falling torrentially on the mountain and the villages around. Charlie was sitting on a sheltered bench with a view of the market. He watched the rain swiping at the last of the blossom of a jacaranda tree and the yellow blossom of a tipu tree. An hour earlier, when he had first sat there, it had been one of those glorious sunny days that intersperse the short rains; fresh and golden for being well-watered, everywhere resolution springing from the lusty earth. Charlie had been meditatively studying his fingernails, cleaning them with a matchstick and looking forward to seeing Jennifer Collins on the tomorrow evening, when mid-afternoon, the rain had swept down from the mountain without warning. He waited until the rain eased then he made his way to the nearest pub.

Charlie had entered a world he didn't know existed, and his heart was joyful. His countless disappointments were forgotten in a ferment of arousal, and he was whistling tunelessly as he left the pub for his house. Some arbitrating angel had, at last, decreed reward for his charitable nature. Not that he had ever looked for reward, he told himself, but surely he deserved something nice to happen to him every once in a while. He wasn't tired of giving of himself to those forever queuing up to take, but, sometimes, he despaired at the lack of appreciation afforded him. But, now, all that he had given was being returned a thousand fold and the world, for once, seemed to balance in his favour.

Jennifer was happy again and her life was getting back to normal. Inspector Wamiru was somehow responsible because everything had improved from the moment he had ended his telephone conversation with him. What Wamiru had done and how he had done it was a mystery, one day Charlie vowed to ask him. Jennifer was showing him genuine affection. He could tell that it was genuine because he had encountered so much of the other kind. She had been visiting him on site, vicariously enjoying the concept and construction of the accommodation block and already, they had had a number of nights out together and most of them in Katamara. And they were good nights, full of laughter and tomorrow, they were meeting in The Taifa Bar in Donya Sabuk because Charlie had the truck. Jennifer didn't want a watch or a night out at the Hilton. Had Charlie, at last, found a woman with a good heart, capable of unconditional kindness? He dared to hope that he had and that was why his own heart was full of joy. He had heard rumour that Esmeralda was back with her people in Uamani but he hadn't seen her and didn't miss her.

As he made his way home, the night was only an hour old and was already sprinkling with stars while an emergent moon embraced the earth tenderly, timelessly. He had spent the whole day in a state of euphoria. Never had he shaken so many hands, and never had so many children been rewarded in his wake. He had done a little shopping, a little drinking and a lot of talking. There was laughter in his voice and lightness in his step that the people had not seen for some time, and they commented on it as he divided his time among them. They were glad about it, for Charlie Carter in a happy frame of mind was good news. The alcohol warmed his blood as he grew nearer to the house, but it was not its beguiling effects that made him blink and doubt his eyes. Someone, or something, had moved through the night-shadows of the porch. He stopped and froze as he perceived movement again, and his mouth dried and his heart beat madly in his breast. Was she here again, the girl? It could not be; the dead are shy, they know they shock the living?

It could not be Titus either, too early, and it was not Freddie, he would know of it if Freddie had returned. There was no one in the house but there was someone hiding in the shadows of the porch. Charlie's heart withered, more beer was needed for him to face a ghost. He turned back towards the village; he would wait for Titus on the bridge. But courage is mutable; sometime strong, sometimes weak, and often absent altogether, but conditioned as it often is by feelings of well-being, it was stronger in Charlie than it had ever been in all his life. Turning on his torch and whistling again, he walked purposefully in the direction of the house. He stopped before ascending the steps but there was no sound and nothing could be seen. As the beam of his torch searched the black corners of the porch, he called to Shula softly. Was it his imagination, had it been imagination all along? There was no movement, and no sound but the echo of his voice and his heart began to beat again. And then a shape unravelled, and, although enlisted in dark shadow, it was manifestly human. Now he froze and his heart beat madly again. It was a girl, whispering with a tremor in her voice, 'It is you, Mr Charlie?'

Charlie croaked soundlessly as a girl materialized in the light of his torch. It was the girl that he had seen that day with Freddie, the spectre at the window.

'Yes,' Charlie breathed. He played the beam into the girl's face and she dropped her head. Charlie was still afraid. 'You have been to this house before.'

The girl did not answer or raise her head. Charlie put his hand to her arm, and her flesh was cold, but it was living flesh. He guided her to the door, and, inside, he lit the oil lamp, his fingers fidgety and nervous with the matches. Now he could see her clearly; she was slim and graceful, quite tall and very pretty, she might have been twenty-twenty-one years old. Who was she? She would not raise her head and she was trembling.

'I have been in this house three times before, each time with Freddie.'

'Freddie?' Charlie puzzled. 'And why are you here now?'

'Oh, I have been waiting outside since morning.'

'Since morning! But why?'

'For Freddie.'

Charlie took her to his room and sat her gently on a chair. Perching on the edge of his bed, he faced her. For the first time she raised her head, and he could see that her soft brown eyes were fearful.

'You have been waiting for Freddie since morning?'

'I was about to leave when I heard you whistling. I thought it might be Freddie, but when I saw that it was you I feared you, and tried to hide because I was fearing your anger too much.'

She was cold; she was shivering. From a closet Charlie took a heavy woollen jumper and draped it over her shoulders. She took the sleeves and pulled them tightly around her. Of course she was cold, she had been waiting on the porch since morning; she would be hungry too. Her lips parted, but words failed and her eyes were fixed upon her fingers now entwined together in her lap. Such was the abundance of love in Charlie's heart that he could not feel anger for anyone, much less a cold and hungry girl.

'Why should I be angry with you?'

'Mr Charlie, I am not Shula as you think.'

'I know that now.' Answers to unasked questions were settling incredulously but agreeably in his rationale. Already he knew that somehow he had been duped by Freddie and he chuckled inwardly at his own stupidity. 'Then who are you? What is your name?'

'I am Aisha.'

'And you were here with Freddie on that first day here at this house?'

'Please forgive me, Mr Charlie, it was not my wish but we have been fooling you this long time now.'

This time he laughed with bitter humour, 'You and Freddie?'

'Please forgive me, for I am not a cruel girl.' She looked so contrite, so forlorn, he wanted to comfort her, hold her, but like a captive bird, she trembled and fear and alarm, although subdued, were just below the surface.

'I know you are not a cruel girl, and I know I have been fooled, but how?'

Encouraged by his kindness, bolder words began to tumble from her lips: 'That day you saw me first, we came early, for Freddie wanted to show me where he was going to live. We were early so that you would not see us, no one would see us. Even I ducked low in the truck as we were passing you at your work, and even through the village. No one saw us, so quietly and quickly did we pass that day. Freddie would leave his stuff at the house and we would return to Nairobi. I was a secret girl. It was Freddie's wish that I be known to no one. And that was how we came to fool you. That day you came home from work early and you saw me at the window as I was looking around. We heard you calling for a dog and, oh it was such a shock to see you coming up the path. Freddie did not panic: "Just hide," he told me. So I hid in his room until all the stuff was emptied from the truck, then, when you went to wash after your work, we drove back to Nairobi with me ducking down again. And you thought I was the poor girl Shula, who had perished here so long ago. But I was the ghost girl, and Freddie thought it such a joke, and how he laughed and laughed. Every time he met me in Nairobi he had another tale to tell about you, believing in a ghost girl and hearing her knocking in the middle of the night. Freddie thought it was all so very funny—'

Charlie cut in, 'And the photo in the upstairs window, that was you.' Her brown skin reddened, her fingers wrestled.

'This is my big shame, Mr Charlie, for it was never my wish to fool you more. You were away the day it happened. You were away with a girl called Esmeralda. I was here for the day, but I must be returned before nightfall because of Titus. I came and went by *matatu*, all so very secret. In the afternoon Freddie saw Titus about to take pictures of the house, and I was pushed up those stairs into the room above. Freddie was laughing, the way he does when he is about to play a joke on people. I thought I was to hide again, but Freddie made me go towards the window, I was to be the ghost of Shula at the window. Then he heard nothing and he thought the photo had failed but after some time Freddie told me that the photo had been a success, and that you believed everything he had planned for you. He said that you were going mad, seeing ghosts and hearing knocking, and believing that the house was haunted. I swear, Mr Charlie, I hated what he was doing but I was helpless, still a secret girl. Then I did not see him anymore and I thought it was because of the jokes we had played on you. Oh, I have been so worried about those jokes we played on you, I thought even that you might have gone mad and that I would be blamed for being so cruel. And I have not seen Freddie for this long time now. I thought the only way was to be brave and come to this house. I wanted so much to see him again, to ask him where he's been this long time and also to explain to you these things that have worried me so.'

She was whimpering; she was about to cry. Once again, Charlie was moved to comfort her. This time he edged forward and touched her lightly on the back of her hand.

'I'm not angry with you, not even with Freddie.' He wasn't even angry with himself for being so naive. 'Yes, I truly thought this house was haunted. There is an awful story about a girl who was murdered here. I know that story to be true.'

Aisha was sniffling and dabbing her eyes ineffectually with a wet tissue. The jumper had slipped from her shoulders; Charlie stood up and replaced it tenderly. A large moth danced around the flame of the lamp, projecting alarming shadows on the ceiling and from outside the manic cackle of a chimp. He laughed shortly, derisory at the thought of himself moping through gloomy rooms, communicating with a dead girl. All along she was a living girl and the knocking that he had heard was that just the echoes of his own sad lament?

'Mr Charlie, I don't want you to think bad of me, I am a good girl. I have always been so frightened that because of circumstances

I might go the same way as my poor sister Elizabeth. For many years I was in a convent, my wish was to be a Holy Sister but then my sister got so ill, I had to leave to help look after her. Freddie has been the only one in all my life and he brought me here another time too, and I stopped the night. It was another night you were away. I think you were again with the girl, Esmeralda. I stayed the night, even with Titus at the door. Always quiet, always out of sight until I felt that I must be a ghost-girl after all.'

Tears began to appear in the corners of her eyes and when she blinked they flowed down her cheeks, fresh tears that had nothing to do with regret at her innocent duplicity, Charlie knew that she did not fear him anymore and he took both her hands in his and squeezed them reassuringly.

'Oh, Mr Charlie,' she sobbed, 'I love Freddie so much. He is the world to me, but I have not seen him for so long. He is avoiding me, and I fear my heart will break and I will die of sorrow. I live in Nairobi and we would meet in a certain street, the same street every time, and every day I go there and I wait and wait, sometimes I wait the whole day long, but he never comes. I think, surely, he must come to me again but no, so this morning I think I must come here, and ask him why. Many times I thought to come here and ask for him, but I did not because I was still his secret girl and also I was fearing the truth and fearing you. Oh, Mr Charlie, I know I will never see my love again.'

A wave of sadness washed over Charlie, it came from out of the same sea of suffering where he had once loved Esmeralda, and he understood her pain. No words of consolation could ever heal the wounds in this girl's heart, and he must tell her what he knew to be the truth about Freddie, and the virulent cruelty that lay behind his easy smile.

'Aisha, you must forget Freddie Bristow. He is not for you and he never will be. He has a wife and children in England, and now he is either in Busia or Nairobi, and he is probably with Esmeralda, yes the same Esmeralda who broke my heart as yours is broken now.'

Aisha withdrew her face from the cone of light, from life and the truth she didn't want to face; the life she might have had with Freddie and the truth of his abandonment. 'Oh a wife and children, oh my God, he never told me that.'

Charlie said, 'Aisha, you know Titus, my *askari*, well he will be here soon. You may stay here the whole night if you want; sleep in Freddie's room. I don't have the truck but I could take you back to Nairobi in the morning on the back of a motor-bike.'

'No, I cannot stay here the night. I would die, should Freddie return and find me in his bed.'

'Then maybe you can stay at the hospital for the night. I am friendly with the nurse there. She will arrange a bed for you.'

'Is the nurse, Nurse Collins?' Aisha asked.

Charlie turned his head towards her in surprise. 'You know Jennifer Collins?'

'That lady, I met her once when she attended to my sister and another time at a *harambee*. I saw you that day too but you did not see me, I was just in the crowd.'

'No, I don't ever remember seeing you before, except as the ghost in the window.' He shook his head ruefully and smiled grimly at the thought. 'Please stay, Aisha. I'll bring Jennifer to the house to-night. She will be most surprised and happy to see you, I promise.'

'There is *a matatu* soon,' Aisha said, glancing at the clock on the wall. 'It leaves just over one hour from now, and I must be on board for tomorrow I must be back with my family.'

Charlie took her hands again and squeezed them tightly. 'I will get you something to eat before you go, and the jumper you have around your neck, you will keep it. It's my present to you. Jennifer, Nurse Collins, and me, we must see you again. Perhaps not with Freddie here, maybe in the village, or we could meet with you in Nairobi, would you like that?'

She smiled weakly and put a wet tattered tissue in her pocket. 'Mr Charlie, you are good to me and I cannot believe now how I was fearing you so much. Please, I must have something to eat. I am very hungry and it is so important now that I eat well.'

Something in the girl's voice struck a cord and Charlie knew instinctively why she must eat well. He had been smiling. He wasn't now. 'Are you—?' The question loaded, searching.

'I'm with a baby, yes, for almost three months now.'

'Freddie's?'

'Yes.'

'And he doesn't know?'

'I was to tell him today. But it must be me that tells him. Please, please I beg of you, don't tell Freddie of my predicament, I would rather he never know than he be told by someone else.'

'No, I promise, Aisha, I won't tell Freddie.'

Titus knocked on the outside door. His footsteps could be heard, crossing the living room floor. He knocked again on the door of Charlie's room and entered. He looked shocked to see the girl, then a huge smile slowly spread across his face and he held out his hand, 'You are the girl in my photograph. This is the first time I am meeting with a ghost.'

PART FOUR

Shula

Chapter Thirty-Two

*E*xtract from a letter from Charlie Carter to his mother dated sometime March 1975

Mother, what a story I have to tell.

The Norfolk Hotel on Harry Thuku Street is as inescapable a part of Kenya as the Great Rift Valley and the Maasai Mara, an integral peg in the country's history. It was from the Norfolk that the riotous Lord Delamere conducted his lordly settlers to take over the White Highlands when he wasn't drunkenly careering down bar counters, during yet another evening of bawdy festivity.

The hotel had recently acquired another 'museum' piece to add to the ox-wagon and rickshaw exhibited in the garden as examples of hand-drawn, animal-drawn and machine propelled transport used in Kenya since the turn of the century. This new acquisition was a Ford Roadster, a 24-3 model manufactured in 1928, still roadworthy and of curiosity to Josiah Kariuki, who had an aesthetic if not technological interest in vintage jalopies. And it was in the hotel's 'museum' garden that Kariuki had arranged to meet his old friend Sam Wamiru.

After examining and discussing the rudimentary merits of the Model A Roadster they retired to one of the hotel's opulent lounges to reflect on old times and the new-time dynamics of government.

Kariuki had been re-elected as expected, due, he told Wamiru, in no small part, to the enormous success of his political rallies.

True to his word, Wamiru credited the organisational success of his last rally to Adonis Musyoka, the one-man crime-prevention guru of Katamara, a man for whom he now harboured a grudging respect and an intense dislike in equal measure.

The two men drank beer and talked and laughed and, in spite of a stream of well-wishers besieging their table to compliment Kariuki, they enjoyed a convivial and recreational evening.

It was time to go. Kariuki's driver was hovering politely but expectantly in an open doorway, dangling a bunch of keys. The politician acknowledged his chauffeur with a wave and a smile that stretched his trim moustache to twice its length.

Wamiru stood up first and, gripping his friend's hand, said, 'J.M. Please for all our sakes, moderate the criticism.'

The politician looked thoughtful for a moment, before answering wryly, 'I was re-elected, and it was my criticism that did it for me. The job's not done, Sam, it's only just started. I feel things inside me, work that must be done, the way things have worked out for me, as if they were meant to be.'

Wamiru gauged his friend admiringly, the steady eyes, the forthright manner, the fearless sincerity that had made him what he was. 'But give yourself some time, Josiah.'

J.M. grinned crookedly and tilted his head mockingly: 'You trying to say that I'm impulsive?'

'Inflammatory.'

The politician's eyes widened. 'You think I go too far?' He didn't wait for a reply. Wamiru's silence had answered his question. 'Look Sam, enough of politics.' Then, wanting to close the evening with something more valedictory, he hugged the policeman close to him and said accusingly, 'Sam there's one thing missing in your life and I'm not talking about your arm.'

Wamiru did not respond, pretending he did not know what his friend was alluding to.

'I can't believe you're still single.'

Wamiru's smile was apologetic as he nodded affirmatively.

'Sam Wamiru without a woman, it's just not right.'

Intuitively, his friend was probing at the woman-hunger Sam had learned to control. J.M. wanted Sam as he used to be. Sam himself wanted to be as he used to be. One day it will be, he often told himself.

'You haven't got over it?'

Wamiru grimaced. 'No I haven't. Not yet.'

'Well yes, I understand. It wasn't exactly an amicable parting of the ways. There were some extenuating circumstances,' J.M. remarked with grim facetiousness.

'You could say that.' The brevity of Wamiru's reply accentuated the bitterness in its tone.

'How is it now?'

'Still get pain even though it isn't there. Someone throws a ball at me suddenly, or a punch for that matter, someone threw a punch at me in the charge office last week. I raised both arms, still do, raise both arms instinctively to catch a ball or ward off a punch and I'm momentarily surprised when one arm isn't there.' Wamiru lowered his head and continued a little ashamedly, 'I never had a woman since I left the hospital with an arm missing. I've got so I imagine no woman could want me.' He laughed emptily. 'J.M., you've got me whinging about feeling incomplete.' He shrugged hopelessly. 'A woman wants a man that can hold her in his arms, both of them. A man can't say – darling come into my arm – doesn't sound right. I think of being in bed with a naked woman and throwing my stump around her. Silly things like that have got into my head, they've stayed there. Ever since it happened, I've been like a monk or a priest, coming to terms with celibacy. But it's not me, I know it. I think maybe in time I'll get my confidence with women again but it hasn't happened yet.'

'To a woman there's a more important appendage than an arm,' J.M. said and, grinning crookedly again, finished with, 'And if you don't use it – well – you know what they say.'

'Well with three wives, you should know,' Wamiru answered sardonically.

'I don't believe that you haven't got someone in mind.'

Wamiru nodded guiltily.

Kariuki studied his friend suspiciously. 'Who is it?'

There was no need to lie to his friend, waste of time anyway. 'It's the nurse at Katamara hospital, the white woman.'

'The nurse who was suspected of killing the little boy, I saw a photo of her in the newspaper. God, Sam you know how to pick 'em. Look at what the last small, white blonde did to you.'

It's not an offence to love someone and it's not an offence to pretend to love someone else. Christ, it happens all the time. That's why she got let off.'

'Clara should have got life.'

'Please J.M. I don't want reminding of it.'

'OK. This nurse, does she know how you feel?'

'She might guess.'

'What have you done about it?'

Wamiru looked shamefaced. 'That's just it, J.M. nothing. I took her for a drink once in the village. We had a good time, she was under a lot of pressure then but she was relaxed and I could tell that she was enjoying herself. We were close that night. You know when a woman looks you in the eye, she didn't say anything. She didn't have to. It could have happened that night, it should have happened. On our way back to the hospital she asked me if I had a woman. She was giving me another chance, but I didn't take it. I wanted to say something to her, do something, but each time my courage failed me. She couldn't want a man with a stump for an arm, that's what kept cropping up in my head. At the entrance to the hospital I said "goodnight", for God's sake I didn't even kiss her. I was disgusted with myself and I knew that she was disappointed with me. I've regretted it ever since.'

'Sam, don't leave it too late.'

'No. I've made my mind up to do something about it. Charlie the builder, you know of him, he's after her I'm sure of it. Somehow though, I can't see her and Charlie together although you never know. Christmas, that's the time, I'm going to go to Katamara. I'll call at the hospital, just to wish her a Happy Christmas. Hope she'll invite me in, she will, and I'll make my feelings known to her. Even if she rejects me I'll feel better knowing that at least I've done something about it.'

J.M. gripped Wamiru's shoulders. 'Sam, don't hesitate, and good luck.'

The driver, still at the doorway must have been close to his boss because he dared to cough and rattle his keys.

Chapter Thirty-Three

*T*he grey dubiety that had dogged him for most his life had not returned. A cloud of failure had lifted from Charlie. No longer was it his constant companion. The two voices in his head, the strident one advocating action, and the nervous one of restraint began to merge into one of shy assertiveness. For the first time he was contented with his fellow travellers and felt able to deal with what the day might bring. No more did he feel compelled to feed hope like coins into an insatiable slot-machine of relationships, without ever getting a win. Thought of the coming Christmas and New Year was laden with optimism and did not stretch stark and lonely, empty of promise. With Jennifer he didn't have to try so hard, and failure was not a terrifying issue. She accepted him and liked him and he understood at once that his inadequacies were not failures at all but simply facets of his character which, although open to improvement, made him what he was. Suddenly he was talking about them, laughing at them, they laughed together for she had failings too, and their levity was a joint celebration of life that wasn't perfect and never could be. Failure, he had finally realised, could be used to a man's advantage.

He regarded her pleasurably as she sipped at her drink. She was small but not frail, and her fair hair fell luxuriously to her shoulders. She kept things to herself; there was something bad or sad in her past, he was sure of it, he was also sure that there was much more to her than what was presented to the eye. On occasions, as of the moment, her mind would seem to dwell in some impalpable region of remembrance, lingering there, only to leap back in an instance and he felt he could hear binds and bonds snapping asunder, so great was the sudden leap. 'I'm sorry,' she said, 'for a minute there I was thinking of something.'

He studied her. She was not beautiful, she was lovely.

She had told him teasingly that he was lovely, too, and he had taken to surveying himself in the mirror, and, whereas most times he couldn't bear to look, he was telling himself now that he was "not too bad at all" Sure, his head was too big, its globular shape accentuated by its dreadful dome, and his nose was too big, but he had nice blue eyes and his teeth were white, even and all his own, his best feature, so, in future, he resolved to do a lot more smiling.

'You seem back to be contented, with your life,' Charlie said.

Jennifer said, 'For a while there, Charlie, my life was a nightmare with no way out.' They were in the Safari bar in Katamara, drinking to many things including Josiah's Kariuki's re-election and hope for Kenya's future. Low tribal drum music, like the country's heart-beat, thumped quietly in the background. Christmas was at hand but the bar-room was not decorated, there was no Christmas tree and carol singers would not be trooping through the door, but Charlie felt that this would be the best Christmas of his life. He was at ease. The fresh night air drifting through the open door invigorated the shadowy room and flicked at the flames in the oil lamps. Although electricity was now general throughout the village, some commercial premises had declined the luxury; Charlie had deliberately chosen a bar without artificial light because his teeth looked brighter by lamp-light. He was surprised to find himself so relaxed, but was acutely sensitive to Jennifer's needs and to the reaction of others in the bar. Now people smiled and nodded acknowledgement, they bent in passing too, wishing them "Happy Christmas". How things had changed. At Charlie's insistence they moved to a quiet corner of the room, out of earshot, and Jennifer did not question the move, perhaps sensing his need

261

for discretion. Jennifer said, 'After I was in the Jaffa bar with you, Sam Wamiru called. He insisted he take me to the Jaffa bar again. My God, I didn't want to go but he persuaded me and from that night everything started changing. Charlie, it must have been you who told him what had happened.'

Charlie nodded. 'He said he would do what he could. Seems he did.'

Jennifer thought about that evening with Sam Wamiru. My God, How long was it since she had lowered her eyes and crossed and uncrossed her legs towards a man; moistened her lips with the tip of her tongue and dangled a shoe from her toes? She shuddered with grim humour at behaviour which clearly had not worked. My God, she had overdone it. Of course, Sam Wamiru was a cop, a hardened cynic, impervious to the sexual anthropology of a wanton woman. She had acted like a hussy, and on their way home from the pub that night, asking him if he already had a woman, my God, how blatant was that? He was a genuine guy, who, at Charlie's instigation had decided to help restore her reputation, but had no romantic inclination towards her. My God, was it any wonder that he hadn't kissed her good night, at the hospital gates. 'Sorry Charlie, what did you say?'

'Sam Wamiru, he said he would do what he could. Seems he did.'

Jennifer said, 'Somehow I feel that I owe that man a lot.'

Charlie was quiet, thinking. He didn't pursue the topic of Wamiru. He had his own agenda and it must be done tonight. He needed to unburden himself at last. He had tried once before, and only once, because he had been laughed at, ridiculed, but that was by a woman who did not have a kind and open heart. What he had to tell Jennifer was not funny, and neither was it bad, but it was terribly shameful. He hadn't robbed the poor, beat a woman, assaulted a child but something far, far worse; the heaviest and most painful millstone a man over forty can ever have to carry.

He drank his beer, slowly savouring the strong taste and foreswore not to get drunk. Drink would make his disclosure easier, but he did not want his words slurred with melancholia or alcoholic sentiment. This was to be a confession as sanctified as was ever counselled by a priest. How often had he envisaged this submission to another, squirmed at the thought of revealing this most shameful of his secrets, but it had to be done. It would be finally expunged so that, at middle age, he might start again the quest first started as a pimply youth whose head was topped with gingerish hair and filled with forlorn hope.

The bar began to empty, men drifting out, one by one into the night with polite farewells to the two *musungus* in the corner, each with their own idea of what might be going on between them. The bartender closed the door on a village, no more celebratory for it being the festive season. In the dark, quiet room, just the three of them and a myriad of tiny moths paying homage to the lamp light. The bartender busied himself, keeping a discreet distance from his two remaining customers. They were still drinking, albeit not as much as he would like them to, but as long as they were spending money, they could stay all night.

'Do you think we should make a move?' Jennifer said. 'We're the only ones left and maybe he is looking to close for the night.'

Charlie glanced at his watch, it was ten o' clock. 'It's still early, Jennifer.' In deference to the bartender, he ordered two more drinks. When the drinks were served, he began telling her about the arrival at his house of Aisha, about her pregnancy and Freddie's betrayal. They then speculated on what they might do to help her. They also talked about the hospital and the project, discussed the sisters and the volunteers, and the photograph in the window of his house. It was Aisha, it was Freddie's joke. There never was a ghost. But Jennifer was not convinced. A firm believer in the afterlife, an advocator of things spiritual and beyond human comprehension; the image could still be of the ghost-girl, Shula.

'Charlie, I think those barriers between life and death can be weakened by innocence, say the innocence of a child, weakened too by a very good or a very evil person approaching that region of the dead. I believe that you are a good person who awakened

Shula. I am convinced that we live within a spiritual dimension, of which we know virtually nothing. Shula exists in that dimension and is trying to reach you in that house.'

But to Charlie all was small talk, even, Aisha, even the ghost of Shula. Yet convivial and questionable as it was, it was but a precursor to the progeny about to be expunged. A landlord could not call time on that. 'Jennifer, I have something to tell you which for years has been driving me crazy. It is why I am here in Katamara, it is what controls, motivates and destroys my life.'

Jennifer lowered her eyes and a feeling of compassion overcame her. She knew what was coming, somehow she had known from the very moment that they met.

He began to talk of his youth and although his language was not coarse, it was playfully explicit in describing those years of permanent erotic arousal, his crouching like a cripple in order simply to leave a bus. Well, with the years, things might have deteriorated a little but the flame of intention still burned as brightly as it ever did. He still dreamed daily of the woman into whom he would one day lay his seed. She was not refined, or beautiful, or even pretty, even his mind was conditioned in its expectation. No, the woman who most often slunk into his fevered fantasies was a whore, as falsely accommodating and mercenary as any tout. But she was flesh and blood, and dissolute, and she was what he thought he wanted. But it wasn't what he wanted, what he really wanted was a nice woman to settle down with, have a home and children with and a garden full of daffodils like his mother and see his mother overjoyed. Surely he would find such a woman in Africa, but as yet he hadn't.

'When I was seventeen I started to go bald,' Charlie said softly. 'The first thing I did every morning when I got out of bed was to check in the mirror to see how much more of my hair had gone missing during the night. Yes, every morning my bald patch was bigger than it was the night before. But where had it gone? I would check my pillow but there was never a single hair to be found. I became convinced that some kind of imp was coming in the night and stealing it while I was asleep. The worry of it overwhelmed me, I became obsessed: I was like those girls who starve themselves to death thinking they are fat. Whenever I would approach a girl and speak to her, which I did from time to time, whenever I was able to summon up the courage, my only thought was my pink carbuncle of a head, thrusting through the bits of ginger fuzz that was my hair. And I imagined that that was what the girl was thinking too. I've known times when I would suddenly run away in the middle of a conversation. Oh yes, that's how bad it was for me. I had not one scrap of self-esteem and by the time I was twenty-one I was bald, as bald, as I am now. Then I was coming up to thirty and hair was everything. That was when girls were looking for manes of hair, swept back like Elvis Presley. It was impossible for me to get a girl, you know, a steady girl-friend, and I never did.' He paused.

Jennifer did not fill in his pause, neither did she look up from the table, but she was listening. With her glass she was making little liquid circles on the table top, lots of them, interlinked like a crumpled chain. She was listening to a story compelling in its despair.

'What was it? Years ago now, boys and girls jiving to a new kind of music that was exclusive and incredible, and, oh, what I would have given to join them on the dance floor. But it was impossible, I was too ugly, I had no hair. How can a boy dance if he has no hair? But Jennifer, there was an answer to all my troubles.'

At the sound of her name she raised her melancholy eyes to show him that she understood, eyes that remembered well the bold freckles of youth upon her cheeks and she tried to convey to him an empathy that she too had lived a time of wretchedness and hapless hope, when she too was looking for answers.

He laughed bitterly. 'My answer was a wig. I worked in an office and every week I saved up what I could. I wasn't going to buy any old wig, only the best that money could buy. You see, I was going to jive on the dance floor like the other boys, and girls would want to jive with me. I was coming up to thirty and

I was terrified that this wonderful time was going to pass me by. When I had enough money I went to Leeds, where there was shop that dealt solely in wigs, and I was like a kiddie in a sweet shop. My head was measured.' Charlie smiled bleakly at the thought. 'It was just as if I was being measured for a new suit. This wig would be the best that money could buy because the rest of my life depended on it. It was proper human hair and I could have a choice of colour, but I stayed close to my natural hair because I still had plenty of it elsewhere on my body.' He laughed mirthlessly. 'This wig had Velcro tabs so it could be adjusted, extra tabs too, so that it would always be tight to my head. Jennifer, that wig was completely undetectable.'

Jennifer was still silent, examining the liquid circles she had made. The flames of the lamps were upright, the room segmented in shades of dark and light. The background music still played, but was so low it was hardly audible. Behind the bar, the bartender stood patiently, motionless in silence, only the tiny moths were active with whatever compelled them to the lamps; no sound from the village, not even the barking of a dog. From nowhere a cat appeared, rubbed at Charlie's legs then settled at his feet to sleep.

'And so, at last, I had my wig, the answer to my prayers. No one was allowed to see me wearing it, not even my parents who knew nothing about it. You see, it had to have a test run first. Jennifer, it was perfect – I mean perfect, and I was human. Of course, I couldn't wear it at work, couldn't go to a local dance couldn't even wear it in my own home town of Tala. But there were other towns nearby where people didn't know me, a whole new world out there teaming with girls, a world of rock and roll, where, at last, I could be a member.'

Jennifer knew what was coming; what was being carried on the wave of stifled emotion that was Charlie. The fingers of one hand slid across the table top to rest on his hand and her eyes said 'yes' so that the wave, at last, could break upon a redeeming shore.

'One night I went to York, York is about twenty miles from Tala and no one knew me there. It was a Saturday night, and there was a dance at a place called the Assembly Rooms, a really nice place with marble pillars and a proper dance band, you know, Jennifer, men at one side, girls at the other, all weighing each other up. I put the wig on in the lavatory then spent the next hour going back every five minutes to see that it was still in place. It must have been at least two hours before I plucked up courage to ask a girl for a dance, about two hours and six pints of beer. I chose one girl from dozens. It was a girl who hadn't been asked to dance for ages, not good looking or anything, just a girl who I had watched and hadn't been asked to dance for ages. Of all the girls who were there that night, I chose this one, dark haired she was, quite tall, I remember. It was a waltz, of course, I couldn't dance, but she got up with me and we were doing the best we could. The floor was crowded and we were dancing and I couldn't think of a word to say to her when she suddenly said, "I know you don't I?" and I said, "No you don't." She said, "Yes, I've seen you before, I've seen you before in Tala." Jennifer, I couldn't believe it. All those girls and I picked one who knew me from my home town. Then she started looking at me really closely. She started laughing, and said really loudly, "My God, you've got a wig on." She started laughing as if it was a really big joke and she wanted everyone to share it. I was in the middle of the dance floor, with people all around, and I was wearing a wig as if it was a fancy dress or something, and this girl thought the whole thing was hilarious. She grabbed it and, of course, the tabs couldn't stand anybody pulling at them. It came off in her hand and she was just hooting with laughter. Jennifer, I swear I died that night and I think I've been dead ever since. I snatched it back off her and the next thing I remember was, I was standing on a bridge overlooking a river. I flung the wig into the river and got the next train back to Tala.'

Jennifer was overwhelmed by a vague horror. She had witnessed an exorcism, a brutish memory expunged so that a soul might be free to start again. She had the same in her, she needed exorcism too. She squeezed his hand to tell him that he wasn't on his own.

'From that night I would never have a girl, a woman, never. It's why I'm here in Katamara, trying to escape, trying to find a woman who will have me for myself.' He laughed bitterly. 'I got Esmeralda.'

Jennifer knew what he meant. 'That girl will break a lot more hearts than yours, Charlie.'

'Jennifer, I'm still a virgin.'

The disclosure did not come as a surprise because she knew he was. 'But you could have had a girl, there are girls,' she said simply.

'I wasn't worthy. I wasn't worthy of a whore.'

She was silent, her eyes resting on the table top, on the liquid circles that her glass had made. 'Well, maybe not for long.'

Charlie didn't know what she meant and didn't dare to ask.

'There's me, Charlie,' Jennifer said. 'If you'll have me, that is,' she added.

Chapter Thirty-Four

Could Titus spend Christmas with his brother's family in Mavaloni? Of course he could, and Charlie would pay the bus fare for his family there and back. The night was set: Christmas Eve. The time: as night was falling.

The shadows touched lightly on the little houses, and soon the moon would shine its lovely light on Katamara. Jennifer Collins, without a care for who observed her, set off through the village towards the bridge and the house on the mountain; this was the night she had arranged to have sex with Charlie Carter. She felt a stirring of excitement as she passed the houses, a sensation she understood well enough, but had not experienced for some time, which added to her pleasurable anticipation. There were some in the little houses that observed her passing, but not with prying eyes, no air of censure. She was a local woman friendly with a local man, and such a liaison would not raise a single eyebrow – squinting speculation had not yet jaundiced the Kenyan mind. Indeed, the notion was laudable and should a single man and a single woman decide to have sex in that lonely house then who would begrudge them? It was natural and would matter no more or no less than if they were two wild dogs knotted together outside their door. The influence of the British was intrinsically embodied in the Kenyan psyche but somehow their prudish hysteria towards sex had passed the Kenyans by, and the *wanachi* were well advised to leave it that way. Pressing her body forward against the bank of the hill, she neared the house and the drama to unfold. Was there anything on God's earth so wonderful, so satisfying, so disappointing, so disastrous, so comedic as sex. She wondered which of those stories would be told tonight. Lamp light flickered in the windows of his house and she could see the image of Charlie watching, as he waited for her. She waved and he must have seen her for she saw that he jerked away from the window and it made her smile.

There was nothing much to admire about Freddie anymore, his imperfections far outweighed his talents, but when Charlie saw Jennifer coming up the hill, what he would have given to be a bit more like him. Would a rutting buck be daunted at the approaching of a doe? Where was Freddie now? No doubt screwing Esmeralda, or impregnating some other poor native girl. Gist to the mill for Freddie, but the very first time for Charlie and nervousness consumed him. How many times throughout his barren years had he lived this moment in his mind; how many wanton images had fired up his blood? But would he be up to it? The oracles had always said that no one ever forgets the first time. Would his memory be one of joy or one of dread?

He was prepared. Hitherto his mission with women had been to impress, but the cornerstones of his life were never strong enough to support the measures he laid upon them, and he had learned that you usually end up despising those whom you've tried to impress, so no candles, exotic foodstuffs or bottles of champagne. Food and wine were available but were not garnished with any ostentation. She was at the door, the scales of success and failure weighted evenly, but the distance between the two, in all his life, had never been so vast.

The journey from the door, whereupon he greeted her, to his bedroom was without palaver or histrionics. Why, they might have been a long married couple, so without incident was the transition. And there was no parley, Charlie, although nervous and eager, was uncertain of what to do, so Jennifer took the initiative and with unaffected example lay on the bed and invited him to join her. Progress was slow but there was no fumbling with buttons and straps, Jennifer undressed herself. Knowing and understanding his situation, she would ensure he did not fail, he must know no pressure, fulfilment must be natural and unhurried; a rapacious appetite was waiting to be sated and there would be nothing phoney about her response. She relaxed him, and he undressed so unself-consciously he even laid his clothes upon a chair, and yes, for the first time in his life, a naked woman lay waiting for him on a bed. Easily, he slipped into a cradle in which all the treasures of the flesh had lain in wait; a hollow in which he would thrash about and gorge and nothing could still the rapture coursing through his blood. The oil lamp had been left lit: this was a glory for the senses, sight must not be denied. Shadows danced and little leaping flames probed like tongues, the deepest cracks and corners of the room. It was happening and his maleness did not let him down. No longer tractable, the testosterone in Charlie inhibited for so long roared and rampaged like a beast let loose from turgid restraint, and he achieved, at last, his one great goal.

It was over quickly, but it was passionate and intense and satisfying for both. Jennifer had sighed and groaned with honest pleasure at everything he did to her, for what he lacked in finesse he more than made up for with in fervour. Her uplifted eyes were candid in the enjoyment he had given her. The second time it was slower and better and the third time, after a long rest and a cup of tea, was best of all. Charlie collapsed exhausted and peace fell upon him at the exultation of his heart and soul.

This was mastery to rank with works of art, classics of literature and the composition of music most sublime. Forty years in the making, there was triumph in it and such glory that if he was to die that very moment then his life had been successful and he was a great man, as great as any other. The path through life was open, no longer obstructed by trees of doubt, gnarled and twisted in the forest of his mind. Free from the desolation of failure, his life had entered a new dimension and the prescience of his soul was the full and happy life that he deserved. He knew of women now, they were a mystery no more. Henceforth he could live among them without having to hop precariously from one muddling stepping stone of insecurity to another, always in terror of stumbling and falling off.

He slung his legs from the bed, and standing, caught a glimpse of himself in the mirror. Was this the same man, who one night in self-disgust had thrown an expensive hand-made hair-piece into a river, who feared rejection as one would fear a rabid dog? Who was Freddie? He no longer envied Freddie. It was a wondrous discovery and he could see how Freddie had misused it, he had too much of it. Why is an abundance of anything always treated worthlessly? Clearly now, he could see the dangers strewn along this precious path, the distressful pits into which a man could fall, a woman too, poor Aisha had fallen thus. OK, it was late in life, but at last he was empowered with something of immense value and he vowed to use it well, to cherish it and those with whom it would be shared.

They dressed without embarrassment. Jennifer was comfortable naked, confident that her body was as pert and trim as it was when she was a teenage girl. She felt happy and was satisfied; her satisfaction was in Charlie's pride. Charlie had performed well, and had that nonchalant, self-congratulatory air about him that comes with a job well done. He was standing naked and unashamed, his chest swelled and it was amazing what three hours in bed with a woman could do to make a belly disappear. And he didn't feel bald anymore; was he ever bald and what did it matter if he was? He was a real man, and real men don't need a head of hair. His dome was bold and bronzed. A symbol of masculinity and he had all the hair he wanted around his bollocks. His buttocks were small and hard, and he displayed them as he bent to don his clothes and his genitals still felt hot and heavy and forever ready now. They made small talk about the things that didn't matter, and they shared a bottle of wine. They did not talk about what had happened or how they both felt, and although there was a bond between them, they both knew that it was unlikely ever to happen again, but strangely it didn't matter to either of them.

It was late when they left the house. There was warmth from the moon, with its light making pale yellow the sloping banks of the Athi, and mellow its flowing waters.

★

Sam Wamiru had spent Christmas agonising about the woman he loved. He must do what he had promised J.M. he would do. Earlier he had travelled to Katamara, to wish Jennifer Collins a *Happy Christmas* and hoping to talk with her. He had made enquiries at the hospital and had found out where she was; at Charlie's house. He waited. Waited; maybe she would return alone. Late at night when he saw her crossing the bridge with Charlie, he desolately turned his car back in the direction of Nairobi.

Chapter Thirty-Five

When Freddie Bristow left the city to return to Katamara, he was a humbled man. He felt empty after a Christmas time of raw frustration, but he had come to terms with the situation, his pride had lost its battle with Esmeralda's atypical nature. She had likely celebrated Christmas with her saved boy, in the elusive Church of the Ever Open Door, or Embu or wherever. He had spent Christmas pounding hot pavements of familiar streets, looking for a girl called Aisha.

He had first seen Aisha in the street outside his language school. A tall, slim girl was passing him by and he noted approvingly her unassuming grace and the rosy health of her lovely face. Her appeal to Freddie was immediate but he could not approach her in view of the school; too may eyes and too many promises to keep. He kept pace behind her until she was aware that he was following her. Once or twice she gave him a backward glance but did not increase her pace or attempt to cross the road. Freddie knew the signs were good so he followed her a while until, with practised ease, he found a means by which he could arrest her purpose; make her face him. The strap on one of her shoes was loose, that was all he needed. 'Oh dear, who's going to have an accident,' he sang with a faint mocking tone; girls like masquerade, it shows that a man is interested enough to want to play a game with them. With spurious concern he pointed to her shoe.

The girl stopped, blushed and went down on one knee self-consciously, exposing a long brown leg without blemish. As she readjusted the strap, her eyes shyly found his and she thanked him kindly. Freddie joined her and gestured towards the way that she was heading.

'If you don't mind, I'll walk with you a little way,' he said, giving her no chance to refuse.

So forthright were his actions and his tone, it took the girl by surprise but she was instantly attracted. This handsome white stranger could walk with her as far as he would wish.

'May I ask your name?' he asked disarmingly.

'Aisha.'

'Aisha, a lovely name, well my name is Freddie, not such a lovely name at all,' and, stopping her from walking on, he shook her hand with elaborate courtesy. 'I'm new in Nairobi, spending time at a school here, learning *kikamba*.'

The girl put a finger of surprise to her lips and said with a little gasp, 'Well that is my native tongue, I am *Kamba*.'

'Maybe you could teach me better than they're doing at school,' Freddie laughingly suggested. 'Where do you live?'

Well, Aisha lived in a shanti town called Kibera but she didn't choose to say so. This dark-haired, dashing white must not know that she lived in abject poverty, in a vast slum on the outskirts of the city, and that she had no job and, in spite of her undeniable beauty, had little likelihood of finding one. 'It is a place quite far from here,' was all that she would tell him.

And that was how Freddie and Aisha met, a beautiful young Kenyan girl and a white man almost twice her age, who she thought handsome, funny and confident. Freddie found out that Aisha had a niece at the hospital where he was going to work and he promised to take her to Katamara and show her where he was going to live. That night they had drinks and a meal in the Ambassador Hotel and Aisha was overwhelmingly and irretrievably hooked. The next night they spent in bed at another hotel and Freddie had his first black girl and Aisha had her first man, ever.

Through the living room window, Charlie watched Freddie stop the truck outside. He was going to break his promise to Aisha. Freddie Bristow must know what he had done. Aisha was not going to come back to Katamara. Knowing now that Freddie had a wife and children, she didn't want to hurt him with the news. Well, Freddie deserved to be hurt, and badly. Charlie had never been a vindictive man but couldn't help the pitiless relish, in having as a retributive weapon, news he knew he couldn't keep; really bad news waiting to be unloaded on the unsuspecting Freddie at a time of his own choosing. He wouldn't admit it, even to himself, but he would use it as recompense for the tricks that had been played on him. They would spend the next few days together, albeit in a strained relationship, but bad news would subdue Freddie, and for a change Charlie felt he had the upper hand. They had three days before work on the project was due so start again, so Freddie might return to Nairobi, or somewhere else but he doubted it. The expansive country would have less appeal to him with bad news to brood upon.

Long gone were the days when they would cook and share a meal together, play cards and drink beer, discuss the vagaries of site work in the sun. Their respective adverse attitude to just about everything had come irreversibly between them. From the start they had never been true friends, now they never would be. As Freddie gathered items from the truck, Charlie stepped down from the porch to assist him and remarked casually, 'Oh I forgot to tell you, Aisha was here early December.' He watched closely for reaction.

There was immediate reaction, which Freddie made a poor attempt to disguise. 'Aisha – here,' he questioned. His face was blank but his eyes and mind were agitated.

'Aisha, you know, the secret girl.'

Freddie was shaken. The irony, over Christmas, he had been pacing the streets of Nairobi looking for her. He got over the shock. So, the girl was no longer a secret, so what? He had little respect for Charlie and certainly no fear. 'And what did she want?'

'You.'

'Well, she would, wouldn't she?' he quaffed and with undisguised but exaggerated vanity he brushed past Charlie to his room. Out of sight, he called through the doorway, 'And what did Aisha have to say for herself?' Beneath the overt bravado, his voice sounded a little uncertain.

'To tell me she isn't a ghost and there never was a ghost and a lot of other things.'

Naked to the waist, Freddie appeared at the doorway. As always, Charlie could not help but marvel at his muscled frame.

'Sorry Charlie, but it was too good to resist. The way you were carrying on about dogs, and knocking, and bloody ghosts. I couldn't help but take you for a ride. Really Charlie, you asked for it.'

'If you say so, Freddie.'

Laughing, Freddie disappeared back into his room. 'Lovely isn't she, lovely skin?'

The image of the girl was still fresh in Charlie's mind, and, going to the doorway, he regarded Freddie with distaste. He fought the urge to tell him that the lovely skin would soon be grotesquely stretched with pregnancy. Wipe the grin off those dark chiselled features. Negate the massive pride buttressed as it was by his muscled torso. Not just yet, later, when the mood was more conducive to his undoing. 'Tell me something, Freddie, at the beginning, that first day when I saw you at the house, why, why did she have to be so bloody secret?'

Freddie chuckled. 'Come in, sit down, and I'll tell you a long, sad story. Nothing's secret anymore.' Yes, it was time someone knew of his Rabelaisian history, even if it was only the hapless Charlie and after his lousy, uneventful Christmas, it would be nice to remind someone, especially himself, just what a horny dog he was.

Charlie sat down in the easy chair.

'Want a beer?' Freddie asked, wanting his house-mate in an ungrudging mood to listen to his tale.

Charlie declined the offer. Freddie lay down on his bed, propping himself up with pillows on the head rest. Still stripped to the waist, he stretched his body luxuriously; that tensing of ligaments and tendons that muscular men love to feel, all that potential power. He had denied himself his favourite subject far too long, maybe it was this uncharacteristic inhibition that had ruined his chances with Esmeralda. But he still had Aisha, he told himself, every bit as beautiful as Esmeralda, albeit without the challenge. So Aisha had come looking for him. Esmeralda would be easier to forget when he could carry on with Aisha where he had left off. And Dianne would be waiting for him, she always was. Tempers and passions among the golfing fraternity back home should be allayed enough by now and when he returned, maybe he would finally settle down to married life. Anyway, it was time the people of Katamara knew something about the real Freddie Bristow, especially one young lady, masquerading as the Queen of bloody Sheba.

'My nickname back home is Bumble you know,' he laughed, 'Bumble Bristow, always in and out of honeycombs. Those weekends when I was supposed to be visiting all that Kenya has to offer, I wasn't. I was in Nairobi with Aisha. Sometimes we would go on trips but believe me, Charlie, it wasn't for the view.' He paused, allowing Charlie to respond to his duplicity.

'You always had great descriptions of the places you were supposed to have visited,' Charlie charged.

'Yeah, but surely you must have noticed there were never any photographs. Brochures, Charlie, the staff at Nairobi's Tourist Information Office got to know me quite well. I don't know how the hell you didn't twig. Thought you might check the speedo, but you never did.'

'Never thought to, I trusted you, Freddie,' Charlie said simply.

He waited for Charlie to respond, to get angry or at least complain but when there was no further reaction he continued, 'I'm married with three kids, you know.'

'Of course I know,' Charlie said impatiently.

This news came as a surprise: 'How the hell do you know that?'

'Adonis told me.'

Freddie looked even more surprised. 'Then how the hell does he know?'

Charlie shrugged. 'Adonis seems to know everything. Don't ask me how.'

'Adonis, he's a strutting little bastard, yes, he does always seem to know a lot more than he's entitled to know. Before I leave here, I'll do for that jumped-up little prick.'

Charlie's inward smile was trying to expand. Talk of Freddie's own ribald past had not started too well, and with Charlie's news held in restraint, it wasn't going to end well either. 'Yeah, seems everyone knows you're married,' Charlie said, inviting him to continue.

Shaking his head to free it of the enlightened corporal, Freddie started talking again, unbridled pride creeping back into his tone. 'Yeah, and when I get back I'm going to stay married. Charlie, I've told you before, you couldn't count the number of women I've had in my time, most of them since I've been married. Trouble though. Trouble is, I like women and bigger trouble is that they like me. You know why I'm here, know why I'm slogging my guts out on that bloody building site, you think it's anything to do with love for my fellow man? Humanity, hell no, I'm lying low, Charlie, lying low for a while until things calm down back home. And I work hard because it makes the time go faster.' He laughed shortly. 'Got chucked out of Cravenvale Golf Club, and what for? Got caught shagging the captain's wife and daughter.' He laughed again, full-throated laughter. 'And both at the same time, the wife didn't know about the daughter and the daughter didn't know about the mother, and the captain didn't know about either. There was hell to pay when he found out. It was like one of those bloody *Carry On* films, except no one was laughing. Mind, there was a lot of sniggering going on. Even made the local newspapers, you know— "Golfer found bunkering Mother and Daughter." Got thrown out of the club, had to move to Tala with Dianne and kids. Moved for her really, for Dianne, to get away from the scandal, but it wasn't far enough, my reputation went before me. I had to get away again, but where to? Christ, knows, anywhere.'

Charlie, irritated yet at the same time compelled by Freddie's tale, turned to the window for relief. Outside everything was green and peaceful, small birds flitting in the trees. A glorious butterfly alighted on the sill and flexed its wings and a chimpanzee swung gracefully from one tree to another.

'You listening?' Freddie demanded.

Pleased at having offended him by apparent disinterest, Charlie turned back from the window and said with farcical absorption, 'I'm hanging on every word, Freddie.'

Freddie stretched and yawned. 'As it turned out, I ended up here. When I applied, the agency people had heard about me, they knew how good I was with building work but they also knew how I'd come by the nick-name Bumble; they would only accept me if my wife agreed. Christ, she agreed, she needed to get me out of the way for a while. Had to promise Dianne in front of the agency people that I would behave myself, but what did I do the minute I got here? Saw Aisha in a street outside the language school, followed her, got talking with her, and the next night I'm fucking her in a hotel bedroom. The first black girl I ever had, a virgin too. First black girl, first virgin, first night, first bloody mess, God, thought I'd done her a serious injury.'

Charlie flinched at the indifferent cruelty of the words and felt himself tremble with annoyance. To think, that a tender girl was pining for this boastful oaf. To give, in trust, the only thing she had of worth; how base was Freddie's recollection of that night. He regarded the man in silent contempt, his pitiful vanity; once, above a river Charlie had thrown away his great hope. What a trifle compared to Freddie who long ago had thrown away his soul.

Freddie carried on, 'I had to keep quiet about Aisha. Doesn't matter now, I might go home anyway as soon as we get the roof constructed and fixed, just about had enough of this place. I am improving though. Aisha has been the only girl I've had since I've been here. Hope for me yet, I think.'

'What about Esmeralda?' Charlie goaded.

Freddie tried a puzzled look. 'Esmeralda?'

Charlie snorted. 'For God's sake Freddie, do you think no one knows you've been seeing Esmeralda? You took over from me. Ever since that bloody reference she was taken in with. You've been with her this Christmas.'

Everyone knew? Did everyone know what a fool she had made of him? Was everyone laughing at him as they had done at Charlie? 'I have not been with Esmeralda this Christmas,' he protested with the assurance of absolute truth. 'There might have been a bit of dalliance earlier but that was all. I've never screwed Esmeralda.'

'Well it won't have been for the want of trying.'

'I didn't, I never—' He gave up and his mood changed. He wasn't having Charlie, or anyone else goading him about Esmeralda – too painful.

Charlie observed with trepidation the forceful look in Freddie's eye. He had struck a nerve. He lowered his eyes to his own boots, the laces neatly fastened in bows. He had never noticed before that his laces didn't match and he was surprised. He dare not challenge Freddie, not even with his eyes. A long, brooding silence followed, broken when Freddie threw his legs from the bed and opening a beer bottle, began swigging from the neck. He began to pace around the room. Then he stopped, suddenly sat down heavily on the bed and put his head in his hands, his shoulders slumped forward. Charlie observed him discerningly and his fear of Freddie lifted; Freddie's anger was not directed at him, but at Esmeralda.

'She is the most opportunist girl that I have ever met. Totally self-obsessed,' Freddie muttered through his fingers.

How well did Charlie know the pain which Esmeralda could inflict upon a man, so the girl had done to Freddie what she had done to him, and for the first time he felt a twinge of something;

was it understanding; it certainly wasn't pity? Freddie took his hands from his face and his eyes were dewy with emotion. If the mighty fall with grace they can evoke compassion.

Charlie's empathy was short-lived as Freddie sprang to his feet and began pacing the room again. Eyes dilated he hissed. 'What a bloody man-eater that girl is. Flaunting through life as if she's some kind of bloody celebrity, some tuppence-ha'penny prima donna, life for that girl is one big charade, I hope some drunken local puts her up the stick and she spends the rest of her life in some grotty *shamba* as a baby-making machine, some brute that will make her toe the line. That girl lives in a world of make-believe, she honestly thinks she's some bloody queen of somewhere.'

Charlie chuckled quietly, knowing the dynamics that provoked such rage. He had heard the rumour, and pertinent words of provocation began to gather in his mind. He threw them in the mix, their tenor laced with mock sympathy, 'I heard about that fiasco in the Nairobi Hilton.'

'How the hell did you hear about that?'

'I honestly don't know, Freddie, but as you know, around here all rumours start with Adonis.'

Freddie exploded, intimidating Charlie with his body arched above him. 'Don't mention the bloody Nairobi Hilton. That night cost me an absolute fortune and for nothing, you wouldn't believe what that night cost me. More than a year's subsistence allowance, I can't bear to think about it Most of it paid by credit card so add the interest onto that, that's how much our evening at the bloody Hilton cost. And I never got anything back.'

Charlie's chuckle turned to outright laughter, he couldn't stop himself. Freddie's face was red with rage, but his voice lowered with tension and resolve. A glare cut Charlie's laughter short.

'But I'll get the bitch. I'll get her back for what she did to me – and to you too,' he added, inviting complicity. 'Know what I'm going to do?' He slammed the beer bottle on the bedside table. 'You got a letter from Esmeralda, well I got one too, Lovely letters they were, both of them, never read anything quite like 'em. Well, there's going to be a lovely letter from me to her, and she can read it while I'm on the bloody plane. I'll tell her what she meant to me and how much I'll miss her and no matter how she has treated me, I will always love her and she's so bloody vain she'll swallow every word. And also there will be a big, fat cheque with the letter. I mean one hundred pounds sterling, maybe two hundred pounds, how many Kenyan shillings is that, thousands, she's made for life. Can you imagine Esmeralda flouncing into a bank in Nairobi, waving her cheque? Oh I'll be imagining it all the way home. I'll live off the image for years. For all her craftiness she really doesn't know much about finance. Christ, does she know about credit cards but she will have never seen a cheque before, much less tried to cash one. She won't know it can be cancelled. Imagine her face when the bank tells her that it's worthless.'

Charlie smiled and nodded in agreement, not adverse at all to the plan. A short, sharp shock would do Esmeralda the power of good. He didn't hate her, he couldn't hate her but most importantly, he didn't love her anymore. He had no qualms about her being taught a lesson; a little humility would do that girl no harm at all.

'Need to find her first,' Freddie grumbled.

'She's back,' Charlie told him, 'she's been seen. I've been told she spent Christmas with her family in Uamani. I haven't seen her myself. Maybe she's lying low for some reason because she hasn't been in the village, and she definitely wasn't at the Christmas markets. Maybe she's moved on somewhere else.'

Freddie said. 'She gave me a lousy Christmas, a lousy time, and I didn't deserve it, not after all I've done for her.'

If Freddie had a lousy Christmas, he was going to have a worse new year. Should the devastating news that Charlie had for him be deferred any longer? No, Freddie's glad tidings of seduction should be denigrated by the awful reality of repercussion. Esmeralda deserved a lesson; so did Freddie. But by preference, Charlie was a good news man, delighting in the adrenaline that good new brings. He hated bad news, bad news can sink a man and bring the bearer with him, and he felt ashamed of his earlier gloating while every second an innocent baby was getting bigger in an innocent woman's belly. 'Listen Freddie, I've got something to tell you and you're not going to like it.'

Freddie laughed uneasily.

'Freddie, this is serious.'

Freddie curtained his eyes and face with a blank expression and turned his body towards the door in an unconscious travesty of escape. 'What's serious?' he croaked.

'Aisha, she's pregnant.'

A thousand questions dammed up Freddie's brain and he paled instantly; questions to which he had one instant answer, 'Well it isn't mine.'

'She said it was.'

'Couldn't be, I was always careful.'

'Well, the baby isn't showing. In fact Aisha's very slim but she wasn't lying, I'd have known if she was lying. She was upset. Freddie, Aisha's baby is yours.'

Stunned, Freddie slumped on the bed. 'She might be pregnant but it isn't mine.'

'You said she was a virgin,' Charlie reminded.

Freddie's face was now ashen. 'She was a virgin but there could have been others after me. I haven't been with her for months. There must have been others. She would never tell me where she lived, but I'm sure it's Kibera. Ever seen that place? Every girl over twelve has either got kids already or is expecting one. She'd o' had kids too if she hadn't been in a convent. Kibera, it's teaming with guys walking around with permanent hard-ons, it could be anybody's, it could—' He was disintegrating, the news more debilitating, more crippling than any physical malady. His body, that tower of male potency was dissolving, his hands were shaking his lips were trembling. 'She's lying, it's not mine. Why the hell didn't you tell me sooner?'

'Because she asked me not to, the girl is crazy about you,

Freddie. She hasn't seen you for a long time and she's frantic. The baby's yours and you've got to—' Charlie stopped himself. He was about to lecture Freddie on the merits of doing the right thing for the girl. But Freddie had a wife and children, what was right for them? It was Freddie's dilemma, not his. Charlie did not have any experience to call upon.

But there was no dilemma. Freddie knew exactly what he was going to do. 'First thing in the morning I'm to the office. The agency can book me on a plane. An emergency, one of my kids is very ill, seriously ill. I'll tell 'em that I'm coming back here but I'm not. No part of my life is going to be spent in a shanti town raising a half-caste kid. You understand, Charlie, don't you? I've got a wife and children they are my priorities. It's not that I'm abandoning the girl, I'll see if I can get some money to her somehow, it's not as if I'm abandoning the girl.'

'Of course you're abandoning the girl.'

'I'll get some money to her, I promise. I've been a total shit to Dianne and she's always stood by me, and when I get back I'll make it up to her.' He began pacing around the room, touching things, still pale, still in a state of shock. He had decided on a course of action, but many loose ends had to be gathered in before it could be taken. 'Please, Charlie, please don't say anything about this to anyone.'

Oh Freddie where's your swagger now? What price the notches on your bedpost? The frightened child remains in every man. Freddie's boyish eyes were pleading but Charlie felt no triumph. It was the end of a story awash with sadness.

After piling everything he owned into the truck the following morning, Freddie disappeared from the house and Katamara. The next time Charlie saw him was six days later to pick up the truck and say goodbye to him at Jomo Kenyatta airport. Freddie was going home for good. He never did get his own back on Esmeralda or Adonis, there just wasn't time. Charlie wasn't sorry to see him go, he would miss his expertise on site, but then the agency had promised a replacement. There wasn't anything else he would miss about Freddie, and at least he would have the truck for himself.

★

'Charlie, there will be letters arriving for me at the post box,' Freddie said before boarding his flight. 'Pick them up for me, open them read them if you like. There'll be one maybe two from Dianne. Christ, I haven't even told her I'm coming home. Well I've written to her but I'll beat my letter back. She'll get a shock, I've made up a story why I'm coming home, she'll believe it, she'll be only too glad to see me. These letters, Charlie, there's almost certain to be one from the golf captain's daughter too, she writes once a month and I'm due one, just destroy it please, all letters, just destroy them and please don't send any back to my home address.' He gripped Charlie's hand tightly. 'And, if Aisha comes looking for me again, don't give her my home address. The agency won't give my address away. It's their policy so the only way she could get it is from you. Charlie, I know you don't approve of me, Christ, I don't approve of myself. I'm ashamed of the way I've carried on, and God knows it won't happen again.' He whistled a breath, 'Boy, have I learned a bloody lesson. You will see Aisha again for sure, tell her I've gone back, but don't tell her that I knew about her being pregnant. I don't want her to think too badly of me.'

'I will see her again,' Charlie said. 'Because if she doesn't come looking for you I'm going looking for her. Whatever you do, Freddie is up to you, but I'm going to help her how I can.' The look of relief on Freddie's face annoyed him. 'You must have some idea where she lives.'

'No, I told you. She wouldn't tell me. I'm sure she lives in Kibera. Listen. Don't go wandering about Kibera looking for a young pregnant girl. An old *musungu* like you might not get out alive. Think I once heard her mention Haraka Valley, it's part of Kibera, make some enquiries first.'

'What is her surname?

Freddie shook his head. 'She would never tell me. Think she was afraid I'd go looking for her in Kibera.'

Charlie remembered. 'Jennifer Collins once looked after Aisha's sick sister. She lived in Kibera. Maybe they still have the same surname. I'll start from there.'

There was a passenger flight call over the loud-speaker. Freddie gripped Charlie's hand. 'I'm sorry about lots of things. Sorry for taking the piss out of you with the ghost girl. Sorry for nicking the truck. Sorry for leaving you with the project, but you'll get someone else, the Agency is good like that. I really am a selfish bastard. I'll write to you tell you how I'm getting on. Write back and tell me about things here, about the site, about the people, but for Christ's sake be careful what you write. I don't want to hear a thing about Esmeralda or Aisha. Dianne will read my letters if she can get her hands on them. Goodbye Charlie and good luck.'

'Good luck to you too, Freddie.'

Freddie turned towards the departure lounge. Charlie called him back, 'Freddie, just one thing.'

'Yes?'

'It's been bothering me.'

'What?'

'How the hell did you do the knocking?'

'Knocking?'

'On a night, the knocking I kept hearing.'

'I didn't do any knocking Charlie.'

Chapter Thirty-Six

*L*eaving the airport on his return to Katamara, Charlie found an unexpected sadness had come over him, and he cast his mind about for explanation. Why this strange dejection? He was pleased to see Freddie on his way, and happy knowing that the agency was looking for another *musungu* to replace him and now with the truck to himself he could take Jennifer wherever she wanted to go. He could also set about looking for Aisha. Despite the distraction of careless traffic and pedestrians spilling off the pavements, his mind was elsewhere. If Freddie hadn't been knocking to deliberately unnerve him then who had, surely not Titus? Was the house haunted after all, or was that knocking only in his head?

Was anything changed by the departure of Freddie? He pulled into a layby on the outskirts of the city and addressed his tangled thoughts. What did he really want? He had wanted Esmeralda, but he could never have her. He wanted Jennifer but knew in his heart that he could never have her either. He wanted Aisha. A compulsion overwhelmed him, stronger than whim, he was being guided. He felt himself being guided, a voice infusing his spirit with overwhelming conviction. He was needed, and, as if controlled by concealed hands, the vehicle started up and headed for Kibera. There was something he wanted above all else.

Charlie had never been in a shanti town before. He had never had a cause to. He had passed Kibera many times by road, a sink of squalor he had never felt the urge to investigate. The second biggest slum in the whole of the African continent, he knew it only by location and reputation, white men did not feature in Kibera's mountain of scrap metal, plywood, plastic and planks, flattened by the need to form a township; a multitude making it their home. No sanitation, no electricity, no running water, no basic social or civic structure, and little hope of work; the *wanachi*, scratching an existence on a tip face, because society and God had wiped their hands of them. The toxic township was divided into villages. Haraka Valley was one of them. Where was Aisha and her unborn child amid this deprivation? Knowing of Haraka, the search might be narrowed down a bit.

Parking his truck at the roadside, Charlie walked to the edge of the locality for advice. He had heard of whites with ghoulish interest venturing into the squalor, only to be beaten up and robbed for their pains, and of one white, driving deep inside for a better look, accidentally killing a child who ran in to his path; he was lucky get out alive. He would make an excursion to the outskirts of the township to find out where Haraka was, then return the following day with daylight hours left; bring Jennifer with him for directions and moral support. At the locality's periphery, the stench in the late afternoon heat was overpowering. Hardened mud streets and paths littered with garbage and human and animal waste stretched out before him. Children played in them, dogs and chickens ferreted for anything they could eat, cats stayed clear on rooftops, eyeing proceedings balefully, knowing they could be eaten too. Adults carried on as they would on the street of a little English hamlet in lilac coloured springtime because they were just the same, human, resilient and hopeful. Sharp rocks protruded through the rutted streets and at each side raw sewage flowed sluggishly through gutters. He had heard that people had to pay for access to open pit latrines. No money: better to hold on until nightfall, then defecate into plastic bags and throw them on the street. Drink, dope; violence, prostitution, suicide, despair but here and there, bright defiance reflected in the colour of the ramshackle houses, a light of expectation amid the dispossessed, beacons to someone, something, for eventual deliverance.

Three miles from Nairobi city centre, he found Haraka Valley off the Thika road. It was a continuation of Kibera, a terminal that stopped the township sprawling into the Nairobi River, a microcosm of grinding poverty the world over, which he dared not enter even in his truck. He returned to Katamara, and, after informing everyone that he was taking time off work, he returned to the township with Jennifer and began his quest. Jennifer remembered the location of the house clearly and if she had ever doubted the paternity of Aisha's baby, it had been ratified by Freddie's sudden unscheduled departure back to his wife and family in England. Yes, Jennifer would help in any way she could to look for Aisha. Yes, it was likely that the immediate neighbours of the girl's dead sister, Elizabeth would know where Aisha lived. Except there weren't any neighbours, there wasn't even a street, just a bulldozed acre of land already sprouting new shacks made from old rubbish.

A goat, climbing up a mound of refuse, scavenging for food had caused an avalanche of flammable materials to fall on a charcoal fire left momentarily unattended. Due to the high density of the combustible buildings, the fire spread quickly, destroying all dwellings on either side of the narrow path which constituted the street and beyond, to involve the entire quarter, only to extinguish itself because of natural fire stops at either end. One person had died in the fire and half a dozen were injured in attempting to tackle the blaze but all residents had been compelled to re-house themselves among their extended families and from some council depot a bulldozer materialized to finish the job the fire had started.

There were still people in the vicinity who had known Elizabeth, but only one woman could be found who knew Aisha, although she had no idea where she lived.

'A nation of ten millionaires and ten million beggars,' Jennifer quoted as she viewed the devastation, a black swathe amid multi-coloured privation. She threw her arm out despairingly. 'This is what Kariuki is complaining about and he's right. Are these people any better off for independence? I don't think so.'

'I'll call on Sam Wamiru, I'll find out when J.M.'s next meeting is. I support him and I'll do anything I can to help him. My God but this place is a disgrace to the nation.' Charlie meant what he said. He was not a political animal but he knew right from wrong.

'Charlie, I'll go with you.' Jennifer was more of a political animal than Charlie was and she had a great excuse to see Sam Wamiru again.

Charlie undertook the search for Aisha on his own. Keeping to the outskirts of Haraka, he barely dipped into the rivers of filth that passed as street ways, and, seeking out the most approachable denizens, he gently poked his questions. Poked, at first, as if he was awakening a sleeping animal, which might turn and savage him, prodded and poked and was pleasantly surprised to find the people helpful and friendly, and not the feral creatures who skulked the paths for food and water, as he half-expected. But still, he dared not venture deep inside. How many people lived in Kibera? No one seemed to know. Half a million, a million, no one seemed to know, or care. Certainly half of Nairobi's population lived in shanti towns, with Kibera being the biggest. Then what was the population of Nairobi? No one seemed to know or care about that either.

He was trying to find a teenage girl called Aisha. Aisha? A name never heard called or shouted about the paths of Kibera, a name never gossiped in the markets. What of her native name, her group? Kibera was the result of mass migration from rural lands at the prospect of work, forming little ghettos of common culture; *Bantu, Nilotic, Kikuyu*, her tribe then? *Akamba, Meru, Kikuyu*? Charlie had heard that *Kikuyu* had poor teeth, something to do with the water in *Kikuyu* land. Aisha was not *Kikuyu* for she had fine, white teeth. Not *Maasai*, he knew what *Maasai* women looked like, tall and slim and beautiful, as was Aisha but she wasn't *Maasai*. What about *Samburu, Rendille, Somali*? No, he also knew what those women looked like too. She was *Kamba*, Freddie had told him, and why Haraka, why not Kiandi, Ndogo, Lindi or Marina or any other village that made up the heaving mass of humanity that was Kibera? No one knew of her and he would have to go deep inside Kibera if he hoped to find her. She was young and pretty, well, thousands of girls in the township were young and pretty. And pregnant, which drew laughter, because thousands of young, pretty girls were pregnant too. And who was it made her pregnant? Most certainly it wasn't Charlie. He did not know her surname because she had a different surname to her sister or any other name she might have had. Aisha was not a Kenyan name; was she Asian? No, she was definitely African. The police might know, but he would have to pay a bribe. Never, Charlie had foresworn on his arrival never to pay a bribe to police; Charlie had principles.

There were unofficial primary schools in Kibera, maybe she had attended one and there were records kept, but the schools were situated at the township's core, too deep inside for Charlie. Well, he must find her before the long rains. The Nairobi River might flood and wash the animal and human filth into houses. Aisha would not be happy to greet him if her house was full of shit. But surely there must be official waste and rubbish collection? Does it look as if there is? The government doesn't even acknowledge the existence of Kibera. What! Even though it is situated on government land, and politicians and officials are landlords gathering rent? It is the way. The City Council does not build roads, provide sewage disposal, drainage, water or electricity, oh yes they might supply a bulldozer to mow the houses down. It is the way. There is plenty of water in the Nairobi River which is on the doorstep of Kibera, sluggish and polluted just now – why, often you might see a body floating past, but things will be better in a few weeks when the long rains come. But then, of course, it will be worse if the river floods.

It might be the way but Freddie's child could not be raised in this environment. It must not be exposed to typhoid, hepatitis, cholera and worms. What about malaria? Malaria? No, not malaria; Nairobi is at high altitude, mosquitos cannot thrive. Well, thank God for a small mercy, anyone might think that God had abandoned this monument to neglect, injustice and exploitation altogether. And the child must not be exposed to the lack of sanitation. Privately owned holes in the ground where up to five hundred people at any one time might pay to squat were not for Freddie's kid, Charlie's kid.

He returned to his truck and for a while, he observed black kites gliding and soaring on the thermals. Evening was nigh and attracted by smoking fires on tip faces they sought small mammals seeking to escape, a last meal to see them through the night. They had made Kibera their own and their shrill whistles heralded nightfall and the end of a scavenging day.

So Aisha was lost amid the human flotsam of a shanti town, and he would only find her if she came looking for another man. Could Freddie Bristow know what he had done? Could he ever be aware of the chasm between the life of a child in Kibera, Kenya, and one in Tala, England? It was a crime to abandon his child in a foreign land, a crime of colossal irresponsibility. His seed shot without consequence into a woman that would have to take the liability. Freddie must know what he had done.

Freddie, self-satisfied at home in Tala, playing with his children, indulged, as he would be, by his long-suffering, devoted wife Dianne; he must be made aware of his other woman, his other kid condemned to desperation. His nights should be sleepless with worry, his days wracked with guilt. Fate, so disparate in its dispensation, cannot be trusted, but Charlie could. Spineless, selfish Freddie would not return to face the sordid music, so it would be taken to his door. Charlie would write and tell him what he'd left behind. He went to his room and wrote a letter.

It began as an angry missive of accusation, but did not finish so, for Charlie in his writing reflected on his own recent conquest. It did not matter that it had been his only conquest, had he considered consequence as he stood triumphant above the supine form of Jennifer Collins who was likely to be still of child-bearing age? Would it have made one iota of difference in his intent or commission if she had been twenty years younger and black? The answer was no, and he had to admit it to himself. He was no different to Freddie and he felt ashamed. It is man's appalling legacy of reckless imprudence that causes so much misery to women, and he was no less blameless than the others. So he abridged the letter and ended it as judgemental of all men, himself included. He did not care that Freddie's wife might read it. The letter would be posted in the morning, for that much was owed to Aisha.

Late morning he drove to the post box, his letter to Freddie sealed and stamped. There was only one letter for Freddie, and, from the handwriting on the envelope it was from his wife. Charlie had hoped there would be one from the golf captain's daughter which would make titillating reading but there wasn't, he would have to make do with the one from Dianne. It was short and to the point and he had to read it three times before the enormity of what was written sunk in. Halfway down the one and only page one sentence mattered above all others – *'Freddie I'm afraid it is finally over between us, I have met another man.'*

Everything had changed. Everything was suddenly on its head. Thank God he hadn't posted Freddie's letter. Freddie was now free. He might already be on his way back. But Charlie didn't want him back and he tore his own letter into little pieces.

Did Charlie, do any of us, truly understand our underlying motives? Do we not all live lives of expediency, only changing course when drastic situations affect us? He was going to send that letter, wanting Freddie's wife to read it. It had been moderated but it was still a vengeful letter. And, in truth, the letter was being sent not for Aisha, but for Charlie. He didn't want Freddie back in Kenya, doing the right thing for Aisha and their child, not now that he was free to do so. That was the last thing Charlie wanted. He wanted Aisha for himself, he also wanted Freddie's child; a wife, a child, a home in England, in Kenya, even in Kibera.

Chapter Thirty-Seven

*A*fter taking up a stance of self-aggrandizement on the decking outside a pub, Adonis, observed with sullen vexation, the provincials and visitants invade his marketplace. Today, he wasn't in the mood for people. He was not happy. He was still a corporal.

And he wasn't slipping. No. No one knew where Esmeralda was, but he did. She had gone to Nyeri. She had left immediately after Christmas to visit her aunt, and had not returned. He had kept quiet about it because long may she remain there, he was miserable enough.

The long rains were due. There was a bigger buzz in the marketplace than ever and an air of optimism all around, but not for Adonis. Empowered by his neatly pressed uniform and inscrutable persona behind dark shades, he surveyed the bustling scene with routine sovereignty, but nothing could penetrate his gloom. His mandate was, as ever, police supervision and control, and no one moved in Katamara on a Sunday afternoon unless he knew about it. But his confidence had been undermined. He had put things right in the village for Wamiru but somehow, couldn't help but think that the inspector in some way had manipulated him and, if he had put a good word in for him at HQ, he hadn't received any benefit yet. Inspector Wamiru might be a top investigative officer but he did not understand the concept of deterrent. Maybe Adonis should move to somewhere where his tried and trusted preventative matrix was more appreciated.

Now enjoying steady employment at the *musungu* house, Titus had sufficient standing in the community to approach the corporal without fear of rebuff. 'Adonis, how are you this day, I hope you are fine?'

Without losing any of his rigid dignity, Adonis accepted Titus' hand in traditional *Kamba* fashion and answered, 'Fine, fine, and I hope you and your family are pushing on with life?'

Titus said, 'I am proceeding well with life, and my family is well, OK, and is pushing on with life.'

Adonis looked gravely upwards to where some fluffy white clouds were fussing about the mountain top, and said, as if the weather also came within his jurisdiction, 'The rain will come three days from now and the first fall will be very heavy.'

Titus' gaze joined the corporal's. 'It will be good, the short rains were not good, but the long rains will be fine with the blessing of Almighty God. Adonis, I remember many poor rains of my childhood, when the maize and beans dry up, the grass and leaves dry up, and drinking water dry up. I remember my mother footing five miles for water, five miles footing this way then five miles footing that way, this way, that way for water. Adonis, I work hard as an *askari* by night and hard by day in my *shamba* to kick hunger ever from my door.'

'It is good to kick hunger ever from your door, Titus,' Adonis replied. 'In Tala, where I come from, and where my *shamba* lives, the land is very fine. The grass is fine. Everything is fine including the goats that are the finest in the land. Yet, in Tala we too pray for good rain.'

'Good rain is important,' Titus concluded, nodding his head towards the clouds in grave support.

It was another very hot day, the days progressively hotter as they headed for the rain. The marketplace was bright, cheerful and buoyant with camaraderie, and as Adonis looked over Titus' shoulder, hoping to find someone more important to talk to, he visibly stiffened. His unerring eye had spotted something untoward, something that aroused his ire more than a phalanx of barbarians taking on his manor. Was that Esmeralda? He took off his shades as if he doubted his eyes. 'Titus, see that disgraceful girl is back, look at her, she is this way, that way, talking, talking and see how she is leading the other girls to damnation.'

Titus squinted into the gaudy heat. Indeed it was Esmeralda. He had not seen her during this New Year, not since rumours abounded that she was seeing Freddie, not since Charlie's heart-break. She was back and Katamara would be agog with the news.

'I have not seen her this long time now. I heard that she was back with her family at Uamani for Christmas time, but after that— '

'She was back at Christmas and then she left for Nyeri and that's where she should have stayed, not back in my place causing trouble.' The muscles in the corporal's face had tightened, irritation ignited in his eyes. 'She will have been doing bad things in Nyeri, maybe she has fled the law, maybe I will be notified so that I can arrest her.' Then, as the group of high-spirited girls led by Esmeralda came closer, he nudged Titus heavily in the ribs. 'Titus, look, look. I knew this would happen one day, and the mamas always said it. Look.' There was horror in his eyes.

Titus looked. 'What?'

'What she is wearing.' The corporal's jaw snapped shut and his teeth grated. Putting his shades back on as if to obscure the offending sight, he ferreted in a pocket of his tunic for cigarettes, sticking one at the centre of his lips and pointed it at her like an accusing finger or the barrel of a gun.

Titus smiled. Esmeralda, the rebel, the trend-setter, was wearing tight trousers. No wonder other girls were gathered about her; they had missed her, as all groups miss their leader. His smile broke into laughter, 'She will have got those tight things in Nyeri.'

Adonis had real anger towards this girl. Just to see her in the distance caused hatred spontaneously to combust his mind. What enraged him most was that she didn't hate him, wasn't afraid of him and would treat him with indifference should he permit it. But he wouldn't permit it, ever. He began spluttering abuse but stopped, unable to find words sufficiently vituperative to give his gall the justice to which it was entitled. The last time he had spoken to her, he was standing at the same spot and she below him answering back, unflinching. The girl had no shame and no fear, flaunting her unbridled discordance as if it were a banner, calling other girls, good girls of the villages who knew their place, to emancipation and schismatic disregard. Now, back again and in overt provocation to acceptable standards, wearing tight trousers, so tight they looked as if they might split with every movement of her saucy body. Oh they were tight, bright red and tight about her thighs; how did she get into them, how could she get them off? She should be whipped for wearing them. As the girls were slowly and playfully making their way towards him, he reined in his arousal. He knew where she had been, which would surprise her. To gain immediate advantage he needed to unsettle her, knock her off her perch. He couldn't bear it, if she just walked by with her nose in the air like the nurse.

'No *musungus* in Nyeri, Esmeralda,' he called out mockingly as the girls drew abreast of him. Sensing the animosity in his tone, Titus took a step backwards, disassociating himself from any semblance of allegiance. 'No *musungus* in Nyeri to cheat and rob,' Adonis taunted again.

Esmeralda stepped out from among her companions, '*Jambo*, Adonis,' she called, either not hearing or refusing to acknowledge his barbs. With her hand outstretched, she made to mount the decking to greet him, but was stopped by his hand remaining at his side and the disagreeable expression on his face.

Adonis thrust his pelvis forward and tongued his unlit cigarette into the corner of his mouth. 'Huh' so you come back to my town.'

'Adonis, so you've missed me,' Esmeralda said, in mocking recognition of his antipathy.

'So you are back from Nyeri. The last time I saw you was months ago and at this very place but dressed more respectable.'

'Adonis, and you're still here, it is so good of you,' she retorted cheekily and the girls behind her chuckled into their hands.

He would not have these upstarts laugh at him but still Adonis would not respond angrily. He would respond with cutting rhetoric. 'Who would want to see you?' he sneered, 'Mr Freddie, he's gone back to England, knowing you was coming back, and Mr Charlie knows you now for what you are, so no more Mr Charlie. No *musungus* in Nyeri to buy you things, so you come home here with your tail between your legs. Try Nairobi Hilton, for I understand you like to vomit there. Who would want a girl who vomits in a posh place like the Hilton Hotel? Who would wait for a disgusting girl like you?'

'It's OK, Adonis, I got a *musungu* to clean it up for me.'

'A disgusting girl and now returned in disgusting troosers.'

'But I thought you might be still here, Adonis, so I wear them especially for you,' Esmeralda retorted whimsically and the girls around her laughed encouragingly as she wiggled her bottom in his direction.

Adonis would not lose his temper, taking off his shades and spitting out his cigarette, he stepped down a pace. 'Troosers, you think Adonis Musyoka cares what you cover your fat arse with to bring disgrace to the villages and your parents?' His hands gripped the bannister rail; it relieved the tension in his voice.

'Oh, Adonis, you being here to welcome me, what a lucky girl I am.'

He still had the upper hand. He must not lose his temper. 'You wonder how I know you vomit in the Hilton, you wonder how I know you visit Nyeri. I know much about you, girl, and you should fear me.' He turned to Titus for corroboration but Titus, seeing the policeman's eyes bulging and his hands, white knuckled on the bannister, regarded him with mounting alarm, and disappeared into the shadowy bar room behind him.

Adonis was fooling no one. He was in a rage and the gathering of girls, in the face of such overt wrath, retreated to a safe distance except for the smallest girl in the group who, with Esmeralda, stood her ground in defiance.

Esmeralda was getting rattled too: 'Oh, it is for a long time now you feared to see me in tight troosers. Oh, you feared the market might fall like Sodom and Gommorah and maybe you hope, like Cain, I will be banished like the Bible say to the Land of Nod. Maybe I find a *musungu* in the Land of Nod who like to see me in tight troosers and buy me more.'

Adonis dismounted from the decking, and, so conspicuous was his inner vehemence now, that people who had gathered in speculative wonder, began to edge away. He thrust his face into Esmeralda's, forcing her backwards. 'Anywhere you will look to find *musungus* to buy you watches and cameras and jewellery, even in the Land of Nod. And so much gin as to make you spew it like a fountain all over the city of Nairobi. You, a *Kamba* chick who should know how people talk of you, and the bad things they say. You, fooling white people with wobbling that fat bottom so as to rob them, as if your hands was permanently deep inside their pockets. You – you—'

The small girl stepped between them, hands on hips and chin jutting forward, a stranger to Adonis. 'Let me tell you, policeman, you say such bad things about my cousin Esmeralda but you do not know her. You don't know that she has been caring for my family in Nyeri. My mother is sick, and Esmeralda, she sells all her things so that we can pay for the care of my mother. A camera she got from Mr Freddie she sells, and a watch she gets from Mr. Charlie she sells, jewellery she sells and fine clothes, and if *musungus* give her those things, then fine for them, for they go to a good cause through Esmeralda to whom my family owe a lot. She is an angel sent from heaven to help the poor. She even—'

Adonis drew himself to his full height, and holding his hand out, fingers extended, he used a signal acquired at training college to stem the flow of words as he would traffic. The girl looked tiny by comparison.

'And who are you, small girl to be coming to my town and misbehaving? You do not know of the trouble this girl, Esmeralda, causes in my place. Already a good white, Mr Freddie who was here helping the holy sisters has fled back to his mother country to get away from her devilish ways, and another good man, Mr

Charlie, she got him so crazy from robbing him, he started seeing ghosts. And you, small girl, will be in my station soon and having a hard time at my expense.'

Esmeralda pushed forward to separate them. The sizeable crowd moved back a little further. Adonis' status was being challenged and this was unheard off in Katamara. 'Oh my God, Adonis, this girl is my cousin only from Nyeri, here to have a good time in the villages around this place. She has not come here to be stigmatized by your silly talk. You polarize my senses with your nonsense.'

Aware that the crowd was judging him, and that the two girls facing him were not afraid, Adonis moderated his tone. He was losing the argument but might yet win the battle. 'Esmeralda, you cause all this commotion with your cheeky ways and your cheeky dress. It is my duty to prevent you causing trouble in this market. All I ever say is that you should settle down with a good man, who would put you in your place and not allow you to do such things as wear those troosers in public and vomit in posh places.'

'You think I could be with a man who puts me in my place, maybe he beat me. You think I am a dog to be beaten and wag my tail for more?'

'Maybe it would do you good to be beaten, Esmeralda. You should be beaten about those troosers with a stick.'

'Take off your troosers, cousin and give them to him so that he may beat them as hard as he would wish,' the small girl laughed, and, reaching up grabbed Adonis by the tie. Pulling his face towards hers, she said, 'You say my cousin should be beaten like a dog. Well, I say you are a dog. Oh yes, a bad girl is Esmeralda, and she selling all her worldly goods to help her family and her friends. Oh Mr Policeman, know that God loves Esmeralda and know that if she fails him then He will forgive her. But you Policeman, you fail the devil and he does not forgive. Fail the devil at your peril.'

Adonis wrested the girl's fingers from his tie, straightened up and adjusted his cap. This confrontational debacle had degenerated to farce and humiliation. The crowd around them were

301

sniggering; he could arrest her, but if he did there was a danger that the disaster would escalate to catastrophe. He should have known better than to tangle with Esmeralda.

Sensing outright victory, the small girl turned to the crowd, 'The Bible says, *For God doth know that in the day ye eat thereof then your eyes shall be opened and ye shall be as Gods knowing good and evil.*' She swung back. 'Do you know good and evil, Mr Policeman? Do you know who in this world is an angel and who is a devil? Then I tell you. Esmeralda is the angel and you is the devil. You the dog, you hear me, a dog in uniform.' She addressed her friends who were grouped together, in awe of what they were witnessing. The crowd were closing in, aware now of who was going to win, and wanted to be present so that later they could talk about it. 'So Esmeralda gets trinkets from *musungus* who is here to help us. Well that is good, because, for oh so many years, the whites did not help us, but plunder our lands and plunder our very people, they—'

Adonis cut in weakly, 'No good girl would plunder *musungus* for revenge.'

'My cousin would not plunder a white man for revenge.' She held Esmeralda forward as paragon of virtue, and asked of the crowd, 'Does this girl look as if she plunders, does she?' She turned to her cousin, 'Esmeralda, have you ever plundered a white man?'

Esmeralda hesitated: 'Well, sometimes I've plundered a bit,' she admitted honestly.

Undeterred, the girl continued. 'But white men kill her father, who knows that? Her real father, when she was just a little baby, but God has blessed her with beauty and white men give her gifts, but does she store them up like a mountain of gold so that she might reach the gates of heaven? No, she gives it all away so that she is left with a mountain of nothing but nearer to heaven for it. Her heart is a mountain that will reach the gates of heaven first. Esmeralda, my cousin is not an evil girl but an angel.'

Adonis had lost and his loss was ignominious. Villagers were laughing, a laughter that would soon spread to the whole of Katamara and the villages beyond. What could he do to abrogate this impertinent outsider, Esmeralda's cousin from Nyeri? Well, this very day, he would start by getting aboard the station bicycle and cycling to Uamani, there to complain to Esmeralda's parents about their daughter appearing in the village wearing tight trousers. Also, together with her cousin from Nyeri, causing trouble and verbally attacking an officer of the law. So, her father was her step-father but he was still responsible for his girl's behaviour. He would be imposed upon by a representative of the Kenyan police force to take a stick to his girl, and for the benefit of the whole nation, beat the pride and vanity out of her; make her sweet, obedient and compliant as other country girls. And the odious cousin, still standing defiantly in front of him, well, although he didn't want to use it, he still had one ace to play. The village must know that Corporal Adonis Musyoka was not a man to be trifled with. Fight or run? He would fight. He rattled the handcuffs attached to his belt. 'You girl, in a minute will be under arrest for attacking a policeman. You pulled my tie.'

For Adonis, could things possibly get worse? Yes. The girl appeared delighted at the prospect and offered her hands to him, wrists together, inviting handcuffs. 'Oh, my knees tremble with fear at being arrested by the great corporal of Katamara.' She hoisted her skirt and wriggled her knees for the crowd who encouraged her by clapping their hands, 'Adonis Musyoka of the abattoir, how we fear him.' Facing him squarely, her little face contorted with ridicule, she carried on, 'You remember Elijah Gichuru, well, that man is my father, the chief slaughterer at the same place that you worked in Nairobi. And he tell me what a great man you was, with a sweeping brush and mop, and while he slaughtering big beasts that could turn on him at any moment, you follow behind cleaning up and mopping the floor. My father, he moved to Nyeri from Nairobi five years ago and bring his stories with him. He also tell me that here in Katamara you torture people, well, only talk, talk talk.' She now addressed the people: 'The screams you hear from the prison cells is the screams of piglets dying in the next-door *shamba*, he has them taped as my father has this corporal taped. He never torture no one.'

The crowd had grown thick around them and the commerce of the marketplace seemed suspended. Many people appeared embarrassed, others puzzled for there were many of them that had heard screams coming from the police station. But some glowed with pleasure at the policeman's downfall, only little children stared at them in wide-eyed uncertainty. Esmeralda's eyes were now sympathetic to the man but her cousin was relentless: 'So arrest me and take me to your cell. Arrest me, Adonis Musyoka, in front of all these people, and for what for, telling the truth?' She turned her face to the people again. 'And if you hear me screaming, do not be concerned for it is only little piglets on a tape.'

Adonis needed a rejoinder quick and clipped but it eluded him. Before the *wanachi* of Katamara Adonis Musyoka had failed, his position was now untenable. He embodied the reputation of the Kenyan police, the perpetuation of his legendary cruelty, his zero tolerance now a sham. He had let everybody down. How could he have let chits of girls browbeat him? He was so enfeebled he couldn't even pretend to lose his temper. He was trembling, his lips were trembling, he might even cry. Disabled by the girl's fluent, scathing diatribe, he must retreat. Climbing back up the decking, and, knowing that you only lose if you look and act as if you've lost, he gazed over heads into the far distance, and tried to look as the captain of a mighty ship might regard the ocean, or a victorious general survey a vanquished army; were not a gaggle of giggling girls beneath contempt? He fumbled for another cigarette and adjusted his shades. But his posture of command, his air of ascendency fooled no one and he knew it, his trembling fingers had dropped the cigarette but, clinging desperately to his pride, he could not break down in tears.

The small girl again. 'Adonis, Adonis.'

Would she not leave him alone? His gaze remained authoritative, steadfast in the distance and he was conscious of the people beneath him, some laughing, beginning to disperse.

'Adonis, Adonis.'

His throat was bone dry, but, 'Corporal Adonis to you, girl,' he managed and he deigned to lower his eyes to hers. Then, returning his shades to the bridge of his nose, he resumed his contemptuous demeanour.

Esmeralda was unsuspecting as her cousin swivelled her around and bent her down so that her tight-trousered rump faced the policeman. 'Adonis – please – Esmeralda wants to know—' She paused, ensuring that she held the policeman's attention along with everyone else, and when she was satisfied that she did, she repeated, 'Esmeralda wants to know—' then added '—does her bum look big in this?'

Laughing unreservedly, the rest of the girls skipped away, the whites of their big brown eyes catching the sunlight and Adonis' skin prickled with humiliation. There would be gossip around the villages and now, Katamara really was wide open to the villain. He could no longer face the humiliation. He went into the dimly lit bar room behind him and sat down doleful in the dark. From the shadows, Titus joined him, not to comfort or console him, even though Titus could see the pain in the man's eyes; no, it was not the place of a common *askari* to offer solace to a patriarch, but he had heard what had gone on and was sorry for Adonis and did not want him to feel he was deserted.

'Maybe we could have a beer,' Titus said.

Adonis declined. Outside, the ripple and bombast of the marketplace with all those who had been witness to a policeman's undoing, infusing the free-speaking current of conversation with demeaning calumny. He deserved his exalted status around Kilimambogo, he had earned it. Since his arrival on the scene, Katamara had enjoyed an era free from criminality due to a pro-active crime prevention strategy based on reputation. How many wrong-doers had balked on the outskirts of Katamara and turned away, opportunity for knavery plentiful elsewhere, without fear of painful retribution. 'I'm thinking of applying for a posting somewhere else,' he told Titus wearily and a solitary tear slipped uninvited down his cheek.

Titus, with elbows on the table and his chin propped in his hands, regarded the crumbling myth before him with sorrow in his heart. How many of us, like Adonis, are the originators architects, creators, maintainers and begetters of our own disasters? He was not, and never had been a knife-wielding, axe-chopping nemesis of the animal world. And torture? That fettering of unfortunates and that rattling of chains, why no, that's Corporal Adonis with his cups and saucers, he who often makes the tea, and electricity at last, what a boon for making toast. How image does make half-wits of us all.

Adonis, head lowered, sighed deeply. All his hopes and dreams had come to nothing. Let down by Inspector Sam Wamiru and now sniggered at by the very people he had gone to such lengths to protect. All the hard work he done on their behalf. An exhaustive catechism of facts and data secured to protect them. Could they ever know of the trouble he had gone to in surreptitiously opening letters and correspondence at the post office in the middle of the night, a manoeuvre not for the faint hearted, why, he could have been caught at any moment and think of the disgrace. And what use now, all those recordings he had made? All that time spent on his belly taping piglet squeals. Those villagers, did they know that for every human-like wail of pain and terror, a dozen tapes had to be discarded? How on earth had Elijah Gichuru, his old boss, got to know of that? And the fixing of hooks in the ablutions: the probing with a skewer, finding joists, why, the ceiling looked like a pin-cushion by the time he had finished. Dried blood on the cell floor, it was red wine and expensive. Life was so unfair. He should be a sergeant now and maybe married to a comfortable village girl, possibly holding hands in the doorway, watching their children playing in the dust. He was a dutiful father and a loving husband and he had never laid a finger on his wife, well, except for the odd time she had disrespected him.

He sighed again. He was not appreciated, or respected and now, still living on his own, lonely in Katamara, he never would be.

Adonis stood up to go. 'Walk with me, Titus. We'll go the back way.' And so they left by way of the rear exit of the bar into an alley full of empty bottles and debris. They did not speak until they neared the police station and there, they perceived a young girl walking towards the bridge, a stranger, immediately alerting the corporal's circumspection and investigative sensibilities, 'Do you know who that girl is, Titus?'

Titus peered. The girl was familiar.

'Is she looking for Mr Charlie?'

Titus smiled joyfully. The girl was fatter, a little heavier than the last time he had seen her, then, he remembered she was pregnant. 'Her name is Aisha and she will be looking for Mr Freddie, but Mr Charlie is at home and he will be very pleased to see her.'

He was.

Chapter Thirty-Eight

*B*rownie's back.'

'Wow, when?'

'She was outside on the porch this morning, wagging her tail as large as life, as if she'd never been away.'

'Must be a year almost, are you sure it was Brownie? Those dogs all look alike.'

'I knew immediately that it was her. I couldn't believe my eyes. Don't know where she's been all this time.'

'So you'll be expecting the bats back tonight then?' Jennifer laughed.

Charlie laughed, then scowled at the thought. 'I wouldn't be surprised. Like the dog, they left as Freddie came, will they be back now that he's gone?'

'Shula came with Freddie as well. Has she gone away with him?'

'No Jennifer, Shula hasn't gone anywhere.'

Shula hadn't gone away for he had heard her knocking again last night. She was still in the house, she was in his room, as she had been since the day that he arrived, had been there since the day she died. She had been waiting until the right man arrived, until she knew what kind of man he was, before making herself known to him. Where did she abide? For the first time, unafraid, he had got out of bed and lighting the oil lamp had looked around the room. Did she dwell, cradled in the faint light of a region which a mortal might call dreamland, coping with eternity in a timeless sleep? Did she awaken as a mortal might awaken to a nightmare but without the mortal solace of relief? Or was she one of the black faces in the photos on his wall? To Shula what might have happened in an awful dream really had happened; a lowly girl, another innocent among the martyred millions that had gone before and those that were yet to come, unspoken of and forever without justice. The tap, tap tapping that he heard should be the thrashing clawing protest of a terrified girl but in the sound there was no outrage, no resonance of hopelessness; so was the tap, tap tapping a last feeble pitch at the knell of life, a despairing call to someone to know and understand? The call came from the afterlife and was made to Charlie alone because she understood him. He was the only one to hear and now he understood her too.

'Jennifer, it's not Shula but Aisha that I want to talk to you about. She's going to live here with me, certainly until she's had the baby. I'm going to clear it with the Agency. I'll tell them the circumstances, I'm sure they will be OK about it. They are good with things like this, she cannot stay in Kibera. She cannot have the baby, raise the child in Kibera. Her family will be welcome to visit her I'll even collect them in the truck. She's agreed to stay here, at least until the baby is born. Jennifer, I'm really happy about this but, I'm going to need you to help me with her.'

'Where's the new *musungu* going to stay?' she asked.

'That's the help I'm going to need. Among others.'

'You want me to find him room at the hospital.'

'If you could.'

'I'll have to ask Mother Veronica, but I'll do my best, there is a room he could use, the one that Sam Wamiru used when he was here.'

'There's more, Jennifer.'

Jennifer Collins would not turn Charlie down. Of course she would help. It was her vocation. Kibera, her mind dwelt a little while on that awful place, and saw it pulsing with disadvantage, then her mind went to a place in her heart and there was room for a young girl and a baby.

They were at the hospital entrance where Charlie had asked to speak to her. A sister had brought them together. Charlie sighed then said tonelessly, 'I just can't bear the thought of her living in that place, I know her family will look after her, she said as much yesterday, and most of the people I have met in Kibera are decent people, kind, they were helpful to me when I was looking for her but – my God – the place itself – Jennifer, I want help for her when the time comes.'

'Yes, I'll help Charlie. I'll see to it that the baby is delivered in the hospital and that Aisha has everything she needs.'

'Will you come up to the house tomorrow evening to talk?' Charlie asked. I'll prepare something nice for you? I'm getting to be a better cook, Titus has been teaching me. I'm getting good with herbs and spices, vegetarian food. I'm starting to enjoy it myself.'

She had a little work to do early evening. Was 7:30 OK? Should she bring some wine?

Charlie's face lit up with expectation. 'No, I've got wine, white and red. It stays cool in the shower house. I want things to be nice for her. The place needs a woman's touch, you can advise me. Jennifer, I want her to stay after the baby is born I want her to stay. If she'll let me, I want to look after them both and for as long – as long – oh forever...' His voice trailed away.

Aisha would have her baby in the clean environs of a hospital, under the auspices of holy sisters and a trained nurse, with all the sterile accoutrements of birth at hand. And Aisha would return to a clean house; Charlie would make a great effort to make the kitchen cockroach free. She would live in the house and he could hear the baby gurgling in her lap; he could see her breast-feeding and he could see himself averting his eyes. She would live as Charlie's friend and, no longer a secret girl; she would live openly as a legitimate tenant until the project was completed. When the project was over he would lose the house, then Aisha would have a choice to make. Stay with Charlie somewhere else or go back home to Kibera. It was the 'or' that would give him sleepless nights.

Earlier that day, he had called at Titus' house and told him to take the night off, because, although he was ashamed of what was lurking in a deep corner of his mind, there was a remote possibility that Jennifer might want another union with him. He dared not think of naked sex, or sweat, or bodily fluids, he only dared think of a union: any other thoughts would be too much of a betrayal to the woman. She just might, and he owed it to the maleness in him to be prepared. Titus' eyes had narrowed in disappointment. Mutely, they asked, would Titus spy, would Titus eavesdrop? And Charlie was doubly ashamed that his lascivious thoughts had compromised his friend.

Everything was ready when, on the dot, Jennifer turned up at his door. He took her coat and seated her at the table. 'Bats turn up?' she enquired, slyly smiling.

'No, but there's time yet. Brownie turned up again though this evening, he's a regular again.'

With genuine affection for each other they ate and sipped red wine. There was a new contentedness about Charlie, an aura that life favoured him at last; Charlie's life had turned a corner. They made plans about Aisha coming in one week's time and talked of other important things, and, when concerted decisions had been made, their conversation turned to small talk and a second bottle of wine made talking easier still.

Then Charlie sensed that Jennifer was preoccupied with something, or was she tired, or worse still bored? 'I'll take you home whenever you want,' he offered.

'Charlie, I don't want to go home, I want to stay here until I've told you something. I listened to you, now I want you to listen to me and to understand but I don't quite know where to begin.'

Charlie had known for some time that Jennifer had a story, one that had always troubled her. He said, 'Just tell the story like I did.'

So Jennifer offloaded her demons onto Charlie just as he had done with her.

As the reptile had got inside Clarissa seventy years earlier, it had got inside Jennifer Collins too. But, unlike Clarissa, it failed to destroy her. She found it within her, controlled it, and then derailed it, but it was still in her and always would be. She could feel it writhe with impotent frustration, forever regretting the power it had lost, and she would delight in every opportunity she could find to confound it more. How many miseries had she endured that time that it was rampant in her life, but how many weapons had it blunted on her resolve? For some years, malignant and parasitic it had consumed her. It had not entered a portal to her soul through a fissure of weakness like jealousy, pride, indulgence or greed. Instead, it had entered through hurt and sorrow inflicted by the unthinking cruelty of others. Blow by blow by blow it had gained entry, sinking ever deeper, ever more trenchant. Blows by her loving mother and her sister and then her father, blow by blow by blow over weeks then over months, blows by neighbours, nuns and priests until the reptile squatted at her core, did they know what they were doing to her with those hammer blows? She would tell Charlie her story and feel the reptile cower lower beneath the light of both their souls. 'I don't quite know where to begin,' she said.

'Begin where it hurts the most,' Charlie repeated, 'just like I did.'

'I had a baby once,' she started. 'It was a baby girl and they let me have her for a full six weeks after she was born. Oh, that was the cruellest thing that has ever been done to me. For six weeks I knew such love, and then they took her away and I never saw her again. Oh Charlie, I have never got over it and I know I never will.' She paused, as she saw, in her mind's eye, a tiny hand stretched out to her forever, the same hand that had grasped her breasts those days, those tiny nails that had scratched her skin that awful, final, day and she heard again her screams at God at such abomination. Bending her arms on the table she rested her head on the back of her hands to hide her face and then began to cry softly. She had waited a long time to cry as she was doing now, not in self-pity, but in release.

Strangely, Charlie did not feel awkward but he hated to see her so upset. His hand pulled gently at one of her fingers until she released it from beneath her head; it was wet with tears. He wondered should he say something, he wondered what to say. 'How old were you?' he asked. It was cliché, it was stupid, but the question was asked and could not be recalled and he was most relieved when she upturned her eyes and answered.

'I was only fifteen, and such a scandal it was.'

'And in Catholic Ireland too, oh Jennifer, I can imagine it.'

'You can't,' she said.

No one could imagine it. They could imagine how it happened. It happened the once only, with a boy, a little older. A warm evening, it was, on a patch of warm grass and the sun was setting, golden on the sea and yellow on the sand. Just talking, laughing and joking they were, indulging the simple fragility of adolescence, those little trespasses of the flesh, so delightful because they were prohibited and to be acknowledged before God on Saturday morning and worth no more than one Hail Mary each at most. And then something erupted, and a kind of fire consumed them, and nothing would ever be the same again.

But did she at any time try to prevent this terrible thing from happening? Well, no, because it wasn't terrible at all, it was quite wonderful in fact. But she must have cried out, defenceless as she was, with a boy and a mountain towering above her. Of course she cried out, they both did, that groaning cry of hers and that triumphant cry of his. But it was only heard by sea birds. And it was over so quickly. It is absolutely impossible for anything untoward to happen when something is over as quickly as that was. And that was what they told each other, repeatedly, that balmy summer evening as they walked home where the Wicklow Mountains finish in the sea.

Who was it that had done this monstrous thing to her? Like darts, the names were thrown at her, but none would stick because the boy who was rightly named had done nothing to deserve the awful judgement waiting to befall him, and the more relentless the torture to reveal his name, the more she set her face against it. Well, it was always said that Jennifer Collins would come to no good. She had always been disrespectful and confrontational, an incorrigible renegade who deserved her downfall and the whispers that were going around: Jennifer Collins is pregnant, she is growing fat. She had to rush out of class last week and could be heard being sick in the lavatory. Her peers worried for her, but not their parents who wanted it to be true, because where Jennifer was concerned, she could be used as an example, a warning to their own girls; in that respect she was invaluable. These parents were mean-spirited and small-minded, and they had nothing better to do than wallow in the scandal of a girl's distress. The once only, indeed, oh, the day she told her mother that the rumours she had heard were true, that was the day she wished that she was dead.

'See Charlie, I wasn't a fallen woman I was a fallen girl, so much worse, and it was made quite clear to me, that my family did not want the terrible shame of a child born out of wedlock. Mammy and Daddy did not want to be grandparents to an illegitimate child, and my sister Mary was much more forthright, she did not want to be aunty to a bastard.'

So she would have to go away of course, there were special places for people like her, prisons, well, they were not called prisons, but they were prisons nonetheless. She would not have to go until she began to show, or until six weeks before the birth was due. Until that time she would go to school as normal, but once she got home she would stay indoors, except to go to church on Sundays and Holy days. She would stay in her room, study her schoolbooks and pray to God for forgiveness. Not allowed to join her family, meals would be laid outside her bedroom door. Well, she could join her family at meal times if she told them who the filthy boy was. She chose to eat in her bedroom.

When she became like a beast heavy with calf, her parents and a priest took her to a cold, grey building in Dublin, built of cold, grey stone where other beasts were corralled. Everything was cold and grey, the garb of her mother and father; their cold, grey eyes. Then everything turned black, the black of winter; lights out in the dormitory and the black of night; the black scowling of the

Sisters of Mercy and the clerical black of the priests bringing not a sliver of light into the blighted lives of the girls. And with the hammer-blows of piety they drove the sharpened stake of shame into her soul. Blow by blow by blow they put her down, the sneer, a reminder of her degeneracy, the scold, a manifestation of her debasement, the snub, proof of her worthlessness. This was the special place, a temple to the bully, a monument to weakness and to spite. And then the rules, lights out, beds made, meals taken, prayers said. No smoking, no talking and absolutely no laughing and the rules of the ablutions, oh the rules of the ablutions. No holy place on earth could hold a candle to the rituals and etiquette to be observed in that revered shit-house and the Lord help any unfortunate who might deign to question the unwritten commandments that secured its esteem. Rules inviolable, cooking, cleaning, washing ironing, scrubbing floors and more rules, always rules.

'Charlie, the first things that will be found in hell is uniforms and the second things that will be found are rules and they will be small and petty and mean and there will be lots of them.'

Blow by blow by blow the reptile was driven ever deeper, forever thankful to the tyranny of virtue. She was immured in a blur of vestments, the livery of canon law, and in the spirit of repugnance a young girl was never more defenceless and alone. But she was not a young girl anymore, belly distended, she was a beast and about to give birth.

'There was one nun who, for whatever reason, hated me. She wasn't just disgusted with me, she really hated me. One day I came right out with it and asked her. I said, "Sister Michael, why do you hate me so?" She hadn't got an answer and there was panic in her eyes when she couldn't find an answer. After that, things got worse, she was constantly watching for me to break a rule, and forever finding little ways to punish me. The two things we girls looked forward to the most were our baths and our visits. My parents and my sister didn't visit me too much. It was the same with most of the girls. We were pariahs you see. But we got visits from our friends and I still had lots of young friends outside, and we looked forward to them so much. This day Sister Michael was in charge of bath duty and she allocated me to be the last. She told me visiting time had been delayed, and that I could stay in the bathroom as long as I liked. And I really was a long time, because you were normally in and out to make way for someone else, so I made the most of being last, especially with visiting time being delayed and I thought how lucky I was. Except that visiting time wasn't delayed at all, and she would not allow the visitors into the dormitory room until I was finished in the bath. The other girls were livid with me because I was taking such a long time. It was a rule, you see, one of the rules of the ablutions, every one of us had to be bathed and laid neatly on the bed before the visitors could come in. Wasn't I the selfish one, but no one called for me, no one knocked on the bathroom door, because they were not allowed to do so by Sister Michael. And when I came out in my robe all the girls were so angry with me, and who was angriest of all? Yes, Sister Michael, she made such a fuss about me being so selfish. You see Charlie, that's how they used the rules to get at us, to bring us down and there seemed to be more rules for me than there was for the others, Sister Michael saw to that. She turned the other girls against me, as if that hell-hole wasn't bad enough.'

Charlie felt he should say something but couldn't find any words. Instead, he listened with head bowed, knowing his expression was as sepulchral as his mood.

'One day a new priest came to see us, say Mass. Hear our confessions. Give us Holy Communion. A couple of days before my baby was born he came to see me. "Tell me your sins, child," he said to me. So I confessed to him all my sins, and they were only little ones, venial sins they're called. There was no way we could commit a mortal sin in that place, although there were many times I wanted to, especially the one against the fifth commandment. When I had finished he said to me, "Have you forgotten something, my child?" I don't think so, Father, said I. "You know what I'm talking about," he said. "The reason you are here, your sin against the sixth commandment." But I told another priest about

316

that last week, and also the week before and I was forgiven. Does God want me to confess this sin for the rest of my life? Do you know I expected him to get angry with me but he didn't, he said, "Child, God had forgiven you and you need never confess that sin again, God blesses you and loves you." You know Charlie, of all the advice, guidance and forgiveness I have ever received in the confessional, or anywhere else, nothing had ever had more spiritual impact on me than that.'

Charlie looked at her closely and his heart was filled with love for her. He hadn't noticed but, while she was talking she must have let her hair down; it was tousled at her shoulders and thin strands were clinging to her tear-stained face. Nothing carnal would happen between them tonight, or ever again and he was deeply ashamed to have let the thought even enter his head. This woman would be there for Aisha and her baby, just as she was there for him, and every child except her own. Why should such a woman be given a life so fraught with misery because of one childish mistake? He was starting to believe in God and the God he believed in wouldn't think of it as mistake. He would think of Sister Michael as a mistake, and Jennifer's parents and her sister too. Charlie wondered about her little girl, was she alive or dead? And if she was alive, then, what a terrible shame that she would never know her mother. And he wondered about those who had taken her away, the sisters of anything but mercy, and the kind of God that they imagined they were married to.

Jennifer brushed hair from her face and dabbed at her cheeks with a handkerchief. 'There was one kind sister though, but for the life of me I can't remember her name. She had really thick glasses, like bottle-bottoms they were, which made me feel that she was looking at me through a magnifying glass. I felt it was a kind look because it made me feel special, as if I was in a shop window and worth looking at. Those glasses were so thick I couldn't see her eyes, but they must have been kind eyes because she was kind. See Charlie, she bent a lot of those stupid rules and we all loved her. One or two of the older girls smoked in the lavatory and this nun knew of it but never let on to anyone. All the hate and bitterness is gone now, Charlie, so one day I'll go back to that prison and if she's still there I'll thank her.'

Charlie snorted. 'And what if Sister Michael's still there too?'

'What does Sister Michael matter now? If I was nice to her, I think it would make her remember how unkind she was to me. That would be my victory, to cause her to remember how awful she was, but if I savaged her, there would be no difference between us? In fact I'm sure that in her heart it would justify what she did to me, to us. I would be kind to her, Charlie, that's what I would do.'

Charlie nodded and understood what she was saying.

'The girls were allowed to keep their babies for six week after they were born, but they were not allowed to breast feed them. They could nurse them from time to time, bathe them, change them, but could not to bond with them. There were two doors in the nursing ward, and when the six weeks was up a girl would leave by one door and her baby by the other and they would never see each other again. That's what we were told and even though we saw it happen we didn't believe it, we were convinced that it was just another punishment, another rule, and that the girl and her baby would be re-united again once they were outside. She was so beautiful, Charlie. This tiny, beautiful, living thing was in my arms and I had made her and I was so proud. It had all been worth it; all the sneers and the scorn didn't matter when I had a baby with a face and tiny hands and feet, and I couldn't believe that she was mine. All I wanted to do was hold her to my breast and feed her and I just couldn't understand why they wouldn't let me do it. Oh Charlie, the day that it happened to me, Sister Michael took her from me, not a word, and I remember thinking, well, I'll get her back as soon as we are outside. I went out one door and my little baby girl went out the other. Outside I waited and waited. I was worrying; but surely, these people are human, it is unthinkable that they would steal my baby, I am her mother and I love her, surely all this talk about them taking babies away is so much nonsense, no one could be that cruel. I went back to the hospital and hammered on the door, but for a long time no one came to see me. When eventually someone did come it was Sister Michael, and she wouldn't tell me anything. I never saw my child again, Charlie. I could never give her a name. I could never even meet the people who had stolen her. I went down on my knees on the wet grass outside the hospital and looked up into the sky. I cried, 'Heavenly Father, how could you do this to me?'

Charlie's own self-pitying life arose accusingly to face him, could he have ever overcome such pain? Jennifer Collins would never forget, but how was she able to forgive? 'Yet now you're working happily with nuns.'

'I am, yes, the nuns are kind and lovely.'

'Then how?'

Jennifer raised her head, and a half smile flitted briefly across her face. 'I honestly don't know, Charlie. I've wracked my brains thinking about it. I think it is because these nuns are not Irish and I'm not pregnant. There is something about a young, pregnant Irish girl that incenses Catholic clergy, turns them into unfeeling monsters. I don't know, maybe it's because the joy of a sexual relationship is denied for them, they resent it in others.'

'But you're over it now.'

'Yes, the hatred and the bitterness are over, only because I've learned to control them. It's hard to describe, but when I knew that there was no way I could ever get my baby back, something evil, like a creature, occupied my soul: the reptile, I could feel it inside me, slithering and gloating, I knew exactly where it lived, along my spine, close up to my neck and people with uniforms and petty rules had put it there. Oh, how miserable I became, how full of hate. I went mad, a mad girl wandering the streets of Dublin, looking into prams, despising all those proud young mammies beaming over their babies. This thing inside me kept telling me that I would find her, she was just around the next corner but she never was, try another street, another corner, another pram, you'll find her there, but I didn't and so on and so on and so on until I was crazy with depression. I was sitting on the edge of a well and this thing was telling me just give up, just sling my legs over and drop into the well, everything will be fine down there, away from this lousy world and I don't know what it was that stopped me. I slung my legs the other way Charlie, back onto God's earth and I looked into the sky again and this time I asked the Heavenly Father to help me and He did. Suddenly I thought, who am I to be walking this world in perpetual misery? I thought of myself as a tiny ant among billions of others, like those ants, that night, that you saw Charlie. I was one of those and if I was stepped on then what would it matter, what had I done with the life I had been given, to have made it worthwhile? I was ashamed at how little I had done, and how little I would do in the future if I should live. How little I would do if I continued to live a life consumed in despair. It came to me; it was like a shock and it shocked me out of my misery. It is not who we are, or who we think we are, or who we'd like to be that is important, it is only what we do that is important. It is the choice we have. Our only immortality is what we do while we are here. What could I do? Denied my own child, I could give my time to other children. My depression lifted and I made sure that it was never coming back. I was happy again, and while I was caring for children I would never be unhappy. I was driven, Charlie. That thing, that reptile, was still inside me, but it was helpless. The story about what was done to Shula, the thing that got inside Clarissa, it was the same thing inside of me, it's is in me now, but it is helpless and always will be as long as I am able to give. It is Satan, Charlie, and he makes us do the most awful things. Give, give, give, Satan hates that more than anything else. Give to others and he is defeated. Honestly, Charlie, I just wanted to do good; I thought that if I only do good things all my life then nothing can happen to me, then children die in my arms and a village turns against me. Now I think that the more good things you do in your life, the more you can expect to be punished.'

'Then?'

'Then take the punishment, Charlie, and keep giving.'

'But many have nothing to give,' Charlie said, 'I don't have anything to give.'

'Yes, you do Charlie, and you give it all the time. It's what you've got. Then good things can happen, they are not related and are always unexpected. But they *do* happen.' She dwelt a short while in quiet contemplation then raising he head quickly said, 'Something good has happened to me, I've something nice to tell you.' She did not wait for him to answer but spoke words which fell over each other, so keen were they to be expressed. 'That night at Christmas when we were together here in the house, Sam Wamiru was looking for me. He called at the hospital and he was told that I was visiting you. He waited all that time hoping that I would come back over the bridge on my own. Remember how late it was when you escorted me home that night but when he saw us together he immediately drove back to Nairobi. Charlie, yesterday he came to see me, out of the blue it was. There is something between us, something really lovely, I think—'

Charlie interrupted: 'I remember hearing a car start up that night.'

'Charlie, I love him.'

'I'm pleased for you, Jennifer.'

'Charlie, we love each other. We are meeting next weekend in Nairobi and I'm so excited.'

'I'm pleased for both of you, Jennifer,' Charlie said. And he was. He straightened. 'What the hell was that?'

Jennifer straightened. 'It's outside.' A scuffling sound and hushed voices, then a massive boulder smashed through the doorway, tearing the door from its hinges and splintering the frame. Men invaded the room. Charlie was struck violently on the head and fell to the floor unconscious.

Chapter Thirty-Nine

*F*rom the highest point in his *shamba* Titus looked about him. Below him, in a sheltered dip, the roofs of his small homestead shone in the moonlight like a cluster of yellow toadstools, and he could feel the warmth rising from his little patch of land. Centre stage in the midnight sky, the misty moon had told its story of the rain and had bowed out, shyly now, behind draping clouds, but the leaves of the trees still rippled with applause. Nature's voice was joined by the murmuring of mating bugs before being shattered by the night-splitting o-ooo-hoo- of a hyena coming from grasslands; garden plants stretched upwards providentially and a night breeze scattered his little piece of ground with the litter of the day.

It is more pronounced in some than in others, but everyone possesses an intuitive sense when something is not right, a foreboding, like an unexpected death, the portent of something sinister, like the shudder of a footfall on a man's own grave. It was not the answering maniacal bark of a second hyena that tightened Titus' body and checked his breathing, but the presentiment of danger that the haunting sound evoked. Was the crouched, shadowy forms caught in a strand of moonlight and moving towards the distant bridge animal or human? From his vantage point he strained his eyes: the shapes had reached the bridge but were not on the bridge – unless they were crouching, loping across. Then, at the other side of the bridge, they were upright and were unmistakeably human and could only be moving towards the house, where he should be on guard. He had been given the night off, but he had not welcomed it as he had done before. This had not been Christmas leave or the sickness of a child, he had not been wanted and Titus was a man that needed to be wanted. His shame of the night of the ants had never left him, and never would, not until a night came where he could redeem himself. Something was not right. Was this his night?

Quickly, he returned to his house and to the bed where Josephine was sleeping soundly. Shaking her gently, he awakened her. 'I think I have seen something strange crossing the bridge towards Charlie's house, bad men maybe. Charlie and Nurse Collins, they are there alone. Maybe they are robbers and maybe there are others waiting. I will take my bow and arrows and creep up to the house and check but I will not disturb Charlie and the nurse and if everything is very OK, then I come back to you and everything will be fine.'

Josephine raised herself on an elbow, and blinking her eyes said, 'Titus, take your bow and arrows and please, you be careful.'

'I am an *askari*, Josephine, you must understand, it is my duty.'

'And your umbrella,' she reminded, then fell from her elbow and was asleep again.

Titus left his little house clutching his bow and arrows but not his umbrella, it would not rain tonight. The crouching moon peeped from behind a cloud and shed a nervous light upon his path.

At the same time, Corporal Adonis sat on the edge of his bed with his mind delving deep inside itself and hating what it brought up to the surface. He had not slept properly since the incident in the market with Esmeralda and her odious cousin from Nyeri. It was the same last night and the night before, and it would be the same tonight; how can a man sleep with a bee-hive for a brain? On impulse, he had posted to Headquarters in Nairobi, a request for transfer to another district, because what use was he now in Katamara? His letter, written in hopelessness, had not been specific: had given no reason or any preferred district, and in response some senior officer had rung him for further explanation. He had not pre-prepared answers and the senior was curt with him, brusquely dismissing his request as trivial and misplaced, the tone of the man's voice was implicit with disdain. Now, as well as Inspector Wamiru, there was another senior officer in Nairobi harbouring a low opinion of Adonis.

He got up from the bed, and opening the window, slumped forward on the sill despairingly. He couldn't tell this senior officer that he could no longer look the *wanachi* of Katamara in the eye, and that those villagers who once feared him now looked upon him with disdain and why? He had been rendered impotent by a couple of cheeky girls on market day. Oh how awful it is to find that you are not the man you thought you was. The fear-factor was no more, and what would happen now to the levels of crime and violence in Katamara? Well, they would go through the roof and who would be blamed? Why, Corporal Adonis of course. He needed to be transferred somewhere where he could re-establish the matrix of authority, reuse the same background reputation, the despotism of the slaughter house. And wherever he was transferred to, there just couldn't be another Esmeralda to bewitch and forever thwart him.

What was the diminutive Titus doing on the street after midnight, armed with his bow and arrows? Adonis called to him, and Titus came over, greeting him with a handshake through the open window.

'Where are you going so late at night, Titus?' Adonis asked.

A tissue of moonlight ignited the *askari's* great white smile as he answered, 'I am footing to the house of Charlie, because I am overcome with a feeling that something is unwell. As God is my witness, I saw some shapes on the bridge heading to that house and I must do my duty, even though I was dismissed by Charlie for this one night only.'

'Who is at the house now that Freddie's gone?' Adonis asked, as he remembered the girl making for the bridge.

'Only Charlie, but he has the hospital nurse with him tonight.

I will only check if everything is fine, and then I will return to my wife and children. And you, Adonis, why are you so watchful at this late hour?'

'I cannot sleep,' Adonis told him mournfully, 'at this moment, my head is thinking so much I fear it will burst out through my ears. And my thoughts are not good. I am thinking that I am no longer the man for Katamara.'

'Thinking too much at night is very bad for sleeping,' Titus agreed sagely, then smoothing the flights of his arrows continued, 'so, as you can see Adonis, I am very prepared. It is good to be prepared.' Shaking hands again through the opening, Titus turned and headed for the bridge. A hyena wailed again, a dog answered with a howl and a heavy wayward cloud plunged the village into darkness.

Sleep still impossible, Adonis returned to his bedside. To lie down sleepless, thinking, worrying, or to dress and prowl the streets of Katamara still thinking, worrying. Better for him to face the watching eyes of night than the gremlins of self-doubt, too many of them in his little bedroom. He started to get dressed.

Titus had taken out his torch and its beam unfurled the path before him. He trod carefully, warily, and he thought of Inspector Wamiru and how he had lost his limb to a spitting cobra. The arms of the night closed in on him, as high trees and thick bush splintered the moonlight. He stopped; froze, a fracturing crash unmistakeably coming from the house. His heart thudded in his breast and his mouth went dry. Dropping his torch, he loaded an arrow into the string of his bow. It had happened. Bandits were attacking. He had never heard such a sound before but he knew what it was, a great boulder smashing through the front door of Charlie's house and he and Jennifer Collins were alone inside, defenceless. His foreboding was right. Titus was very afraid.

Half dressed, Adonis heard the crash too, distant and faint but laden with menace, only audible because of the open window. It had happened. Law enforcement in the village had collapsed, this was bound to happen, yet he did not think that it would come so soon. Cursing Esmeralda, her insolent cousin, and the faithless people of the village, he laced up his boots, put on his uniform jacket and reached for his gun.

Titus sprinted up the hill, stopping when the insubstantiality of the house filtered into view. Keeping close to the brush, he crept forward. There was noise from the house, no shouting, but male voices, muffled in harsh, raised whispers, as if whatever horror was inside those walls should not be heard beyond. A sudden scream rent the air, the scream of a woman; not of one beseeching help – one of protesting rage. It was immediately followed by the whining scream of a man in pain and a voice raised high in terrible anger. Titus reached the porch. A question was being asked of him: was he brave or not? He did not know. He had never been tested. His first inclination was to run back across the bridge for Adonis. But was Titus a man, a courageous *askari*? He didn't know but now was his opportunity to prove that he was, to Charlie, to everyone, but most of all, to himself. After it was all over, the consensus was that Titus had been very brave indeed and his reputation as an *askari* was without parallel. His bravery that night was commented on in the national press and he would be a legend in the villages forever more.

Whatever was happening was happening in Freddie's room for eerie shadows danced macabrely in the lamp-lit window. There were more shadows just inside the entrance door spilling onto the porch, the outlines of at least two men. A woman's scream again, it could only be Nurse Collins, followed by groaning expletives from a male. Nothing from Charlie: what had happened to Charlie? Titus had to draw the men outside, get them in range. Leaping onto the porch with an arrow attached to his bow string he yelled at the top of his voice, 'POLICE, *ASKARI*, POLICE,' his voice echoing off the *mabati* roof. Shadows merged and the doorway filled with dark growling shapes. With maximum tension on the bowstring, Titus released an arrow into the shapeless mass. The arrow unmistakeably thudded into something hard, he had missed. A menacing shape loomed over him. There was a rumble of noise from inside the house and, with fumbling fingers Titus tried to fit another arrow to his bow string. The shape had something raised in its hand and filled the doorway. The groove of the second arrow wouldn't fit the string and the arrow hung useless in his fingers. He tried to reclaim it. The shape was hovering above him and something heavy crashed into his skull and Titus was dead before he hit the floor.

Minutes later gun in hand, Adonis raced across the bridge and up the hill, then stopped in amazement as figures began tumbling from Charlie's house. Momentarily, the moon was clear of cloud, and he could see two men disappearing around the corner of the house, two more stumbled towards the mountain. Unbelievably, almost comically, another man followed, scrambling, clutching at his trousers which were around his knees. There was nothing predatory about these men, they appeared to be in panic; fleeing the house in great fear. A figure was on the porch, slumped motionless. It could be Titus, who had gone before him. Charlie and Jennifer Collins were nowhere to be seen and there was no sound from within the house. Adonis shouted a warning for the fleeing men to stop which went unheeded; then he raised the barrel of his gun.

Chapter Forty

Chief Superintendent Simon Nydivo felt aggrieved. Who's was the authoritative voice summoning him by Tannoy to his own office? He hadn't been able to settle into the new job and already he was beginning to regret his unexpected promotion to Head-quarters. Preparing indignation in proportion to the abasement of the summons, he bore down upon his office door, stern-faced and stoking up authority. A new man must start as he means to go on, and the upstart awaiting him would, very soon, be able to convey a potent message to others at Headquarters who might deign to usurp his senior position. Taking a deep breath and throwing the door open, he stood, legs apart, in the doorway and was astonished to see two men, one black, one white, in civilian clothes seated behind his desk. He waited in the doorway, view-ing them as a wren might view two cuckoos in her nest. Surely they should stand up and introduce themselves. Surely they had mistakenly seated themselves at the wrong side of his desk. With a slight gesture of a finger, the black man invited him to sit in the chair facing them, the visitor's chair, and Ndivo's feigned loftiness was seen as a sham dissolving instantly. The black man leaned forward with his elbows on the desk, while the white man leaned back, and crossed one leg over the other. Simon Ndivo might be the new Chief Superintendent, and this might be his own office, but there was no question as to who was in charge. He sat down quickly and obediently, surprised at his own meekness, as two sets of eyes beheld him, one set deep brown, almost black, and the other ice blue: expressionless, exuding an authority transcending rank and station, exclusive to those with absolute power over those with none.

'Good morning,' the black greeted from a fat face that draped like melting chocolate.

'Good morning,' Nydivo answered, stopping himself from adding 'sir'. He hated being intimidated by their presence and wondered how he might re-empower himself. He had been caught wrong-footed. He should have asked them immediately, who they were, and what they were doing at his desk. He must assert himself, quickly, or flounder for the foreseeable future in a gradation of subservience. 'I am Chief Superintendent Simon Nydivo,' he said, without trying a disarming smile. 'I am newly appointed here from my previous position in Nakuru.'

'We know who you are,' the black man said, without a trace of expression, and for a moment Nydivo thought that he might yawn and the white man put his hands behind his neck. 'Have you seen a newspaper this morning?' the black asked.

'Haven't had time, a lot to do, settling in.'

'But you will have seen the placards.' The white spoke with the sovereign tone of the colonial British which so intimidated the native peasant. Nydivo was not a peasant but these two made him feel like one.

'I see that the body in the mortuary has been identified,' Nydivo guessed hurriedly. 'Coming here this morning, I saw the news on the placards. As soon as I saw it, I immediately thought J.M.? It has been on the cards ever since that body was found.' But when the two men remained implacable he stumbled, 'Thought J.M. at once. Thought must buy a paper but haven't been able to get around to it.'

The black took his elbows off the desk, stroked his chin and addressed the white, 'Such a tragedy for the country.'

'The rumours, they were right, myself, I knew it all along of course.' Nydivo's nerves were feathering. Who the hell were these men? Their dress and demeanour implied that they were not policemen. Neither did they look like military men. Could they be government men? If they were, then he had never seen a photograph of either of them in a newspaper or on television but whosoever they were, they were from the very top of something. Theirs was not an act.

The white man, his skin the colour of wet putty, swung his leg from his knee, removed his hands from behind his neck, and, leaning forward, said with unexpected but suspicious friendliness, 'We congratulate you on your promotion, Mr Nydivo, and we welcome you to Nairobi. Time we had some new blood at the top. Yes, we have lost our beloved Josiah Kariuki, a fine man, and indeed a tragedy, a man who had the potential to rise to the very highest office in the land. He has left three wives and many children you know, he will be missed, not only by his family but by the nation. It is about J.M. that we are here to speak to you.'

Now, surely they must introduce themselves, Nydivo thought, but they didn't. The black man, speaking sadly through his fingers, said, 'A great speaker, an orator, his rallies attracted thousands. Tell me, Mr Nydivo, have you ever heard J.M. speak?'

Nydivo stiffened uncomfortably. He was a policeman, not a politician. He knew nothing of the political machinations of post-colonial Nairobi. Yes, he had attended two of J.M.'s rallies but did not ascribe to his ideologies. Better to be circumspect. 'Don't have a great interest in politics,' he told the men cautiously. The men's eyes narrowed in disbelief, surely a Chief Superintendent of Police must have some political intelligence. 'Well no more than I should have,' Nydivo stumbled hurriedly. 'Oh yes, I once heard him speaking in Nakuru,' he remembered. 'Excellent speaker, although I can't say I agreed with everything he said. Some of what he said, yes, maybe—' His mouth was dry, he was gambling. Then the black smiled and suddenly the two men seemed almost human, less intimidating, less like jackals homing on a kill. Nydivo felt his heart steady and he began to relax a little.

The white took over again: 'He was a man of vision. He was once Kenyatta's private secretary? He was at the core of government.'

'Yes I do know that, sir,' Nydivo answered. He had said *sir*, he couldn't help himself. The word *sir* made him subordinate and foolish. Two men of whom he knew nothing, he a Chief Superintendent and calling one of them *sir* and a white at that, no way back now. 'Did you say that you were here to speak to me about J.M.?' he asked, quickly, to cover his embarrassment.

'We want you to lead the police investigation into his death,' the black man said. 'You're probably the right man for the job – but—'

The disclosure fell sweetly onto Nydivo's desperate ears, but he had learned to be wary of all praise which ended with 'but'.

'But we have to know that we can trust you,' the black man finished.

'It's why you got promoted here,' the white man said with a glance at his colleague.

The black took over again. 'There will be a full investigation into J.M.'s death, the people will demand it. A Parliamentary Select Committee will be established into the circumstances, with the police playing the major part. You will be a member of a small group representing the police. We haven't decided which of you will head it yet. It might well be you.'

Small mysteries began unravelling in Ndivo's brain. 'Well of course, I will be only—'

'In good time,' the white said, holding up his hand. 'Another matter now entirely. You have an Inspector Wamiru here on your staff. In fact, we know that he is in his office, now, here in this building. Have you met him yet?'

'No, I haven't had time to meet any of my staff formally. I know of him as the policeman with only one arm, and I saw him yesterday, briefly, but, apart from bidding him "good morning", I have not spoken to him. Everyone knows of Inspector Wamiru, and how he lost his arm to a spitting cobra. I have done a little research into my staff.'

The black man flexed a smile which did not reach his eyes. 'Wamiru's arm got chopped off with a panga.'

Nydivo felt himself biting at his bottom lip.

The white took over. 'We're not going into detail. There was very little in the press, that's the way we wanted it. Wamiru was handcuffed to a man on remand, Lance Allenby, remember him? He was being taken to court, road blocked on the way, men masquerading as police. Wamiru was the original arresting officer, deeply involved in the case, chief prosecution witness. So his cohorts couldn't get him away, he was handcuffed to Wamiru. Sergeant Wamiru, as he was at the time, brave, threw the key to the handcuffs into a ravine, bad decision; they chopped his fucking arm off with a panga. He'd been set up by the man's mistress. Wamiru had fallen love with her, he had no idea she was Allenby's mistress. This woman Clara, she knew everything that was going on, had done for months, everything, including which route the car was taking, she was following in her own car. Allenby jumped into her car with Wamiru's arm still dangling from the handcuffs. Wamiru had been a fool, a brave fool. Anyway, some consolation, they made him an inspector when he finally got out of hospital.'

Nydivo bit deeper into his lip.

The black again. 'Allenby got shot at a road block trying to cross the border into Tanzania. Clara, she got away with it, brilliant lawyer, she left the country. She's in South Africa now. The story is Wamiru lost his arm to a spitting cobra, less embarrassment to the police. Keep it that way, Mr Nydivo.'

The white changed the subject. 'Wamiru was a good friend of Kariuki.'

'A very good friend,' the black commented ambiguously and with a confirmatory nod at his confederate, said, 'Right now, we want you to send Inspector Wamiru to an incident. The incident is at Katamara Hospital, Wamiru knows it well. There is a Constable Kitonyi waiting in a jeep in the yard to take him. Tell the inspector that something serious has occurred there, that's all you need to tell him. He is to set off immediately, then you come back here to the office and we'll tell you a little more. Now that it is public news that the dead man is indeed J.M., we must act quickly. He paused: 'You are the man we think you are, a man we can trust.'

Of course they could trust him. They were inviting him to become part of a team. He was a team man and a team man doesn't have to be in charge. Already he was in with the in-crowd and would co-operate fully. 'Of course I can be trusted, sir.'

'That's all we need to know,' the black man said dryly.

Then the two men waited. Nydivo wondered what they were waiting for. Of course, they were waiting for him to do their bidding. He stood up clumsily, almost knocking his chair over. He didn't even know where Wamiru's office was. He almost bowed as he left through the door. In the corridor he gestured to a woman, with papers in her hand, who approached him deferentially. She directed him to Wamiru's office.

The office was in another part of the building, and it was there that Nydivo gave Wamiru his assignment. Now, from a window of the same office, he watched the inspector walk through the sunlight of the station yard to where a jeep was waiting. He watched with disquiet the flapping of his jacket sleeve. Under Nydivo's uniform, his shirt stuck uncomfortably to his skin and his palms were sweaty: those men had made him perspire alarmingly. He had restored some self-esteem at the expense of Wamiru; he hadn't bullied him, but simply shaken his only hand, thankfully his right hand, firmly, and adopted a superior air but shuddered at the thought of how much pain the man had suffered having his arm hacked off with a panga. He waited at the window until the jeep got swallowed up in traffic, then he began an unfamiliar trek back through the building to his own office where the strangers waited. He was in no hurry. Rain began beating on the windows of the corridors. Turning issues over in his head, he looked outside: no sunshine, cloud had rolled in very quickly. He wished he had stayed in Nakuru. He was in charge in Nakuru.

'He's on his way,' he told the men on entry, and by eyeing them both together avoided saying *sir*. He sat down without being invited. Despite misgivings, he had been included and should appear a little bolder: 'This business in Katamara?' He raised his eyebrows.

The white man had his hands behind his head again, and Nydivo thought he looked a little irritated at this show of emergent confidence. The man's skin was very pale, unhealthy almost, as if he had spent his entire life indoors, flesh stuck on the bones of his face like a wet, white flannel. He smiled obliquely with bloodless lips at his colleague, malice hinting in the moist corners of his mouth. 'Now we can tell you what we want you to know.'

This was a double-act and it was the black man's turn. 'A Corporal Adonis Musyoka, the policeman in charge of a village rang here in the early hours of this morning. The village is called Katamara, it's about eighty kilometres north of here on the Garissa Road. The door of a house was smashed in. Around here in rural parts, that's the *modus operendi*. Middle of the night, a great boulder is smashed through the main door of the house terrifying the people inside. Gangsters were involved, but strangely the main motive this time doesn't appear to have been robbery but the gang-rape of a *musungu* woman who was in the house at the time, maybe they knew that there wasn't much in the house worth stealing. Carnage apparently, one man dead, the *askari* at the house, another man, the white that lived there, he's got a severe head wound, and the white woman, who was the focus of the attack, she's been battered about a bit but apparently gave a good account of herself. She seems to be OK.' He chuckled mirthlessly. 'The attackers this time didn't fare too well. If they are the gang that has been causing so much mayhem around the mountain then they're finished now. One almost had his balls torn off by the woman; another got a bullet in his arse. The one with ball-ache gave himself up, couldn't run,' he laughed again, inviting his colleague to join in, 'three escaped to the mountain and this policeman, name of Adonis, is apparently after them now.'

Taking his hands from behind his neck, and beginning with a tight-lipped smile, the white cut in, 'This Adonis, like the name, did a fantastic job, single-handed too, although at this stage we only have his own word for it. We don't know the details, we don't know names. We'll get further information from Machakos. The police from Machaos are dealing with it.'

'Anyway, Wamiru's on his way now,' the black said as if wanting to put an end to the Katamara incident.

Rain smacked heavily onto the slightly open window above him, showering the desk. The white stood up and closed it. He was thin and frail-looking and small. Smaller even than Nydivo. Sitting down again, he continued, 'Chief Superintendent, you need not concern yourself with what has happened in Katamara. You are here to assist in investigating the untimely death of Josiah Kariuki and you will be given all the assistance you need. You will hear gossip and rumour, and you will have to put up with a number of red herrings. You are new and fresh and you will report to us anything you find, before it gets into the public domain. I'm sure I don't have to tell you just how sensitive this matter is.'

'We have decided we can trust you,' the black man said.

'The right man for the job,' the white added.

'Yes sir,' Nydivo concurred. A little more confident now, he inched his chair forward.

The black carried on, 'We will monitor your findings and decide what can be made known, and what cannot. We have our own men to help you.'

'Perhaps if we could have Wamiru to help us when he finished in Katamara,' Nydivo suggested. 'If he was a friend of J.M.'s, he might be quite helpful.'

The two men looked at each other, neither answered. Nydivo had raised Katamara again and he wondered if he had said the wrong thing. 'Or maybe, I should leave it to you gentlemen, you will know what's best,' he adjusted with a weak smile of appeasement.

'When you told Wamiru about Katamara, was it news to him?' the white asked, as if something had just occurred to him.

The black added, 'Someone could have contacted him directly that we don't know about.'

'No, he knew nothing about what had happened, he asked me, but of course I knew nothing myself but he looked a little worried as he left the office for the jeep.'

Chapter Forty-One

Shifting his weight from foot to foot, and excitedly twisting his watch strap, Corporal Adonis stood, expectantly, in the corridor outside Chief Superintendent Ndivo's office as he waited to be called inside. The last three days had been the most eventful of his life, the most triumphant too; Katamara, and the villages around, were awash with his praise. Virtually single-handed, he had apprehended the scourge of Kilimambogo, and for the first time in years the people of the mountain could sleep safely in their beds. Overnight, from the abyss of desolation, he had risen to heights of distinction he could not have thought possible. He had already received written citation from Police Headquarters, and now he awaited verbal praise which must surely be a prelude to even greater acclaim, and hopefully some more tangible reward. How mercurial is fate as she deals the cards of life.

As he was mutely rehearsing epithets of oblique self-praise masquerading as humility, a crisp, well-spoken voice invited him to enter and he found a surprisingly small man in full regalia, standing behind a desk awaiting him. 'Corporal Adonis Musyoka, sir,' he announced, snapping smartly to attention and saluting.

The senior man did not return the salute, but on seeing how tall Adonis was, immediately raised himself on his toes in an attempt to match his height, and, across his desk, crushed Adonis' fingers in a handshake. 'Congratulations Corporal, please sit down. I am Chief Superintendent Nydivo, recently appointed here from Nakuru. Although I know hardly anyone here at HQ yet, or at any of my departments, I already I know of Corporal Adonis Musyoka of Katamara.'

Adonis lowered his eyes submissively and glowed.

'I know the investigation is now being dealt with by officers from Machakos, but it has been reported to me that your conduct that night was outstanding, exemplary, and I want to hear your story, Corporal. Those evil men I understand, have been terrorizing the district of Kilimambogo for some years.'

'For many, many years, sir, the villages around the mountain have been in terror. Only Katamara had escaped. Then they foolishly think to come to Katamara and make a big mistake; thank God that they have at last been dealt with.'

'A little thanks to you as well I think,' the Chief Superintendent said graciously.

'Sir, I have only been in Katamara some few years and, until now, those men have not dared to come near my town. But I only did what any policeman of Kenya would do, who is devoted to his job, his force, the *wanachi* at large, and his country as a whole. And proud I am to have been at such service.' Adonis had used the first of his pre-set pieces but he had more.

'Before you leave here today I want you to tell me about that night. I want to know exactly what happened. From what I have heard up to now, there is something that doesn't quite fit.'

'I can tell you the whole story, sir, as I have not slept properly since it happened. The whole thing running over and over in my head like a news-reel, also I have volunteered my services to the Machakos police as I know so much about the people in Katamara and the villages around the mountain and what villainy they are capable of. I know my services will be of much assistance.'

'The Machakos men are dealing with it. Leave it to them. You did your job, Corporal. The Machakos men have now taken over.' The chief's voice was still kindly.

Warming to the subject and the man, Adonis continued, 'These men I have arrested, sir, are very bad and I'm thinking even they might have had something to do with the death of Josiah Kariuki, a very great man, sir, who only recently was at Katamara and it was I, the very policeman, who organised the event, even bringing goats from Tala for the feast. I am also available if requested to help in the investigation into J.M.'s death because already I have many theories and suspicions.'

Nydivo, for the first time, appeared irritated and silenced his subordinate, saying, 'A Parliamentary Select Committee has been established to look into the death of Josiah Kariuki, If anyone needs your advice, Corporal, no doubt they will be in touch and ask for it.'

Adonis shuffled in his chair, Nydivo's words falling like clunking bricks into his reservoir of bubbling fervour. You're overdoing it, he told himself. He'd overdone things before. He must not let verbosity get out of hand. He was only a corporal and by the tone of the chief inspector's voice, he had been rudely reminded so. 'Of course, sir,' he finished tamely.

Nydivo, in a 'now to matters-in-hand' approach, took a paper from his drawer and placed it squarely on the desk in front of Adonis, saying, 'This memo has been brought to my attention only this very morning. It is dated ten days ago, and it is your request for transfer to another district. I have given it due consideration to the request and in view of your remarkable performance in Katamara, where the people all around the mountain owe you an enormous debt of gratitude, I have decided to grant it and you can take up a new position in Nanyuki on the first day of next month.'

Adonis groaned inwardly as his spirits thudding to the pit of his stomach. What had he done? Not only had his exalted position in his own village and the surrounding villages been restored, it had been enhanced. He was the new King of Katamara and was being crowned daily. Girls were flocking to his feet, the *wanachi* were falling over each other to talk to him, and the marketplace, when he was able to fight his way through fans, was as water when he walked upon it. Why, even the sisters at the hospital were talking to him, only yesterday Mother Veronica thanked him personally for going to the assistance of Nurse Collins. His crowning glory to date, the austere officers from Machakos paying homage and a written citation from Nairobi; where was he going to reign now? A dusty out-of-the-way backwoods in Nanyuki? This was a disaster of his own making; no more the conquering hero, the memo in the chief's hand, a ticket to oblivion and anticipation of his new start in life flowed with sluggish discontentment through a desolate alley of his mind. 'I don't think I want to go now, sir,' he blurted.

Nydivo, a man of no irony and little humour looked surprised: 'So you've changed your mind?'

Adonis coughed and, searching the chief's eyes and voice for the drollery, found there wasn't any. Relief tumbled from his head to his heart and with the chief's next few words, a warm glow of reprieve settled in his senses.

'So, shall we leave you where you are then, in Katamara?'

'Yes sir, thank you, sir. I think I am better positioned there to continue with my good work and prevent further attacks.'

Nydivo crumpled up the memo and threw it in a bin. 'That's settled then. OK, now I want to know from you exactly what happened that night? It's made the national newspapers but most of that is speculation. You're the man who wrapped thing up single-handed. Tell me how you did it.'

'Sir, single-handed as I have been since I arrived in Katamara but I only did what any policeman would do who is devoted to his job,' then – remembering that he had already used this preamble – he juggled in his mind for others. Then for the next fifteen minutes he talked non-stop, beginning with the distant sound of the crash and the splintering of timber. He kept to the truth as far as he knew it, interjecting his story with snippets of detraction and self-deprecation which he felt would do him no harm at all in summing up his own humble, inadequate, but unquestionably outstanding, performance. He concluded by expressing deep regret that he didn't get there soon enough to save the *askari's* life. 'It was most unfortunate sir, as poor Titus had been given that night off.'

'So I understand. Head sliced in two with a panga.'

'Most unfortunate, sir.'

'And the lady, she wasn't raped, seems she put up a fight but from what I've heard, the men had left her alone and were fleeing out of the building as you arrived.'

'Luckily I was awake when I heard the crash and as I've already told you, sir, dressed very quickly. Remembering to bring my gun I footed very fast across the bridge. Never had it happened in my patch before but I knew well what was happening at that house.'

'Certainly you got there just in time. How is the woman now?'

'She is very OK sir but is very upset. sir.'

'Understandable, under the circumstances.'

'About the attack on her side she is very OK, it is what happened to Titus that upsets her also she is much upset that Inspector Sam Wamiru has not been to visit her. She seems to be very much heart-broken in that department.'

Ndivo raised an eyebrow: 'Were she and the inspector good friends?'

Adonis shrugged and said, 'The inspector, sir, he like that woman. After he cleared her of the death of a little boy, he took her to Nairobi and another time he took her to the Jaffa Bar for drinks. Seems, sir, that they were close but seems, sir, maybe they were closer.' Further intimacy of this liaison, if such had taken place, had surprisingly escaped his notice.

'So the woman is OK.'

'From the statements taken, Nurse Collins fought like a wild-cat. One of her attackers almost had his bollocks twisted off. It is known that three men had her on the bed, you see, each would have his turn, until she got one by the bollocks, excuse me, sir the use of that word but that is what she had him by and that is the word I have used in my report and the word she used in her statement. Then there was only two men, sir, and somehow they did not pursue the penetration. And then she was very OK and back at the hospital, wanting to start nursing as normal and pushing on with life and facts were kept from her until she recovered somewhat. Then she heard about Titus. She collapsed when she

341

heard about Titus – then she collapsed some more and yelled out loud for Inspector Sam,' crying that he had not visited her.

'Mmmm, I'm sure he will visit her in due course.' Nydivo was now leaning back in his chair, with his hands around his stomach. Was he satisfied with Adonis' account of events? Not yet. 'And the *musungu* builder, Charlie Carter?'

'It was thought a fractured skull but only yesterday he left the hospital where the Holy Sisters have been looking after him, and the doctor there said that he was well, OK, and pushing on with life. He called at the station only this morning, to thank me for what was done on his behalf by me, that night. He was struck with a club and not a *panga* like Titus and his head recovered quickly. Later I found that very club in the bush outside the house and secured it as evidence and the policemen of Machakos thanked me fine for that service.'

'So Charlie Carter is back home already. He was very lucky.'

'He is very well, OK, and seems he will be soon living at his house with a young Kenyan lady who has found herself to be a bit pregnant, but as I understand not by Mr Charlie but by another *musungu*, who penetrated her in times gone by. All the good people that was injured is now OK except for Titus who is dead.'

Nydivo said, 'I understand, that from the statements, it appears this time the object was not so much robbery but the rape of the nurse.'

'Although officers from Machakos are now dealing with all this matter, it was I that took the original statements and it was I who discovered that nothing was stolen, thanks be to God, Now I am leaving those officers to it. It was my opinion that those bad men were out to rape the nurse and was prevented. But you can see, sir, what a job I had to do that night, so unaided and to do so without panic was a surprise even to myself. Imagine, an injured man, Mr Charlie and a dead *askari*, Titus. Add to that a lady suffering shock. Then, there was one bandit who could not walk for twisted bollocks, and another with a bullet in his bottom that I shot myself after careful aim. And then from what I could see, that still left three bandits, all ready to rampage. Oh it's a wonder how I coped.'

'Well you did cope,' the Chief Superintendent conceded without a trace of satire.

Adonis continued animatedly, 'I arrested the man with the injured bollocks and the man with the bullet in his arse, another man gave himself up when he saw what he was faced with and two escaped up the mountain. When I got back to the station I dispatched trusted villagers to set off in hot pursuit so that I was able to direct further operations from my post in Katamara. Telephone HQ in Nairobi about what had happened and what I had done to prevent further bloodshed. Send people back to see to Charlie and to Titus. Arrange at the hospital for the nurse and the guy with a bullet in his bottom' – he laughed – 'oh, and the guy with the twisted bollocks, he was complaining most bitterly. Not that any of this was special, sir, as I was only doing my duty as a professional and devout policeman.'

'Your conduct that night was honourable and brave, Sergeant, and to the high standards expected of the Kenyan Police Force.'

Sergeant? Had Adonis heard him right? Did the Chief Superintendent use the word *Sergeant?* The garland rolled over in his mind, gathering magnitude; it was the most beautiful, most wondrous word that he had ever heard. *'Sergeant'*, oh this godlike, Chief Superintendent from Nakuru; a third stripe, the tap of a sword on the shoulder of distinction, Sergeant Adonis, Inspector Adonis, Chief Inspector Adonis; how long before he had a pair of leather gloves and the scrambled egg of high office adorning his epaulettes and cap. A vision of eminence strolled elegantly through the rank and file of his reverie while minions looked on in envy; destiny, this day, was knocking at his door. 'I'm sorry sir, but did you say – did I hear you correctly, Sergeant?'

'You have earned it.' Then Nydivo endorsed the adjudication with a smile, and the word again: *'Sergeant.* When you get back home you can add your third stripe immediately.'

Oh the voice of his benefactor, ensuring days and nights of

delirious cogitation, transmuting the want of power to the reality of influence and premiership and already a shopping list of office was being assembled in his mind. A new girlfriend was waiting for him outside and she would be the first to know; she would be at his side to proudly observe his investiture. Oh, and he must get a swagger stick.

Words were forming in his mind, words of gratitude and jubilation but, strangled by emotion, they could not be released.

Nydivo was deadly serious. 'But I must have one thing explained to me. I have heard your story and I have heard other stories, but as yet I have not read any witness statements. There is one thing that doesn't make any sense at all, one question that I have already hinted at but must be answered to my satisfaction.'

Adonis looked up earnestly, but knowing what the question was, he dreaded it. He simply didn't have an explanation. He was glad that the men from Machakos had taken over when they did, let them try to explain the unexplainable.

'Yes, sir,' Adonis asked despondently.

The Chief Superintendent's eyes darkened with, what to Adonis, looked like mistrust; and already he had cautiously reined in his expanding empire and was back in Katamara treading the beat as a corporal. 'I think I know the question, sir, and it is very difficult to answer.'

Hanging on to his dubious expression, 'This is what puzzles me,' Nydivo began. 'The *musungu* Charlie Carter, is unconscious with a blow to his head and Titus the *askari* is dead. Another has had his testicles injured by the woman, the other villains, it figures, are still attacking the woman on the bed. Yet when you arrive, a minute later, they all appear to be tumbling out of the house together. What caused them to suddenly scramble from the house, leaving the woman alone to give evidence against them? What was it alerted them? This matter seems most strange to me.' He paused, then added, 'My question is what caused them to suddenly run from the house What happened just before you got there?'

And it was the question Adonis had feared most, but he had schooled himself sufficiently in case it should arise, 'It is a most strange case, sir, and I swear to God it is better answered by a senior officer from Machakos. But I will tell you what Nurse Jennifer Collins told me in her sworn statement, which is now in senior hands. And sir, this woman is a respectable lady whose word cannot be doubted. Charlie Carter, he says in his statement that he had all along suspected that a ghost was in that house, and now, even me, I am somehow thinking the same. Sir, there is a devil at work in that house, a devil that is still there.'

Intrigued, Nydivo nodded for him to continue.

Hesitantly, Adonis took up his tale, then, when he was not interrupted, he carried on with more authority of tone, 'Men have Nurse Collins on the bed, two men are holding her while another begins bad business so to penetrate her, but she is struggling so hard, biting, scratching, all those things, that he cannot penetrate her body in the place that he would wish. In fact, it is in the statements that this man appeared much frustrated by his efforts at penetration. All the men are much aware that something has happened outside on the porch but they remained waiting, sir – you see each would wait their turn and all this I know from the sworn statements that it was my duty to obtain by the statutory laws of Kenya.'

Nydivo appeared more intrigued than ever.

'Then sir, it happened.'

'What happened?'

'Out of nowhere a young girl appears in the room, the same room that the men are penetrating in, a young girl sir, eighteen maybe, she comes from nowhere and is standing by the bed and watching, crying silently, saying nothing, only watching and crying. The men, sir, they are very frightened of this strange girl who has suddenly appeared. One man goes to grab her but his hand goes right through her body. Very frightened, these men, they jump off Nurse Collins, and the man who has mounted the nurse, he does not even have the time to pull his trousers up.

Such a scene as they all stagger out of the house, they are falling over each other to get away. It is at this point in the proceedings as I arrive to do my duty. I shout for them to stop, I shout again, and my gun all this time is raised towards them. They do not obey as they are in too much hurry to get away from that house. I fired at this bare bottom, sir. It was very big and bright in the moonlight and a very good target for a bullet. I hit the guy, who was doing the penetrating, as he had not time to pull his trousers up.'

Nydivo held up his hand: 'Stop there. Who was this girl?'

'It was not known at the time, but in the witness statements of Nurse Collins and Charlie Carter, it is stated that the girl is known as Shula.'

Ndivo frowned. 'This is the first time I've heard mention of another girl. And of course this Shula was required to give a statement too.' The Chief Superintendent was beginning to sound impatient but for the first time there was a trace of sardonic humour in his words.

Adonis convulsed in swallowing. 'Well, no, sir.'

Nydivo's eyes looked upon the answer coldly. 'Why not?'

Adonis was gulping again. 'Because this girl disappeared as fast as she had arrived, Nurse Collins saw her go. Like a wisp of smoke, she came and then she went.'

The chief inspector drummed his fingers on the desk. Adonis was becoming increasingly uncomfortable with his explanation. His outstanding performance that night was about to be denigrated by his own admission, but what could he do? He couldn't take a statement from a ghost.

'Why did you not find this girl, get her statement?'

'We couldn't.'

'Couldn't? Why?'

'Because, sir, she has been dead for seventy years.'

Nydivo flinched as if cold water had been splashed upon his face. Was this young pup playing a game with him? His toes curled, his fingers curled on the desk, and his lip curled in repudiation.

A fog of disbelief had pervaded the milieu of the room and the aura of goodwill was dissipating fast.

'What are you talking about, Corporal?'

The spirit in Adonis sank. He had been demoted back to corporal and much more of this nonsense and he would be constable again. He was gripping tightly the arms of his chair and he was sweating, his credibility now very much in question. 'Sir, it is in all the statements. Even those bad men say the same. One of them even thought it was the Virgin Mary. But It must have been the devil in that house.'

'Doesn't sound like the devil to me,' but the lip had curled again. Nydivo had just completed a Criminal Justice and Law Enforcement doctorate degree, and could not recall divine intervention being included in the syllabus.

'Shula is a ghost, sir,' Adonis tried despairingly.

'There are no ghosts in Kenya.'

'Of course not, sir.'

Nydivo coughed and began picking at imaginary specks on the sleeve of his uniform. Adonis was one of them. 'And the men from Machakos, have they been fed this bloody nonsense too?'

'It is what is written,' Adonis gulped. 'All the statements made say much the same thing. Of course, sir, I very much doubted it myself but—' He had wrecked his chances now. The expression on the senior officer's face was not so much of disbelief, but of disgust at being expected to ingest such a fatuous absurdity. Promotion had been but a few words of promise, demotion but a few words more. 'Sir, it is what I know to be true.' Adonis pleaded in a last throw of persuasion.

The Chief Superintendent scratched his nose. There was no doubt in his mind now that the young man sitting nervously before him was telling the truth, or what he thought to be the truth, and as he looked upon the troubled face he wondered how many others had succumbed to this supernatural farce. Witchdoctors he could countenance, but not seventy-year-old ghost girls. 'Who from Machakos is in charge of the investigation?'

This was a question Adonis could answer and awash with gratitude, he blurted, 'Chief Inspector Julius Mathu, sir.' And, with the flick of a finger, he was dismissed to the corridor, to wait until he was called for.

His story was outrageous, yes, but it was true. Had he thrown everything away with a rush of stupid but inescapable truth? Would his story be corroborated by the chief inspector from Machakos? His future life depended on it – could the greatest week of his life yet come to a sorry end? He was the King of Katamara, no, the King of Kilimambogo, with the villages in the palm of his hand, girls flocking around him, he could take his pick, was it all to end so sadly? He seemed to have been waiting in the corridor an inordinately long time as he desperately tried to eavesdrop but to no avail.

Ndivo replaced the telephone receiver and sat back in his chair in contemplation. Julius Mathu of the Machakos police, during his investigations, had spoken at length to an old *mzee*, a Moses Nyjonjo who mended punctures for a living. Yes, some seventy years earlier, a young girl had gone missing from the house on the hill, and yes, her name was Shula. She was the old man's elder sister. She had been murdered by two *musungu* women, one the wife of a White Highlander. The old man didn't know anymore but from files left by the British, Julius Mathu found that the three had left Kenya in a hurry and nothing was heard of them again. The old man told Julius that the spirit of his sister had never left the house. He said it never would.

It seemed an age before Adonis heard Nydivo's voice calling for him, and he tried to determine the tone, was it upbeat and friendly? No, the tenor sounded churlish and unforgiving. Gingerly he opened the door, hardly daring to step inside, hardly daring to breath.

Nydivo looked up, his face was serious and for the rest of his life Adonis would remember the next few words he spoke.

'I have talked with Chief Inspector Julius Mathu and the case is still much under investigation. Do not discuss this case with anyone until it is resolved. The matter of the second woman is also very much under investigation and yes, a ghost-girl, at this stage, cannot be discounted.' And the next few words above all others Adonis would remember for the rest of his life. 'You can go back to Katamara now, Sergeant.'

Sergeant, Sergeant Adonis Musyoka, the words were a delirious drum beat in his head. Next step, Inspector. He would be like Wamiru. Wamiru was not his nemesis he was his mentor, a man who didn't need hyperbole to do his job. Wamiru was a good honest Kenyan copper and henceforth Adonis Musyoka would be a good honest Kenyan copper too.

He couldn't wait to tell his girl. He took the stairway three blissful steps at a time and leapt out into the gilded city. Oh golden day. His whole being, his brain, his very essence glowed with the triumph of the moment and he threw open the door to a world kindled with sunlight. At last he had got his just deserts. He had been promoted to sergeant, his life was fulfilled. Nothing could stop Adonis now. What could possibly go wrong with life now that he was sergeant and his heart was full of joy as he skipped across the road to tell his new girlfriend of his triumph: 'Esmeralda, such news I have,' he called.

Chapter Forty-Two

*T*he bandages had been removed but Charlie's head still ached and he had been told that the angry red scar on his bald dome was permanent. He had a lot to tell Aisha, he would tell her as they were driving back to Katamara. He must tell her what had happened at the house in which she was about to live.

The time was drawing close to when he must drive to Kibera and pick her up with all her things. Would she be waiting for him, was she packed and ready? Maybe she wouldn't be there. Maybe she had changed her mind.

Thanks to Jennifer Collins, the new *musungu* who was expected in a couple of weeks would be accommodated at the hospital and Aisha would live in Freddie's room, with every vestige of Freddie's tenancy removed. The Agency had been accommodating, just as Charlie knew they would be. At his request they had provided a new mattress and bedlinen and with the wooden floor freshly polished and the walls draped with *kangas* and batics, the room was fresh and homely and it smelled nice too. He so much wanted Aisha to be happy in her new mountain home.

She would be spending time in the kitchen so Charlie had attacked the cockroach problem with genocidal ferocity. Unscrewing and shifting a heavy shelved cabinet, he had found the culprit and cause of the unremitting infestation, a giant brown mother, and yes, as big as a baby's foot: too big to crush, too fast to catch. He watched in horror as it moved with lightning speed to disappear beneath the gap under the door. It was outside now; to prevent its re-entry, he caked the threshold with doom-powder and if it did come back, he knew now where it lived.

How he worried. How would Shula react to another woman in her house, no, worse, another pretty girl? Shula was pretty; she was young, slim, pretty and wearing a light blue dress. He had badgered Jennifer for a description and that was how she had described her, gossamer and seemingly transparent as she had stood weeping by her bedside. Did she speak, did she move? No, she appeared out of nowhere to manifest an evil that couldn't face itself and then she went back to the unknown. Her work was done. But although Shula had lived in the house for seventy years, she was still a teenage girl and would still think as a teenage girl. Going to the aid of a violated woman she had shown herself clearly, but once and dramatically so, but was back in hiding now. Would she appear to Aisha? Would that Charlie could find her, talk to her and explain about Aisha. Titus would soon be with his parents beneath the orange trees in the warm earth of Mavaloni but where did Shula lie? Shovelled somewhere underground in Nyeri with the Highland hills as witness to her shameful death but her spirit had returned to Katamara, to the house of her last words, her last breath. Her ghost was in his room, his bedroom, as it always had been and again he looked for her. She would not live in the kitchen or the godless room above and not in Freddie's room. Freddie might have been handsome and athletic and everything a girl would want in a man but Shula would have known, sensed his true character, known that he could not be trusted; Charlie couldn't bear to think of Shula alone with Freddie in his bedroom. No, she had chosen his room because she trusted him, yes, she was somewhere among the many black faces with bright eyes watching him from the photos on the wall. She moved about his room, he knew it, for sometimes the brightly coloured *kangas* fluttered as if disturbed by phantom hands.

His attention dwelt now on the large coloured photo of a wedding feast that he had attended soon after his arrival in the village.

He had been invited as the guest of honour and his was the only white face among a sea of black ones. The distinction of *guest of honour*, he had been reminded, was conditional on him taking along his truck for it was honour indeed to be selected to transport the betrothed to and from the church. Also it would add to his esteem should he happen to bring his camera; how eminently regarded was the official photographer at a *Kamba* wedding feast. Oh, and if he would freight the old and infirm back to their *shambas* when the celebrations were over, then his standing would be complete. That day Charlie was a most honoured man indeed.

Shula was in this photograph because often, almost imperceptibly, he felt he saw an insubstantial flickering entity moving through the people. It was the slight and furtive figure of a girl in a light blue dress who did not belong, who did not want to be seen but yet had every right to be there to play a tiny part in what was going on. But he could never find her, never pin her down. But each day now he looked for her, talked to her as if he might be praying; he honoured and revered her as he would a saint. He was to Shula as the sisters of the hospital were to God. This was faith and to Charlie it was wondrous.

Very soon now Aisha would be living here with him in this house and would know of what had happened. Already the story of the ghost girl who had saved a woman's life was speeding through the villages and beyond the mountain to the towns. Suddenly, surprisingly, all worry lifted from him and he felt at peace. This was what the murdered girl had wanted, her story to be told; there would be no more knocking now. Aisha and her baby would be safe and cared for. Shula was a ghost no more but a part of a family; a guardian angel and a guardian angel doesn't haunt a house.

Starting up the engine of the truck, Charlie set off to Kibera but first he would visit the accommodation block. Work had stopped since the night of the attack and no one had been inside. He had no real reason to investigate the unfinished building apart from the possibility of damage from the heavy rain, but something told him that he should.

Epilogue

*T*he sky, a black beast sat heavily upon the earth and the earth, pale and needy and wanting, opened up. Roaring mightily, the beast blackened the day and rent the sky as it emptied but still the earth was not assuaged. She had waited too long for this and she thrust herself upward and was silent in submitting to the torrents and would not be satisfied until the beast was spent.

Of course the young policemen had never heard of him because Peter Kitonyi wasn't a policeman. Of course he wasn't, his clothes didn't fit, something Wamiru should have realised when he first got into the jeep. Stranger still was the barrel of a gun being pointed at his chest, why was Kitonyi pointing a gun at him? Above, rain thudded in an endless reverberation on the *mabati* roof. Wamiru tried to speak, tried to push the barrel of the gun to one side. The rain was getting heavier and what was the sudden mighty explosion because it wasn't thunder? Why was he being propelled backwards by an unseen force to slam against the soil-brick wall? Something terrible had happened to him but he did not feel any pain, only profound shock. The rain was really battering the *mabati* roof. What the hell had hit him, and why was he on the floor with his back slumped against a wall? He was sitting in a pool of water; he was soaked. He tried to get to his feet but couldn't, this was what happened in nightmares. The young boy had turned on him, but why? The barrel of the gun was now only inches from his nose. The hand that held the gun had perfectly manicured fingernails, why should he notice that the finger on the trigger had a perfect quarter-moon beneath the cuticle? Wamiru heard a voice; it could only be the constable's. 'I was told to tell you that you should never have threatened to go to the newspapers.' The rain on the roof was getting worse. The *mabati* could not withstand the force much longer. Then, there was another deafening explosion.

THE END